A Regency SCANDAL

THEY DARED TO TASTE
THE FORBIDDEN...

Inspired by Lundy, a beautiful island in the Bristol
Channel, with a fascinating and romantic history,
international bestselling author Nicola Cornick has
penned two thrilling novels about the passionate feud
between the Mostyn and Trevithick families.

Lady Allerton's Wager
'A fast-paced romance with passionate, intense
characters... Captivating.'
—*The Word on Romance*

The Notorious Marriage
Nicola Cornick's first UK bestseller and voted
one of the Romantic Novelists Association's
Best Reads of 2002
'...without a doubt a most engaging romp that
is sure to delight ardent Regency readers.'
—*Writers Unlimited*

Nicola Cornick is passionate about many things: her country cottage and its garden, her two small cats, her husband and her writing, though not necessarily in that order! She has always been fascinated by history, both as her chosen subject at university and subsequently as an engrossing hobby. She works as an university administrator and finds her writing the perfect antidote to the demands of life in a busy office.

NICOLA CORNICK
A Regency SCANDAL

MILLS & BOON®

*MILLS & BOON and MILLS & BOON with the Rose Device
are registered trademarks of the publisher.*

*Harlequin Mills & Boon Limited,
Eton House, 18-24 Paradise Road, Richmond, Surrey, TW9 1SR*

A REGENCY SCANDAL © Harlequin Enterprises II B.V., 2005

Lady Allerton's Wager and *The Notorious Marriage*
were first published in Great Britain by
Harlequin Mills & Boon Limited in separate, single volumes.

Lady Allerton's Wager © Nicola Cornick 2001
The Notorious Marriage © Nicola Cornick 2002

ISBN 0 263 84951 1

108-1005

*Printed and bound in Spain
by Litografia Rosés S.A., Barcelona*

Lady Allerton's Wager

Chapter One

The Cyprians' Ball was scarcely an event that featured on the social calendar of any of the debutantes of the *ton*, although more than one bitter chaperon had observed that it was the only place outside the clubs where all the eligible bachelors could be found. The most unobtainable of gentlemen, who would scorn to step inside the doors of Almack's Assembly Rooms for fear of ambush, showed far greater alacrity in striking up an intimate acquaintance of quite another sort, and a masquerade was ripe with all sorts of possibilities.

It was late in the evening when Marcus, sixth Earl of Trevithick, joined the crowds of revellers milling in the Argyle Rooms. Being neither a callow youth nor particularly requiring an *inamorata*, he had seen no need to hurry to be first through the door.

The room, with its elegant pillars and lavish decoration, seemed as gaudy as the birds of paradise that flocked there. Marcus knew that he was already drawing their attention. With his height, stature and wicked dark good looks it was inevitable, but he felt little pride in the fact. Once his name was whispered amongst the Cyprians he knew that some would lose interest and hunt for bigger game, for they were motivated by cupidity rather than lust. He had the looks and the title but he had little money, for he had inherited estates that had gone to rack and ruin.

'Been rusticating, Marcus? I had heard you were still in northern parts!'

It was his cousin, Justin Trevithick, who had clapped Marcus on the shoulder. Justin, the only child of a scandalous second marriage between Marcus's Uncle Freddie Trevithick and his housekeeper, was a couple of years younger than his cousin. The two had never met as children, for Marcus's father, Viscount Trevithick, had disapproved of his brother's morals and had steadfastly refused to acknowledge his nephew. When Marcus was twenty-two he had bumped into Justin at White's and they had hit it off at once, to the amusement of the *ton* and the despair of the strait-laced Viscount and his wife. Now, eleven years later, they were still firm friends.

Marcus and Justin shared the distinctive lean Trevithick features, but whilst Marcus's eyes and hair were the sloe-black of his pirate forebears, Justin's face was lightened by the fair hair and green eyes that in his mother had captured the attention of Lord Freddie. He turned and took two glasses of wine from a passing flunkey, handing one to his cousin. Marcus grinned, inclining his dark head.

'I have just returned from Cherwell,' he said, in answer to Justin's enquiry. 'I was there longer than I had intended. The tenant there has been fleecing the estate for some time, but—' he gave a sardonic smile '—it won't be happening again!'

Justin raised his eyebrows. 'I don't believe our grandfather ever visited that house. Towards the end he never even left Trevithick. It led the unscrupulous to take advantage.'

Marcus nodded. He had inherited from his grandfather a bare fifteen months before and had swiftly discovered that people had indeed taken advantage of the late Earl's infirmity in his last years. It seemed ironic that his grandfather, whose soubriquet had been the Evil Earl, had himself been cheated in his old age. The Trevithick estates were huge and the subsequent confusion had taken until now to sort out. There were still places that Marcus had not had the time to visit, business that remained unfinished.

'Do you intend to stay in London for the little Season?' Justin asked.

Marcus pulled a face. 'I should do, as it's Nell's debut. I would like to, but—'

'Lady Trevithick?' Justin enquired.

Marcus took a mouthful of his wine. 'It is damnably difficult to share a house with one's mother after an absence of fifteen years!' He grimaced. 'I have already asked Gower to find me a set of rooms—preferably on the other side of town!'

Justin smothered a grin. 'I saw Eleanor at Almack's earlier this evening,' he said, tactfully changing the subject. 'Pershore and Harriman were dancing attendance, to name but two! She seems to have taken well, which is no surprise since she has all the Trevithick good looks!'

Marcus laughed. 'I do believe that Mama is uncertain which of us to make a push to marry off first, though I believe she will have more success with my sister! I don't look to take a wife just yet!'

'Well, you certainly won't find one here,' Justin said,

turning back to scan the crowds. 'Women of another sort, perhaps...'

'Perhaps.' Marcus allowed his gaze to skim over the ranks of painted faces. 'It is a complication I could do well without, however.'

Justin grinned. 'There's one that would be worth it!'

Marcus turned to follow his cousin's gaze. The ball-room was packed and the dancers were executing a waltz, which was the excuse for much intimate and pro-vocative behaviour. Yet in the middle of the swirling crowds, one couple stood out, for they danced beauti-fully but with total decorum. The gentleman was tall and fair, but he did not have much of Marcus's attention. The lady in his arms was another matter, however.

She was taller than most of the women present and only a few inches short of his own six foot. She wore a silver mask and her silver domino swung wide as she danced, revealing beneath it a dress in matching silk that clung to a figure that Marcus could only describe as slender but voluptuous. Her face was pale with a hint of rose on the cheekbones and her ebony black hair was piled up on top of her head in a complicated mass of curls that was just asking to be released from its captiv-ity. Marcus grinned. Her hair was not the only thing that looked as though it would benefit from being given its freedom—the silk dress hinted at all sorts of delightful possibilities and he was already entertaining the idea of peeling it off her like the skin of a ripe fruit. Glancing around, he realised that at least half the men in his vi-cinity were thinking along the same lines and his grin broadened. Perhaps they had tasted the fruit already, for the very fact that she was at the Cyprians' Ball marked her as no lady. Marcus shrugged. It mattered little to him who had been before him, but he had every intention of being next in succession.

'Setting your sights, Marcus?' Justin Trevithick enquired, a smile in his voice. Like the Earl, he was watching the dancing couple. 'From what I've just overheard, you are at least tenth in the queue!'

'I don't like waiting in line,' Marcus murmured, not taking his gaze from the girl's face.

'Who is she, Justin?'

'Damned if I know!' Justin said cheerfully. 'No one does! The guesses are inventive and range wide, but no one can put a name to the face!'

'What about the lady's escort?'

Justin was laughing at his cousin's persistence. 'Now, there I can help you! The fortunate gentleman is Kit Mostyn! A shame we are not on terms with the Mostyns and cannot beg an introduction!'

Marcus gave his cousin an incredulous look, then laughed in his turn. 'Mostyn! How piquant! Then it will be doubly enjoyable to take the lady away from him...'

Justin raised his eyebrows. 'Is this love or war, Marcus?'

'Both!' his cousin replied promptly. 'They say all is fair, do they not? Well, then...'

The dancers were circling closer to them now. Marcus thought that the lady looked very comfortable in Lord Mostyn's arms, for she was talking eagerly and smiling up at him. Marcus's eyes narrowed. He had nothing against Kit Mostyn personally, but there had been a feud between the Mostyn and Trevithick families for centuries. Marcus knew little of the detail of it, and just at the moment he had no interest in healing the breach. He waited until the couple were directly beside him, then made a slight movement that attracted the lady's attention. She looked up and their eyes met for a long moment before she deliberately broke the contact. Marcus had the impression of a wide, smoky gaze, a slightly deeper silver colour than her dress. A moment later, she looked back at him over her shoulder, with what he could only interpret as a gesture of invitation.

Justin laughed. 'A result, I think, Marcus!'

Marcus thought so too. He watched as the music ended and the lady and her partner strolled to the edge of the dance floor, then, without haste, he made his way towards them through the crowd.

'Your servant, Mostyn.' There was a mocking edge to Marcus's drawl and he saw the younger man stiffen slightly before he returned his bow with the very slightest one of his own. Marcus's attention had already moved to the lady, which was where his real interest lay. At close quarters she looked younger than he had imagined, but then he realised that it was not so much a youthful quality but an impression of innocence. Her eyes lacked the knowing look that characterised so many of her profession. Marcus reflected cynically that that air of innocence must be worth a great deal of money to this particular lady. Gentlemen would pay over the odds to possess so apparently unspoilt a beauty. It amused him, for in his youth he had become entangled with a Cyprian who had pretended to a naïveté she simply did not possess and had tried to sue him for breach of promise. Such candour was appealing but ultimately an illusion.

He held out his hand to her and after a moment she took it in her own.

'Marcus Trevithick, at your service, ma'am. Would you do me the honour of granting me a dance?'

Marcus felt rather than saw Kit Mostyn flash the girl

a look of unmistakable warning. She ignored him, smiling at Marcus with charm but absolutely no hint of coquetry. Grudgingly, Marcus had to admit that she might have been at a Dowager's ball rather than a Cyprian's masquerade. She had an inherent dignity. As she smiled, a small, unexpected dimple appeared at the corner of her mouth.

'Thank you, my lord. I should be delighted.'

He bowed slightly and led her on to the floor, where a set was forming for a country dance.

She carried herself with a poise that contrasted starkly with the flirting and ogling that was going on all around them and Marcus found it oddly touching—until he thought that this was no doubt all part of the act. Innocence, dignity… It was a clever way to set herself up as out of the ordinary. Nevertheless, her artfulness mattered little to him and he was confident that they could come to an understanding. Sooner rather than later, he hoped. He was beginning to want her very much. He studied her bent head and the way that the ebony curls brushed the nape of her neck. He wanted to touch her. Her mouth was as sultry as her figure, promising sensuous delight. He felt a powerful impulse to kiss her where they stood.

'Will you give me a name for a name?' he asked softly. 'You already know who I am.'

Her smoky grey gaze brushed his face and made him feel suddenly heated. She smiled a little, the dimple flashing. 'My name is Elizabeth, my lord. In fact, I am known as Beth.'

'Yes? And…?'

She considered. 'That is all I wish to tell you. There are no names at a masquerade. You have already broken the rules once by telling me your own identity.'

Marcus laughed. He had no problem with breaking any of society's rules that he did not agree with.

'What is Mostyn to you?' he asked, as the music brought them together again. 'I would like to know—before I attempt a trespass.'

He felt her fingers tremble in his before she freed herself and stepped away from him. She danced most gracefully.

'Kit is very dear to me,' she said, when eventually they came back together.

'I see.'

'I doubt it.' Once again that silver gaze pierced him. 'He is a friend. Closer than a friend—but that is all.'

An old lover, Marcus thought, with a vicious rush of envy. That would explain why they looked so comfortable together, yet had none of the heat of sensuality between them. Old passions had burned themselves out, leaving only the flame of friendship. It made him jealous to think of their past relationship, yet it also implied that there might be a vacancy...

'And is there anyone else?' Foolish question, when she probably had a dozen admirers paying for her favours! Yet her cool gaze searched his face and she answered quietly.

'I do not care to discuss such matters here, my lord.'

Marcus allowed his gaze to hold hers for several long seconds. 'Then may we discuss it in private? I confess that would suit me very well...'

He felt that he might reasonably have expected some encouragement at this point, even if it was only a smile, but Beth gave his suggestion thoughtful consideration, and then inclined her head.

'Very well. There is a study off the hallway—'

'I know it.'

She nodded again. The dance was finishing anyway, but no one paid any attention as she slipped from the line of dancers and went out into the entrance hall. Marcus waited a few moments before following her, pausing to see if he was observed. It seemed that everyone was too preoccupied with their own *amours* to be concerned about his.

He picked his way through the entwined couples and crossed the checkerboard black and white tiles of the hall. He vaguely remembered that the study was the third door on the left and he was just in time to catch the faintest swish of material as Beth whisked through the door, leaving it ajar for him.

Marcus smiled to himself. The situation was most promising and, despite his cynicism, he had to admit that there was something intriguing about the lady's air of aloof mystery. Perhaps it was all assumed simply to whet jaded appetites, but it was working on him and he was more world-weary than most. He quickened his step, went into the study and closed the door behind him.

It was a small room with a mahogany card table and chairs in the middle and matching mahogany bookcases about the walls. Long amber curtains shut out the night and the only light came from one lamp, standing on a side table.

Beth was standing beside the window. She had taken the dice from their box on the table and was tossing them lightly in one hand. She did not look up when Marcus came in and for a moment he thought he sensed something tense and wary in her stance, though the impression was fleeting.

He took a step forward. 'Would you care to indulge in a game of chance, sweetheart?' he asked.

She looked at him then, a stare as straight and pro-

tracted as the one she had first given him in the ballroom.
Marcus was amused. He knew of few men and even
fewer women who were so direct. Her eyes were a shadowed silver behind the mask, her gaze as deliberate and
fearless as a cat.

'If you are sure that you wish to play, my lord.'

They were talking in *double entendres* now and
Marcus appreciated her quick wit. It made the pursuit
even more enjoyable. He wondered if she knew who he
was, even though he had given only his name and not
his title. It was entirely possible. She had focused on
him from the first and he did not flatter himself that it
was simply because she was attracted to him. She might
well consider that his status and physical attributes out-
weighed a lack of fortune. And fortune was relative anyway. He could pay her well enough.

He kept his eyes on her face and smiled slowly. 'I'm
sure. Which game do you prefer?'

The lady smiled too, the dimple quivering again at the
corner of her deliciously curved mouth. Marcus suddenly
wished he could cut to the chase and simply kiss her. It
was a high-risk strategy and might backfire, but it was
very tempting. He took a step closer. She took one back.

'Hazard might be appropriate,' she said coolly, tossing
the dice from one hand to the other. 'One throw of the
dice. The winner takes all.'

Marcus hesitated. It was clear from her words that she
would be his prize if he won and he considered it very
sporting of her to offer her services for free. The reckoning would come later, of course, if they suited each
other: the villa, the carriage, the jewels...

But if she won the wager...

'I like your terms, but first I need to know what you

want from me if I lose,' he drawled. 'I do not have a fortune to offer. What would you settle for, sweetheart?'

He waited confidently for her to name her price. A necklace of diamonds, perhaps, to outclass the exquisite but tasteful grey pearls already around her neck.

She moved closer until he could smell her perfume. It was a subtle mix of jasmine and rose petals, warm as the sun on the skin, and it sent his senses into even more of a spin. Damn it, whatever the price, it had to be worth it.

'I don't want a fortune,' she said sweetly, 'just a small part of your patrimony. I want Fairhaven Island.'

Marcus stared. It comprehensively answered the question of whether or not she knew who he was, but it seemed an extraordinary suggestion. Fairhaven fell in the part of his estate that he had not yet had time to visit, but as far as he was concerned, it was a storm-swept isle in the middle of the Bristol Channel that supported a few people, a flock of sheep and nothing else. There was no earthly reason he could see why it should appeal to a courtesan. It was worth absolutely nothing at all.

Part of his mind prompted him to ask a few questions and get to the bottom of the mystery. The other part, tantalised by her perfume, suggested that there was no need to cavil and he was bound to win the bet anyway. Even if he lost he was fairly certain that he could persuade her to humour him. The time for a discussion on land and property was not now, when he wanted to sweep her into his arms, but later and best left to the lawyers.

'Very well,' he said, adding slowly, 'Do you always honour your bets?'

She looked away for the first time. 'I do not usually gamble, my lord. Do you honour yours?'

Marcus laughed. No man would have dared ask him that question but, after all, he had questioned her integrity first. And she still had not really answered him.

'I never renege,' he said. He took her hand in his and felt her tremble slightly. Her skin was very soft; he turned the hand over and pressed a kiss on the palm. 'But you did not answer my question.'

There was a flash of something in her eyes that almost looked like fear but it was gone as swiftly as it had come. She raised her chin.

'I will pay my debt, my lord—if I lose.'

Marcus nodded. He drew her closer until one of her palms was resting against his chest.

'And if I wish to take something on credit?' he asked, his voice a little rough.

'Then you might find yourself even further in debt since there is no guarantee that you would win.' She looked him straight in the eye. 'If you are willing to take the risk—'

It took Marcus only a split second to decide that he was. He bent his head and brought his mouth down on hers.

He was experienced enough not to try to take too much too soon. Even a Cyprian liked to be courted and he was no naïve boy to pounce without finesse. He kissed her gently, exploratively, holding her like china until he felt the tension slide from her body and she started to respond to him. She tasted soft and sweet and very innocent. She even trembled in his arms. It had to be an illusion, but it was such a beguiling one that Marcus felt his self-control slipping dangerously. He deepened the kiss and, after a moment's hesitation, she kissed him back tentatively, pressing a little closer to him. Desire surged through his body, so powerful it pushed all other thoughts aside and he pulled her to him fiercely, careless now of gentleness. But it was too late— she was withdrawing from him, as elusive as she had ever been. Marcus stifled a groan of frustration.

'The game, my lord?' Her voice was husky.

The game. He had forgotten. Intent on a different game of his own devising, he had not been certain that she would persist in their wager. Still, he was quite willing to indulge her.

'If you wish.' Marcus shrugged. 'All on the one throw.' He gave her a slight bow. 'I will concede you the honour of calling the main, madam.'

Beth threw him one swift glance. 'Then I call a nine.'

She took the dice up and cast them on to the walnut table. Marcus watched them spin and settle on the polished wood. A five and a four. She really had the devil's own luck. He could not believe it. He smiled a little. 'Will you play for the best of three?'

'Certainly not.' She sounded breathless and as she turned into the light he saw the expression on her face. He had expected triumph or greed. What he saw was relief.

'Fairhaven,' she said, on a questioning note. 'You will honour your bet, my lord?'

Marcus did not reply. For the first time, doubt surfaced in his mind, faint but troubling. She had come close to him again; her skirt brushed against his thigh. Part of him responded to her proximity, but he clamped down hard on his desire and tried to concentrate.

'Why do you want it?' he asked.

She laughed then and he saw the triumph that had been missing a moment before. 'Your question comes a little late, my lord! Surely that is academic now.' She took a step back and her silken skirts rustled. 'My man of business will call on yours on the morrow. Goodnight, my lord!'

She turned to go, but Marcus caught her arm in a tight grip and spun her round to face him. He tore the mask from her face with impatient fingers. Without it she was even more striking than he had supposed. Her face was a pure oval, the smoky eyes set far apart beneath flyaway black brows, the nose small and straight, the sultry mouth that was not smiling now. She was breathing very quickly and he could tell that she was afraid. And that she was not the courtesan she pretended to be. For some reason that took all the anger out of him.

'One of us is in the wrong place, I believe,' he said slowly.

'It is I,' she said simply. 'Did you truly believe me a Cyprian, my lord?'

Marcus started to laugh. He could not help himself. 'Assuredly. Until I kissed you.'

That gave him the advantage. He saw the colour come up into her face and she tried to free herself from his grip. He stood back, letting her go with exaggerated courtesy. No, indeed, this was no courtesan, but even so he still wanted her. He had no idea whom she was, but he intended to find out.

'You will honour your bet?' she asked again.

Marcus grinned, folding his arms. 'I will not.'

He saw the fury come into her eyes and held her gaze steadfastly with his own.

'I will *make* you do so!' she said.

'How?' Marcus shifted slightly. 'Are you telling me that you would have honoured yours had I won? If so, I would press you to play me for the best of three!'

She blushed even harder at that but her mouth set in

a stony line. 'What I would have done is immaterial, my lord, since you lost. You claimed never to renege!'

Marcus shrugged. 'I lied.'

'A liar and a cheat,' Beth said, in a tone that dripped contempt. 'I repeat, my man of business will call upon yours on the morrow, my lord, and will expect you to have ready the title to Fairhaven to hand over.'

The study door closed behind her with a decided snap and Marcus heard the quick, angry tap of her footsteps receding across the marble hall. He picked the dice up casually in one hand and sat down in one of the chairs. A whimsical smile touched his lips. He could not believe that his judgement had been so faulty. To mistake a lady for a Cyprian, even given the circumstances... He had been thoroughly misled by his desire, like a youth in his salad days. Led by the nose—or some other part of his anatomy, perhaps. It had never happened to him before.

He tossed the dice absent-mindedly in his hand. So he had been richly deceived and for an intriguing reason. He wanted to know more about that. He wanted to know more of the lady. Damn it, he still wanted *her*. Marcus shifted uncomfortably in his chair. And he needed a drink. Urgently.

Justin found him in the refreshment room after he had already downed a glass of brandy in one swallow. Justin watched him take a refill and despatch it the same way, and raised his eyebrows.

'Unlucky in love, Marcus?'

'Unlucky in games of chance,' Marcus said feelingly. He took Justin's arm and drew him into the shelter of one of the pillars, away from prying gossips. 'Justin, you know more of West Country genealogy than I! Tell me, does Kit Mostyn have a sister?'

Justin nodded. 'He has a widowed younger sister, Charlotte. Allegedly a blonde beauty, but she lives retired so it is difficult to say with certainty.'

Marcus frowned. Beth had never been a blonde and she could scarcely be described as retiring. Perhaps she was Mostyn's mistress after all. Yet something in him rebelled at such a thought.

'What is all this about, Marcus?' Justin was asking, looking puzzled. 'I thought you were about to make a new conquest, old fellow, not indulge in a mystery play!'

'So did I,' Marcus said thoughtfully. His face lightened and he held up the glass. 'Only find me the bottle and I will tell you the whole story!'

'I cannot believe that you just did that, Beth.'

Christopher Mostyn sounded mild, but his cousin knew full well that he was angry. She had known him well enough and long enough to tell.

Beth sighed. 'It was your idea to escort me there, Kit—'

'I may have escorted you to the Cyprians' Ball, but I did not expect you to behave like one!'

Now Kit's voice sounded clipped, forbidding further discussion. Beth sighed again. Kit was head of the family and as such she supposed he had the right to censure her behaviour. The fact that he seldom did owed more to his easygoing nature than her obedience.

Beth rested her head back against the carriage's soft cushions and closed her eyes. Truth to tell, *she* could not believe that she had behaved as she had. And she had only told Kit half the story, the half relating to the wager. She knew that if she had told Kit that Marcus Trevithick had kissed her, very likely he would have stormed back and challenged the Earl to a duel and matters would be immeasurably worse.

Beth opened her eyes again and stared out of the window. They were travelling through the streets of London at a decorous pace and the light from the lamps on the pavement skipped across the inside of the carriage in bars of gold and black. It hid her blushes and a very good thing too, for whenever she thought of Marcus Trevithick, she felt the telltale colour come into her face and the heat suffuse her entire body.

Not only had she overstepped the mark—by a long chalk—but she knew that she had been completely out of her depth with such a man. She had a lot of courage and, allied to her impulsive nature, she knew it could be her downfall. However, her nerve had almost deserted her in that secluded room. If he had won the bet… Beth shivered. Like as not he would have demanded his prize there and then on the card table or the floor… But he had not won. She took a deep, steadying breath.

Marcus Trevithick. Children of her family were taught to hate the Trevithicks from the moment they were born. There were tales told at the nursemaid's knee—stories of treachery and evil. The Earls of Trevithick were jumped-up nobodies, whereas the Mostyns could trace their ancestry back to the Conquest and beyond. The Trevithicks had stolen the Mostyn estates during the Civil War and had wrested the island of Fairhaven from them only two generations back, taking the family treasure and the Sword of Saintonge into the bargain. No good had come to the Mostyns ever since—their fortunes had fallen whilst the Trevithicks had flourished like an evil weed.

Marcus Trevithick. Beth shivered again. She could not believe that he was evil, but he was certainly dangerous.

He was also the most attractive man that she had ever met. Having been a child bride, her experience was necessarily small, but even so she was certain that he could stand comparison in any company.

The carriage drew up outside the house in Upper Grosvenor Street that she had rented for the little Season. Kit descended and helped her out with cold, studied politeness. He did not say a word as he escorted her up the steps and into the entrance hall. Beth bit her lip. She knew she was well and truly in disgrace.

Charlotte Cavendish, Kit's sister, was sitting in the red drawing room, her netting resting on the cushion beside her. She was reading from Oliver Goldsmith's *The Vicar of Wakefield* but cast the book aside with a smile as they came in. Like her brother, she was very fair with sparkling blue eyes, slender and tall. A scrap of lace was perched on her blonde curls as a concession to a widow's cap.

'There you are! I had almost given you up and gone to bed...'

Her smile faded as she looked from her brother's stony face to Beth's flushed one.

'Oh, dear. What has happened?'

'Ask your cousin,' Kit said shortly, stripping off his white gloves. 'I will be in the book room, enjoying a peaceful glass of brandy!'

Charlotte's gaze moved round to Beth. 'Oh, dear,' she said again, but there was an irrepressible twinkle in her eyes. 'What have you done, Beth?'

Beth wandered over to the big red wing-chair opposite and curled up in it. She was beginning to feel annoyed as well as guilty.

'It is all very well for Kit to act the moralist, but it

was his idea to go to the Cyprians' Ball in the first place—'

Charlotte gave a little squeak and clapped her hand to her mouth. 'Beth! You told me you were going to Lady Radley's rout!'

'Well, so we did, but then Kit had the idea of the Cyprians' Ball!' Beth wriggled uncomfortably under her cousin's horrified stare. 'We were masked, so I thought there would be no harm...' She looked defiant. 'Very well, Lottie, I admit it! I was curious!'

'Oh, Beth,' Charlotte said in a failing voice. 'I know I cannot accompany you about the town, but I thought you would come to no harm with Kit!'

'Well, you were wrong!' Beth said mutinously. It suddenly seemed much easier to blame the whole thing on her cousin. 'None of this would have happened if Kit had not decided to have some fun!'

'None of what?' Charlotte asked, in the tone of someone who was not entirely sure they wanted to know the answer.

Beth yawned. She was very tired and suddenly wanted her bed, but equally she wanted someone to confide in. Her cousin had been as close as a sister this year past, closer than they had ever been in childhood when Charlotte's five years' seniority had put Beth quite in awe of her.

Beth, Kit and Charlotte had grown up together, but time and differing fortunes had scattered them. Charlotte had married an officer and followed the drum, Kit had spent several years in India and Beth had been orphaned at seventeen and left penniless. Friends and relatives had murmured of schoolteaching or governessing, but two days after her bereavement, Sir Frank Allerton, a widower whose estate marched with that of the Mostyns, had called to offer her an alternative future. He had not been a friend of the late Lord Mostyn, but Beth knew that her father had esteemed him as an honest man, and so she had accepted.

She had never regretted her decision, but she did regret the lack of children of her marriage. Her home and parish affairs had given her plenty to do, but when Frank had died, leaving her a widow at nineteen, she had been lonely. Though Kit had inherited Mostyn Hall and the title he was seldom at home, and it was Beth who kept an eye on the estate. Then, a year into Beth's widowhood, Charlotte had lost her husband during the retreat from Almeira and had come back to Mostyn. Fortunately she and Beth had found that they got on extremely well. Charlotte was cool and considered where Beth was impetuous and tempered some of her cousin's more madcap ideas. Beth's liveliness prevented her cousin from falling into a decline.

'So what has happened?' Charlotte asked again, recalling Beth's attention to the lamp-lit room. 'You went to the Ball...'

'Yes. We only intended to stay for a little, although I think Kit might have lingered if he had been there alone!' Beth said, with a sudden, mischievous grin. 'At any rate, it was not as I had imagined, Lottie! There was the most licentious behaviour—'

Charlotte looked exasperated. 'Well, what did you expect, Beth? You were at the Cyprians' Ball, not a Court Reception!'

Beth sighed. 'Yes, I know! Everyone was staring at me—no doubt because they thought me a demirep!' she added, before her cousin could make the observation herself.

'Yes, well, it was a reasonable assumption—' Charlotte

looked at her frankly '—and you do have a lovely figure, Beth! The gentlemen—'

'Spare me,' Beth said hastily, remembering the disturbing heat in Marcus Trevithick's eyes. 'I thought you wished to hear what had happened, Lottie?'

'Yes,' her cousin said obligingly, 'what did?'

'Well, Kit and I had a few dances and, as we were waltzing, the behaviour was becoming more and more uninhibited so I decided it would be wise to come home. Then a gentleman came up to us and asked me to dance.'

Beth looked away. When Marcus Trevithick had first approached her she had been amused and some dangerous imp of mischief had prompted her to play along. She had not known his identity then, but she had been tempted by the atmosphere, tempted by *him*...

She looked back at Charlotte, who was waiting in silence. 'We danced a country dance together and he introduced himself as Marcus Trevithick. I had had no notion—I have never met Trevithick before, and although he knew who Kit was he did not know me, though he made strenuous attempts to find out my name...'

'I'm sure he did,' Charlotte said drily. 'Did he proposition you, Beth?'

'Lottie!' Beth looked shocked, then smiled a little. 'Well...'

'Well, who could blame him?' Charlotte seemed torn between disapproval and laughter. 'The poor man, thinking you Haymarket-ware and no doubt getting a setdown for his trouble!'

'It was not quite like that,' Beth admitted slowly. 'Yes, he did...make his interest plain, but I did not discourage him exactly...' Suddenly, foolishly, it seemed difficult to explain. Or at least difficult to explain without giving some of her feelings away, Beth thought hopelessly. And Charlotte was no fool. She would read between the lines and see all the things that Beth had not admitted.

'It is just that I thought of Fairhaven,' she said, in a rush. 'You know that I had been intending to make Trevithick a financial offer for the island! Suddenly I thought how much more fun it would be to make a wager...' She risked a glance at her cousin from under her lashes and saw that Charlotte was frowning now, all hint of amusement forgotten.

'So I suggested that we step apart, and then I challenged him to a game of Hazard, with Fairhaven as the stake—'

'Beth!' Charlotte said on a note of entreaty. 'Tell me this is not true! What did you offer against his stake?'

Beth did not reply. Their eyes, grey and blue, met and held, before Charlotte gave a little groan and covered her face with her hands.

'Do you wish for your smelling salts, Lottie?' Beth asked, uncurling from her armchair and hurrying across to the armoire. 'You will feel much more the thing in a moment!'

'I feel very well, thank you!' Charlotte said, although she looked a little pale. 'I feel better, in fact, than you would have done if Trevithick had claimed his prize! I take it he did *not* win?'

'No, he did not!' Beth felt the heat come into her face. 'I won! And if I had lost I should not have honoured the bet! It was only a game—'

'No wonder Kit cut up rough!' Charlotte said faintly. 'Stepping aside with a gentleman who already thought you a Cyprian, challenging him to a game of chance, offering yourself as the stake...' She took the smelling salts and inhaled gratefully. The pale rose colour came back into her face.

'I have shocked you,' Beth said remorsefully.

'Yes, you have.' Charlotte's gaze searched Beth's face before she gave a slight shake of the head. 'Each time you do something outrageous, Beth, I tell myself that you could not possibly shock me more—and yet you do!'

'I am sorry!' Beth said, feeling contrite and secretly vowing not to tell Charlotte any more of the encounter. 'You know I am desperate to reclaim Fairhaven!'

'Not so desperate, surely, that you would do anything to take it back!' Charlotte sat back and patted the seat beside her. 'This obsession is ridiculous, Beth! The island was lost to our family years ago—leave it in the past, where it belongs!'

Beth did not reply. She had learned long ago that Charlotte was practical by nature and did not share the deep mystical tug of their heritage. Beth could remember standing on the cliffs of Devon as a small child and staring out across the flat, pewter sea to where a faint smudge on the horizon signified the island that they had lost. The tales of her grandfather, the dashing Charles Mostyn, and his struggle with the dastardly George Trevithick, had captured her child's imagination and never let it go. Lord Mostyn had lost the island through treachery and, fifty years later, Beth had vowed to take it back and restore the family fortunes. In her widowhood, a woman of means, she had twice offered George Trevithick, the Evil Earl, a fair price for the island. He had rejected her approach haughtily. But Beth was persistent and she had fully intended to repeat the offer to his grandson, the new Earl. It was one of the reasons that she had come up to London. Fate, however, had intervened…fate, and her own foolish impulse.

But perhaps it had not been so foolish, Beth thought. Whatever the circumstances Fairhaven was hers now, won in fair play. And she intended to claim it.

'What sort of man is Marcus Trevithick, Beth?' Charlotte asked casually. 'What did you think of him?'

Beth jumped. She was glad of the lamp-lit shadows and the firelight, for in the clear daylight she did not doubt that her face would have betrayed her.

'He is perhaps of an age with Kit, or a little older,' she said, glad that she sounded so casual herself. 'Tall, dark… He has something of the look of the old Earl about him.'

'The Evil Earl,' Charlotte said slowly. 'Do you think that his grandson has inherited his character along with his estates?'

Beth shivered a little. 'Who knows? I was scarce with him long enough to find out.'

'Yet you must have gained some impression of his nature and disposition?' Charlotte persisted. 'Was he pleasing?'

Pleasing? Who could deny it? Beth remembered the strength of Marcus's arms around her, the compelling demand of his lips against hers. He was a man quite outside her experience. But he was also a liar and a cheat. She saw again his mocking smile. She turned her hot face away.

'No, indeed. He was a proud, arrogant man. I did not like him!'

Charlotte yawned and got to her feet. 'Well, I am for my bed.' She bent and dropped a soft kiss on Beth's cheek, pausing as she straightened up. 'You did not tell Lord Trevithick your name?'

'No,' Beth said, reflecting that that at least was true.

'And though you were with Kit, you were masked.' Charlotte sounded satisfied. 'Well, at least he will not know your identity. For that we must be grateful, I suppose, for it would cause the most monstrous scandal if it were known that you had attended the Cyprians' Ball! People would assume—' She broke off. 'Well, never mind. But perhaps you will think twice in future before you play such a hoyden's trick again!'

The door closed softly behind her. Beth lay back on the cushions and let out her breath in a huge, shaky sigh. Charlotte was in the right of it, of course—it would be very damaging for it to become known that she had been at the Cyprians' Ball. And what Charlotte did not know was that whilst she had not given Trevithick her name, he had seen her face without the mask. Beth stared into the fire. Well, it mattered little. She would send Gough to call on the Earl's man of business in the morning, and once the title to Fairhaven was in her pocket, she would leave for Devon without delay.

Even though he had said he would not honour his bet, Beth could see no reason why Marcus Trevithick would decline to surrender the island to her, for it could not be worth much to him. He had lands and houses far more valuable and there was no sentimental reason for him to hold on to the least important part of his estate. If he persisted in his refusal, however, she was still prepared to pay him, and, Beth thought with satisfaction, one could not say fairer than that. She had heard that his pockets were to let and she was certain that he would see the sense of the matter.

She raked out the embers of the fire, doused the lamp and went upstairs to bed. It should have been easy to put the matter out of her head but for some reason the

memory of the encounter—the memory of Marcus
Trevithick—still lingered as she lay in her bed. She told
herself that she had seen the last of him, but some unnerving instinct told her that she had not. Then she told
herself that she did not wish to see him again and the
same all-knowing voice in her head told her that she lied.

Chapter Two

'A gambler, a wastrel, a rake and a vagabond!' the Dowager Viscountess of Trevithick said triumphantly, ticking the words off on her fingers.

There was a short silence around the Trevithick breakfast table. The autumn sun shone through the long windows and sparkled on the silver. There were only three places set; one of Marcus's married sisters was coming up from the country for the little Season but had not yet arrived, and the other had gone to stay with friends for a few weeks. Only Marcus, his youngest sister Eleanor and the Dowager Viscountess were therefore in residence at Trevithick House.

'A vagabond, Mama?' Marcus enquired politely. 'What is the justification for that?'

He thought he heard a smothered giggle and looked round to see Eleanor hastily applying herself to her toast. Although she appeared to be the demurest of debutantes on the surface, Marcus knew that his sister had a strong sense of humour. It was a relief to know that the Viscountess had not crushed it all out of her during Marcus's years abroad.

'Traipsing around the courts of Europe!' the

Viscountess said, giving her son a baleful glare from her cold grey eyes. 'Drifting from one country to another like a refugee…'

Marcus folded up his newspaper with an irritable rustle. He had a headache that morning, no doubt from the brandy that he and Justin had consumed the night before, and Lady Trevithick's animadversions on his character were not helping. In fact, he was surprised that she had not added drunkard to the list.

'I scarce think that a diplomatic mission accompanying Lord Easterhouse to Austria constitutes vagabondage, Mama,' he observed coolly. 'Your other charges, however, may be justified—'

'Oh, Marcus, you are scarcely a wastrel!' Eleanor protested sweetly. Her brown eyes sparkled. 'Why, since your return from abroad I have heard Mr Gower say that the estates are already better managed—'

'Enough from you, miss!' the Dowager Viscountess snapped, chewing heavily on her bread roll. 'You are altogether too quick with your opinions! We shall never find a husband for you! As well try to find a wife for your brother! Why, Lady Hutton was saying only the other day that her Maria would be the perfect bride for Trevithick were it not that Hutton would worry to give her into the care of someone with so sadly unsteady a character! So there is no prospect of *that* fifty thousand pounds coming into the family!'

Marcus sighed. It was difficult enough having a parent who was so frank in her criticism without her holding the view that he was still in short coats. How Eleanor tolerated it, he could not imagine. He knew that if he had been in her shoes he would have taken the first man who offered, just to escape Lady Trevithick. Marcus was also aware that his friendship with Justin did not help either. The Dowager Viscountess had never got over her disapproval of her nephew and barely acknowledged him in public, a sign of displeasure that Justin cheerfully ignored. Families, Marcus thought, could be damnably difficult.

As if in response to that very thought, Penn, the butler, strode into the room.

'Mr Justin Trevithick is without, my lord, and enquiring for you. Shall I show him in?'

Marcus grinned. 'By all means, Penn! And pray send someone to set another cover—my cousin may not yet have partaken of breakfast!'

The Dowager grunted and hauled her massive bulk from the chair. 'I have some letters to write and will be in the library. There is the possibility that Dexter's daughter may be a suitable wife for you, Marcus, but I have some further enquiries to make!'

'Well, pray do not hurry on my account, Mama!' Marcus said cheerfully, gaining himself another glare from his parent and a covert smile from his sister. 'Miss Dexter would need to be very rich indeed to tempt me!'

'Marcus, you make her much worse!' Eleanor whispered, as the Dowager Viscountess left the room. 'If you could only ignore her!'

'That would be difficult!' Marcus said drily. 'I curse the day she appointed herself my matchmaker!' His expression softened as it rested on his sister. 'How you tolerate it, infant, I shall never know!'

Eleanor shook her head but did not speak and, a second later, Justin Trevithick came into the room. He shook Marcus's hand and gave Eleanor a kiss.

'Eleanor! I'm glad that Lady Trevithick did not whisk you away—'

The door opened. 'Her ladyship requests that you join

her in the library, Miss Eleanor,' Penn said, in sonorous tones. 'Lord Prideaux has called and is with her.'

Eleanor gave her cousin and brother a speaking glance, then dutifully followed Penn out of the room. Marcus gestured towards the coffee pot. 'Can I offer you breakfast, Justin? And my apologies for my mother's transparently bad manners at the same time?'

Justin laughed. 'Thank you. I will take breakfast—and for the rest, please do not regard it! The only thing that concerns me is that Lady Trevithick considers Prideaux more suitable company for Eleanor than myself! He is a loose fish, but then, I suppose his parents were at least respectably married!'

'So were yours,' Marcus commented.

'Yes, but only after I was born!' Justin leant over and poured some coffee. 'How do you feel this morning, old fellow? Must confess my head's splitting! That brandy was nowhere near the quality it pretended!'

'The coffee will help,' Marcus said absently, reflecting that the brandy had proved to be the opposite of his mysterious adversary of the previous night. She had been Quality masquerading as something else and today he was determined to get to the bottom of that particular mystery. He had told Justin an expurgated version of the whole tale the previous night over the maligned brandy bottle, and his cousin had been as curious as he as to the lady's motives. Justin had been closer to the fifth Earl than Marcus because their grandfather had taken Justin up deliberately to spite his elder son, but despite his far greater knowledge of the old man's estates and fortune, he could throw no light on why anyone would want the island of Fairhaven.

The door opened for a third time as Penn came in.

'Mr Gower is here to see you, my lord. He says that it is most urgent.'

Marcus frowned, checking the clock on the marble mantelpiece. It was very early for a call from his man of business, but if Gower had managed to find him rooms well away from Albemarle Street, then the earlier the better. Remembering the previous night, his frown deepened. There was another reason why Gower might have called, of course...

'Thank you, Penn, I will join Mr Gower in the study shortly,' he said.

The door closed noiselessly as Penn trod away to impart the message. Justin buttered another roll. 'Shall I wait here for you, Marcus, or do you prefer to join me at White's later?'

Marcus stood up. 'Why don't you come with me to see Gower?' he suggested. 'I have the strangest suspicion that this relates to the business last night, Justin, and I would value your advice.'

His cousin raised his eyebrows. 'Your mysterious gamester, Marcus? Surely she does not really intend to claim Fairhaven!'

'We shall see,' Marcus said grimly.

Mr Gower was waiting for them in the study, pacing the floor with an impatience that set fair to wear a track through the rich Indian rug. He was a thin, aesthetic-looking man whose pained expression had come about through years of trying to make the irascible old Earl see sense over the running of the Trevithick estates. There was a thick sheaf of papers in his hand.

'My lord!' he exclaimed agitatedly, as the gentlemen entered. 'Mr Trevithick! Something most untoward has occurred!'

Marcus folded himself negligently into an armchair.

'Take a seat and tell us all, Gower!' he instructed amiably. 'What has happened—has one of the housemaids absconded with the silver?'

Mr Gower frowned at such inappropriate levity, but he took a seat uncomfortably on the edge of the other armchair, placing his shabby leather briefcase at his feet. Justin strolled over to the window, still eating his bread roll.

'This morning I had a call from a gentleman by the name of Gough who has chambers close to mine,' Mr Gower said, still agitated. He shuffled his papers on the table. 'He is a most respected lawyer and represents only the best people! He came to tell me of an agreement between one of his clients and yourself, my lord, an agreement to cede the title deeds to the island of Fairhaven, which is—'

'I know where it is, thank you, Gower,' Marcus said coolly. He exchanged a look with Justin. 'Gough, is it? Did he tell you the name of his client?'

'No, sir,' the lawyer said unhappily. 'He told me that his client expected—*expected* was the precise word used, my lord—that I would have the deeds to the island ready to hand over immediately. Naturally I told him that I could do no such thing without your consent, my lord, and that you had issued no such authorisation. He therefore suggested…' Mr Gower shuddered, as though the suggestion had been made with some force '…that I call upon you to gain your approval forthwith. Which I am doing, sir. And,' he finished, apparently unable to stop himself, 'I do feel that I should protest, my lord, at the cavalier manner in which this transaction appears to have been handled, putting me in a most difficult position with a fellow member of my profession!'

There was a long silence. 'You are right, Gower,'

Marcus said slowly. 'The whole matter is damnably out of order and I apologise if it has put you in a difficult situation.'

'But the island, my lord!' Gower said beseechingly. 'The deeds! If you have an agreement with Mr Gough's client—'

'There is no agreement,' Marcus said. He heard Justin draw breath sharply, but did not look at him. 'Tell Gough,' he said implacably, 'that there is no agreement.'

'My lord...' Gower sounded most unhappy. 'If there is any way that such a contract could be proved, I do beg you to reconsider!'

Marcus raised one black eyebrow. 'Do you not trust me, Gower?' he asked humorously. 'At the very most it could be construed as a verbal contract and there were no witnesses.'

Gower blinked like a hunted animal. 'None, my lord? Can you be certain of that?'

A smile twitched Marcus's lips. 'Perfectly.'

'But even so...' Gower glanced across at Justin. 'A verbal contract, my lord...'

'I think Mr Gower feels that you should honour your pledges, Marcus,' Justin said, with a grin. 'Even in a game of chance—'

'A game of chance!' Gower looked even more disapproving. 'My lord! Mr Trevithick! This is all most irregular!'

'As you say, Gower,' Marcus murmured. 'Have no fear. Gough's client will never sue. I would stake my life on it!'

Justin grimaced. 'Can you be so sure, Marcus? She sounds mighty determined to me!'

Gower, who was just shuffling his papers into his briefcase, scattered them on the carpet. 'She, sir, *she*?'

he stuttered. 'Good God, my lord, not even the old Earl would have indulged in a wager with a female!'

'He was missing a trick then,' Marcus said coolly, 'for I found it most stimulating!' He rose to his feet. 'Good day, Gower. Give Gough my message and if you find his instructions are that he persists in his claim, refer him direct to me. Penn will show you out!'

'Marcus,' Justin said, once they were alone, 'do you not consider this a little unsporting of you? After all, the girl won the bet, did she not?'

'She did,' Marcus conceded. He met Justin's eyes. 'Truth is, Justin, I would like to meet her again, find out about this passion she has for Fairhaven. It intrigues me.'

'And this is how you intend to flush her out?'

'Precisely!' Marcus grinned suddenly. 'I could go to Kit Mostyn and ask for his help, of course, but I would wager he will not grant it! So…if I refuse to honour the bet, my mysterious opponent may show her hand again!'

Justin's lips twisted. 'You're a cunning devil, Marcus! But what is your interest in the lady herself?'

Marcus's grin deepened. 'That depends—on the lady and who she turns out to be!'

'And you would recognise her again?'

'Oh, yes,' Marcus said slowly. 'I would recognise her anywhere, Justin.'

'Pull your chair up a little closer, my love,' Lady Fanshawe instructed her goddaughter, gesturing her to move to the front of the theatre box. 'Why, you will not be able to see anything at all from back there! But do not lean out too far! It is not good to lean excessively, for the gentlemen will stare so! Oh, pray do look, Beth!' Lady Fanshawe leant as far out of the box as she could without falling. 'It is Mr Rollinson and Lord Saye! I do believe they will call upon us in the interval!'

Beth edged her chair forward an inch and leant backwards at the same time. She had every intention of effacing herself until she was practically invisible. The invitation to the theatre was a longstanding one and could not be avoided, for Lady Fanshawe had been her mother's closest friend. That was the only reason why Beth had come to Drury Lane that evening, although the play, Sheridan's *The Rivals*, would normally have been sufficient to tempt her out. Normally, but not now. The matter of Marcus Trevithick and her ill-conceived wager with him had suddenly become so very difficult that she had no desire to risk meeting him again.

Beth chanced a glance over the edge of the box at the crowded auditorium below. Fortunately it would be easy to be inconspicuous in such a crush. People were milling around and chattering nineteen to the dozen: dandies, ladies, courtesans... Beth drew back sharply as a passing buck raised his quizzing glass at her in a manner she considered to be odiously familiar. Lady Fanshawe did not notice for she was waving excitedly to an acquaintance in the crowd.

It was already very hot. Beth fanned herself and looked around idly. Kit had escorted her again that evening but as soon as they had arrived he had left her in Lady Fanshawe's company and could now be seen in a box to the left, chatting to a very dashing lady in green silk with nodding ostrich feathers. Lady Fanshawe had taken one look and remarked disapprovingly that one met with any old riff-raff at the theatre and that Kit need not think to foist his *chère amie* on their attention! Beth had been a little curious, but had tried not to stare. She thought that the dashing lady looked rather fast but, given her own performance at the Cyprians' Ball, she was scarcely in a position to comment.

As time wore on without mishap, Beth started to relax a little. She felt comfortably nondescript in her rose muslin dress. She had chosen it deliberately because it was so unremarkable and she had tried to disguise herself further with a matching rose-pink turban, but Charlotte had positively forbidden her to leave the house looking such a dowd. Beth sighed. It was a terrible shame that Charlotte could never accompany them, but her cousin had had a fear of crowds ever since she was a girl and the glittering hordes that thronged the *ton*'s balls and parties terrified her. It was odd, for Charlotte was perfectly comfortable in society she knew, and could travel and visit amongst friends quite happily, but she was never at ease with strangers.

Beth watched as Kit took a fond farewell of his companion and turned to rejoin them for the start of the play. He was just making his way back to their box when Beth saw that his attention had been firmly caught by a slender young lady, very much the debutante, who was just taking her seat opposite. Intrigued, Beth watched as the young lady saw Kit and faltered in her conversation. For a long moment the two of them simply gazed at each other, then the girl gave Kit a half-smile and turned hesitantly away. Beth smiled to herself. Kit seemed smitten and she must remember to quiz him on the identity of the young lady…

She froze, all thought of Kit and his romantic entanglements flying from her mind as she saw the gentleman who had entered the box behind the girl. She recognised his height, the arrogant tilt of his head. She could even imagine those smooth, faintly mocking tones that she had last heard at the Cyprians' Ball, but which had positively leapt from the page of the letter he had sent her via Gough earlier in the week:

'My dear lady adventuress…'

Beth's fan slipped from her shaking fingers and she leant down to retrieve it, trying to shrink into the shadows. Bent almost double, she groped around on the floor and tried to think quickly at the same time. How was she to avoid Marcus Trevithick seeing her when their boxes were almost opposite each other? If she tried to leave now, would she be able to slip away or would she only draw more attention to herself? She cursed the pale pink dress, which had seemed such a good idea earlier but in the dim light seemed to glow like a beacon.

'What are you doing down there on the floor, Beth, my love? Are you feeling unwell? Do you wish to return home?'

Beth straightened up hastily as Lady Fanshawe's carrying tones threatened to attract the notice of the whole theatre.

'I am very well, I thank you, dear ma'am. I had only dropped my fan…' Her words trailed away as, under some strange compulsion, she looked across the theatre and directly into the dark eyes of Marcus Trevithick. There could not be the slightest doubt that he had recognised her. He held her gaze for a long moment, a smile starting to curl the corners of his mouth, then he inclined his head in ironic salutation.

The play started at last and Beth forced herself to look at the stage and nowhere else. This proved difficult as a wayward part of her seemed to want to look across at the Earl of Trevithick all the time and she had to fix her gaze firmly on the actors instead. She soon discovered that she was one of the few people in the whole theatre who was giving their undivided attention to the stage.

The chatter about her scarcely faltered and it seemed that most of the fashionable crowd viewed the play as a diversion from the main business of the evening. Eventually the noise began to grate on Beth, who inevitably found her concentration interrupted. After that it was easy for her thoughts to wander back to the tangle in which she found herself.

When Gough had come to her five days before and told her that the Earl was refusing to honour his bet and give Fairhaven to her, she had been annoyed but not particularly surprised. She had sent the lawyer back to offer a price that she felt was more than fair and had waited, confident that Trevithick would agree this time. It had come as a nasty shock when Gough returned the next day, out of countenance, to relate that he had seen the Earl in person and that her offer had been spurned. Further, the Earl was demanding in no uncertain terms that his client identify herself and discuss the matter with him face to face. This Beth declined to do, but she sweetened her refusal with a far more tempting sum of money. She could afford it and he... Well, she had thought that he would seize the chance to make such a profit. Instead, Gough had delivered the letter.

My dear lady adventuress,

Your offers intrigue me but you should know that I will only do business with you directly. If you choose not to identify yourself it makes no odds; I shall soon know your name and your direction. Then, even if you do *not* choose it, I shall seek you out...

After that, Beth had not set foot outside the house for two days. Glancing across at Marcus Trevithick now, she acknowledged that she had not felt afraid, precisely, more angry and outmanoeuvred. She had won the wager, but he held all the cards. He was not only refusing to give her Fairhaven, but he was also refusing to *sell* it to her, and if he discovered her identity he could ruin her by having it whispered abroad that she, a respectable lady, had attended the Cyprians' Ball. She knew that the wisest thing was to withdraw her offer and retire from the lists, but it seemed that Marcus Trevithick was not prepared to let her do so. She was angry with him, but she was furious with herself for giving him the advantage.

'Do you care to take a walk during the interval, Beth?' Kit enquired, from beside her. 'It might be pleasant to stretch our legs…'

Beth came back to the present, looked around and realised that the curtain had come down at the end of the first act. She glanced across at Marcus Trevithick and saw that he was already moving purposefully towards their box. So much for her half-formed hope that he would not dare accost her there! She took a quick breath.

'A walk? Yes! No…I am not sure… Yes!'

Kit looked understandably confused. 'What the deuce is the matter with you, Beth? You're as edgy as a thoroughbred mare!'

Beth grabbed his arm. She could see that Marcus had been delayed by an acquaintance, but he was still watching her with the concentrated attention of a predator. There could be no question that he meant to approach her.

Beth took one last look and hurried out of the box. 'Yes, by all means! Let us walk! This way!'

She steered her cousin out of the doorway and

plunged into the corridor outside, making for the place where the crowd was thickest.

'Steady on, Beth!' Kit protested, as he was buffeted on all sides. 'You'll have us trampled in the crush!'

It was inevitable that such tactics, whilst they might delay matters, could not put them off forever. It was only a matter of minutes before someone recognised Kit and stopped him for a word, whilst the pressure of the crowd pulled Beth from his side before she had even noticed. Seconds later she looked round and realised that her cousin was nowhere in sight. Marcus Trevithick was, however.

He was leaning against a pillar just a few feet away from her, arms folded, as though he were prepared to stay there all night. His black gaze was watchful and faintly amused. Beth felt her breath catch in her throat. For one moment it seemed as though the press of people would whisk her past him, but then he stretched out one hand in a negligent gesture and caught her arm, pulling her to his side.

'Well, well! My mystery lady—at last! Have you any idea of the balls and routs I have endured these past few days in the hope of catching sight of you, ma'am?'

There were prying eyes and ears all around them. Beth strove to keep her face blank and give nothing away, though her heart was hammering.

'Good evening, my lord! I am sorry that you have put yourself to such trouble on my account!'

Marcus gave her a look of brilliant amusement. 'Thank you! It was worth it, however, for now I have found you again!' He tucked her hand through the crook of his arm and steered her out into the corridor. The crowd had lessened now and they could stroll along without too much difficulty. Beth looked around for rescue, but none was immediately forthcoming.

'I only wanted to speak with you, you know,' Marcus said reproachfully. 'I was utterly intrigued by your offer and wished to discuss the matter with you—'

'Is that not why you employ a man of business, my lord?' Beth asked, keeping her bright social smile in place. 'To relieve you of such onerous tasks?'

'Generally. But this would hardly be onerous.'

Beth found the warmth in Marcus's tone difficult to resist. She glanced up through her lashes and saw that he was smiling at her. It made her feel strangely hot and cold at the same time and she almost shivered. She made an effort to gather her scattered senses.

'If you had but honoured your wager, my lord, such a situation would not have occurred!'

'True.' Marcus bent closer and she felt his breath stir the tendrils of hair by her ear. 'But that would have defeated my object—of seeing you again, sweetheart!'

Beth stopped dead and glared at him. 'Do *not* call me that!' she hissed. 'You must know I am no…no lightskirt for your tumbling!'

Marcus grinned. 'Then why behave like one, ma'am? A dignified request to buy Fairhaven might have elicited a more dignified response!'

Beth could have wept with frustration. What had started as a light-hearted idea—to visit the Cyprians' Ball—had caused more trouble than she could ever have imagined. She wondered what on earth had possessed her to dance with Marcus Trevithick and to further the masquerade. At the time the opportunity to trick him out of Fairhaven had seemed too good to miss, amusing, clever even. She had congratulated herself on her ingenuity—and on her courage! Now she could see that the wager had been the product of too much wine and excitement. She tightened her lips in exasperation.

'It was an impulse! Which I now bitterly regret!'

'Understandably. If you are indeed the lady you pretend to be, what could be worse than a version of the events of that night circulating amongst the *ton*? Dear me, ma'am, it does not bear thinking about!'

Beth coloured up furiously. 'You would not do such a thing!'

'Why not?'

Marcus's tone was mild, but when she glanced up at his face Beth saw that he was watching her intently. It was exactly the problem that Charlotte had hinted at, the one that Beth had not even anticipated. If the Earl of Trevithick let it be known that he had had an encounter with a lady indecorously disporting herself at the Cyprians' Ball, no one would believe in her innocence. And yet some instinct told her that he would not do that to her. Her troubled grey gaze scanned his face and she saw the hard lines soften a little as a smile came into his eyes. Suddenly she was acutely aware of him; of the smooth material of his sleeve beneath her fingers and the hard muscle of his arm beneath that, of the warmth of his body so close to hers and the disturbing look in his eyes.

'Just tell me your name,' he said softly, persuasively.

'Beth, my dear! There you are!' Beth jumped and swung round, tearing her gaze from Marcus. Lady Fanshawe was bearing down on them, her good-natured face wreathed in smiles. Her gaze moved from her goddaughter to the Earl of Trevithick and her smile faltered slightly in surprise, but she recovered herself well.

'Oh! Lord Trevithick, is it not? How do you do, sir? I had no notion that you knew my goddaughter!'

Beth was aware of a sinking feeling as she watched Marcus bow elegantly over Lady Fanshawe's hand. She knew that her godmother, voluble as ever, was about to give her identity away completely.

'It is so delightful to see that the younger generation has ended that tiresome estrangement between the Mostyn and Trevithick families!' Lady Fanshawe burbled. 'I have never quite understood the cause of all the trouble, for it was an unconscionably long time ago and over some trifling matter such as a lost battle—'

'Or perhaps a lost island, ma'am!' Marcus said smoothly. Beth felt his dark gaze brush her face and deliberately evaded his eyes. 'In fact, I was hoping that your charming goddaughter—' there was just a hint of a query in his voice '—might tell me more about our family feud, for I confess it fascinates me!'

Lady Fanshawe beamed, accepting Marcus's other arm as they strolled slowly back towards the box. 'Oh, well, Beth will be able to tell you the whole story, I dare say! All the Mostyns are steeped in family history from the cradle!'

'I see,' Marcus said slowly. Beth could feel him moving closer to his goal, but for some reason she felt powerless to intervene and direct the conversation into other channels. And Lady Fanshawe was so very good-natured, and seemed pleased that the Earl was showing such an interest...

'You must know the family extremely well, ma'am,' he continued.

'Oh, indeed, for Davinia Mostyn, Beth's mama, was such a dear friend of mine, was she not, Beth, my love? It was such a tragedy when Lord and Lady Mostyn were killed in that horrid accident! But then Kit inherited the title and Beth married Frank Allerton...'

Beth felt Marcus's arm move beneath her fingers. She caught her breath.

'You did not tell me that you were Sir Francis's widow, Lady Allerton,' Marcus said gently, smiling down at her. She could see the triumph in his eyes. 'He was a fine man and a great scholar. His treatise on hydrostatics formed part of my university studies. I remember his work well.'

'Thank you,' Beth murmured, looking away. 'Sir Francis was indeed a fine academician.'

They had reached their box now and discovered that the second act of the play was about to start. Kit was already in his seat and looked up, startled, to see both his cousin and Lady Fanshawe escorted by the Earl of Trevithick. The two men exchanged a stiff bow, and then Marcus took Beth's hand in his.

'I should deem it an honour to call on you, Lady Allerton,' he murmured, his gaze resting on her face in a look that brought the colour into her cheeks. 'I understand that you are staying in Upper Grosvenor Street?'

Beth hesitated. 'We are, but—'

'Then I shall look forward to seeing you shortly.' He bowed again. 'Good evening, ma'am.'

Beth bit her lip as she watched his tall figure make its way back to the party in the Trevithick box. It seemed that the Earl was difficult to refuse. And now that Lady Fanshawe had told him everything he needed to know, his position was well nigh unassailable. With a sigh, Beth tried to direct her attention back to the play. She wondered what his next move would be.

'I am not at all sure about these newfangled artists,' Lady Fanshawe sighed, pausing in front of a landscape painting by John Constable. 'Only look at those odd flecks of light and the strange *rough* technique. There is something not quite finished...indeed, not quite *gentlemanly* about it!'

Beth laughed. She rather liked Constable's atmospheric landscapes and they gave her a longing for the countryside and the fresh sea air. It was pleasant to be able to escape the bustle of the London Season for a little and step through an imaginary window into another landscape, even if they were in fact in the Royal Academy and Lady Fanshawe was starting to complain that her feet were aching.

'Why do you not take the seat over there, ma'am, if you are fatigued?' she suggested, gesturing to a comfortable banquette placed over by the window. 'I shall not keep you long, but I should just like to see Mr Turner's collection in the blue room. If you would grant me five minutes...'

Lady Fanshawe nodded, sighing with relief as she took the weight off her feet. 'Take as long as you wish, my love,' she said, sitting back and closing her eyes. 'I suggest we call in Bond Street on our way home. Far more to my taste, but one must be seen here, you know!'

Smiling, Beth wandered through to the second gallery. There was quite a fashionable crowd present, bearing out the truth of Lady Fanshawe's statement on the social importance of attending the exhibition. Beth paused before a picture of seascape and gave a small, unconscious sigh. The water was a stormy grey and the clouds were building on the horizon, and far out to sea there was an island...

'Daydreaming, my lady?' The voice, deep and slightly mocking, caught Beth by surprise. She turned her head sharply to meet the quizzical gaze of the Earl of Trevithick. She could feel a vexatious blush rising to her cheeks and looked away swiftly. It was irritating enough that she had spent the last three days waiting for him to call on her, with a secret anticipation that she had not acknowledged even to herself. She had just begun to relax and think that he had forgotten her, when here he was.

'How do you do, my lord.' Beth smiled politely. She tried not to notice how superbly elegant Marcus looked in a coat of green superfine and the fawn pantaloons that clung to his muscular thighs. 'I hope that you are enjoying the exhibition?'

Marcus took her hand. 'To tell the truth, I came here with the sole intention of seeing you, Lady Allerton. I called in Upper Grosvenor Street and was told that you would be here, and I hoped to persuade you to drive with me. It is a very pleasant autumn day and my curricle is outside.'

Beth hesitated. 'Thank you, my lord, but I am here with Lady Fanshawe—'

'I am sure she could be persuaded to entrust you to me.' Marcus smiled down at her. 'That is, if *you* wish to come with me, Lady Allerton. You might not want to break a centuries-old feud, after all!'

Beth could not help laughing. 'How absurd you are, my lord! I believe I might take the risk, but...'

'I know!' Marcus looked apologetic. 'You are quite out of charity with me because of my ungallant refusal to grant you Fairhaven! But now, Lady Allerton...' he bent closer to her '...now you have the opportunity to persuade me! Will you take the challenge?'

Beth looked at him. There was a definite gleam of provocation in his eye. She frowned.

'It seems to me, my lord, that you have the best of both worlds! You have nothing to lose whereas I may wear myself to a shred trying to convince you of my attachment to Fairhaven and still have no influence over you!'

A wicked smile curved Marcus's lips. 'Believe me, Lady Allerton, you have made quite an impression on me already! I would put nothing outside your powers!'

Beth blushed and looked away. 'Pray do not tease so, my lord.'

'Must I not?' Marcus offered her his arm and they started to walk back through the gallery. 'It is difficult to resist. So, will you take my challenge?'

Beth paused. 'I will drive with you. That would be most pleasant.'

'Very proper. You are not always so proper, are you, Lady Allerton?'

'However, I could withdraw my acceptance. Any more of your mockery, my lord—' Beth looked at him severely '—and I shall do so!'

Marcus inclined his head. 'Very well! We shall instigate a truce! You are a most determined person, Lady Allerton. It is quite unusual.'

'Unusual, perhaps. Most certainly imprudent.' Beth spoke wryly. She was thinking of Charlotte and her strictures on her conduct. 'I think it comes from being an only child, my lord. I was much indulged and given my own way. It bred stubbornness in me, I fear. And then, my late husband...'

'Yes?' Marcus slanted a look down at her. Beth sensed that his interest had sharpened and she managed to stop her runaway disclosures just in time.

'Well, he was very kind and indulgent too...generous to me... I was most fortunate.'

'You must have been a child bride,' Marcus observed lightly, after a moment. 'After all, you are scarce in your dotage now! How long have you been widowed, Lady Allerton?'

Beth turned her head so that the brim of her bonnet shielded her from his too-perceptive gaze. Something about this man made her feel vulnerable, as though he could read into her words all the things she did not say.

'Sir Francis died two years ago. Yes, I was very young when I married. My parents had been killed in an accident and I...' Her voice trailed away. She did not want to reveal how lonely she had felt, uncertain if she was making the right decision in marrying hastily. On the one side had been security and on the other... On the other, she had felt as though she was throwing away all her youth and future by marrying a man older than her father. Yet Frank had been a kind husband, as kind to her as to a favourite niece. All she had lacked was excitement.

'I see,' Marcus said, and Beth had the unnerving suspicion that he did indeed see a great deal.

'My dears!' Lady Fanshawe had watched them approach and now rose to her feet, wincing slightly. She greeted the Earl as though he was a family friend of long standing, which Beth found slightly unnerving. She watched with resignation as it took Marcus all of a minute to persuade Lady Fanshawe to his plan.

'If you have offered to take Lady Allerton up with you I am all gratitude, my lord,' Lady Fanshawe trilled, 'for I am sorely in need of a rest! I was intending to call at Bond Street, but fear I do not have the energy! This picture-viewing is unconscionably tiring!'

They went out of the Academy, Marcus calling a hackney carriage to convey Lady Fanshawe home before handing Beth up into his curricle. It was a fine, bright day for autumn and the pale sun was warm. It was pleasant to be driving slowly through the fresh air of the Park, although it seemed to Beth that they were obliged to stop every few yards to greet the Earl's acquaintances. She knew few people in London, so had little to contribute to this social ritual, and after a while she had been introduced to so many new people that her head was spinning.

At last, when they reached a quieter stretch of road, Marcus turned to her with a rueful smile. 'Forgive me. To drive at the fashionable hour precludes sensible conversation!'

'You seem to have a vast number of friends in London, my lord,' Beth said non-committally, thinking of the elegant ladies who had appraised her with curiosity-hard eyes and the sporting gentlemen who had looked her over as though she was a piece of horseflesh.

Marcus smiled. 'I certainly know a lot of people, but as for friends—' he shook his head '—I could count them on the fingers of one hand! But I almost forgot, Lady Allerton...' His gloved hand covered Beth's and her pulse jumped at the contact. 'I cannot count you my friend, for we are sworn enemies, are we not? Will you tell me more about the feud?'

'Oh, the feud...' For a moment, gazing into those dark eyes, Beth was all at sea. She had forgotten all about it. Then she pulled herself together. This was the point of the whole exercise, after all. Somehow she had to persuade Marcus Trevithick of the importance of Fairhaven to her, and becoming distracted by his company was not going to help at all. She pulled her hand away and saw him smile at the gesture.

'I believe that the feud between the Trevithicks and Mostyns dates back to the Civil War, my lord.' Beth cleared her throat and tried to sound businesslike. 'The

Mostyns were on the side of the King and the Trevithicks were for Parliament. When Sir James Mostyn went into exile with Charles II, the Trevithicks took the chance to steal—I mean to seize—Mostyn land.'

'Steal will do,' Marcus said lazily. 'I fear the Trevithicks always were thieves and scoundrels, Lady Allerton! But they prospered as a result!'

'To profit by the misfortune of others is not honourable!' Beth said hotly. 'Even worse, at the Restoration, the Mostyns regained a little of their former estate, but the Trevithicks managed to persuade the King of their good faith and were not punished!'

'I can see that you have a very strong sense of fair play, Lady Allerton!' Marcus observed. 'Sadly, the way the Trevithicks prospered is the way that fortunes are often made—through double-dealing!'

Beth looked severe. 'That is no recommendation, my lord!'

'No, I can see that my ancestry is doing me little service here. I sense that worse is to come as well. Pray continue!'

Beth glanced at him doubtfully. Although his tone contained its habitual teasing edge, he was looking quite absorbed. She shifted uncomfortably.

'I hope that the tale does not bore you, my lord?'

'Not in the least! I am all attention!'

Beth realised that this was true. Marcus had loosened his grip on the reins and the horses, very well-behaved thoroughbred bays, were trotting at a decorous pace along the path. All of Marcus's attention was focused on her and as soon as Beth realised it she became acutely aware of the warmth of his regard and the disturbingly intent expression in those dark eyes.

'Well, yes…anyway… For a hundred years the Trevithicks prospered and Mostyns struggled, but they still held Fairhaven Island.' Beth glared at Marcus, forgetting for a moment that he had not been personally responsible for wresting it from her grandfather. It was easy to fall back into the stories of her childhood, the enthralling tales of Trevithick treachery. 'Then my grandfather inherited the estate and came up against your grandfather, my lord, the fifth Earl, George Trevithick.'

'Ah, the Evil Earl. I have heard much of his exploits. They say that in his youth he was in league with the wreckers and the smugglers and the pirates and anyone who could help him make an illegal profit.'

'I have no doubt. What is certainly true is that our grandfathers were implacable enemies, my lord, and had sworn to take their fight to the death. One stormy March night my grandfather was sailing for Fairhaven, not knowing that the Earl had already landed there and that the wreckers were waiting for him. There was a gale blowing and in the dark my grandfather did not realise that the shore lights were not placed there by his servants but were a trick of the enemy.' Beth took a deep breath. 'His ship ran aground and all hands were lost, along with the chest of treasure the ship had been carrying. My grandfather was the only one to escape ashore, but he was ambushed by the Evil Earl and cut down in the fight. Then the Earl stole his sword, the Sword of Saintonge, that had been in the family for centuries, and took the island into the bargain! Now, what do you think of that, my lord?'

Beth finished, out of breath, and looked at Marcus expectantly. It was a tale for a dark, stormy night rather than a bright day in the park, and it was difficult to believe that either of them were the descendants of men who had struggled to the death for supremacy only fifty years before. That conflict had been ruthless and atavistic, belonging to a previous and less civilised time. Beth allowed herself to consider the man who sat beside her, looking every inch the sophisticated society gentleman. She wondered suddenly just how much of that image was a façade, for she already knew from her dealings with Marcus that if one scratched the surface there was something infinitely more ruthless beneath. As for herself—how far would she go to regain Fairhaven? The stubborn tenacity of the Mostyns was in her blood. Perhaps both of them were true to their ancestry after all.

Marcus encouraged the horses to pick a bit of speed, then turned to Beth with a smile. 'What do I think of it? I cannot deny that it is a tale that reflects no credit on my grandfather. Yet I have some questions for you, Lady Allerton. What was Lord Mostyn doing sailing in such dangerous waters at night? Why did he have his treasure with him? Was there not something slightly suspicious about his own actions?'

Beth stared. In twenty years she had never questioned the detail of the story. She remembered Maddy, her nursemaid, telling her the tale at bedtimes, by the light of the candle in the nursery at Mostyn Hall. She had imagined the perfidious, flickering light of the wreckers' lamp on the cliff, the smashing of the ship's timbers as it broke up on the rocks, the glint of gold as the family treasure tumbled into the depths of the sea... It had never occurred to her to wonder why her grandfather had been carrying so much money on his journey, nor what he had been doing sailing to Fairhaven on a stormy night. Until Marcus had spoken, she had not even thought of it.

Beth wrinkled up her nose, looking at him thought-fully. 'I must concede that it is odd...'

'Indeed. One is tempted to go to Fairhaven to discover the truth of the whole story!' Marcus flashed her a smile. 'Would you accompany me, Lady Allerton, if I invited you to join me on Fairhaven Island?'

Beth looked scandalised. 'Accompany you? I should think not, my lord! A most improper suggestion!'

Marcus laughed. 'A pity. Yet I do not doubt your loyalty to the notion of regaining Fairhaven for your family.'

Beth clenched her gloved hands together in her lap. 'It is something that I feel I must do, my lord. My grand-father's ghost is unquiet...'

Marcus smiled at her. 'I hope you do not feel that in order to lay the ghost you must foster the quarrel!' Once again he transferred the reins to one hand and put the other over hers. 'I have a feeling, my lady, that you and I might settle this feud once and for all.'

This time Beth let her hand rest still under his. 'I hope that we may, my lord,' she said, deliberately reading nothing into his words. 'Might I suggest that you accept my offer for Fairhaven as a first step? It is a very gen-erous offer...'

'It is.' Marcus let go of her and picked up the reins again. 'Too generous. Fairhaven cannot possibly be worth such a sum.'

Beth shrugged a little. 'How does one assess senti-mental value, my lord? To me, Fairhaven is priceless.'

Marcus smiled. 'I understand that,' he said slowly. 'Fairhaven has become your passion, has it not, Lady Allerton? I wonder just what you would do to achieve that obsession.'

Beth stared at him. Despite the fact that his words

only echoed what Charlotte had said to her previously, it was disconcerting to hear them from a relative stranger. It was even more disconcerting to read the double meaning behind them. She looked at him very directly.

'I am not sure that I understand you, my lord. Are you rejecting my offer?'

'I preferred your original one,' Marcus said coolly.

Their gazes locked. The sun disappeared behind a grey cloud and suddenly the wind was chill. Beth shivered inside her pelisse, but it was not entirely from the cold.

'Are you offering me *carte blanche*, my lord?'

Marcus laughed out loud. 'You are very frank, my lady! I was under the impression that the boot had been on the other foot! You set the terms of our wager—'

'You lost the wager,' Beth said swiftly, 'and it is because you did not honour your stake that I am offering so much more!'

'You are offering more financially, I suppose. As I said, I preferred your original—more personal—offer!'

Beth could feel herself blushing and was vexed. She knew he was deliberately provoking her and was determined to stay calm. It was difficult, however, particularly as a tiny corner of her mind was acknowledging the attractions of such a course of action. To offer herself to Marcus in return for Fairhaven Island. It was immoral. It was iniquitous. And it was definitely tempting...

She frowned.

'The wager was a means to an end, my lord! It is not my usual mode of behaviour to offer myself as part of a bargain!'

'I see.' Marcus had allowed the curricle to come to a

halt under the bare branches of a spreading oak tree. 'In that case it was a remarkably dangerous wager.'

'It was.' Beth held his gaze. 'However, if I had lost, I had only to refuse to honour my stake—as you did, my lord!'

'*Touché!*' Marcus laughed again. 'I must confess myself disappointed, Lady Allerton. I was hoping that you might be persuaded—'

'Were you? You cannot know me very well, then, my lord!' By now there was a warning glint in Beth's eye. 'I have told you that I am no courtesan! I wish you take me home now, if you please!'

'Very well!' Marcus's tone betrayed amused admiration. 'I will not tease you any further, my lady. And if it is true that I do not know you well, time can at least remedy that situation!'

The thought gave Beth little comfort. In the first place, she had a strange and disturbing conviction that Marcus did in fact understand her very well, for all his teasing. As for his pledge to know her better, her instinct told her that that could be a very perilous enterprise indeed.

Chapter Three

Another country dance came to an end and Beth applauded enthusiastically and accepted the escort of her partner back to Lady Fanshawe's side. It was very hot in the Duchess of Calthorpe's ballroom for there were at least two hundred guests and the event was assured of the accolade of being a crush. The Duchess had chosen white as her theme to create the impression of approaching winter, and it was ironic that the temperature resembled that of the tropics. Hundreds of white candles added to the heat in the ballroom, creating such a fire risk that footmen were stationed about the room with buckets of water.

'Are you enjoying yourself, my love?' Lady Fanshawe fanned herself vigorously. 'It is such a sad crush in here, I declare there is barely a spare rout chair to be had! And all this white is quite dazzling to the eye!'

Beth giggled. As well as the white candles there were filmy white draperies that were threatening to catch fire and droopy white lilies that evidently preferred a cooler climate.

'You are in looks tonight, my dear,' Lady Fanshawe

continued. 'That lilac muslin is very pretty and stands out well amongst the debutantes. Poor girls, I fear they will melt into the draperies!'

'In more ways than one!' Beth agreed, gratefully accepting a glass of lemonade from Mr Porson, who had been partnering her in the previous dance. He was a worthy young man and he showed signs of lingering at her side, which Beth did not particularly mind. At least she felt safe with him.

'Mr Porson, do you think—?' she began, only to raise her eyebrows in surprise as the young man shot away with barely a word of farewell. Kit Mostyn came up and took the vacated rout chair at his cousin's side.

'Good gracious, Kit!' Beth said crossly. 'What sort of reputation do you have that scares away my innocent admirers? Poor Mr Porson was only indulging in conversation!'

'I doubt that it was my arrival that scared him off,' Kit said drily. 'The Earl of Trevithick has just come in, Beth. Porson won't want to be seen trespassing on Trevithick's ground!'

Beth glanced quickly at the doorway and looked away equally quickly, conscious that plenty of people were watching her. She was unhappily aware that she had become the talk of the town during the previous ten days, all as a result of Marcus Trevithick's attentions. They had driven in the park twice, attended a concert and fireworks at Vauxhall, met at a musical soirée and danced at a couple of balls. That had been sufficient to set tongues wagging and it seemed to Beth that Marcus had done nothing to quell the speculation. He had behaved entirely correctly towards her on all occasions, and yet Beth was aware of something beneath the veneer of convention, something entirely more exciting and dangerous in his attitude towards her.

The interest of the *ton* was piqued because of the family feud and also because the Dowager Viscountess of Trevithick had made her disapproval of Beth very plain. Only the previous night, the Dowager had cut her dead at the opera and Beth had decided that she would have to avoid Marcus in future. This was not entirely because of his mother's attitude but also because of some belated sense of self-preservation. Beth knew that she found Marcus all too attractive and she had heard something of his reputation and did not want to become another conquest. Now, however, her resolution put her in an awkward situation, for to shun Marcus's company at the ball would be remarked upon. Beth fidgeted, drumming her fingers on the arm of the chair as she tried to decide what to do.

She saw Marcus start to cross the room towards her. He had paused to speak to an acquaintance but Beth saw that although he was talking to the man, he was still watching her with a deliberation that was most disturbing. She got hastily to her feet.

'Kit, will you dance with me, please?'

Kit looked pained. 'Must I? If this is some elaborate charade to avoid Trevithick—'

'Kit!' Beth frowned at her cousin's lack of tact. 'How can you be so unchivalrous? Even if it is, I still need your help!'

Kit grinned at her. 'I only meant to warn you that Trevithick would not be fobbed off! By all means let us dance if we must!'

He took her arm and led her away from Marcus Trevithick, joining the set that was at the furthest end of the ballroom.

'I saw you talking to Eleanor Trevithick when her mother's back was turned,' Beth said slyly, as they took their places. 'If you seek to warn me, perhaps you will take some advice in turn? I hope you do not have a *tendre* there, Kit, for you must be doomed to disappointment!'

She had the satisfaction of seeing a hint of colour come into Kit's lean cheek. He avoided her gaze. 'Don't know what you mean, Beth! Miss Trevithick is a charming girl, but I have no interest there!'

Beth smiled beatifically. 'Of course not! How foolish of me even to imagine that you did!'

'It's bad enough having Charlotte dispensing advice,' Kit said gloomily, 'without my honorary sister joining in as well!'

They danced in perfect accord, though Beth found that she had to concentrate on her steps rather more than usual. Her gaze was drawn with tiresome repetitiveness to the tall figure of Marcus Trevithick as he threaded his way through the crowd and joined his mother and sister over by one of the long terrace windows. It seemed that some strange compulsion made it well nigh impossible for Beth to ignore him, for even when she was not looking at Marcus she sensed exactly where he was. It was only when Justin Trevithick came up to the family group and he and Marcus headed towards the card room that Beth started to relax, but by then the dance was ending. Kit bowed to her, then hastened away to claim another lady for the boulanger.

Beth was about to rejoin Lady Fanshawe, when she saw Marcus emerge unexpectedly from the card room again and start walking towards her through the crowd. She immediately dived towards the door and took refuge in the ladies' withdrawing room, where she fretted and fidgeted for twenty minutes, uncertain whether Marcus would simply be waiting in the corridor outside. He was not. Wrestling with a mixture of relief and disappointment, Beth tiptoed back into the ballroom and saw that Marcus was now dancing with Eleanor. She made her way back to Lady Fanshawe's corner of the room, only to find that her chaperon had disappeared.

Beth sat down, feeling a little self-conscious. She could see Kit, who was dancing with a plump debutante in a pink gown, but was looking over her shoulder all the time at Eleanor Trevithick. So much for his denials of an interest there! Beth smiled to herself. It seemed that she and her cousin were both caught in the same trap.

The crush in the ballroom was lessening now as some of the guests moved on to other engagements, and without the camouflage of the huge crowd Beth felt strangely vulnerable. She watched as the dance ended and saw Marcus look around and fix on her with an almost uncanny accuracy. In a candlelit room of a hundred and fifty people it seemed unreasonable that he was able to pick her out so quickly, but she did not feel she had time to stop and think about the implications. She started to edge towards the doors that led out on to the terrace, then paused, thinking that it would probably not be a good idea to wander out into the dark, especially on a cold autumn night. If Marcus decided to follow her they would end up playing hide-and-seek in the gardens and who could say where that would end. Glancing over her shoulder, Beth saw that he was getting closer to her, moving with a purposeful intent that was most disconcerting. She skittered along the edge of the dance floor, almost tripping over in her attempts to put some more distance between them. What she really needed now was someone to ask her to dance. Someone, anyone…

'Would you care to dance, Lady Allerton?'

Beth turned sharply, her grateful acceptance withering on her lips as she looked up into the smiling face of Justin Trevithick. Out of the frying pan and into the fire. She was certain that Justin had seen her trying to avoid Marcus, but she was also aware that she could not refuse to dance with him without seeming dreadfully rude.

'Oh, Mr Trevithick! I…yes…thank you, sir…'

Beth had met Justin several times in the previous ten days and had taken to him immediately, liking his sense of humour and easygoing manner. Just now, however, she was wishing him at the bottom of the sea. Dancing with Marcus's cousin was getting too close to Marcus for comfort. She looked round and saw that Marcus was now speaking to a fashionable matron in striped red and white silk. He looked engrossed and suddenly Beth began to feel rather silly. Perhaps Marcus had never intended to approach her at all and all her diversions had served no purpose other than to make her look foolish. Probably she was flattering herself by imagining that he had ever shown any real interest in her.

Justin was waiting, a look of speculative amusement in his eyes. Beth hastily wiped all expression from her face and gave him her hand. She was pleased that she managed to keep up a tolerably bright conversation throughout the polonaise, only faltering slightly when she observed Marcus and the stripily clad matron disappearing through the door together. That was that, then. Evidently Marcus had found company more to his taste and had retired to enjoy it in privacy. Beth felt even more out of countenance at the unedifying jealousy that swept through her.

At the end of the dance, Justin guided her off the floor and into the refreshment room.

'May I fetch you a glass of lemonade, ma'am?' he suggested. 'It may be a tame sort of beverage but is just the thing in a hot climate like this! If you take a seat in this alcove I will undertake to be back directly.'

Beth sank gratefully onto the window seat. It was fresher here with a pleasant draught of air that cooled her heated face. She rested her head against the stone window casing and closed her eyes. The noise of the ball swirled around her but she took no notice.

'Your lemonade, Lady Allerton.'

Beth jumped so much that she almost banged her head against the stone. The voice was not Justin Trevithick's, but the deeper tones of his cousin the Earl. Sure enough, Marcus was standing before her, a glass of lemonade in one hand, watching her with the same quizzically amused expression that he had been wearing all evening. Beth felt at a disadvantage and tried to get to her feet, but she found that Marcus was standing too close to her and that any movement would bring her into physical contact with him. This did not seem a very good idea, so she leant back instead and took the lemonade from him with an assumption of ease.

'Thank you very much. How do you do, Lord Trevithick?'

Marcus gave her his devastating smile. 'I am all the better now that I have finally caught up with you, Lady Allerton! I thought that I would never achieve it!'

'I was expecting your cousin's company—' Beth began.

'And did not want to have to tolerate mine instead? I fear I persuaded him to exchange places with me.' Marcus shrugged lightly. 'Now that I finally have you to myself, Lady Allerton, I would be obliged if you would keep still for at least a minute! I would like to speak with you!'

Beth shifted guiltily on the window seat. There was little chance of her escaping anywhere since Marcus was now leaning against the alcove embrasure and comprehensively blocking her retreat.

'In that case you had better sit down,' she said coolly, 'and cease looming over me in that threatening manner!'

Marcus grinned and sat down next to her. 'I will do as you ask on the understanding that you will not run away! What has all that ridiculous rigmarole been about this evening—dodging out of rooms, hiding away, avoiding even looking in my direction—?'

'When I did look in your direction I thought you most preoccupied!' Beth said tartly, before she could stop herself. 'I am surprised that you noticed me at all!'

Marcus laughed. 'I collect that you are referring to me stepping aside with a lady just now? That is my elder sister, Lady Grace Walters. She found the heat too overpowering in the ballroom and needed some fresh air.'

Beth looked away, feeling foolish. 'I am sure that I do not care—'

'Well, you do, or you would not have quizzed me about it!' Marcus sat back on the window seat and stretched his long legs out in front of him. 'And you still have not answered my question, Lady Allerton. What was all that play-acting for?'

Beth flushed. 'I thought it best to avoid you,' she said candidly, trying to look him in the eye. 'There has been so much speculation about our...' She hesitated, trying to think of the right word to describe their relationship.

'Our friendship?' Marcus supplied helpfully.

'Friendship. Yes, thank you. So much speculation

about our friendship, my lord, that I thought it best to subdue it by—'

'By creeping about like an actor in a bad play? You have caused so *much* speculation tonight by your strategies for avoiding me that I am amazed you are not aware of it!'

'Well, if it comes to that, you have hardly suppressed the gossip by cornering me in this alcove!' Beth said, firing up. 'It seems to me that you positively enjoy stirring up scandal, my lord!'

Marcus shrugged his broad shoulders. 'I confess that I seldom regard it. As you should not, my lady! Why should the tabbies concern you? I am minded to kiss you here and now and see what the scandalmongers make of that!'

Beth recoiled slightly. 'Do not jest, my lord!'

'Why should I be jesting? You did not object to kissing me before!'

Beth blushed scarlet. 'My lord! Kindly lower your voice—'

'Come and speak with me in private, then. I want to talk to you about your offer for Fairhaven. It is time that we settled the matter.'

Beth gave him a very direct look. 'I do not believe you, sir! This is just a trick! In fact, I do not trust you! At all!'

'Why not?' Marcus grinned. 'Because the last time we were private together we shared more than just a conversation—'

Beth waved her hands about in mute appeal. 'I believe you must be inebriated to speak thus, my lord—'

Marcus captured both her hands in one of his. 'Not in the slightest! But if you will not speak with me, come and dance with me instead!'

He had already pulled her to her feet and was steering her through the crowded room with one hand resting lightly in the small of her back. Beth was sharply conscious of his tall figure close beside her, so close that her skirt brushed against his thigh as they walked. She tried to move away a little but found that the press of people forced them together. She could feel the warmth of his touch through the thin muslin of her dress, and suddenly she felt hot and vulnerable. It was no state in which to begin a dance, and when Beth heard the waltz striking up she almost turned tail and fled.

'No need to look so terrified, sweetheart,' Marcus murmured in her ear. His voice was warm and persuasive. 'I promise to behave!'

A strange shiver went down Beth's spine. She did not dare look at him. She reluctantly moved into his arms and felt only slightly relieved when Marcus held her at an irreproachable distance from his own body and made no attempt to draw her closer.

They started to circle the floor in time to the lilting rhythm of the music. The faces of the guests spun past them, curious, avid, amused, sharp, and spiteful... It seemed to Beth that the music was whirling faster and faster and that the flickering candlelight washed over them like a kaleidoscope of black and white. Marcus's face was in shadow, his expression inscrutable, almost distant. Yet despite his apparent coolness Beth could feel a current of heat running between them, intense and strong. She shivered again, convulsively.

Beth had intended to keep a decorous distance between them and to avoid the intimacy of conversation during the waltz, but some compulsion made her glance up into Marcus's face as they completed their second circuit of the floor. His gaze met hers for a split second and now it was dark and heavy with a passion he made no attempt to conceal. Beth caught her breath on a little gasp and almost lost her footing. Immediately Marcus's arms tightened about her, pulling her into sudden and shocking contact with his body. His cheek brushed hers, hard against the softness of her skin, causing a feeling of helpless, wanton warmth to flood through her. Beth shuddered in his arms, unable to prevent her body betraying her with its trembling. She saw Marcus's lips curve into a smile, felt his own body harden with arousal against hers and thought that she might well faint with shock and sheer, sensual delight, there in the Duchess of Calthorpe's ballroom in front of one hundred and fifty people. It was terrifying but also strangely exhilarating all at the same time, and she was thoroughly confused. She did not risk looking at Marcus again.

The music was ending, the waltzing couples slowing down, breaking apart and walking away. The chatter rose around her and the room suddenly seemed brighter. Beth tried to break free of Marcus's grip, intent only on putting a little distance between them, but he held on to her, keeping her close.

'You must give me a moment...' his voice was husky '...if you are not to embarrass me...'

The colour flamed into Beth's face. She allowed him to guide her skilfully to the edge of the dance floor, where she plied her fan and desperately tried to think of an innocuous topic of conversation. Her mind was dazed, cloudy with desire, and all she could think of was what had happened between them and how she was still trembling with an echo of the passion she had seen in his eyes.

'It is very warm,' she said uncertainly, and was relieved to see amusement replace the sensual heat in Marcus's face.

'Certainly it is very hot in here,' he drawled, 'and between us, Lady Allerton, I should say that it is almost too hot for comfort!'

Beth's gaze flew uncertainly to his face, but before she could answer, Justin Trevithick appeared, escorting Lady Fanshawe. Beth was tolerably certain that Marcus's cousin had summed up the situation with one comprehensive glance, for his gaze moved from her face to Marcus's and his eyebrows rose fractionally as he picked up on the tension between them. Fortunately Lady Fanshawe was decidedly less perceptive.

'There you are, my dear! You know that we are promised to Lady Baynton's rout and positively must put in an appearance before the night ends!' She beamed at Marcus and Justin. 'Do you gentlemen wish to accompany us, or do you have other plans?'

Beth felt Marcus's gaze rest on her. It was not difficult to imagine just what other plans he might have for her. She schooled her face to remain blank, annoyed that he seemed to be able to make her blush at the slightest provocation.

'Thank you, ma'am, but I believe we are for White's,' Justin was saying, with a smile. 'May we escort you to your carriage?'

It felt cold outside after the stifling heat of the ballroom. Beth drew her velvet cloak more closely around her and tried not to shiver. Marcus kissed her hand before helping her up into the coach, and murmured that he hoped to call on her the following day. She was almost at a loss for a reply, half-longing to see him again, half-afraid of the feelings he could evoke in her.

As she settled back in the coach, Beth reflected that

it seemed strange now, but she realised that she had barely given a moment's thought to physical passion in her whole life. She had married almost from the schoolroom and had considered herself happy with Frank Allerton, but he had rarely troubled her for his marital rights and had treated her with all the indulgence of a fond parent. No hint of passion had disturbed the even tenor of their relationship. From the vague comments that Charlotte had occasionally made, Beth had realised that there could be a great deal more to marriage than she had shared with Frank, but she had largely dismissed such matters as simply not for her. She had met a few personable men during her widowhood and had even enjoyed the company of some of them, but had never felt moved to indulge in a love affair. She realised now that she had even begun to believe that she was simply not very interested in love.

Then Marcus had kissed her and it felt as though a whole new side of her personality, both emotional and physical, had been brought to life. Curled up in a corner of the carriage, listening vaguely to Lady Fanshawe's chatter, Beth reflected that Marcus had awoken something she had not even been aware was sleeping: a hunger to experience emotion and passion in vivid detail.

And it was the first of these that was the problem. If she had only wanted to take a lover, matters would have been simple. Marcus was there and he was eminently suitable, eminently desirable as a lover. Beth felt the warmth steal over her again. It was a tempting thought, yet she knew that she could not accept it. Newly awakened, her feelings were craving satisfaction as much as her body was, and the thought was terrifying. Against her better judgement she liked Marcus. She enjoyed his company, his conversation, his humour. She knew she was in danger of loving him, too quickly, careless of the risk. It was in her nature to be impulsive, but on this one occasion she had to be more careful and protect herself against this danger. For though she knew Marcus wanted her, she could not be confident that his feelings were engaged any more deeply than that. It hurt her to think it, but she knew she was right.

'Would you mind if we do not go on to Lady Baynton's rout, dear ma'am?' she asked Lady Fanshawe in a small voice. 'I am a little fatigued and would prefer the quiet of going home.'

Her godmother shot her a concerned look. 'Of course, my love. You do look rather done up! I suppose that it is country living—you are simply not prepared for such a dizzy round of events as we indulge in here in town!' Lady Fanshawe fidgeted with her reticule. Her voice changed a little. 'Beth, dear, I do not mean to pry, but I feel I should warn you about the Earl of Trevithick...'

Beth shifted slightly on the seat. 'There is no need to warn me, ma'am,' she said sadly. 'No need at all.'

'Beth, I do declare you are in a brown study this morning!' Charlotte Cavendish put down the dress she was holding and viewed her cousin with a puzzled eye. 'I asked you if you preferred the mauve or the green and you said both! Are you not feeling in plump currant? You need only say if you wish us to stop!'

Beth shook herself. They had been wading their way through the dizzying pile of goods sent round that morning by the Bond Street modistes. There were dresses, shawls and spencers, scarves and tippets, stockings and petticoats, gloves, fans and hats. The crimson saloon looked like an eastern bazaar and Beth felt utterly unequal to choosing anything from the selection. Not that her mind was on the task in hand. Not at all. She had spent the best part of the night and most of the morning dwelling on Marcus Trevithick; on his high-handed manner and his infuriatingly mocking tone, on the dark face that could soften into a warmth that took her breath away, on the forceful attraction of a man who was quite beyond her experience. Any minute she was expecting—hoping—that the bell would ring and he would have fulfilled his promise to call on her. And at the same time she was thinking that to foster any hopes of him was the greatest folly.

'The pale blue suits you to perfection, Lottie,' she said hastily, admiring the way that the figured silk mirrored her cousin's bright eyes, 'and I would take the ivory muslin and the grey as well.'

'That is all very well for me, but what about you?' Charlotte questioned. 'You do not seem very interested, Beth, and this is the finest that Bond Street has to offer!'

Beth let a pale green scarf float through her fingers and stood up, moving over to the window. 'I am sorry. I think I am a little tired from last night. We were back very late, you know, and I did not sleep particularly well.'

Charlotte frowned a little. 'I wish I could come with you to all the parties and balls, Beth! Lady Fanshawe is the sweetest person imaginable, but I am not entirely sure she is up to snuff! Why, she told me she was hoping that Sir Edmund Netherwood might make an offer for you, when everyone knows he is the most tiresome old fortune-hunter and has been through three wives and their dowries already!'

Beth giggled. 'You need have no fears on that score, Lottie!' She sobered. 'All the same, it would be so much more fun if you could accompany me about town. I do not like to think of you sitting here on your own whilst Kit and I set the town by the ears!'

'Speaking of which, Lady Fanshawe said that you met with the Earl of Trevithick at the ball,' Charlotte said casually, examining the stitching on a fine pair of kid gloves. 'She said that he was most attentive, Beth!'

Beth blushed. She looked away, down into the street, where a flower-seller was just setting up a stall on the corner opposite.

'Yes... I... Well, I could not really avoid him...'

'Oh, Beth! Did you really want to?'

Beth raised troubled grey eyes to her cousin's blue ones. 'No, not really.' She spoke in a rush. 'I like Lord Trevithick a great deal, Lottie, but I am afraid...'

Charlotte was folding up the material, but now she let her hands rest in her lap. 'Afraid? Of how you feel about him?' she asked shrewdly.

Beth nodded, avoiding her gaze. 'He is just so very different from Frank!'

Charlotte laughed. 'I should say so!'

The doorbell shrilled, making them both jump. Carrick, the butler, strode into the room, carrying a flat packet wrapped in brown paper and tied with string. He proffered it to Beth.

'This parcel has arrived from the Earl of Trevithick, madam. There is also a note...'

Beth shot Charlotte a startled look, and then tore open the envelope. Inside was a single sheet of paper, written in the strong scrawl that she had come to recognise:

Dear Lady Allerton

I enclose your winnings. I have every intention of regaining them in time, however. Pray do not flee

London for Devon before I have time to call upon
you.

Until then,

Trevithick

The note drifted to the floor as Beth slit the parcel
with her letter opener. Her fingers shook slightly. Inside
was a document, dated that very morning, granting the
Island of Fairhaven in the Bristol Channel to Elizabeth,
Lady Allerton, and her heirs in perpetuity. Again, it was
signed in a strong black hand with the one word,
Trevithick. There was also a bundle of other papers,
some of them ancient manuscripts written in Latin on
paper so old and thin that the light shone through. Beth
riffled through them in disbelief, seeing the history of
her beloved island so suddenly and unexpectedly in her
hands.

Charlotte had picked up the note and was reading it.
She looked doubtfully from the letter to Beth and back
again.

'Oh, no! I cannot believe that the Earl is prepared to
humour you in this mad obsession!'

Beth could not quite believe it either. 'I suppose that it
does not matter to him,' she said, a little breathlessly. 'He
has so many other estates more valuable. Fairhaven has
only its sentimental worth, and that only matters to me!'

'I wonder what he means by saying that he intends to
regain Fairhaven,' Charlotte said thoughtfully, 'and what
he wants in return for his gift!'

Beth looked up, startled.

'Why, nothing! He is paying his debt, that is all! He
lost the wager—'

'Do not remind me of it!' Her cousin pursed her lips.
There was a twinkle in her eye. 'Sometimes you are so

naïve, my love! In my experience there is no such thing as something for nothing! Ten to one, Trevithick has some kind of bargain in mind! It might be that he seeks your good opinion, which would be reassuring, or it might be that his intentions are dishonourable.'

Beth could feel herself blushing again. She had not told Charlotte that the Earl had already offered her *carte blanche*, for she knew it would only fuel her cousin's fears. 'Oh, no, I cannot believe—' She met Charlotte's sceptical gaze. 'Well, perhaps…'

'You know you suspect it yourself!' Charlotte said drily. 'What exactly happened during that wager, Beth?'

Beth felt herself blush harder. 'Why, nothing! Only…' She evaded Charlotte's penetrating gaze. 'I suppose he did…does…perhaps admire me a little…'

'Quite so. That being the case, I think you should be careful. Trevithick is not a man with whom to indulge in an idle flirtation! He is far too dangerous!'

Beth was momentarily distracted. 'Is he? I was not aware that his reputation was *so* bad.'

'You never are,' Charlotte said, with a sigh. 'Remember that fortune hunter who tried to attach your interest at the Exeter Assembly? You thought him a very pleasant fellow, as I recall—'

'Oh, but he was not in the least like Lord Trevithick!'

'No,' Charlotte said, opening the door, 'he was harmless! Just take care, Beth!'

She went out. Beth picked up all the documents and walked over to the window seat, sitting down in the mid-morning sun. Outside the street was busy with vendors and passers-by.

She put the papers down on her lap and gazed out at the jumbled spires and rooftops stretching into the distance. It felt very claustrophobic to be cooped up in

London in the autumn. It was a season in which to ride across the fields and feel the sharp breeze on her face, to stand on the cliff tops and look out across the sea, to walk along the beach and hear the hiss of the waves on the sand.

Beth looked down at the papers again. She realised that she felt decidedly odd, but could not work out why. Perhaps it was the shock of having her heart's desire suddenly thrust into her hands, or that the pleasure of owning Fairhaven had overcome her. But it did not feel like that. She realised that she had wanted Marcus to talk to her about it, to tell her what he intended. Now she felt oddly cheated. She had what she wanted but she was uncomfortable about it. And she was not entirely sure why.

The reading room at White's was very quiet that morning and it was proving a most pleasant oasis of calm for Marcus after an eventful breakfast at Trevithick House. The Dowager Viscountess, mindful of her elder son's behaviour at the ball the night before, had rung a peal over him for his lack of filial duty. It was her expressed view that the Trevithicks had not fostered a feud with the Mostyns for two hundred and fifty years simply for Marcus to disregard it by paying attention to a fast little widow, no matter how rich. Marcus, incensed to hear his mother speak so slightingly of Beth, had thrown down his napkin and departed the house forthwith, fortunately bumping into Justin in St James's. The two of them had retired to White's where Justin promptly fell asleep and Marcus buried himself in the *Morning Chronicle*.

After half an hour, Marcus stirred his cousin with his foot. 'How much did you win last night, Justin? When

I left you were ten thousand guineas up against
Warrender. Did you make enough to pay off that vora-
cious opera singer you had in keeping?'

'Twenty-five thousand, all told,' Justin muttered,
without opening his eyes. He slumped down further in
his chair. 'I took the money and Warrender took the girl
off my hands! She was sweet, but too much of a handful!'

Marcus laughed. 'Seems you struck a good bargain!
So, are you clearing your decks in order to settle down,
old fellow?'

'Devil a bit!' Justin yawned. He opened his eyes and
squinted at Marcus. 'Thought you were the one about to
be caught in parson's mousetrap!'

Marcus raised his eyebrows. 'Are you trying to marry
me off by any chance, old chap? Only last night you
were singing Lady Allerton's praises!'

'No harm in marrying a fortune,' Justin said laconically, straightening up. 'Good money but bad blood in
that family! Not that the Trevithicks should criticise the
Mostyns! Pirates and thieves, the lot of them!'

'Call me fastidious, but I would not care to marry for
money,' Marcus said slowly.

Justin bent a perceptive look on him. 'Ah, but you
wouldn't be, would you, Marcus? Never seen you more
smitten, old fellow! After all, you've never given away
an island before, have you?'

Marcus smiled, but did not trouble to reply. Justin
knew him too well to be fooled, but equally he had no
intention of discussing his matrimonial plans just yet.
He shifted a little in his chair as he thought of Beth. He
would call on her in a little while and take her driving.
He wanted to talk to her about Fairhaven, make her
promise that she would not rush away from London to

inspect her new property. His smile deepened as he imagined how excited she would be to have the island in her possession. It pleased him to make her happy and it was a feeling he was not accustomed to. He had always been generous in a careless, casual way, but this protective desire to take care of someone else was entirely new. He grinned. Damn it, he must be getting old, wanting to marry and set up his nursery...

A servant was approaching them with a folded note on a silver tray. The man's face wore a rather pained expression, as though he had been entrusted with an errand that was in poor taste.

'Excuse me, my lord. A person by the name of Gower is without. He asks if you might spare him a moment of your time...'

Marcus raised his eyebrows. He had seen Gower only the previous day when his man of business had reluctantly presented him with the deed of gift by which Marcus had signed Fairhaven away. Gower had begged him to be prudent, to reconsider, to wait... And Marcus, impatient to make Beth happy, had signed the document and sent it round immediately, ignoring Gower's advice. He knew that something untoward must have happened for Gower to seek him out at White's. Wondering if it was to do with Fairhaven or some completely unrelated matter, Marcus felt his own apprehension growing.

The man of business was waiting for him out in the street, turning his hat round between his hands in the gesture he always employed when he was worried or nervous. On this occasion Marcus judged him to be both of these things.

'My lord,' he said jerkily, looking from Marcus to Justin and back again, 'forgive me for disturbing you, but the matter was most urgent. I would not have troubled you else—'

'That is understood, Gower,' Marcus said shortly. 'What is the difficulty?'

'My lord…' Gower looked unhappy. 'There are documents I feel you should see, matters that have come to light—'

'Matters to do with Fairhaven Island?' Justin interposed, his gaze keen. Marcus felt his heart sink as Gower nodded his head.

'Matters concerning Fairhaven—and Lady Allerton, I fear, sir.'

'Well, we cannot stand here in the street discussing it,' Marcus snapped. 'Gower, your rooms are more appropriate than Trevithick House. We will go there.'

They walked to Gower's rooms in Chancery Lane in an uneasy silence. Gower ushered them into his office and a clerk who had been working at the desk moved unobtrusively away. Gower carefully moved some stacks of papers from the chairs and invited the gentlemen to take a seat, but Marcus ignored the suggestion.

'Thank you, I prefer to stand,' he said tersely. 'Now, what is this matter that is of such import, Gower?'

Gower resumed his seat behind his large mahogany desk. He moved a few documents to the right, picked one up, put it down again, then moved the pile left. Marcus felt his nerves tightening.

'For God's sake, man, just get on with it—'

He saw Justin shoot him a warning glance and tried to get a hold on his temper. Shouting at Gower would do no good and the man was only doing his job anyway. Marcus knew that he needed a pernickety lawyer to attend to all the matters that held no interest for him, but when he wondered what Gower was about to tell him about Beth he felt the cold seep through him like water on stone.

'Yes, my lord,' Gower said expressionlessly. He settled his half-moon spectacles on his nose. Behind the lenses his eyes gleamed palely. He picked up the document on the top of the pile and cleared his throat.

'On the matter of Fairhaven Island, my lord... Several weeks ago, when you first mooted the possibility that you might cede the island to Lady Allerton, I instigated some investigations—' Gower's pale eyes flashed '—all in your best interests, my lord.'

'Of course,' Marcus said politely. He resisted the impulse to take the lawyer by the throat and shake him. 'Pray continue, Gower.'

'Yes, my lord. I discovered that the possibility of a sale of Fairhaven had first been suggested some twenty years ago, when Sir Frank Allerton approached your grandfather, the late Earl.'

Marcus shifted impatiently. 'What of it, Gower?'

The lawyer shuffled the papers again. 'It seems that Sir Frank was a notable mineralogist, my lord, and suspected that there might well be valuable resources on the island, mineral deposits that would justify the cost and difficulties of mining there.'

Justin gave a low whistle. 'There cannot be many substances that would be worth such an effort, Gower.'

'No, sir.' Gower permitted himself a small, prim smile. 'Naturally enough, Sir Frank did not inform the late Earl of his precise interest in Fairhaven, but information that subsequently fell into my hands...' the lawyer looked slightly shifty '...suggested that the substance under discussion was gold.'

Marcus expelled his breath sharply. He did not speak, but turned away to look out of the dusty window. There

were some pigeons pecking in the gutter opposite. In the
room behind him he heard Justin say carefully, 'Would
you say that Sir Frank was well informed on the mineral
potential of the Devon area, Gower?'

Marcus swung back round. 'Of course he was,' he
said abruptly. 'Why, even I know that Sir Frank Allerton
was a distinguished expert on such matters! In addition
to work in his native county, he was looking to develop
the Somerset coal field and held considerable concessions in the Cornish tin mines—'

'Concessions which his widow still holds,' Gower finished quietly.

Marcus leant on the desk. 'Very well, Gower. I believe you have reached the crux of your story, have you
not?'

The lawyer looked unhappy. 'Perhaps so, my lord.'
He took a deep breath. 'My lord, I do wish you to know
that I am only looking after your best interests—'

'It is understood,' Marcus said tersely. His mouth was
set in a grim line. 'Please go on.'

'Very well, my lord. As you are aware, your grandfather did not choose to sell Fairhaven to Sir Frank,
claiming that he had only just wrested the place from
the "cursed Mostyn brood", as he put it, and had no
wish to give it up so easily. He had neither the money
nor the inclination to explore the island's potential himself, but was content to leave it unexploited for the following years.' Gower looked up. 'There is an ancient
castle there, my lord, as well as a farm and a rudimentary
village. If you recall, your uncle St John Trevithick holds
the living there and he and your aunt Trevithick live in
the castle. I last visited it some two years ago, when
your factor, Mr McCrae—'

'Please get to the point, Gower,' Marcus said wearily,

subsiding into the chair opposite Justin. He saw his cousin's look of concern and flashed him a brief smile. 'Forgive my abruptness, but what is really of concern is the nature of your allegations against Lady Allerton.' He stopped and looked at the lawyer. 'For I believe that you have some.'

'Yes, my lord,' Gower said again. The paper in his hand shook slightly. 'Some two years ago, shortly after the death of her husband, Lady Allerton petitioned the Earl to buy Fairhaven.'

Marcus raised his eyebrows. 'Yes? She has told me as much.'

'Indeed, my lord.' The lawyer's voice was dry. 'She approached your grandfather twice, in point of fact, and after he refused her offer a second time, she wrote to tell him that she would resort to whatever methods necessary to gain the island. I remember the Earl laughing and saying she was a spirited little filly with more mettle than the rest of her family put together! But for all that he thought it unbecoming that such a young lady should involve herself in business matters, for all that she brought her lawyer with her—the self-same man whom Sir Frank had always used to negotiate his mining ventures.'

Justin shifted uncomfortably. Marcus's eyes narrowed on the lawyer's face. 'I do not find that in any way surprising, Gower. If the man were acting for Sir Frank it would be natural for Lady Allerton to retain his services in matters relating to the estate. It does not mean that she retained an active interest—'

He broke off at the look on the lawyer's face. 'No, my lord,' Gower said lugubriously. 'However, when Lady Allerton was out of the room, the man apparently told your grandfather quite openly that it was their intention to pursue Sir Frank's ambitions on Fairhaven. Lady Allerton still retains the same lawyer,' he added quietly, 'a gentleman by the name of Gough, as you know, my lord. As soon as you mentioned to me the matter of the wager for Fairhaven I was suspicious, my lord, and even more so when I discovered that Gough was involved.'

Marcus let out a long breath. He could see both Gower and Justin watching him with similar sympathetic looks and felt the anger rise in him. It seemed that he had made a fine fool of himself over Beth Allerton and was in danger of appearing even more foolish by his unwillingness to believe badly of her. He remembered the passion with which she had spoken of her love of Fairhaven, the way she had related the tales of her childhood, her fervent intention to regain her patrimony. It seemed that it had all been assumed to hide a more avaricious reason, a convenient tale to make him sympathise with her, to bewitch him, as she had done so subtly, with her smoky grey eyes and her soft, sweet body and her conniving mind. He clenched his fists.

'Is there any more, Gower?'

'Only that I have heard this very morning that Christopher Mostyn has been approaching various backers for a new commercial venture,' the lawyer said slowly. 'It was then that I felt I had to lay all this matter before your lordship. I understand that Lady Allerton signed over all active interests in her late husband's business to Lord Mostyn, although she shares in the profits.'

'And the plans,' Marcus said grimly. 'Could this new venture be the mining of Fairhaven, Gower?'

'I do not know, my lord,' the lawyer said truthfully, 'but it might well be.'

There was a silence.

'It does not look good,' Justin said carefully, after a
moment. He put a hand on his cousin's arm. 'I am sorry,
Marcus…'

Marcus shook him off and stood up. 'There is no need.
Gower, I am obliged to you for your information.
Justin…' he turned to his cousin '…we have a call to
make, I think. In Upper Grosvenor Street. I will take
back the deeds to Fairhaven and give that devious little
witch a piece of my mind!'

Chapter Four

'Excuse me, my lady.' Carrick, Beth's butler, had come into the red drawing room and was looking rather dubious. 'The Earl of Trevithick is here and is asking— rather strongly, my lady—that you should receive him.' The butler's frown deepened. 'There is another gentleman with him, a Mr Justin Trevithick. I was somewhat concerned, my lady, that the Earl was inebriated, for he was most forceful in his demands for entry.'

Beth put her book down and looked at Charlotte in some consternation. The clock stood at ten minutes to two, which seemed somewhat early for a gentleman to be in his cups. It also seemed somewhat out of character.

'I cannot believe that the Earl is foxed, Carrick,' she said forthrightly, gaining a squeak of disapproval from Charlotte at her unladylike language, 'so perhaps I should see him to ascertain the reason for his behaviour.' She turned to her cousin. 'Shall I receive Lord Trevithick in the green study, Charlotte, so that you need not be disturbed? I do not wish you to have to receive two strangers so unexpectedly.'

Charlotte stood up, smoothing her dress with nervous fingers. 'Thank you, Beth, but there is no difficulty. If the Earl is inebriated I would rather be with you to prevent an unfortunate scene—'

The words had scarcely left her lips when the door was flung open with a crash as Marcus stalked into the room, closely followed by Justin, who was looking slightly less than his usual imperturbable self.

'My apologies, ma'am,' Marcus drawled, sketching a slight bow in Charlotte's direction. 'I have no wish to discompose you, but I have an urgent need to speak with Lady Allerton and I was afraid that I would have taken root to the spot by the time your butler saw fit to return!' He turned to Beth and she recoiled slightly from the expression on his face. There was a furious light in his eyes and a very grim set to his jaw. The change from the attentive suitor of two nights before to this hard and angry man was almost impossible to believe.

As she stared at him in bemusement, Marcus said silkily, 'I am glad to find you at home, Lady Allerton, and not halfway to Devon to claim your ill-gotten gains! Will you grant me a private interview or must I rehearse my quarrel with you in front of your cousin and a host of servants? I have no difficulty in doing so, you understand, but Mrs Cavendish might find it somewhat distasteful...'

Beth drew herself up. The reference to her ill-gotten gains puzzled her, for had Marcus not sent her the deeds of Fairhaven only that morning, and with a perfectly amicable note into the bargain? She wondered briefly if Carrick had been correct and Marcus was drunk, but it took only one glance to see that he was stone cold sober. Sober but very angry. It was frightening.

'I have no notion to what you refer, my lord,' she said a little shakily, 'nor have I any wish to hear your impertinent accusations! I think you must be either drunk or mad to speak like this, and I suggest that you return when your temper has cooled!'

Justin caught Marcus's arm. 'Lady Allerton is in the right of it, old chap! Cool reason is better than hot heads! Let us retire for now—'

Marcus ignored him. He crossed the room to Beth and stopped an unnerving foot away from her. She could see the anger and dislike clear in his face.

'Well, ma'am?' he challenged softly. 'What is it to be? A private discussion or a public quarrel? The choice is entirely yours!'

Beth heard Charlotte draw a protesting breath and saw Justin Trevithick move protectively to her cousin's side.

'Beg pardon, ma'am,' she heard him say in an undertone. 'Dreadful intrusion, I know, but there is no reasoning with him when he is like this. The Trevithick temper, you know. The old Earl was renowned for it...'

Beth's gaze flickered to Charlotte and back to the compelling anger in Marcus Trevithick's face. She drew breath to give Marcus a blistering set-down, but Charlotte spoke first.

'Beth dear, it does seem that the Earl has some pressing matter to discuss with you. Perhaps you could take him into the study, whilst Mr Trevithick stays here with me? Carrick, would you bring tea?'

The prosaic suggestion seemed to restore some sense of normality. The tight rage lessened slightly in Marcus's face and he walked over to the door and held it open for Beth with studious courtesy. Carrick moved away with his customary composed tread to fetch refreshments. Beth saw Justin take Charlotte's hand and start to introduce himself formally, then the door closed behind them with a snap and she was alone in the hall with Marcus.

'If you would step this way, my lord,' she said, a little faintly, gesturing towards her book room, 'I am sure that we can resolve this problem, whatever it may be...'

The study faced south and had a warm fire burning. Earlier that morning Beth had taken the deeds to Fairhaven and placed them on the desk, intending to read them thoroughly in the evening. She had wanted to see Marcus first and talk to him about his gift. And now it seemed that she had the opportunity, but not exactly as she would have wished it...

She saw Marcus's gaze go to the pile of papers and saw a frown crease his forehead as though he wanted to snatch the deeds up and simply walk off with them. For a moment her mind was filled with the ludicrous picture of them tugging on opposite ends of the papers until they tore across and fluttered to the ground. And for what? She was still utterly confused about the nature of his quarrel with her.

Marcus drove his hands into his jacket pockets. 'Lady Allerton, I have come to ask for the return of the deeds to Fairhaven Island,' he said, in tones of measured dislike. 'It seems that you have obtained them under false pretences and so our agreement, such as it was, is null and void. The wager, the gift...' his dark gaze dwelled on her face for a moment in a look that made Beth feel curiously vulnerable '...everything. I do not expect to see you again or have any further debate about the ownership of the island.'

Beth sat down weakly in the nearest chair. She raised her eyes to his face. 'I do not understand you, my lord. You made me a free gift of the island only this morning—'

Marcus spoke through his teeth. 'It was a mistake. I am rescinding it.'

The indignant colour sprung into Beth's face. 'But you cannot do that! There is no reason— Why, how dishonourable can you be? First to renege on the wager and then to cancel your gift—'

Marcus came across and bent over her chair. His furious dark eyes were only inches from hers. 'If we are talking of honour, I would like to know how a woman who lies and cheats could possibly know anything of such a quality!' He turned away from her, his movements so full of repressed rage that Beth quailed. 'I have heard about your plans to exploit Fairhaven for financial gain! So much for your touching protestations that you were wishing to regain your lost patrimony! And to think that I believed you—' He stopped and ran a hand through his disordered dark hair. 'Well, I was richly taken in, but not any more!'

Beth got to her feet. Her eyes were wide and puzzled. 'Truly, my lord, I do not understand—'

Marcus spun round and caught her wrist. 'Not understand? Do you deny that your late husband tried to buy Fairhaven because he wanted to mine gold there? Do you deny that you went to my grandfather and told him that *you* wished to buy the island for the same reason? Do you deny that your cousin is even now looking for investors for such a project, now that you have tricked me out of Fairhaven—?'

'Yes, I do deny it!' Beth wrenched her wrist out of his grasp. 'I knew nothing of Frank's business concerns, nor do I know anything of Kit's! I do not wish to! I want Fairhaven for all those reasons I told you, my lord, and as for telling your grandfather otherwise—' she swallowed a sob '—I never said anything of the sort!'

Her gaze searched Marcus's face and saw the unyielding disbelief there. She could tell that she was wasting her breath. 'It seems, however, that you have no wish to trust me,' she finished quietly.

Marcus moved over to the writing table. 'I will take these with me—'

Beth whisked across the room before he could reach for the deeds to Fairhaven, and inserted herself between Marcus and the desk, blocking his way. She put her hands behind her and leant back against the desk's smooth surface to steady herself. Marcus looked at her for a moment, then raised an incredulous eyebrow.

'So determined to keep your island, my dear? I have not forgotten exactly what it was you offered me when we made our wager! It seems you will do anything to achieve your ambition!' His gaze swept over her with contemptuous familiarity, from the black curls piled up on her head to the kid slippers peeping from beneath the hem of her pale blue muslin gown and Beth felt as though he was stripping her naked. He moved forward until she was completely trapped with the writing table behind her and Marcus in front of her. Beth drew back as far as she could, but she felt the sharp edge of the desk digging uncomfortably into the back of her legs. A second later she forgot all about the discomfort as Marcus moved in closer, so close that Beth could feel his thigh pressing against hers through the thin muslin gown. She drew an outraged breath.

'My lord, kindly let me go!'

Marcus smiled with wicked amusement. All his anger appeared to have gone now, replaced by a devilish enjoyment that Beth suddenly found even more frightening. She tried to lean away from him, but the desk behind her blocked her path completely, and when she attempted to slide sideways Marcus simply leant both arms on the desk on either side of her, effectively pin-

ning her down. As Beth tried to arch away from him she
saw his gaze drop to the neckline of her dress and linger
there on the soft swell of her breasts.

'My lord!' Beth's voice came out as a desperate
squeak. 'This is not fair!'

Marcus leant closer. She could feel his breath soft on
her heated skin. He raised a hand and traced one lazy
finger down her cheek, continuing down the line of her
neck to her collarbone. His eyes were dark with desire.

'Would you have honoured the bet if you had lost,
sweetheart? Would you?'

'No!' Beth gasped. She felt his fingers pause at the
hollow in her throat, felt him stroke the pulse there.

'Your skin is all flushed.' Marcus's voice had sunk to
a husky whisper now. 'You are as hot as you were the
other night. I do not believe you, Lady Allerton. I think
you are as shameless as you pretended to be at the
Cyprians' Ball…'

Beth's gasp of fury was lost as his mouth came down
on hers. This time his kiss was hard and hungry, as demanding as the one at the ball had been gentle. He
forced her lips apart and she felt his tongue invade her
mouth and her senses spun under the onslaught. She
brought her hands round to grip Marcus's arms, intending to push him away, but he leant his weight against
her so that the table caught her behind the thighs and
she was borne helplessly back, to lie amongst the scattered papers and rolling inkpot. She felt her dress gape
and her hair come loose from its pins and fan out across
the wooden surface, and she could neither struggle
nor scream, for Marcus's weight was on top of her,
holding her still, and his mouth still plundered the softness of hers.

It was only when his lips left hers, to follow the line his fingers had traced earlier and brush against the sensitive softness of her throat, that Beth realised she had no will to struggle anyway. The touch of his hands and lips was exquisite pleasure and she wanted more. She tangled her fingers in his hair and pulled his mouth back up to hers so that she could once again touch and taste him.

She had no idea how long they lay locked together before Marcus moved with single-minded concentration to strip the dress from her shoulders. Beth felt the little puffy sleeves slide down her arms to the elbow and a moment later Marcus had slid one warm hand inside the gap in her bodice and cupped her breast. Her involuntary moan was lost against his lips as he thrust his tongue deep into her mouth. His fingers found her hardening nipple and he pulled the bodice of her dress down before his mouth left hers to fasten over the pink tip he had exposed. Beth squirmed in delight and desperation as he bit down on her sensitised skin. There was an exquisite pain in the pit of her stomach and she was lost in the sensations of pleasure that he was creating. The remaining papers went flying from the desk as she writhed with excitement.

There was a sudden noise out in the hall and Marcus eased away from her with a purely involuntary movement. It was enough to bring Beth down to earth. Suddenly she was horribly aware of something digging into her back, of the papers scattered beneath her hands, the dress that had almost slipped to her waist. She wriggled again but this time in a desperate attempt to stand up, and Marcus stepped back and put out a hand to help her to her feet. Beth flinched away.

'Don't touch me!' All her horror at what she had done was in her voice. She could not believe it—could not believe her own behaviour and could not forgive him his. She saw Marcus recoil and knew that finally, she had the upper hand. She gestured towards the door. 'Lord Trevithick. Please leave. Now.'

She tidied herself with trembling fingers and watched as Marcus smoothed his hair and straightened his clothes. His eyes met hers and she saw that they were as dazed and dark with passion as she knew her own must be. Suddenly she wanted to throw herself into his arms, to make all well again between them, but she drew herself up haughtily and simply waited for him to go.

'Beth—' Marcus put out a hand to her, but Beth turned her shoulder and stared blindly out of the window. 'Beth, I am truly sorry—'

'No!' Beth's eyes filled with tears. She did not know whether he meant that he was sorry for his actions or for his earlier suspicions but whatever the case, she *did* know that she would cry in another instant. 'I do not want to hear it!'

She heard Marcus open the study door and she turned round quickly. Before he went there was something she had to say to him, something that had to be absolutely clear.

'Lord Trevithick.' Her voice shook. She could not help it. She took a deep breath and ploughed on. 'Lord Trevithick, I intend to travel down to Devon immediately. Fairhaven Island is mine and I am going to claim it.'

She watched with misgiving as Marcus straightened up and gleam of amusement came back into his eyes. He sketched an ironic bow. 'Very well, my lady. You are going to Fairhaven. I am going to Fairhaven. We shall see which of us manages to claim the island first!'

And before Beth could say another word, he was gone.

Charlotte was very good. She did not ask why Beth had ink stains on her blue muslin dress, nor why her hair, so prettily arranged *à la Greque* earlier in the day now looked as though it had been dragged through a hedge, nor even why her cousin chose to lock herself in her room for several hours, emerging pale and wan for dinner. She patted Beth's hand, told her that if she wished to discuss anything she was always happy to talk, and tactfully went off to the kitchen to confer with the cook about menus.

Kit joined them for dinner and seemed inclined to quiz Beth over her pallor and lack of appetite, but a well-aimed kick from his sister soon put paid to his questions. He was more voluble about the use to which the fine dessert wine had been put in removing the ink stains from a certain blue muslin dress, but when Beth pointed out that it was her wine cellar he did not pursue it. Beth herself felt inclined to take the rest of the bottle and drink it straight down, but her natural good sense suggested that she would soon feel the worse for it. Besides, she found dessert wine too sweet and reflected wryly that if she wished to become intoxicated for the first time in her life, she should find a more enjoyable way of doing so.

Beth felt miserable and as weary as though she had been awake for a week, but most of all she felt furious at the injustice of Marcus's behaviour. To make wild accusations and not even do her the courtesy of explaining them properly; to give Fairhaven to her only to try to take it away again; to behave in a less than gentlemanly fashion—but here she blushed hotly even in her thoughts and hastily turned her mind to something else.

After dinner, Beth sought Charlotte out in the red drawing room where her cousin was sitting placidly embroidering at her tambour frame. Charlotte was working on a piece of white muslin, sewing the hem with exquisite neatness, and Beth smiled a little as she remembered her own hopeless efforts at needlework. She plumped herself down next to her cousin, curling up and hugging one of the red velvet cushions.

'Charlotte, I have been thinking,' she began. 'I intend to leave London tomorrow and go home to Devon. I know that Kit has business to finish here, but I have no more taste for parties and balls, and it would be better to be home in good time for Christmas.'

She saw her cousin's penetrating blue gaze resting on her and blushed slightly. 'Well, there is no reason to stay…'

'I know that you are doing this to avoid Lord Trevithick,' Charlotte said calmly, cutting her thread. 'I do not really understand the nature of your quarrel, Beth, for Justin Trevithick had too much delicacy to speak to me of it, but if you wish to run away from your troubles that is your affair!' She fixed her cousin with a severe regard. 'However, running away does not generally solve anything!'

Beth hugged her cushion harder. 'No, I know you are right! But I do not believe I can resolve my dispute with Lord Trevithick, for he is utterly indifferent to my explanations! Indeed, he scarcely gave me the chance to offer any! Oh!' All her pent-up frustration came out on the word. 'He is the most arrogant and tiresome man imaginable!'

'Strange, when his cousin is so courteous,' Charlotte

observed, with a little smile. 'Mr Trevithick is all that one could wish for in a gentleman of quality!'

Something about her tone of voice struck Beth, despite her preoccupation. She gave her cousin a penetrating stare.

'Charlotte, are you developing a *tendre* for Mr Trevithick?'

Charlotte blushed. 'Certainly not!' she said with dignity. She bent her head over her tambour frame. 'Besides, we are speaking of your concerns, Beth, not mine!'

Beth had not missed the colour that stained her cousin's cheeks. She smiled. 'I would far rather talk of the impression that the *gallant* Mr Trevithick made upon you than the shortcomings of his kinsman, the Earl!'

'Humph!' Charlotte seemed put out of countenance for the first time. 'I know you are only seeking to distract me, Beth! Mr Trevithick was very charming, but I doubt that I shall see him again. Now…' she recovered herself '…you mentioned returning home to Devon, but did you intend to go to Mostyn Hall—or to Fairhaven Island?'

Beth narrowed her eyes. Her cousin's powers of perception were disturbing at times. 'Well, I confess I had thought to visit Fairhaven first… That is, the Earl granted the island to me, so it is mine now! And though he now wishes to rescind his gift, I do not see that I should make it easy for him…'

Charlotte selected another thread from the sewing box open on the seat beside her. 'I see. So what do you intend to do? Take Fairhaven by storm and defend it against him? Really, Beth! This is the nineteenth century! You are not in the Civil Wars now, you know!'

Beth got up and walked over to the window. She was not going to admit it, but there was something powerfully tempting about Charlotte's suggestion. Things must have been so much easier when one could round up an army of retainers and take the fight to the enemy. Perhaps she had been born in the wrong century but, army or not, she was determined to claim her island.

'It would not be like that, Lottie,' she said, with more confidence than she felt. 'I'll warrant that there is no tenant on Fairhaven—who would want to live in such an out-of-the-way place? And doubtless the villagers will be pleased to have someone take an interest at last…'

Feeling restless, she pulled back the red velvet curtain and looked out. It was dark in the street outside and the lamplighter and his assistant were making their rounds. The lamplighter had rested his ladder against the stand and passed the oil container down to his assistant for refilling. The boy was pouring oil slowly from the jug, his tongue sticking out of the corner of his mouth with the effort of concentration. Beth smiled a little.

'Anyway, I still have the deed of gift to Fairhaven,' she said slowly, 'signed by the Earl himself. It is a legal document and he would find it difficult to explain it away in a court of law—'

Charlotte looked horrified. 'You would not take this matter to the courts! Think of the cost! Think of the scandal, and all for what? Beth, surely you cannot mean it?'

Beth turned back to the candlelit room. 'No, Lottie. I would not go so far, but I do intend to claim Fairhaven.' She pressed her hands together. 'It is just that Trevithick's behaviour has been so *unfair* and I have the greatest dislike of being bested!'

'I had observed it,' Charlotte said, very drily. 'Oh, Beth, can you not just let it go? If you truly do not believe you can come to terms with the Earl of Trevithick, then concede gracefully and let us go home to Mostyn!'

There was a silence. The fire crackled and spat. 'Does that mean that if I were to go to Fairhaven you would not come with me?' Beth asked, after a moment. 'I know you disapprove, Lottie…'

Their eyes met. Charlotte looked pained. 'Oh, Beth! Yes, I do disapprove! Most heartily! *Why* must you go?'

Beth looked unhappy. 'Because it is a point of principle. Because I cannot let him win!'

'Those are not good reasons!' Charlotte almost wailed. 'Of course Trevithick will win! He is the Earl and he holds the island and he has all the advantage! You are tilting against windmills!'

Beth's mouth set in a mutinous line. 'Perhaps so. But I have to try!'

Charlotte screwed her face up. 'Why? Such stubbornness is so unbecoming!'

Beth laughed. 'Stubbornness, impetuosity… Oh, Lottie, you have been trying to improve me this age! I do not know why you bother, for I shall never become more ladylike!' Her smile faded. 'But if you do not wish to come with me I shall understand. There is no reason for you to have to compromise your propriety just because I am a hoyden!'

Charlotte pushed the tambour frame away and got to her feet. 'What, am I to let you go jauntering about the countryside alone and in even more of a hoydenish manner? I shall go and start my packing!'

Beth rushed across the room and gave her an impetuous hug. 'Oh, thank you!'

Charlotte hugged her back. 'Do not thank me for being as foolish as you! Why, it will take us at least six days to get there at this time of year—'

'Oh, no, only three! And the weather is not so bad at present!'

'And the inns will be dreadful and the sea will be rough and like as not we will end locked in a dungeon! Oh, Beth…'

'There will be no difficulties,' Beth said, with far more confidence than she was feeling. She did not think that this was the moment to tell Charlotte that the Earl of Trevithick had indicated that he too would be travelling to Fairhaven, so that another confrontation was inevitable. 'I have it all planned! I will ask Gough to formally register the transfer of the island from the Earl of Trevithick to myself, so there will be no questions about the legality of the situation! Gough will take care of everything!'

Charlotte looked unconvinced. 'It seems to me that there is every doubt! However, if Gough will deal with it, I suppose we may be comfortable on that score!' She brightened a little. 'Now, if we were to wait until your legal title to the estate was established…'

Beth shook her head. She knew that Charlotte was right; it was the most sensible course of action and by far the safest. She also knew that the Earl of Trevithick was eminently capable of opposing her at every turn and that the ensuing struggle might last for months. And possession was nine-tenths of the law…

'It would never serve, Lottie. I could be waiting for ever!'

Charlotte sighed, apparently accepting the inevitable. 'Very well! I suppose I shall have a few days on the road to try to change your mind!'

Beth smiled. 'I have it all planned out! Kit can keep

the house open here for as long as he has business in town and meanwhile I will send to Mostyn Hall for some of the servants to join us on Fairhaven! We shall go across and tell the islanders that the property has changed hands—it will be exactly as though I had purchased the estate!'

'Not precisely,' Charlotte said drily. She looked at Beth with deep misgiving. 'A disputed deed of gift is hardly the same as an acknowledged sale! However, I can see that there is no reasoning with you! This whole plan will go horribly awry! Mark my words!'

On the first night of their journey the inn, the Castle and Ball in Marlborough, was of good enough quality to meet even Charlotte's specifications. They had a neat private parlour, well away from the public tap, and a bedroom on the quiet side of the inn so that they would not be disturbed by the comings and goings in either the main street or the coach yard.

Charlotte had wanted to put up for the night at Newbury and had argued that there was no necessity to push on to Marlborough, but Beth had been adamant that they needed to cover as much distance as possible. Their departure had already been delayed by two days, for it had taken far longer than she had expected to make all the arrangements for their journey. Firstly she had had to discuss her plans with Gough, who had raised any number of legal queries about the deed of gift. Then she had had to send a messenger to Mostyn Hall to ask the estate manager to arrange for a group of servants to be ready to join them on Fairhaven once she gave the word. She could imagine the raised eyebrows that letter would cause when it was received. Finally she had to attend to her own packing and all the preparations for the journey, which all took twice as long as she had expected. Then, when they were about to depart, Kit had expressed his severe disapproval of the plan and all but threatened to forbid them to go. The quarrel that ensued had ended with him telling Beth that she was headstrong to the point of madness and with Charlotte telling both of them that they were as bad as each other. It had not been a good start to the venture.

Beth sighed. Downstairs in the inn parlour, a clock chimed seven. They had set off at eight o'clock that morning and had been travelling for almost nine and a half hours, with barely time to snatch a drink or something to eat when they stopped to change the horses. Charlotte had frowned at Beth's urgency and both of the girls had become increasingly tired and irritable as the day had worn on. However, when they had arrived at Marlborough, a pitcher of hot water, a change of clothes and the promise of a good meal had made them both feel much better, and Beth was looking forward to a peaceful night's sleep.

Charlotte stuck her head around the bedroom door. 'Are you ready to come down to eat, Beth? Our supper is on the table.'

The most delicious smell of roasting lamb filled the corridor and Beth's stomach gave an enormous rumble. She went gratefully into the little parlour and allowed the bowing landlord to escort her to her seat. The table was already laden with covered dishes, the candles were lit and the room had an altogether welcoming feel to it. Beth was glad to see that Charlotte seemed much happier now that they were settled and that the accommodation was everything that she could have desired.

Neither of them spoke for about ten minutes, for they were far too busy applying themselves to the food and drink. Eventually Charlotte accepted a second glass of wine and a second portion of lamb, and smiled across the table at her cousin.

'Thank goodness! I feel so much better! And this place is a most superior establishment! I was afraid that they would not treat us so well, travelling alone and without any gentlemen to bespeak rooms for us!'

Beth shifted a little on her chair. Like her cousin, she was aware that their arrival had caused some curiosity, travelling as they were with only a couple of servants and without an escort. She knew that it made Charlotte feel vulnerable and whilst she did not believe that they were in any danger, it was certainly more comfortable to have Kit's company when travelling. He had always been the one to bespeak rooms, arrange meals and deal with payment. Beth was in no way a retiring female, but she had not travelled a great deal and so had little experience to draw on. Fortunately the inns at which they planned to stay were all reputable ones and there was no doubt that her title and evident wealth were most useful in smoothing their way. She did not anticipate any trouble.

The dishes were removed and a fine apple pie brought in. Beth considered another glass of wine and regretfully decided that it would make her fall asleep at the table. Charlotte yawned prettily.

'May we travel a little less precipitately tomorrow, please, Beth?' she pleaded. 'I am shaken to pieces from the journey, for all that the coach is so comfortable! Surely we could stop at Trowbridge or Frome? There is no need for us to hurry in this madcap way!'

Beth toyed with a spoonful of pie. She had still not told Charlotte that the Earl of Trevithick had threatened to journey down to Fairhaven himself and that it was her main aim to reach the island before him. When they had left London that morning she had been reassured to know that Trevithick was still in the capital—Kit had seen him at a ball only the night before. Beth had begun to wonder if, in fact, the Earl did not intend to go to Fairhaven at all. He had never evinced any interest in the island for its own sake, and his only aim had been prevent her from claiming it. It was a matter of pride to him as well as to her. But perhaps, Beth thought, it was not important enough to him to come chasing after her. Only time would tell.

She reached for the cream jug and poured a little on to her remaining piece of pie.

'I had hoped to reach Bridgwater tomorrow night—'

'Bridgwater!' Charlotte seldom interrupted for her manners were too good. This time, however, she was staring at her cousin with incredulous eyes. 'Why, that must be all of eighty miles! Why on earth do we need to go so far in one day?'

Beth sighed. 'It is simply that I had hoped to reach Fairhaven as soon as possible.' She avoided her cousin's gaze. 'When we last met, the Earl of Trevithick indicated that he was intending—well, that he might be thinking of travelling to Fairhaven himself. So—'

'Trevithick going to Fairhaven himself?' Charlotte interrupted for a second time. She stopped eating and put her spoon down slowly. 'Why did you not tell me this before, Beth?'

Beth toyed with her food, still evading her cousin's eye. 'I thought you would only worry if you thought we were engaged in some sort of race. Matters were bad enough as they were…'

'Yes, but if Trevithick is going to be at Fairhaven that will not be so bad at all!'

Beth looked suspiciously at her cousin. For a moment she wondered if Charlotte had had too much wine, but although her cheeks were becomingly pink and her eyes bright, she did not appear inebriated.

'Whatever can you mean, Lottie? How could it possibly be a good thing for us both to be there together? We would come to blows within minutes!'

'Well…' Charlotte started to eat again. 'It will not be so much like an invasion this way, more a house visit—'

'House visit!' Beth stared. 'Good gracious, what can you mean? It will make things twice as bad!'

'Oh, surely not! For we may all sit down together and discuss the matter calmly!'

Beth stared all the more, wondering which of them was mad. 'Lottie, you saw what the Earl was like when he came to the house in London! How can you imagine that we would be able to discuss anything calmly?'

Charlotte frowned. 'Well, I realise that the Earl was suffering under some strong emotion then, but surely he is perfectly reasonable under normal circumstances!'

Beth grimaced. She could not imagine how their situation could be interpreted as normal and was afraid that Charlotte was clutching at straws. Should the Earl of Trevithick appear and throw a rub in their way, it would prove decidedly awkward. Beth's fervent hope by now was that the Earl would not care enough for Fairhaven to put himself to the trouble of going all the way to Devon in winter. The little Season was in full flow and Christmas was approaching and surely he had better things to do with his time than pursue a wild goose chase?

Before she could put this view to Charlotte, however, there was a rumble of wheels in the courtyard outside and the flare of carriage lamps in the darkness.

'Ostler!' a deep masculine voice shouted. 'Look lively there!'

Beth got up from the table and hurried over to peer through the diamond-paned windows. A curricle was standing in the yard outside, a superb vehicle in dark blue or green livery, with four elegant horses of a quality to match. As she watched, the driver handed his reins to his passenger and swung down from the seat. Beth's stomach suddenly felt hollow for all the excellent meal she had just eaten.

She turned back to Charlotte who had also started to look apprehensive.

'You may judge for yourself how reasonable the Earl of Trevithick is, Charlotte,' she said slowly, 'for I do believe that he is here now!'

In an excess of propriety, Charlotte had whisked her cousin away from the window, drawn the curtains tightly and ordered the servants to remove the dishes and to serve tea. She and Beth now sat in the wing chairs on each side of the fire, clutching a cup in their hands and looking at each other with ill-concealed nervousness. Both of them knew that good manners demanded that they make themselves known to the new arrivals. Neither of them had moved to do so.

The whole inn seemed to have come alive with the gentlemen's arrival. Beth could hear Marcus out in the yard, chatting with the grooms and ostlers and accepting many complimentary comments on the quality of his horses. Lights flared, doors banged and Beth reflected uncharitably that it was typical of the Earl to make as much fuss as possible wherever he went. She sipped her tea, wondering how on earth Marcus could have reached Marlborough that night and with his own horses. Then she told herself that she did not want to know. She did not want to speak with him and preferably she did not want him to know that she was even there. Her appetite for a confrontation seemed to have vanished completely.

Beth heard Justin Trevithick's voice in the corridor outside, bespeaking supper for two and rooms for the night. Charlotte heard it too; Beth saw a hint of colour come into her cousin's face as Charlotte busied herself pouring fresh tea. Then Beth heard the door of the tap-room open and a gust of laughter flow out, and for a moment she thought that they were safe and that the gentlemen had chosen to take a drink in the bar. She was swiftly disabused.

'The ostler tells me that there are some other travellers staying tonight, landlord.' Beth heard Marcus's voice sound from further down the corridor. She realised that the maid had left the parlour door slightly ajar when she had removed the dishes. She crept towards it and put her ear to the crack.

'Yes, my lord.' The landlord spoke above the hubbub coming from the taproom. 'There are two ladies staying with us.'

'Beth!' Charlotte whispered urgently from behind her. 'What are you doing?'

'Hush!' Beth put her finger to her lips. 'I am trying to eavesdrop—'

'Real ladies or the other sort?' Beth heard the amusement in Marcus's voice. Evidently the landlord did as well, for this time his tone was scandalised.

'Beg pardon, my lord, but I don't run that sort of a house! And these are very definitely real ladies!'

'My apologies.' Marcus had erased the amusement from his tone. There was a rustle of something and a mutter of thanks from the landlord.

'It is just that some friends of ours are on the road and we are trying to catch up with them,' Marcus continued. 'We traced them through the toll houses and the posting inns and wondered if they had already arrived here…' The rustle sounded again. 'Two ladies, young… attractive… The younger is very striking, with black hair and silver-grey eyes…'

Beth felt herself warming and pretended that she was hot with indignation that Marcus should be speaking so freely of her. She had a small suspicion, however, that it was his compliments that made her face glow. She was not totally immune to his admiration. And the landlord had evidently recognised her from the description. She heard him clear his throat and speak obsequiously.

'Yes, sir. I do believe you are describing our guests… A most beautiful young lady, sir. Most striking.'

Beth drew in her breath silently. She had not suggested to the staff in any of the inns that her journey was secret, so they had no reason not to give out information, particularly if Marcus smoothed the process with the kind of tip that she could imagine had just changed hands. The landlord was still talking, evidently anxious to please his open-handed visitor.

'The ladies have the private parlour, sir, so you will find them there. I dare say they may be retiring soon though, as they've already partaken of supper and have been travelling all day—'

'Of course they have,' Marcus murmured. Beth could tell he was coming closer. 'But I am sure that once they know we are here, the ladies may be persuaded to share their parlour with us…'

Beth shot away from the door like a scalded cat. Charlotte was watching her with a frown between the eyes. 'What is it, Beth?' she hissed.

Beth closed her eyes and opened them again sharply. 'Oh, Lottie, I think we should have retired when we had the chance—'

There was a step right outside the door, then Justin's voice came even closer at hand. 'Marcus, can you come out to the stable for a moment? Stephens tells me that there is a problem with one of the horses—'

A cold draught swirled through the parlour as the door to the courtyard opened and closed again. The gentlemen's footsteps could be heard outside on the cobbles. Without a pause for thought, Beth grabbed Charlotte's hand, pulled her from her chair and bundled her out of the room and up the stairs. Charlotte, out of breath and protesting, sank down on to the big four-poster bed as Beth closed the bedroom door behind them and leant against it, breathing hard.

'Beth! What on earth was all that about? Why could you not just greet Lord Trevithick in a civilised manner?'

Beth was not sure of the answer to that. All she knew was that she felt unequal to the task of confronting Marcus that evening and that any such meeting would have to wait until the morning when she would be stronger and better prepared. She did not have the first idea of what she would say to him or how the conflict between them might be resolved. What she *did* know, however, was that she was certainly not going to agree to go tamely home just because Marcus had caught up with them already.

There was a knock at the door and Beth's heart jumped into her throat. The cousins looked at each other.

'Well, go on,' Charlotte said, a little impatiently. 'Pray answer! I cannot believe that even Lord Trevithick would beard a lady in her bedroom!'

Beth privately thought that that was exactly what Trevithick would do, but she went over to the door and peeped round. To her relief there was only the maid on the landing outside. The girl dropped a slight curtsy. She was carrying a tray with two beakers of steaming liquid, and now brought them into the room and placed them on the table by the window.

'His lordship's compliments, ma'am, and he wondered if you would both care to take a nightcap that is sovereign against the aches and pains of the road.'

Beth stared suspiciously into the cup. The smell was delicious, a mix of mulled wine and spices. Charlotte came across and stood looking over her shoulder.

'Oh, how thoughtful! Pray thank Lord Trevithick for his consideration!'

The maid dropped another curtsey and went out, and Charlotte, smiling, picked up one of the cups and took a sip. She gave a sigh.

'Oh, that is truly delicious! Beth, you must try some!'

Beth took a careful taste. The liquid was warm and soothing, easing away all the aches of the journey just as the maid had promised. Suddenly it seemed churlish to be suspicious of Marcus's motives. Beth drained the cup to the dregs.

Charlotte was yawning widely. 'Goodness, I feel tired! I am for my bed.' She gave Beth a kiss. 'Do not forget to lock your door, Beth—and I am in the next room should anything untoward happen! I am sure we can resolve this situation with Lord Trevithick in the morning. Goodnight!'

Beth closed the door behind her and after a moment bolted it. She hesitated over calling the maid but felt too

weary to bother. She donned her nightdress in a somewhat haphazard fashion, and half-climbed, half-tumbled
into the big bed. She had barely blown out the candle
before she was asleep.

Chapter Five

Beth awoke feeling warm and comfortable. The room was full of sunlight and shifting shadow, and for a moment she was puzzled until she realised that she must have fallen asleep before she could draw the bed curtains. Certainly she remembered that she had felt extraordinarily weary the night before, which she supposed was no great surprise since she had been travelling for an entire day with little rest. Now, however, she felt miraculously restored and quite capable of dealing with the problem of seeing Marcus Trevithick again. She swung her legs over the side of the bed and hurried to ring the bell for some hot water.

It was whilst she was waiting for the maid to appear that she heard the clock downstairs in the parlour strike twelve. Beth paused in the act of brushing out her hair, then counted very carefully as the faint chimes of the church clock out in the square echoed the same twelve strokes. She put down her brush and flung open the bedroom curtains.

Her window looked out on to a small kitchen garden with rows of neat vegetables and a chicken scratching in the dust. The sun was bright and high, and Beth could feel its October warmth through the glass pane. High noon. There could be no doubt. She had slept for fifteen hours.

Beth frowned. She had been intending to breakfast no later than seven-thirty and be on the road by eight. If they were to reach Bridgwater that day... But there was no possible chance of reaching Bridgwater now, or even Glastonbury. They would be lucky to make thirty miles that day and meanwhile Marcus would be halfway to Devon. No doubt he was on his way already.

Beth's eye fell suspiciously on the cup that had held the mulled wine. She picked it up and sniffed the dregs. They smelled of nothing but the same delicious honey and spice scent that had tempted her the previous night. Sovereign against the aches and pains of the road, the maid had said, but perhaps they had been sovereign against more than that...

There was a knock at the door and the maid appeared, clutching a large pitcher of water.

'Good morning, milady! And a lovely day it is—'

'Is my cousin awake yet?' Beth asked urgently, dispensing with the greetings somewhat precipitately. 'It is far later than I had imagined and we had intended to be on the road hours ago!'

The maid, a large, untidy country girl, put her hands on her hips and surveyed Beth with a certain puzzlement.

'Lords lawks, ma'am, there's no need to go hurrying about the country on a lovely day like this!' Her accent was as rich and soothing as butter. 'Mrs Cavendish only woke a few moments ago—just like yourself, ma'am!—and ten to one you'll be needing some luncheon before you set out!'

Beth fidgeted with the curtain cord. Charlotte was a

notoriously slow riser and if she had only just woken it would be at least an hour until she was ready to go. It was with difficulty that Beth restrained herself from rushing into her cousin's room and exhorting her to hurry up, but she knew there was no point in harassing Charlotte, who would proceed at her own unflappable pace.

The maid shot her a curious look, then started to pour the water into the basin. 'His lordship sends his compliments, ma'am, and asks that you join him in the parlour—when you're ready, of course.'

Beth paused. 'His lordship? Lord Trevithick is still here?'

'Yes, ma'am.' The girl lowered the pitcher. 'Some problem with one of his horses, so I'm told. Still, there's no rush, is there, ma'am? I'll tell him that you'll be down shortly!'

Beth sighed. However polite Marcus's request, she suspected it hid a rather more emphatic order and there was little point in resisting.

She came down the stairs fifteen minutes later, her travelling dress neatly pressed and her hair demurely plaited. The door of the parlour was closed and there was no sound within, and after a moment Beth decided that she had no wish to beard Marcus in his lair just now, and went out into the sunshine.

There was a busy market in Marlborough High Street and Beth resolved to take a look at the stalls that lined either side of the wide cobbled road. She was in no hurry. Charlotte would not be ready for ages and as far as Beth was concerned, the longer she put off her meeting with Marcus, the better.

Plenty of cottagers had brought their vegetables to

market and turnips, onions and potatoes spilled out of baskets and across makeshift wooden trestles. Cheek by jowl with these were the vendors of bootlaces, nutmeg graters, cough drops, corn plasters and any number of necessities that Beth had never realised that she needed. She wandered along the row of stalls, pausing to chat with everyone and admire their produce and their children. A persuasive street trader almost convinced her that she would like to buy a small, mewling kitten—her heart was broken at the thought of it ending up in a drowning sack—but common sense suggested that it would not make a comfortable pet, particularly on a journey. It was whilst she was explaining to the trader that he must on no account sell the kitten to a bad home, that a gentleman paused beside them and Beth realised with a sinking heart that Marcus Trevithick had caught up with her at last. Her authoritative instructions wavered and faded away as she completely forgot what she had been talking about.

Marcus was watching her with an expression of amused indulgence in his eyes. He was bare-headed and in the bright sunlight his thick dark hair gleamed a glossy blue-black. He was immaculately dressed in buckskins and an elegant coat of blue superfine, and his Hessians had a mirror-polish that reflected the sun. As Beth watched, he handed the kitten's owner a coin and said gravely, 'Take the little creature to the Castle and Ball Inn. It can earn its keep catching mice in the stables.'

He offered Beth his arm. 'Good morning, Lady Allerton. Have you completed your purchases, or are there more desperate animals that you wish to rescue? I noticed a small piglet at the stall on the left—if you do not buy it, it will surely end in the pot…'

Beth took the proffered arm a little gingerly. 'Thank you, my lord. I am not in a position to establish a sanctuary for animals at the moment and I do not believe I require any more candles, or bootlaces—'

'Or corn plasters or tin trays!' Marcus finished for her. He smiled down at her. 'It is tempting though, is it not? I have purchased a box of cigars and a carved walking stick and have no clear idea of how I came to part with my money!'

They were walking away from the bustle of the market now and down the hill towards where the river curled its lazy way through the fields. The water sparkled in the sunlight. Beth wondered how long it would be before one or other of them came to the point. After all, they could scarcely pretend that this was a chance encounter. Yet Marcus did not speak, and when she risked a glance at his face she saw that he was watching her with thoughtful consideration.

She paused on the bridge and looked down at the ducks splashing in the shallows beneath.

'Oh how pretty it is here!' she said impulsively. 'I would almost like to stay…'

She looked up, caught Marcus's eye, and bit her lip. She had no wish to give too much away.

Marcus leant back against the stone parapet and smiled at her.

'Is your journey too urgent to let you linger here?' he asked. 'Tell me, Lady Allerton, are you making your way home to Mostyn Hall—or, as I suspect, to Fairhaven Island?'

Beth held his gaze. 'We are travelling to Fairhaven!' she said. She raised her chin. 'Now that I have the deeds to the island I consider it my own! I told you that I would not give in easily, my lord!'

Marcus straightened up. 'Truth to tell, I should be immensely disappointed if you did,' he said softly.

The breeze rippled along the river and raised an echo of a shiver along Beth's nerves. A few dead leaves swirled down onto the water and floated away. She found that she could not look away from Marcus's compelling gaze, could not break the contact between them. Then Marcus shifted slightly.

'However, there are difficulties in your way,' he said. 'Did you expect that I would just let you sail to Fairhaven and stake your claim? I warned you that I would be travelling there myself!'

'I thought to get there first,' Beth said defiantly. The cold autumn wind had whipped the colour up in her cheeks. 'And I was not sure that you cared sufficiently for Fairhaven to put up a fight, my lord!'

Marcus laughed. 'But I have to defend my property against invasion—'

'Oh, do not be so melodramatic!' Beth snapped. She turned away from him, frowning down at the eddying water. 'The truth is that you do not wish to be bested, my lord! You care nothing for the island, but you have some cock-and-bull notion in your head that I cheated you in some way and you do not wish me to win!'

Marcus drove his hands into the pockets of his coat. 'It is true that at first I thought you had lied to me, Lady Allerton—'

An angry sparkle lit Beth's eyes. 'You have such a way with words, my lord! Pray do not spare my feelings! You made your opinion of me quite plain before!'

'And the evidence against you is very strong...' Marcus's gaze was thoughtful on her. 'If it were not that my own instinct is to the contrary, I should say that you had to be guilty.'

Beth turned her back on him. 'I do not wish to discuss this with you, sir. There is no point in doing so! You did not do me the courtesy of presenting your apparent evidence to me before, so I do not feel I need to listen to you now!'

Marcus shrugged elegantly. 'That is only fair, I suppose! So, how do we resolve this conflict, Lady Allerton? You wish to claim Fairhaven. I wish to prevent you from doing so. We are here together. So…'

Beth pressed her lips together. It seemed a frustrating and faintly ridiculous situation in which to find herself. She could rush back to the inn and leap into her carriage, but she could not prevent Marcus from following her. Similarly he could hardly force her to go home to Mostyn. It seemed that they had reached deadlock.

'This problem would never have happened if you had not got here so quickly!' she burst out. 'You were in London only yesterday morning, and yet you were here in Marlborough by nightfall and with your own curricle and team! It is not possible—' She broke off and looked at Marcus stormily as he started to laugh.

'I fear that your information is faulty, my dear! I was *not* in London yesterday morning.'

Beth frowned. 'But Kit said that you had been at Lady Paget's ball the night before!'

'That's true. After the ball, Justin and I drove through the night to Bradbury Park, a place I have close by Reading. We rested the horses for a few hours before pressing on to here. We did not wish you to get too far ahead of us, you see!'

Beth stared at him, anger and indignation warring within her. 'But how did you know where to find us?'

Marcus took a step closer to her. 'We could not be sure, of course, but when we asked at the post houses they were able to tell us of two ladies, travelling alone, who were anxious to press on with their journey.' He shrugged. 'It might not have been the two of you, of course, but given that you had told me you would be travelling into Devon and I knew you would not wish to linger, it seemed likely.' He raised a hand and touched Beth's cheek. His voice grew softer. 'Besides, you are very memorable, you know, sweetheart. At least three of the landlords knew exactly whom I was describing when I spoke of the beautiful lady with ebony black hair and smoky silver eyes!'

Beth gazed at him, trapped equally by the warmth of his regard and the softly mesmerising tone of his voice. In all her life she had never ever considered herself to be beautiful and had certainly never imagined that any-one else would think so. She broke the contact with an effort and turned away, resting her clasped hands on the parapet of the bridge and feeling the chill of the cold stone through her gloves. She did not want this confusion of her senses. It undermined her resolve to oppose Marcus and made it so very difficult to be angry with him. It simply was not fair. She deliberately recalled his behaviour in London, his lack of trust and his unfair accusations, and then she felt able to harden her heart.

'I do not believe your compliments sincere, my lord!' she said coldly. 'Indeed, I have the gravest suspicion that you are not to be trusted at all! That mulled wine that you sent up to us last night—can it be a coincidence that both Charlotte and I slept the clock round?'

Marcus was laughing again. 'I can only assume that you slept so well because you were tired, Lady Allerton, and no wonder if you will dash about the countryside at such speed!'

Beth smiled sweetly in return. 'And what a fortunate

thing for you, my lord, when one of your own horses had gone lame and needed a rest! On your own admission you would not have wanted us to get too far ahead of you!'

'Indeed,' Marcus agreed affably, 'for how could we escort you if that were the case?'

Beth stared at him. The breeze was ruffling his silky dark hair and there was the beginning of a smile curling the corners of his mouth. She frowned a little. 'Escort us? What new nonsense is this?'

'It is an idea I have just had.' Marcus's smile grew. 'Would you not be far more comfortable on your journey with Justin and myself to smooth out any difficulties?'

Beth raised her eyebrows. In some ways the answer was a definite yes, but in others there was no doubt that Marcus's company was the last thing she sought, the most unsettling thing imaginable. Besides, it was simply not possible when they were adversaries.

'Well, it is most kind of your lordship to offer us escort, but—'

Marcus's hand covered hers on the stone parapet. 'Please don't refuse me, my lady. It would be my pleasure.'

Beth looked up at him and away quickly. The conventional words were given a completely new meaning by the sensual intensity in his eyes. She tried to slide her hand from beneath his.

'It would not be appropriate, my lord. How could you escort us? After all, we are in competition to reach Fairhaven first and can hardly travel together!'

'Need we be rivals?' Marcus queried softly. His fingers tightened over hers. 'I am sure we can find another solution…'

Beth held her breath. 'Such as?'

'Well...' Marcus looked thoughtful. 'With autumn so far advanced you might reconsider a sea voyage. Then we could escort you home to Mostyn for Christmas—'

Beth wrenched her hand from his. 'Oh, I understand your motives very well, my lord! You wish to persuade me to give up my quest! Well, I have already told you I shall not! Nor have I forgotten the slighting way you spoke to me when last we met! You are the last person whose escort I should accept on any journey, I assure you!'

She whisked past him and took the path up the hill towards the High Street, trying to hurry without the indignity of slipping on the cobbles. She was all too aware of Marcus's step close behind, his hand steadying her when she nearly lost her footing on some damp leaves, as she had known she would. By the time she reached the road, her cheeks were flushed with exertion and she felt hot, bothered and cross. Marcus, in contrast, was sauntering beside her, looking cool and infuriatingly amused.

Beth stalked across the road, narrowly missed being crushed by a cart that was clattering between the market stalls, and shot in at the door of the Castle and Ball with the intention of sweeping Charlotte up and driving off immediately. As she paused briefly in the corridor, she heard Charlotte's voice and pushed open the door of the private parlour.

Charlotte and Justin Trevithick were seated at the table partaking of luncheon. There were two other places set and an array of cold meats, cakes and fruit on dishes before them. As Beth burst through the door, Charlotte looked up and smiled at her. She looked pink and pretty and turned her glowing face to her cousin.

'Beth! And Lord Trevithick! Pray join us for some

luncheon!' She drew out the chair beside her and smiled at Beth. 'The most excellent news, Beth! Mr Trevithick and his cousin are to escort us for the rest of the journey! What do you think of that?'

'This is ridiculous!' Beth grumbled, leaning back against the carriage's comfortable green velvet cushions and glaring out of the window at the passing scenery. 'How can we possibly be involved in a race to claim Fairhaven Island if we are accepting the escort of the very gentlemen we wish to outrun? Really, Charlotte! I never heard anything so foolish!'

Charlotte surveyed her placidly. She suddenly seemed much happier and Beth sighed inwardly with resignation. Charlotte did not have the temperament for risk or competition and now that she had the Earl and, more importantly, Justin Trevithick, to take care of all arrangements, she was much more comfortable.

'I do not see why we needed to become involved in a silly race in the first place,' Charlotte said comfortably. 'Everything will be so much better now!'

Beth wriggled crossly. 'Certainly it will, for unless we can shake off the Earl we shall not be going to Fairhaven at all and shall end by going quietly home!' She looked out of the window, saw Marcus pull alongside on a raking black hunter, and hastily looked away. She wished that she had selected a book to pass the time, but it was such a lovely day that she had wanted to look out at the view. Unfortunately, the view seemed to consist of Marcus most of the time.

Justin Trevithick had taken the reins of the curricle for the time being and Marcus had chosen to ride. It was impossible for Beth not to observe that he had a magnificent seat on the horse and that he rode with an au-

thority and elegance that was instinctive. She turned her
gaze away from him and concentrated rather fiercely on
the pretty Wiltshire scenery. Even though most of the
trees had lost their leaves by now, it was still an attractive scene. It was a fresh day with a pale blue sky and
the countryside shone in the weak warmth of the sun. It
had not rained for several weeks, so the road was dry
and the going good. The cows grazed in the fields and
they rolled through several villages where the children
played at the cottage gates. Charlotte dozed on the seat
opposite. Beth reflected that she was the only one who
seemed to be sitting underneath a private rain cloud.

They passed another tollbooth and drew up at the next
inn to change the horses. Marcus appeared at the carriage
door.

'Lady Allerton, it is such a fine day that I wondered
if you would care to drive with me? I am leaving the
hunter here—it belongs to the Castle and Ball anyway,
and Justin is happy to take a turn in the carriage. What
do you say?'

'Oh, do let Lord Trevithick take you up, Beth!'
Charlotte said, before Beth could decline. 'You know
you would prefer to be out in the fresh air and you are
well wrapped up.'

This was true, but Beth could not help wondering how
much Charlotte's eagerness owed to the prospect of
spending some time with Justin. Marcus was holding out
a hand to help her descend from the carriage and appeared to have taken her acquiescence for granted. Beth
could not be bothered to argue, at least not for the time
being.

They had some steaming hot coffee to warm them,
but Charlotte declined a hot brick for her feet, saying
that the day was mild enough for it not to be required.

Nevertheless, when Marcus handed Beth up into the curricle, he was solicitous for her comfort, wrapping a blanket around her and ensuring that she had scarf, gloves and hat to keep her warm. Soon after they set off Beth realised that there was a great difference from travelling in the carriage; the speed was exhilarating, but it did generate a breeze, and because there was no shelter in the curricle it was considerably colder.

They had gone several miles when Marcus broke the silence and turned to her with a smile. 'I hope you are enjoying the journey, Lady Allerton! If you are too cold you need only to say, and I shall hand you up into the carriage again.'

Beth turned her glowing face to his. 'Oh, no, indeed, this is most enjoyable!' She looked around. 'Everything is so much more immediate, somehow, when one is in the open air! And Wiltshire is such a very pretty county…'

'It is,' Marcus agreed gravely. 'Do you know this area at all, Lady Allerton?'

'Oh, no, for I have travelled little and then only on the way to London and back.' Beth looked with lively interest at some curiously shaped little hills that lay close to the road.

'Only look! What odd-shaped mounds! I believe that these must be the mysterious barrows and hills that I have read about! They date from…oh, thousands of years ago! Is that not intriguing!'

Marcus laughed. 'It seems that history must be your subject, Lady Allerton! Was it an interest that you shared with your late husband?'

Beth turned her face away. For some reason she felt vulnerable when she spoke to Marcus about her marriage to Frank Allerton. It was as though no matter how little she said, Marcus could always see what lay beneath her superficial answers. Not that she had anything to hide, she told herself sharply. Her marriage had been no worse and no better than many others, May and December perhaps, but developing into mutual respect, if not love.

'Oh, Frank had little interest in the arts,' she said lightly, 'whilst I had no aptitude for mathematics or the sciences!'

'Complementary interests can be stimulating, however,' Marcus observed. 'There is much to talk about.'

'I suppose there could be.' Beth knew she sounded uncertain and for some reason honesty prompted her to add, 'Frank was too wrapped up in his studies to have much time to discuss matters with me.'

'Did you not find that disappointing?' Marcus enquired. Although Beth was not looking at him, she sensed that he was watching her rather than the road.

'Not particularly. A lady does not expect...' She glanced at him and her voice trailed away at the look in his eyes, for she was sure that she could see pity there.

'Surely it is reasonable—desirable—to hope for a certain sharing of interests? Life would be damnably lonely otherwise.'

Beth felt a strange pang inside her. She *had* been lonely at Allerton during the long weeks when Frank was absent, and even when he had been at home they had shared nothing more than an undemanding companionship. Marcus's words had given her a sudden glimpse of a different world, an existence where ideas were discussed and shared, giving mutual enjoyment. It was the sort of relationship that Charlotte had once described, something far beyond Beth's experience. Suddenly she felt as lonely as she had ever done at Allerton and she tried to cover it with a light laugh.

'Your ideas are somewhat unconventional, my lord! I can think of any number of married ladies and gentlemen who would be appalled by your suggestion that they speak to each other!'

Marcus smiled. 'Perhaps I ask a lot of the lady I would marry... An elegant and informed mind as well as gentleness, wit and charm! Am I then unlikely to find such a paragon?'

'Impossible!' Beth looked away. Marcus's references to his future wife made her feel peculiarly out of sorts.

'And since Sir Francis's death have you not felt inclined to remarry, Lady Allerton?' Marcus persisted. 'Doubtless you must have met plenty of gentlemen eager to persuade you?'

Beth shrugged, trying to hide her discomfort. 'Oh, I have no inclination to wed! I have my home and my cousins and plenty to interest me! What else could I want?'

It was a rhetorical question, but Beth wished she had not asked it when Marcus answered quite seriously.

'Companionship? Love?' His voice dropped. 'Passion?'

Beth shifted a little. 'Oh, love and passion are the most ephemeral and unreliable of things!' she said, with what she hoped was a worldly-wise air. 'I do not look for happiness there! Besides, I believe my nature must be cold—'

She saw Marcus raise his eyebrows in disbelief and almost immediately regretted her words. The memory of the kisses that they had shared seemed burnt on her mind. She looked about quickly for a distraction.

'What town is this that we approach, my lord? Can we be in Trowbridge already?'

They chatted easily until they reached the next stop,

when Marcus insisted that, as darkness was falling, Beth should resume her place in the carriage to avoid becoming cold. She did not demur, changed places with Justin, and an hour later they arrived at the King's Arms in Shepton Mallet.

The King's Arms was much smaller than the inn in Marlborough, but it was a handsome building, clean and well cared for. Beth saw Charlotte nodding her approval as Justin escorted her inside, but then Beth thought Charlotte was wont to approve everything at the moment. Beth herself found that her earlier good mood had vanished as they settled into their room. She had wanted to press on to Wells, but Marcus decreed that they had gone far enough; she wanted to set off bright and early the next day whilst Marcus had already observed cheerfully that there was no hurry to be away in the morning.

During dinner, the other three chatted whilst Beth sat quietly and mulled over the frustrations of the situation. She could see no way of shaking off Marcus and Justin and getting ahead of them again, but on the other hand it seemed nonsensical to accept their escort all the way to Fairhaven. Such a course of action could never result in her claiming the island, for she would be there as Marcus's guest and not as the new owner. That was assuming that they had not worn down her resistance in the meantime, of course—Beth was determined that not even the combined persuasion of the other three would persuade her to go tamely home to Mostyn Hall.

She had to admit that Marcus had outmanoeuvred her, but only for the time being. She would think of a plan to escape him, of that she was quite determined.

The idea came to her after dinner, whilst she and Charlotte were waiting for the gentlemen to rejoin them to partake of tea. Charlotte had been asking idly how it was that Marcus and Justin had caught up with them so quickly and Beth had explained that they had travelled through the night. And whilst she was speaking she had suddenly thought that if Marcus could do that, so too could she... All that was required was that Fowler, the coachman, should be ready—and should keep the secret.

Beth had considered asking Charlotte to come with her and had reluctantly rejected the idea. Her cousin was so much happier now that she had Justin Trevithick's escort and Beth knew that she would kick up such a fuss at the plan that it would not be worth mentioning. It was in no way desirable to plan to travel alone, without either escort or companion, but Beth argued to herself that she would be able to reach the coast the following day, take ship for Fairhaven, and that would be that. She would have Fowler to protect her and plenty of money to ease her passage, and Marcus would not find out until it was far too late. The plan was perfect.

Before retiring, she went out to stables to apprise her coachman of the new arrangements and the need for secrecy. Fowler had been in the Mostyn family for many years and was accustomed to receiving orders unquestioningly, but even he commented that it was a powerful bad idea to be travelling at night in winter, and it took a lot of persuasion on Beth's part to convince him. Eventually he went off to the tack room, muttering under his breath, and Beth crept back inside the inn intending to sit out the night until two of the clock.

Although it was not yet late, Beth could discern a certain change of atmosphere in the inn. The gentility that had been so apparent during the early evening had now vanished. Earlier the corridors had been cleanly swept and bright with lamplight. Now they were gloomy and full of smoke, the stale smell of beer hung in the air and the sound of loud voices and coarse laughter, both male and female, roared from the bar. Beth scuttled in from the courtyard and made for the stairs, taking care to keep in the shadows, for she was not sure where Marcus was now and she had a particular reason for not wishing to draw attention to herself.

She had only ascended three steps, however, before she saw the shadow at the turn of the stair and checked as a man came down towards her. Her heart sank. Naturally it had to be Marcus Trevithick. It really seemed that there was no escaping him.

Marcus and Justin had evidently settled down in privacy to enjoy their port, for Beth registered that Marcus had discarded his jacket and loosened his stock. The pristine whiteness of his shirt seemed only to emphasise the bronze of his face and the unreadable darkness of his eyes. Beth felt her heart start to race as a mixture of guilt and some other more disturbing emotion stirred within her. She swallowed hard. She considered trying to slip past Marcus without having to stop for tiresome explanations, but knew it was a vain hope. Sure enough, as they drew level, Marcus put out a hand to block her escape up the stairs.

Beth instinctively stepped back and felt the hard wood of the banister against her back. In the dim light she could see nothing of his expression but felt rather than saw the intensity with which his gaze rested on her flushed face. She wondered if he and Justin had been drinking copiously. Not ten minutes previously she had hoped that they would be so sunk in their cups that they would not notice or suspect her escape. Now it seemed that that was all too likely—and rather dangerous.

'A moment, Lady Allerton.' Marcus spoke silkily. 'I

have just been up to your room to check that you and Mrs Cavendish had everything for your comfort and I was concerned to find you absent. I cannot believe that it is appropriate for you to be wandering the corridors of an alehouse alone at this time of night! Whatever can have prompted you to venture out like this?'

Beth raised her eyes to his face in a look that she hoped was innocent. 'I was merely checking that all was well with my servants and carriage for the onward journey, my lord,' she said.

There was a pause. Marcus was still looking at her quizzically and Beth had the unnerving feeling that he was not convinced.

'I see. Well, I shall be very happy to attend to such matters myself and spare you the trouble.' Marcus shifted slightly and Beth backed away as far as she could. It had the reverse effect from the one she was trying to achieve, for Marcus took hold of her arm and drew her closer to him. 'Be careful that you do not fall over the banisters, my lady. They are a little rickety.'

Beth pulled her arm away. 'I am perfectly safe, I thank you, my lord.'

'I would dispute that,' Marcus said, giving her a smile. His gaze appraised her with disconcerting thoroughness. 'I think I should see you to your room, Lady Allerton. This inn is no place to be loitering alone. It has a somewhat…raffish…clientele in the evenings.' As if to underline his words the taproom door opened and a couple fell out into the corridor, laughing and amorously entwined. Beth looked away.

'There is no need to come with me,' she said a little abruptly. 'I can find my own way! Goodnight, my lord!'

Marcus stepped back and she brushed past him and hurried up the remaining steps. When she looked down, he had reached the bottom of the stairs but he was still watching her and the mocking light was back in his eyes. He raised a hand.

'Goodnight, then, Lady Allerton! Sleep well!'

'And you, my lord!' Beth said politely.

Marcus's grin widened. 'Oh, Justin and I will no doubt sleep like tops once we have polished off our brandy!' He disappeared down the passage and Beth heard the parlour door close behind him.

She let out the breath she had been holding, and slumped against the banister, moving quickly away as it creaked protestingly under her weight. What to do now? She was certain that Marcus suspected something, but there was no chance that she would give up her scheme. It was tonight or not at all. Beth sped away up the stairs to pack her trunk and put her plan into action.

It was pitch black. Beth crept down the stairs, feeling for each tread and clutching the banister tightly so that she should not fall. Every creak of the steps sounded like a thunderclap and she was sure it was only a matter of moments before a door was thrown open above and she was discovered. Her trunk seemed very heavy and she could feel it nudging against her leg and threatening to push her down into the darkness beneath as she tried to steal silently down to the hall.

There was no sound in the passage but for the scratch of a mouse in the wainscot and the uneven tick of the parlour clock. Beth tiptoed to the door and drew back the bolt stealthily. She could see a faint light shining in the stables but there was no sound and the carriage was certainly not waiting in the yard for her. Perhaps Fowler had decided it would cause less of a stir to set off only when she was ready. Beth shivered. The moon was riding high amidst the stars and a cold breeze was swinging the weathervane on the stable roof. It was a frosty night.

Beth slipped out of the door and across the yard. The moonlight was very bright and it was easy to pick her way past the water trough and in at the darkened stable door. One torch still burned at the far end of the stables. A couple of the horses heard her approach and shifted in their stalls, bumping against the wall. There was the chink of harness. Beth paused, then went through the wide doorway into the coach house.

Here also a torch still burned, high on the wall. Her carriage was standing in the middle of the cobbled floor, exactly where it had been five hours previously when she had come to give Fowler his instructions. The door was open but of the coachman there was no sign and it was quite evident to Beth that she would be going nowhere other than back upstairs to bed. Fury and disappointment swept over her. It had been such a good opportunity to get ahead, with Marcus and his cousin no doubt dead to the world and unlikely to wake for hours. For a moment she toyed with the idea of harnessing the carriage horses herself and driving off, but she knew it would not serve. She had taken a gig out alone on more than one occasion but the idea of driving a coach and four was clearly unworkable. She almost stamped her foot in frustration.

Just as she was turning to leave the coach house Beth heard a sound emanating from inside the carriage itself. She froze, staring into its dark interior. There was no movement, but then the sound came again, a soft scraping that turned her blood cold. Someone was inside.

For a moment Beth wanted to turn tail and flee, but then she was seized by the conviction that the unfortunate Fowler must have fallen asleep about his work—

or, worse, was dead drunk and was even now sleeping off his excesses in her coach. She marched up to the carriage steps and peered inside the open door.

'Fowler! Wake up at once! How dare you sleep when I require you to be working—?'

Strong hands grabbed her and pulled her inside the coach before she even had the chance to finish her sentence. All the breath was knocked out of her so that she could not have screamed even had she wished. In a hair's breadth of time she found herself tumbled on the velvet seat, pinned under a hard masculine body. She struggled and the cruel grip tightened, forcing her back against the cushions until she could not move. It was too dark to see anything of her assailant and her hair was blinding her anyway as it came loose from its plait and fell about her face. She drew a ragged breath, intending to call out or at the very least make a small yelping noise, but she suddenly froze, overwhelmed by the message that her senses were passing to her. Her assailant was none other than Marcus Trevithick.

Beth could hear him breathing and could smell the faint aroma of smoke and brandy that overlaid the more elemental scent of his skin. As soon as this impinged on her she felt herself weaken hopelessly in a way that was both inappropriate and unhelpful to her current circumstances. She let her breath out on a shaky sigh.

'Lord Trevithick!'

Immediately the ruthless grip eased and Beth heard the sound of flint striking sharply. A flame flared, then settled to a warm glow. Beth sat up and looked around.

The interior of the carriage, which was not particularly large in the first place, looked even smaller and oddly intimate in the glow of the lantern. Marcus adjusted the wick, then sat back in the corner. He was watching her with a mixture of amusement and calculation.

'That was…interesting, Lady Allerton. How did you recognise me?'

Beth had no intention of telling him, just as she had no intention of allowing him to gain the advantage. She edged towards the doorway and his hand immediately shot out and took her by the wrist.

'Not just yet. I believe you have some explaining to do!'

'I!' Beth looked him straight in the eye. 'It is your actions that require explanation, Lord Trevithick! Lurking in darkened stables, attacking innocent women…'

'And all in the middle of the night!' Marcus finished laconically. 'You start, Lady Allerton! Or perhaps I can help you?' His voice took on a sardonic inflection. 'When we last met you had apparently been checking on the welfare of your coachman. Perhaps you are repeating the exercise? To my mind it shows an unconscionable consideration for one's servants to come out to visit them at two in the morning!'

Beth sighed angrily. 'That was not my intention, as well you know.'

Marcus shifted on the seat. He was still holding her wrist and Beth had the unnerving impression that he would not let go of her until she came up with an adequate explanation. It was likely to be a long wait.

'So your intention was—what, precisely?'

Beth flushed at his tone. She was conscious that her hair was tumbled about her face and that Marcus was looking at her in a speculative manner that just made her feel all the more self-conscious.

'By what right do you quiz me anyway, my lord?' she demanded. 'It is not your place to question my conduct!'

There was a loaded silence, then Marcus shrugged. 'I suppose not, Lady Allerton. And as a matter of fact I do know the reason for your appearance here. You had asked your coachman to be ready to depart in the early hours, no doubt wishing to gain a march over us!' He smiled politely. 'I am sorry that your plan has failed, but, you see, Justin and I felt that Fowler was deserving of several glasses of the best brandy as a reward for the work he had done today, and alas…' He shrugged. 'It has such a detrimental effect on one's ability to drive a coach in the dark!'

Beth's eyes narrowed furiously. 'I see that you are intent upon corrupting my servants, my lord, as well as laying violent hands upon my person!'

Marcus was still smiling with infuriating calm. 'It was in your best interests, Lady Allerton! Driving in the dark is not a good idea and I was anxious to save you from harm. I believe that there is a frost tonight and the going might have been slippery. As for laying hands on you, well—' his gaze swept comprehensively over her '—I confess that it is tempting…'

Beth tried to pull away from him. 'I did not mean now.'

'I am well aware of what you meant.' Marcus looked rueful. 'However, you have put the idea into my head…'

Beth tried to draw away. The thought of Marcus fulfilling his threat gave her a feeling of nervous excitement that she tried hard to quell. She summoned up her most severe tone.

'This is foolish, my lord! We are in a carriage in a stables in the middle of the night…'

'True,' Marcus said, sighing. 'By all means let us be sensible and go back inside the inn.' He let go of Beth's hand and she immediately felt both disappointed and cross with herself. Marcus picked up the lantern, jumped down from the carriage and held a hand out politely to help Beth descend.

'Take care, Lady Allerton. It is dark and the steps are steep.'

Beth was never sure whether she slipped first or if he tugged on her hand, but as soon as the words were out of his mouth, she lost her footing on the carriage steps and fell into his arms. This did not appear to cause Marcus any problems; he held her pressed close against him for a second, a second during which Beth became acutely aware of the strength of his arms and the hardness of his body against hers. Then he slowly let her slide down the length of him so that her feet were once more on the cobbles but the rest of her body was still in startling proximity to his. Beth tried to step back and regain her balance, but Marcus simply moved closer so that her back was against the side of the carriage and he had a hand against the panelling on either side of her.

'My lord!' Beth's voice came out as a squeak.

'Yes, my lady?' Marcus's voice was barely above a whisper. His lips grazed the skin just beneath her ear, sending shivers rippling all over her body. He raised one hand to brush her hair gently back from her face.

'You said you would not!' Beth tried to sound authoritative but knew she simply sounded dazed. 'You said you would not lay a finger on me—'

Marcus stepped back a little and spread his arms wide in an exaggerated gesture of surrender. 'I am not doing so.'

Beth frowned slightly. 'Then...'

Marcus bent his head and kissed her.

It was like putting a flame to tinder. Beth's lips parted instinctively as his mouth came down on hers, its first light and persuasive touch deepening swiftly into passion. She reached out to him and his arms closed about her, holding her tight and fast. Beth gasped at the sensation of sensual pleasure that swept through her and Marcus took immediate advantage, tasting her, teasing her, exploring her with a languorous expertise that left her weak with delight. A wave of heat washed over her that had nothing to do with shame and everything to do with a more primitive emotion.

Beth struggled against the compelling demand of the kiss, the invitation to lose herself in the intense web of desire that surrounded her. She had almost forgotten that they were in a stables in the middle of the night; almost, but not quite. She had no intention of allowing Marcus to seduce her in the hay, which she was sure he would do without any compunction at all. She freed herself and Marcus reluctantly let her go.

'What is it, sweetheart?'

Beth frowned. 'It is just that it is not right, my lord!' She cast him a fulminating look. 'We are meant to be at odds—we *are* at odds—over Fairhaven and it is simply not appropriate for you to—' She broke off hopelessly. In the torchlight she could see a faint smile curving Marcus's mouth and it quite made her forget what she was talking about.

'To kiss you?'

'Yes! To kiss me and to make me forget…things.'

'Things?'

Marcus stood back for her to precede him through the coach house door.

'Things such as the reason why I was angry with you in the first place—apart from the matter of Fairhaven, I mean.'

'Ah.' Marcus sounded pensive. 'I think we may put that behind us now.'

'Well, I do not! If I could remember what it was…' Beth tried to marshal her scattered thoughts, but they remained obstinately elusive. 'When I do remember—'

'Beth? What on earth is going on?'

It was Charlotte's plaintive voice, emanating from the back door of the inn. 'I woke up and found you missing—'

She broke off as the light from Marcus's lantern illuminated their little group. 'Oh! Lord Trevithick! Good gracious! Whatever is going on?'

'I am sure your cousin will explain all to you, Mrs Cavendish.' Marcus politely held the inn door open for them. 'May I encourage you both to return to your chamber? And do not worry about an early breakfast! There is no hurry to depart in the morning.' He turned to Beth. 'Goodnight—again—Lady Allerton!'

'Whatever happened?' Charlotte whispered urgently, once they were back in their chamber and the door closed behind them. 'Beth, you are chilled to the bone and trembling! What were you doing in the stables—and with Lord Trevithick? I can scarce believe it!'

Beth told the story as concisely and unemotionally as possible, pausing only to allow for Charlotte's unavoidable exclamations.

'Fowler was apparently in his cups,' Beth said bitterly, as she reached the end of her tale, 'as a result of Lord Trevithick's generosity! And Lord Trevithick was in the coach, waiting for me!'

Charlotte gasped and pressed a hand to her mouth. 'Oh, Beth! What happened?'

'Nothing!' Beth said, shortly and untruthfully. 'Damnation! It was such a good idea.'

'Well, I do not think so,' Charlotte declared, 'and I can only be grateful that it has not come off! Driving off in the middle of the night! Whatever next!' Her gaze softened. 'Oh, let us talk about this tomorrow, for we are both tired and upset!'

Within ten minutes she was asleep again, but Beth lay awake for much longer. In part she was preoccupied with the infuriating failure of her plan, for she could not see how she would get another opportunity to get away. Her predominant thoughts, however, were of Marcus and of the devastating effect that he appeared to have on her. It made it even more imperative that she should escape him, and soon. She could not trust him and she could not trust her own reactions. Beth stared into the darkness of the bed canopy. Her body ached with an echo of the need that Marcus had aroused in her, a need that was both new and powerfully demanding. With a suppressed groan, Beth turned on her side and curled up. She was not accustomed to lying awake and suffering the pangs of frustrated desire and at that moment it was an experience she would happily have done without.

Chapter Six

The weather changed later that morning. The skies were grey when they set off from Shepton Mallet and by the time they reached Glastonbury the rain was falling and a strong westerly wind was blowing.

'I do not envy the gentlemen,' Charlotte said, peering out of the carriage window through the squally rain. 'Their curricle will be full of water! If the weather becomes much worse, I believe the roads will become waterlogged and we shall have to stop at the next inn.'

Beth did not reply. She had only had a couple of hours' sleep and was convinced that Marcus had roused them to set off at a particularly early hour because he knew she would still be half-asleep. Despite telling them that there was no hurry to depart, he had been knocking on the door at seven-thirty.

Beth felt tired and cross-grained but she did not want to vent her bad temper on Charlotte, who did not deserve it. They had already had one difficult conversation that morning; Charlotte had been hurt and reproachful that Beth had even considered leaving her behind. Once they had patched up that quarrel, Charlotte had almost undone all the good work by trenchantly expressing the view that Beth's plan had been foolish, impulsive and utterly unworkable and Beth had had to bite her tongue hard to keep silent. It did not help that she knew there was a lot of truth in Charlotte's words. She knew she could be rash and impetuous, and that Charlotte considered her conduct unbecoming to a lady. She even accepted that she was thoroughly obsessed with Fairhaven and that that might also be considered inappropriate.

Beth wriggled crossly on the cushions. Today, for some reason, the carriage felt so much more uncomfortable. Her hours of insomnia the previous night had not led to any useful thoughts, either—she was still completely baffled as to how she might shake Marcus off and reach Fairhaven before him. Beth looked out at the pouring rain and sighed. Matters were not going at all to plan. The journey to Fairhaven, which had appeared so romantic and exciting to her only a few days earlier, had assumed a resemblance to a farce. Marcus held all the cards and she might as well give up now, which was no doubt what he intended her to do.

Then there was Marcus himself. She knew that the longer she was in his company, the greater her danger. She was as untried in love as a young debutante and no matter how fiercely she tried to defend herself against him, she was fighting her own feelings as well as him. She found him all too devastatingly attractive but, whilst she was certain he might try to seduce her, she had no confidence about reading his feelings. She stared glumly out at the rain. Perhaps Marcus even viewed her seduction as part of the challenge of the situation.

Just as she was thinking of him, the coach lurched to a halt and Marcus appeared at the window. His strong brown face was dusted with raindrops and his dark hair was plastered to his head. The rain was running in rivulets off his caped driving coat. Beth pushed the window down.

'Lady Allerton, Mrs Cavendish—the weather is far too inclement for us to continue. I have a friend living a short distance away in the village of Ashlyn. If you are agreeable, we shall call at the vicarage and beg shelter, at least until the storm stops.'

'Only fancy Lord Trevithick having a friend who is a clergyman!' Charlotte commented when the plan had been agreed and the carriage was in motion once again. 'He cannot be so dreadfully wicked if he keeps company with a man of the cloth!'

Beth laughed. 'Really, Charlotte! I sometimes think you are thrice as naïve as I, despite your greater years! There are plenty of clergymen far more wicked than Lord Trevithick will ever be!'

Charlotte looked affronted but did not argue. The coach had turned in at a neat entrance gate and was making its way up a drive to a substantial stone house, far grander than most of the vicarages Beth had known.

'I believe Lord Trevithick's friend keeps a certain style,' she commented, as they drew up outside the pedimented front door.

This impression was reinforced once they were inside the house. A neat housekeeper had gone to alert the Reverend March to their arrival and the visitors had time to admire the marbled hall, the sweeping stairway and the fine family pictures on the wall. Beth was just looking at a gold-framed portrait of a winsome child, when there was a step along the passage and a small gentleman hurried towards them, blinking myopically through thick reading glasses. His face broke into a smile of great sweetness as he saw Marcus, and he held out his hand.

'Marcus, my boy! How delightful to see you again!

And Justin!' The Reverend March swung round on Justin Trevithick and shook his hand with equal enthusiasm. 'Your dear mother will be so delighted to see you! I was taking tea with her only the other day and she said it was high time you were bringing home a wife—' The Reverend broke off and peered at Beth and Charlotte. 'Upon my word, how remiss of me! Forgive me, ladies, I scarcely saw you there! My tiresome eyesight, you know... How do you do?'

Marcus stepped forward, smiling slightly. 'Lady Allerton, this is the Reverend Theophilus March who, for his sins, was once my tutor! Sir, may I present Lady Allerton and her cousin, Mrs Cavendish? We are travelling to Devon and have been in some distress from the weather, so thought to throw ourselves on your mercy...'

'Of course, of course!' Theo March seized Beth's hand and shook it firmly. 'Allerton? Cavendish? No relation of Hugo Cavendish, I hope, ma'am?'

'A distant cousin of my late husband's, sir,' Charlotte confirmed, looking slightly bemused. 'I have never met him myself.'

'Another of my tutees, I fear!' The Reverend Theo wrung his hands. 'A hopeless case! Quite wild and ungovernable as a boy and set fair to ruin himself as a man! You are to be congratulated on the fact that there is no close acquaintance there, ma'am!'

'I am sure that all your tutees drove you to distraction at times, sir,' Marcus said feelingly. 'I know that I was a sadly lacking in any academic ability!'

'Good at mathematics, but no application in Greek!' the Reverend Theo observed. He turned to Beth with a smile. 'I believe I knew your husband, Lady Allerton. A man of ideas, devoted to his studies. We were all very surprised when he married. Now, may I ask Mrs

Morland to show you to your rooms? I am sure you will want a little time to rest before dinner.'

'I am sorry if you were offended by Reverend Theo's remarks,' Marcus whispered in Beth's ear, as Theo went off to call the housekeeper. 'He is tactless, but his heart is in the right place.'

Beth laughed. 'I did not take any offence and I am sure that Charlotte feels the same. Reverend Theo is quite a character, and more than generous in offering us all shelter!'

She saw Marcus relax slightly. 'I am glad you see it that way. He has offended many people from his pulpit, but the family is rich and owns the benefice and those who take him in dislike can find no way to remove him!'

Mrs Morland arrived then to show them all upstairs, and Beth found herself in a prettily appointed bedroom that faced south towards the Quantock Hills. The clock showed that there were several hours before dinner, and with a sigh of relief Beth removed her damp clothes and lay down to catch up on some sleep. The bed was soft and downy and before long she had drifted into a feverish dream where Marcus was pursuing her along a beach and into the sea itself. She woke up feeling hot and bothered and found herself tangled up in the bedclothes and feeling very little refreshed. It was now only a half-hour before dinner, and Beth forced herself to get up, wash her face and prepare to go downstairs. She had only brought one good evening dress with her, a confection of silver and lace, and though it was a little crushed it lifted her spirits to wear it. She called the maid to press the worst of the creases from the dress and arranged her own hair in a simple matching silver bandeau.

Everyone was already assembled in the drawing room and Beth was glad that she had taken trouble to repair as much of the ravages of the journey as she could. The gentlemen were elegant in their black and white evening dress and Charlotte always had the ability to look as immaculate as though she had just stepped out of a Bond Street modiste's. At her side, Justin Trevithick already looked proud and proprietorial and Beth smiled to herself. No matter what the other outcomes of the journey, that was one romance that she would wager would reach the altar.

Marcus came across to her side and took her hand. His gaze was admiring and Beth felt doubly glad that she had made an effort.

'Lady Allerton, you look very beautiful tonight. May I offer you a glass of Theo's excellent ratafia?'

It became apparent during dinner that the Reverend Theo kept an excellent wine cellar as well as a very good table. As dish succeeded dish, all accompanied by the most exquisite wines, the clergyman kept up an entertaining flow of conversation about parish life, then started to reminisce about Marcus's exploits as a youth. By the time that the gentlemen retired to take their port everyone was fast friends, and even Beth had almost forgotten that they were engaged in a contest for Fairhaven. The thought popped into her head as she was preparing for bed, but for once she dismissed it and as a result slept soundly and dreamlessly, leaving her worries to be confronted in daylight.

'I feel wretchedly sick!' Charlotte said miserably, the following morning. She was sitting up in bed and her pretty face was creased with pain and distress beneath her lace cap. 'It is all my own fault, for I knew I should not have had the sherry trifle last night! And now it has brought on the megrims and I have the most dreadful headache—' She winced as Beth pulled back the curtains a little and a bar of sunlight fell across the bed. 'Oh, Beth, pray do not! I fear my head will burst!'

Beth hastily pulled the curtains together again and went across to sit on the edge of the bed. It was a beautiful morning and she wanted nothing more than to be out in the fresh air, but she knew that Charlotte could not bear the light when she had one of her headaches. Besides, Charlotte was being more than generous in blaming the trifle. Beth suspected that it was the strain of the journey and the necessity of meeting new people that had done her cousin up and she felt more than a little guilty.

'Can I fetch you anything, dearest Charlotte? Some rose water or something to drink?' She saw the spasm that went across Charlotte's face as she shook her head. 'No? I shall leave you in peace, then.'

Beth went out and closed the door softly. When Charlotte was poorly it usually took at least a day for her to recover, so there would be no travelling to Devon that day. Beth knew that she would just have to be patient. It was not one of her usual virtues, but under the circumstances it was the only course. She hoped that the Reverend Theo would not mind prolonging his hospitality.

The house was very quiet. Beth went downstairs and into the breakfast room. Marcus was alone, sitting by the fire and reading a newspaper. He put this to one side immediately as Beth came in and stood up to hold her chair for her, his dark eyes intent on her face.

'Good morning, Lady Allerton. I trust that you slept well?'

'Exceptionally well, thank you,' Beth said truthfully.

'I am afraid, however, that my cousin is in poor health this morning and will be staying in her room.'

'I am sorry to hear it.' Marcus looked grave. 'It is a relief for me to find that you do not expect to move on today, however. Justin has gone to visit his mother over at Nether Stowey and the Reverend Theo has been called to the sickbed of a parishioner whom he assures me thinks himself at death door at least twice a month! It has become a ritual for them, I believe. Theo takes a couple of bottles of claret and the two of them sit drinking 'til the cows come home! I doubt we shall see him again this side of dinner!'

Beth looked at him a little uncertainly. 'Then we are...on our own?'

'To all intents and purposes.' Marcus's smile was faintly mocking. 'I will not inflict my company on you, Lady Allerton—not unless you wish it! Is there any possibility that you would like to spend the day with me?'

Beth hesitated, trying not to smile, but she could not prevent herself. It sounded a most attractive option. She reached for a piece of toast and buttered it slowly. 'Well, I could be persuaded...'

'Excellent!' Marcus smiled broadly. He handed her a cup of tea. 'Theo keeps as excellent a stable as he does a wine cellar, if you would like to ride!'

Beth's eyes sparkled. It was indeed too fine a day to sit inside and she relished the thought of a ride across country.

'Very well, then. I am sure we shall get on splendidly, my lord, provided that we do not quarrel over Fairhaven!'

Marcus smiled and got to his feet. 'Then we shall not mention it for the whole day!' He walked over to the door. 'Excuse me. I shall go to see to the saddling of the horses.'

As soon as Beth had finished her breakfast she hurried upstairs to change into her riding habit. The anticipation was buzzing through her body, as light and bright as the sunshine.

To spend a day with Marcus without the tension of Fairhaven between them seemed almost too good to be true. Maybe it was a temporary truce rather than a resolution of the conflict, but whatever the case, she intended to make the most of it.

They rode out all morning, taking an old green lane from Ashlyn towards the sea at Holford. They did not speak much. There was no need, for the sun was warm and the birds sang and the colours and wood smoke smell of autumn was all around them. Beth felt curiously content, more tranquil than she could ever remember. Her enjoyment sprang from the pleasure of Marcus's company, the warmth of his smile, the cadence of his voice and the light touch of his hand on her arm whenever he pointed out a view or something of interest. It was a more gentle feeling than the disturbing awareness that Marcus's presence habitually engendered in her, but Beth knew that under the calm surface ran the same attraction that was always between them.

After a while they started to speak more and Marcus told her a little about how he had felt when he had had to give up his diplomatic career to take over the responsibilities of the Trevithick estate. In return, Beth told him about Mostyn and her relationship with Kit and Charlotte. The time passed all too quickly and soon Marcus suggested that they return to Ashlyn for luncheon. It seemed a shame, but the exercise had given

Beth an appetite and she reflected that they could always go out again in the afternoon. Or perhaps she might challenge him to a game of billiards, for she had spent many a long afternoon alone practising when Frank had been away from home and was tolerably certain that she could beat Marcus. She sighed. No doubt that was considered unladylike too.

Mrs Morland had set out a simple meal for them of bread, cheeses and Somerset cider; and as Charlotte was still prostrate with the migraine, Beth and Marcus ate alone. Marcus seemed preoccupied and quiet, and when Beth looked at him she thought he seemed rather stern. The thought was quelling. Perhaps the delightful morning had been a prelude to something more unpleasant— perhaps Marcus had only been kind to her because he was about to spring on her the fact that he was prepared to fight her through the courts before he let her have Fairhaven...

'Lady Allerton?' Marcus's quizzical tone recalled her to the present. 'There is something I wished to say to you. I know we agreed that we would not mention Fairhaven today, but—'

Beth jumped to have her suspicions confirmed so promptly. She closed her eyes to ward off the blow.

'But I wanted to tell you that I will not oppose your quest to regain the island,' Marcus continued. 'You won Fairhaven in a just, if unorthodox, fashion...' there was an undertone of amusement in his voice '...and I know it means a great deal to you.'

Beth realised that she still had her eyes closed and opened them now, to see that Marcus was watching her with quizzical humour.

'Lady Allerton? Are you quite well?'

'I... Yes, indeed...' Beth floundered. It was the last

thing that she had expected and it left her quite lost for words.

'That being the case,' Marcus continued, his tone steady, 'I would still like to escort you to the island in order to arrange a smooth transfer of the estate. I trust that that will suit you?'

'Oh, yes, of course...' Beth knew she sounded totally bemused. She simply could not believe that he had capitulated in such a way.

'Good!' Marcus smiled, getting to his feet. 'Please excuse me for a moment. I believe that Mrs Morland has a message from Theo...'

As he closed the door behind him, Beth sat staring at the panels, a lump of cheese still clasped unnoticed in her hand. Marcus's statement had been so unexpected that she had not gathered her wits to question him properly and already the doubts were creeping in. Could he be in earnest or was this just another cunning ploy to set her off her guard? She had been so certain that his tactic would be to try to persuade her to relinquish her claim and go home. Now she was thoroughly confused.

Beth nibbled the cheese absent-mindedly. Did she trust Marcus? He had played her false before. Yet she wanted to believe him. Her instinct told her to let go of her doubts and have faith in him, but that was dangerous, too dangerous for her to contemplate at the moment. It involved admitting to other emotions that made her feel totally vulnerable. Beth suddenly felt as though she was on the edge of a precipice where her own intuition was prompting her to step into the unknown but her natural caution was holding her back.

She sighed. If only Charlotte were not feeling ill she would go and ask for advice, but what was the point of that anyway, when she already knew what her cousin would say? Charlotte had never liked their escapade and would fall on Marcus's suggestion with cries of relief. Her advice could not be impartial. And there was no one else whom Beth could ask.

Still mulling over the problem, Beth went upstairs to see how her cousin was faring. Charlotte was asleep, so Beth came back down again. Mrs Morland was just crossing the hall as she reached the bottom step.

'Oh, Lady Allerton,' the housekeeper said, 'there is a message from the Reverend March. He anticipates being at Hoveton for the rest of the afternoon and begs your pardon.' She smiled. 'He especially asked that Lord Trevithick go down the wine cellar to select a particular claret to have with the dinner, plus a dessert wine and some more port! His lordship is down there now, if you were wondering where he had vanished to, my lady!'

'Thank you, Mrs Morland,' Beth murmured. She watched the housekeeper hurry off back to the kitchens and wandered slowly towards the drawing room, still turning the problem of Fairhaven over in her mind. It was as she reached the drawing-room doorway, when she actually had her hand on the door frame, that she was struck by an idea; an idea so outrageous, so daring, that she was not sure that even she would put it into execution.

There was Fairhaven and there was Marcus. She might trust him, or she might not...

Beth tiptoed down the corridor to the wine cellar. The heavy oak door was wide open, the cellar steps yawning below into darkness. Beth could faintly discern the flicker of a candle flame far in the depths of the vault and she heard the dusty scrape of glass on stone. Marcus was evidently engrossed in the task that Theo had set.

Only the previous night, when Theo March had been

extolling the virtues of his wines, Beth had heard him joke that there was only one key to the cellar to prevent envious friends sampling his collection. That key was now in the door...

Beth stared. She crept forward and swung the door closed. It shut silently on oiled hinges. Beth turned the key, extracted it from the lock, and put it in her pocket.

A strange kind of madness took her and she almost laughed aloud. She ran up the stairs—she had not unpacked her trunk completely and now she threw her possessions in at random, squashing them down and slamming the fastening closed. She paused only to pen a hasty note to Charlotte and all the time she was listening intently, waiting for the inevitable shout from below that would show that she had been found out. None came. She hurried back down the stairs, her trunk bumping clumsily on every step, and shot out of the front door.

And all the while she was exulting in her escape and the fact that she had won.

It was only a step into Ashlyn village, but Beth hurried, glancing over her shoulder all the time, convinced that someone was watching her and about to ruin her plan. She had quickly considered and discarded the idea of asking Fowler to harness the carriage horses—that would take too long and be too noisy. Instead she was banking on the fact that there was a carter in Ashlyn who would be able to take her to Bridgwater.

At the forge she found exactly what she was looking for. An old cart was already standing waiting, half-loaded with sacks, the piebald cob chewing placidly on some hay whilst the carter chatted to the smith. Both of them looked up curiously as Beth hurried forward.

'Excuse me, sir! Can you take me to Bridgwater, if you please? I can pay you well...'

The carter was an elderly man and he was not to be hurried. He looked at the blacksmith, who gave him a significant look in return. He took off his hat, scratched his head, and put his hat back on again. Beth was almost dancing with frustration.

'Aye,' he said, after a long moment. 'I can take you there, missy.' He threw her trunk in the back, climbed slowly into the seat, leant down to give Beth a hand to scramble up beside him, then flicked the reins for the horse to set off. It seemed to Beth that the big cob was resentful of the sudden departure and moved with deliberate, agonising slowness.

'I believe it is but five miles to the sea?' she ventured, as they turned on to the road.

'Aye.'

'And we can go straight there?'

'Aye.'

Beth glanced over her shoulder. The village was receding, slowly, and no one was running down the main street and shouting after her. She started to relax a little. After all, there was only Charlotte and the servants at the vicarage. Charlotte was so poorly that she would not wake up for hours and the kitchen was well away from Theo's wine cellar. It could be some considerable time before anyone realised Marcus's predicament and even then she had the only key. It was heavy in her pocket.

As the cart lumbered down the country lane, Beth sat back with a sigh. The moment of exhilaration had gone, leaving her feeling oddly empty. She told herself that it was only because she felt so nervous at venturing off on her own, but her heart gave her another answer. They had been in complete accord, she and Marcus. It had been such a perfect morning. He had told her that he would not oppose her in the matter of Fairhaven. But…she had not trusted him. And she had ruined everything with her impetuous flight.

Beth gritted her teeth. She had won now. That was the important thing. The Reverend Theo would not return for hours and, even if he did, the door to the cellar was stout and could not easily be broken down. Marcus was trapped and she would definitely reach Fairhaven before him now. It did not matter if he had genuinely intended to give her the island or not, for she had won.

Beth swayed backwards and forwards with the movement of the cart and wondered what would happen next. In all likelihood Marcus would not even trouble to follow her. Probably he would never wish to see her again. Certainly he would never speak to her, unless to haul her over the coals for her appalling behaviour. And it had been appalling; Beth could see that, now that she had plenty of time for reflection. To have locked him in the wine cellar was bad enough, but to somehow betray the memory of their happiness that morning, to distrust him, that was her real offence. She reminded herself that she had finally outwitted him, but all she could think of was that the price had been so very high. She found that she was totally confused by her conflicting feelings and was almost in tears.

They lurched their way along the country roads towards the sea. It became clear to Beth that her idea of a direct journey and that of the carter was slightly at odds—he detoured to several farms on the way to unload his sacks and stood around chatting for what seemed like hours to Beth. After a while the sun dipped behind the clouds and a sharp wind sprang up, bringing with it the first hint of rain. Beth huddled down on the seat of the cart, but there was no shelter. She was cold, for her gloves, hat and scarf were in the trunk and the wind seemed to blow right through her coat. By the time the carter dropped her on the quay in Bridgwater it was getting dark and Beth felt more miserable than she had done for a very long time.

'How could she do such a thing?' Charlotte Cavendish wailed, pressing a small and inadequate lace handkerchief to her eyes. 'I know that Beth can be rash and impulsive, but she has never behaved like this before! Never!'

'Your cousin, madam, has all the self-restraint of a wayward child!' Marcus said, through his teeth. He was trying to remove some clinging cobwebs from his jacket and was tolerably sure that it would never be quite the same again. Certainly it was no longer a glowing tribute to Weston's tailoring.

'It is this absurd obsession with Fairhaven!' Charlotte lamented. 'I fear that it has quite taken over Beth's thinking! If only we could find some way to distract her attention—'

'I will give her something else to think about when I catch up with her!'

Marcus's gaze fell on Charlotte's apprehensive face and his own hard features softened a little. Mrs Cavendish had only risen from her sickbed a half-hour previously, and to find that her cousin had abandoned her and locked him in the cellar into the bargain was a shock that might have justifiably sent her into a fit of the vapours. Yet she was quite resolute, if pale, and Marcus admired her for that.

'Have no fear,' he said, in a gentler tone. 'I will find Lady Allerton and I will escort her to Fairhaven just as

I had intended and I will also marry her! So you need have no concerns for propriety, Mrs Cavendish…'

Charlotte looked slightly winded at this rush of events. '*Marry* her! I cannot conceive why you would wish to do so, my lord—'

'Neither can I at this moment!' Marcus said feelingly. 'But it is inevitable, I fear! Would you be so good as to pass me those scissors, ma'am? There are several loose threads…'

Charlotte snipped assiduously for a moment. 'How did you remember the other entrance to the cellar, my lord?'

Marcus laughed. 'A relic of my misspent youth, I confess, ma'am! I remembered Reverend March once telling us that there was a passage from the cellar to the icehouse in the garden and one day when I was about fourteen I had sought it out. This time it seemed much smaller!'

Charlotte shuddered. 'Reverend March! Whatever will he say when he returns and finds the key to his wine cellar missing?'

'I leave you to smooth that over, ma'am!' Marcus said cheerfully. He looked up as Justin came into the drawing room. 'Is the curricle ready, Justin?'

'It's waiting for you,' Justin said, with a grin. 'I've sent a messenger to meet McCrae in Bridgwater, so he will be expecting you and will also have started to instigate a search. Don't worry, ma'am—' he turned swiftly to Charlotte '—I am sure Marcus will find Lady Allerton before she comes to any harm!'

Marcus clapped his cousin on the shoulder. 'Sorry to leave you so precipitately, old fellow, but I know you will deal admirably with Theo, and see Mrs Cavendish safely home.' He did not miss the look of guilty pleasure that passed between the two of them and smiled a little to himself. 'Mustn't let the horses chill! Oh, and Justin...' he paused in the doorway '...I'll wager that Theo will be more distraught at being debarred from his own wine cellar than by aught else! Pray tell him that I will send his key back to him as soon as I have wrested it from Lady Allerton's grasp!'

Although it was late afternoon and growing dark, Bridgwater quay was still busy with traffic from the river. Beth picked her way between barrels of herrings and piles of coal, trying to ignore the curious stares of the sailors and their occasional coarse remarks. She had thought that it would be a relatively easy matter to charter a boat to take her to Fairhaven, but now she realised that she had no idea where to start. There were plenty of ships tied up at the quay, but she knew she could not simply pick one, go aboard and ask the captain if he would take her to Fairhaven Island. Her trunk was weighing her down and seemed twice as heavy as it had done earlier. Eventually, when she had walked all the way down the North Quay and was wondering what to do next, she came to a brigantine whose captain was busy coiling a huge jute rope whilst his crew unloaded a cargo of lemons in big panniers. The captain looked up, smiled at Beth and touched his cap; emboldened by his courtesy, Beth hurried forward.

'Excuse me, sir. Could you tell me if there is a ship sailing past Fairhaven that might be prepared to land me there?'

'There's a ship sailing for Fairhaven on the morrow, ma'am,' the captain said, peering through the dusk. 'Moored just down the quay, past the square rigger. Over there, see—' And he pointed to a ship that was tied up some fifty yards away. 'Tidy craft, is that,' he said approvingly. 'Lovely job. Built originally as a French privateer, they say, and quite old now but as neat and as quick as they come…'

Beth stared, transfixed. The ship was very trim indeed and on the port side could be read the name *Marie Louise* next to a painting of seagull in flight. At the back of Beth's mind a voice echoed, the voice of her nursemaid all those years ago at Mostyn:

'Your grandfather had a beautiful ship called the *Marie Louise*, named for his French mother… It has a drawing of a seagull on the side, *La Mouette*, in French…'

So the evil Earl of Trevithick had stolen the ship along with the island and the sword. Beth let out a small gasp of shock and the captain looked at her in some concern.

'Are you feeling unwell, ma'am?'

Beth did not—could not—reply. She had seen two men, who were standing on the quay beside the *Marie Louise*, deep in conversation. One was thin and almost concave, dressed in an old-fashioned brown waistcoat and serviceable dark trousers. The other was tall and elegant despite his working garb of a rough frieze coat over his white linen shirt. The sea breeze ruffled his black hair. Beth pressed one hand to her mouth and took an instinctive step backwards, almost tripping over the coil of rope. Her movement caught the eye of the thin man, who caught his companion's arm and swung him round.

It seemed impossible to Beth that the man whom she had locked in a wine cellar only a few hours ago could be here on the quay at Bridgwater, seeing to the provisioning of what could only be his own yacht. How could Marcus possibly have escaped in the first place, let alone reached the port before her when she had a head start? All this went through her mind even while she spun around, ready to run away. Marcus was too quick for her. He had already halved the distance between them and when she bumped clumsily against a stanchion and nearly fell, Marcus's arm went around her, scooping her clear of the ground.

Beth gave a small sob of mingled fear, annoyance and strangely, relief. 'Lord Trevithick—'

'Lady Allerton?' Marcus sounded savage.

The thin man came running up, panting. 'My lord…'

'All right, McCrae.' Marcus's tone was clipped. He did not put Beth down. 'Would you call off the search, please? And take care of Lady Allerton's luggage. I will see you in the Sailor's Rest later…'

He looked down into Beth's face and she saw that his eyes were blazing with fury. She instinctively shrank back from the anger she saw there.

'As for you, Lady Allerton,' Marcus said smoothly, 'I will settle with you now! And in private! You are about to wish you had never been born!'

The inn was not like any that Beth had previously encountered in her travels. Although it was only late afternoon it was already full and smelled overwhelmingly of ale and tobacco. The noise was deafening— there was raucous laughter and loud conversation that quickly became lewd repartee when Marcus pushed his way thorough the throng, still carrying her.

'That's a pretty little moppet you have there, my lord, and no mistaking! When you've finished with 'er, pass 'er on…'

Beth struggled in Marcus's arms. 'Put me down at

once, Lord Trevithick! How dare you subject me to the comments of these people—?'

'You have brought all this and more upon yourself through your own behaviour,' Marcus said, through shut teeth. 'You will oblige me by keeping still, my lady, or I shall drop you into the nearest lap and let them have their way!'

This dire threat led Beth to turn her face into Marcus's shoulder, close her eyes and try to blot out the coarser comments of the crowd. In a moment the noise faded and Beth realised that they had left the taproom and were going upstairs. Marcus was carrying her with about as much consideration as a sack of potatoes—her feet bumped against the wall and she scraped one elbow painfully on the banister. She opened her mouth to protest, saw the look in Marcus's eye and closed it again.

Marcus pushed open the door of a tiny chamber and dropped her unceremoniously on to the bed. Beth bounced on the mattress and came to an undignified rest with her skirts all tumbled about her and her hair falling from its pins.

'Oof! Is it really necessary to treat me with such lack of consideration, my lord? And what can you mean by bringing me to this low place? I demand to return to Ashlyn at once—'

'No, madam,' Marcus said, still through gritted teeth. 'You were the one who was so determined to be here that you would take any steps to achieve it!' He kicked the door closed and turned to survey her, his glittering dark gaze raking her ruthlessly.

'I have no real wish to speak to you now, but there are a few things that I must say. Leaving aside your inexcusable behaviour in locking me in Theo March's wine cellar, you have the gross folly to try to run away

and arrange passage for yourself to Fairhaven! Alone!'
Marcus ran a hand through his hair. 'Have you any idea
of the distress you have caused your cousin? Do you
even care? You have no more sense than a spoilt brat
and you deserve a good spanking!' Marcus drove his
hands into the pockets of his coat as though to prevent
himself from doing her an injury. 'I would administer
one myself were it not for the fact that I should probably
enjoy it far more than I ought!'

Beth blushed bright red. 'My lord!'

Marcus shot her a furious look. 'My lady? It is about
time that someone told you a few home truths! You are
easily the most infuriating and exasperating woman that
I have ever met! Now, I am going to meet with McCrae
to arrange tomorrow's sailing, and I shall be locking you
in here for your own safety! Do you object?'

Beth stared at him, quite cowed into silence. 'I...
Marcus, I am sorry—'

'I do not wish to hear it!' Marcus stalked over to the
door, then turned back to her. 'Speaking of keys, I
should be obliged if you would hand over the key to
Theo's cellar—at once!'

Beth fumbled clumsily in her pocket, aware that
Marcus was watching her efforts with the same angry,
implacable regard. When she put it into his hand she
heard him make a noise of disgust, and he took it from
her without a second glance.

'We shall speak later, if I regain my temper sufficiently to do so without shouting!' he said, over his
shoulder. 'In the meantime I suggest that you draw as
little attention to yourself as possible. No leaning out of
windows and begging for rescue! Do you really wish for
that pack of villains to come upstairs for you? It is about
time you learned some sense, Lady Allerton!' And, so

saying, he slammed out of the door and Beth heard the key turn with finality in the lock.

Marcus had not returned by eleven o'clock that night. Shortly after his departure a slovenly maid had appeared with a tray of greasy beef stew and Beth ate some half-heartedly whilst she listened to the noise swell downstairs as even more seafarers joined the throng gathered below. The tiny room was cold and dirty, but she had absolutely no wish to effect an escape and go straight from the frying pan into the fire. It was unnerving not knowing what Marcus intended. She did not believe that he had locked her in in order to take advantage of her, but she felt uncomfortably vulnerable.

She still could not understand how Marcus had reached Bridgwater before her, but then it seemed that there was a lot that she had overlooked. It was apparent now that Marcus had intended to sail for Fairhaven right from the start, either with or without her, for he had had a boat and a crew waiting. Beth stared miserably into the meagre fire. He had told her only that morning that he intended to escort her to the island, but she had only half-believed him. Yet perhaps his intentions had been honourable all along. She had already begun to regret her impetuous flight and particularly her lack of trust, and now she felt ashamed. But the damage was done. Marcus was deeply angered by her behaviour, and with good reason.

Beth shivered miserably. If Marcus had been acting honourably all along, her lack of trust would have been particularly wounding to him. Locking him up would hurt his dignity but distrusting him went deeper, much deeper. And just at the moment he was so angry he would not even let her apologise.

The fire had burned out and Beth slowly prepared for bed by the light of the one candle. The bedding looked none too clean and she was almost certain that she saw a flea jump from the mattress when she turned the sheets down, so she decided to lie under the bedspread and try to keep warm as best she could. This proved none too satisfactory; even fully dressed she was cold and uncomfortable, and had only drifted into a light doze when the door opened and Marcus came in.

'Lady Allerton? Are you awake?'

Beth opened her eyes and tried to discern whether or not Marcus was drunk. Certainly a strong scent of spirits had entered the room with him, but when the candle flame flickered briefly on the expression in his eyes, she saw that he was frowning and looked sober enough. His tone of voice was as abrupt as when he had gone out hours previously and Beth's heart sank as she realised that his temper had not improved. She struggled to sit up as Marcus sat down on the edge of the bed and started to pull off his boots.

'Oh, what are you doing—?'

Marcus shot her an irritated look. 'What does it look as though I am doing? I am coming to bed!'

Beth clutched the bedspread to her. 'Here? But what will people think?'

This time the look that Marcus gave her combined exasperation and a certain grim amusement. 'Believe me, Lady Allerton, none of the occupants of this alehouse care a jot for your reputation! They already believe that I have ravished you thoroughly and have been pressing me for the details!' He threw his boots into the corner of the room and started to unbutton his jacket. 'Besides, it seems a little late for you to be worrying about such things! A hoyden who dashes about the countryside barely chaperoned, who tries to run away in the middle of the night, locks gentlemen in wine cellars and wanders about a port alone after dark clearly has no consideration for propriety!' His frown deepened. 'Just tell me one thing—do you have so little faith in me that you disbelieve everything I say to you? I had thought that there was more trust between us than that!'

Beth stared at him in the candlelight. His face was set in hard, angry lines, but behind that she thought she glimpsed another emotion: hurt perhaps, or disappointment. It made her feel wretched, doubly so for mistrusting him and for causing him hurt. A big lump came into her throat and she looked at him, unable to speak. For what seemed like a long moment they stared at each other, then Marcus turned away with a sigh.

'Just why are you fully dressed and why are you *on* the bed rather than *in* it?'

Beth let out her breath on a sigh. Marcus was evidently so cross with her that he would find fault with anything.

'It is cold and there are fleas in the bed! Not that it is any concern of yours, Lord Trevithick! Why do you not sleep on your ship?'

Marcus laughed abruptly. 'What, would you have me leave you here all night unprotected? Is that the lesser of two evils?'

Beth turned away from him. 'Well, if you must stay, I am persuaded that you will find the chair comfortable enough.'

Marcus made a rude and derisive noise. 'Do not be ridiculous! And kindly move over! You are taking up all the space!'

Beth squeaked and rolled away quickly as the mattress sank under his weight. He was still in shirt and pantaloons, but he suddenly seemed too big and far too close. He was even closer once he had put out a lazy hand and pulled her back to his side. The treacherous mattress tumbled her into his arms.

'Why, you *are* cold...' Marcus's voice had softened as he felt the chill in her body and tucked it closer to his. He pulled the bedspread over the two of them. 'There, we shall warm up soon enough and be asleep...'

Beth was warming up far too quickly. Her head was on his shoulder and she could feel the heat of his skin through the thin shirt where the palm of one hand rested against his chest. His breath stirred her hair. The prospect of sleep now receded as she became acutely aware of every line and curve of Marcus's body against hers and felt the beat of his heart strong and steady against her ear. She had never gone to sleep in such a position before. Frank had never shared her bedroom and seldom her bed. On the infrequent occasions he had troubled her for his marital dues, he had left immediately afterwards.

Beth lay still, torn between arousal and comfort. She was keenly aware of Marcus's arm about her, his hand resting just below her breast. The awareness kept her awake whilst the corners of her mind started to cloud with warmth and drowsiness and comfort. Marcus turned his head a little and spoke drily.

'Try to breathe a little, Lady Allerton, or you may find yourself in difficulties. Unless...' his voice changed subtly '...your clothing is too tight to allow ease of breathing? If you wish to take anything off—'

Beth gave a protesting squeak and tried to pull away, but he held her tightly. 'Never fear. I do but tease you. But you should try to get some sleep, for the voyage tomorrow will take the best part of the day.'

Beth's eyes flew open. 'Tomorrow? So we do sail for Fairhaven?'

'Of course.' Marcus sounded sleepy. 'I said we would and so we shall.'

'But—'

'No buts…' He shifted slightly so that Beth's head was more comfortably pillowed on his shoulder. 'And no more discussion. I am exhausted, even if you are not. Talking can wait until tomorrow.'

Beth heard his breathing deepen almost immediately and realised that he had fallen asleep. Part of her, a very small part, was affronted that he could so easily ignore the fact that she was in his arms. Evidently he was used to being in such a situation, whereas she was tormented by his proximity. Another part of her mind was grappling with the implications of sailing for Fairhaven in Marcus's company the following day. She tried to think about it, but she was so weary with the events of the day that drowsiness overcame all resistance. At last she was warm, comfortable and safe, and she soon fell asleep.

Marcus awoke as the grey dawn light started to filter in through the bedroom window. The quay below was already noisy with the business of the new day. He opened his eyes and saw that they had both moved in the night; Beth was now tucked in front of him and they were lying very close and snug, like spoons. Her silky black hair was spread out on the pillow and in sleep her face was as clear and untroubled as a child's. Marcus smiled to himself. He had to admit that he had treated her very badly indeed.

When he had first seen Beth on the quay he had been so angry that he had not cared a jot about her feelings.

As soon as she had tricked him and run away from Ashlyn he had known immediately what she intended and at first could not believe that she could be so foolhardy. He had thought that he had made it clear that he would take her to Fairhaven, yet clearly she had either disbelieved him or simply not wanted his company. Either way he was hurt and angry, but he was also worried. Very worried. A woman alone wandering around the quay at Bridgwater would soon find herself receiving several offers, none of which would be passage to Fairhaven. Passage to the nearest whorehouse, perhaps, and the invitation would be phrased in a way to brook no refusal.

He looked down at Beth's sleeping face. He wondered if she had even considered such a possibility or whether her obsession with reaching Fairhaven had blinded her to all good sense. She was no child to be unaware of the perils of journeying alone, though perhaps she had been so sheltered that she did not truly know what could so easily have happened to her. He had known it, and he had had men on every corner, in every inn, looking for her. He had been terrified that he would not find her in time, or that some accident had already befallen her on the way to Bridgwater.

Then he had seen her and his anger had increased tenfold because she was so obviously unharmed and still unaware of the danger she was in. He had wanted to take her and shake her hard, to force her to recognise her own folly, to punish her for the fear and misery she had made him suffer. He had wanted to kiss her and make love to her despite the hurt of her betrayal. So he had locked her in and left her until his anger had subsided, and then he had come back and seen her and wanted her all over again...

Marcus shifted uncomfortably. Beth was pressed against him, very soft and sweet, the curve of her buttocks resting tantalisingly against his thighs. Marcus was already half-aroused and now felt himself harden further as he considered their relative positions. He reminded himself sternly that there were several layers of clothing between them but this did not help as it simply made him think of removing them all. Then there were the fleas… That was better. His tense body relaxed slightly. He had locked Lady Allerton in a flea-ridden room in a rough alehouse on the quay in Bridgwater and had spent the night with her there. He smiled a little to think of the reaction of the society gossips to such a story.

He smoothed the hair away from Beth's face with gentle fingers and she turned her head slightly, snuggling closer to him. Marcus obligingly adapted the curve of his body to hers. He knew there could only be one ending to Beth's adventure now, now that she was so thoroughly disgraced. It did not disturb him, since it was what he had intended almost from the first moment he had met her. How Beth would react to his proposal was a different matter, however. Marcus frowned. He was not at all sure if she would accept him. Most importantly, she was still obsessed with Fairhaven and he did not want to have to contend with such a rival. So they had to go to the island and Beth had to find out the truth about her grandfather and then perhaps she could put the whole matter behind her and concentrate on the future. A future with him. Marcus sighed. It should have been easy but he had the deepest suspicion that it would not be. Where Beth Allerton was concerned, nothing was that simple.

Chapter Seven

Beth sat in the shelter of the wheel-house, out of the wind, a blanket tucked about her legs. Marcus had suggested that she stay below in one of the cabins and at first she had complied, but once they were clear of the land the wind had picked up and the boat had started to pitch alarmingly. Beth had soon started to feel nauseous and had moved out into the fresh air, where one of the crew had taken pity on her and arranged the makeshift seat from a few wooden crates. Now, although the horizon still dipped and soared with sickening regularity, Beth could at least feel the refreshing spray on her face and breathe deeply of the salty air.

She had quickly noted that Marcus seemed quite unaffected by the movement of the boat. He had been in the wheel-house for quite some time talking to the helmsman and he had also taken his turn at doing whatever job was required; casting off, trimming the sails or simply giving a hand to the other members of the crew. And she saw that the men appreciated it. There had been a quick compliment for his skill from one of the hands, and at least one glance between the crew that showed their approval. It was a side of Marcus that Beth had not seen before.

Unfortunately his attitude towards her was in stark contrast. She and Marcus had barely spoken that morning, except for one humiliating conversation over the stale bread and porridge that had constituted their breakfast in the inn. Beth had requested to be taken back to Ashlyn. Marcus had looked at her stonily and said that she could return there if she wished, but that he was travelling to Fairhaven and she might as well accompany him since she had gone to such an unconscionable amount of trouble to get there. That had been the end of the conversation and Beth did not dare question him further about the trip. His face had assumed the same forbidding expression that it had worn the previous night and she knew that she was still in deep trouble. When the meagre breakfast was over she had gone with him out on to the quay where the boat was waiting. They had cast off and now turning back was impossible.

Beth shivered a little within her fur-lined cloak. Ahead of them there was nothing to see but the grey of the ocean, and on the port side the land was slipping away, the hills of Devon growing smaller all the time. Marcus had said that it would take them the best part of the day to reach Fairhaven. To Beth that seemed as nothing after so many years of waiting.

After an hour or so she fell into an uneasy doze and woke feeling queasy and a little befuddled. The sun was peeping through thin cloud overhead and the wind was strong. A rich smell of stew filled Beth's nostrils and her stomach lurched. She turned away as Marcus appeared before her, his bare feet braced on the wooden deck, a plate of food held in one hand. He took one look at her face and smothered a smile. Beth glared at him.

'Oh, dear, you look distinctly sickly, Lady Allerton...'

Beth tried to ignore the persistent smell of the stew but was forced to resort to holding her nose. She spoke with a distinct lack of dignity.

'Lord Trevithick, I would be obliged if you would go away! Now! And take that repellent plate of food with you!'

Marcus sauntered away, grinning. 'Pray call me if you require a bowl, ma'am!'

Within a half-hour Beth was too chilled to sit still any longer. She was tempted to go down to a cabin and try to sleep, but the thought of the enclosed stuffiness below decks made her feel even more seasick. Instead she wandered over to the rail and leant against it, staring into the flying spray below. She felt cold, sick and lonely, and it was a far cry from the way she had imagined arriving on Fairhaven Island.

Now that she thought about it, she realised that she had given very little thought to the practicalities of the journey. Her imagination had flown ahead of her, skipping over the difficult bits like a rough sea crossing, and had pictured some triumphant return to her grandfather's castle. She felt a little foolish. It did not help that Marcus had ignored her for the best part of the day and that his crew, apart from a few sympathetic glances, had left her to her own devices.

As much to occupy her mind as to keep warm, Beth wrapped her cloak closer and strolled around the deck, watching the seabirds that whirled and screamed in the ship's wake, scanning the horizon for land or for any other passing ships out of Bristol. The afternoon dragged by.

'Land ahoy!'

Beth had been staring at the sea for so long that she

felt almost mesmerised by the time the call came. She swung round. Marcus was strolling towards her across the deck, a telescope in his hand. 'Fairhaven is visible from the starboard bow, Lady Allerton. Would you care to see?'

Beth went with him across to the rail, took the spyglass a little gingerly in her hand and searched the horizon. Sure enough, the great granite cliffs of the island were visible above the tossing of the waves. Everything looked grey: sea, sky, land. The clouds were lowering and clung to the island like a veil. But it was beautiful.

'Oh!' Beth handed the telescope back to Marcus, her eyes shining. 'I can scarce believe it! It looks very beautiful, my lord!'

There was a strange expression on Marcus's face, part amused, part rueful. 'If you think that, Lady Allerton, you must love Fairhaven very much indeed! To my mind it looks a damnably lonely place!'

He turned away to issue some instruction to the helmsman about avoiding the shoals around Rat Island and anchoring in Fairhaven Roads. Beth hardly paid attention. She was clinging to the rail as the island slowly grew bigger in front of her. Within minutes she was soaked by the spray and the drizzle that was falling from the grey sky, but she barely noticed. She was so close to achieving her dream of reaching Fairhaven that she had no thought for anything else at all.

As they grew closer the island took on a clearer shape and Beth could even distinguish the chimneys of the castle and the roofs of the houses in the tiny village that huddled at the top of the cliff. The whole of the eastern side of the island was now spread out before them and Beth could see what Marcus meant—there were no trees, no shelter, only the plunging cliffs and the screaming seabirds.

'There are no trees…' she murmured, when he came back to her side. 'Does nothing grow here?'

'Colin tells me that the crops grow well enough,' Marcus said, nodding in the direction of Colin McCrae, 'and my aunt tends a small garden in the shelter of the castle walls. She always complains that the sheep take the greenest shoots!'

Beth frowned. 'Your aunt?'

'Why, yes.' There was a mocking smile curling Marcus's mouth. 'Did you imagine Fairhaven quite uninhabited, Lady Allerton? My uncle, St John Trevithick, has been the vicar of Fairhaven for donkey's years and his sister Salome keeps house for him at Saintonge Castle.' He gave Beth an old-fashioned look. 'Did you imagine that I was bringing you to a place quite beyond the pale? The truth is rather more prosaic, I fear!'

Beth looked away. She was not entirely sure what she had imagined, but her thoughts had not encompassed meeting any of Marcus's relations. She doubted that they would be pleased to see her. Certainly she had not supposed that she would be evicting a vicar who had served the community for decades, nor supplanting his spinster sister. It looked as though her image of Fairhaven as a bleak and neglected place had been embarrassingly at fault.

By now they had reached the shelter of the island and the sea swell abated a little as they anchored in the lee of the great cliffs. A rowing boat was lowered and Marcus and Colin McCrae assisted Beth down the ladder to a place in the stern. It seemed the work of moments for two burly seamen to row them ashore and pull the boat up on the shingle of the beach. A cart was already waiting at the bottom of the cliff and they lurched up a rough track that seemed carved into the face of the rock, Beth clinging to the sides of the cart whenever they turned a corner and the wheels seemed to skim the thin air. Suddenly the walls of the castle rose before her, Saintonge Castle, built by her forebears so many years before. A lump came into her throat and for a moment she was afraid she would cry.

There was a reception party waiting for them at the bottom of the castle steps. It seemed that every man woman and child on the island had assembled to greet the new Earl. Beth became suddenly and devastatingly aware of the figure she must cut as she crouched in the back of the cart, her hair straggling from her bonnet in rats' tails and her soaking dress and cloak clinging to her body in a manner far too voluptuously revealing. No doubt the good villagers of Fairhaven would think the sailors had brought their concubine with them! As for what Marcus's relatives would make of her... Uncharacteristic reticence made her hang back, but it was too late, for Marcus was climbing down from the cart and had cheerfully swept her up in his arms, to deposit her right in front of the curious crowd. Beth suspected that he had done it on purpose.

'Marcus, by all that's holy!' A voice boomed from behind them. 'I never thought to see the day! The lord moves in mysterious ways!'

Beth and Marcus both spun round. An elderly woman was descending the steps from the castle entrance. She was not fat so much as large, and recognisably a Trevithick from her very dark brown eyes, high cheekbones and the luxuriant dark hair that was coiled in a huge chignon in the nape of her neck. She was improbably dressed in pink satin with matching embroidered slippers, and a scarlet cloak was thrown carelessly about her shoulders and was now flapping in the strong wind. Beth found that she was staring.

'A plague upon this weather!' the woman said cheerfully, grasping Marcus to her and kissing him enthusiastically on both cheeks. 'Seven plagues upon it! My, my, how you've grown!'

'Aunt Sal,' Marcus said, grinning, 'it is such a pleasure to see you again!'

'And you, dear boy!' Salome Trevithick looked round and her bright brown gaze fell on Beth. 'Bless me, a stranger in the desert!' Then, at Beth's look of puzzlement, she added, 'Isaiah thirty-five, verse six, my dear.'

'Aunt Sal, this is Beth Allerton,' Marcus said formally. 'Lady Allerton, my aunt, Lady Salome Trevithick.'

'Welcome, my dear!' Salome Trevithick extended a hand sparkling with diamonds. She looked Beth over approvingly. 'A veritable angel, Marcus, albeit a rather sodden one!'

Beth blushed.

'Aunt Sal writes all my uncle's sermons,' Marcus explained in an undertone, 'so her conversation is always peppered with Biblical allusions! Indeed, she quotes the Bible at every available opportunity!' He raised his voice. 'Is Uncle St John not with you, Aunt? I was hoping—'

'Alas, St John has taken a journey into a far country,' Salome said, beaming. 'He has been called to the Bishop at Exeter, my dears. Apparently the poor man had heard that St John was drunk in the pulpit last month and demanded an explanation!'

'Nothing else to do on Fairhaven!' a voice from the back of the crowd shouted.

Marcus turned back to the villagers, who had been waiting with good-humoured patience. 'Thank you for such a warm welcome to the island!' His voice carried easily to everyone. 'It is good to be here at last, even on such an inclement day!'

'You should see the place in really bad weather!' the voice at the back of the crowd responded.

Everyone laughed. 'I am sure I shall!' Marcus said, grinning. 'For now, I am happy to see you all and to introduce Lady Allerton, who is to be the new owner of Fairhaven.'

To Beth's horror, Marcus pulled her to his side. 'I know that many of you will remember Lady Allerton's grandfather, Charles Mostyn, and be glad that the days of a Mostyn landlord are to return!'

A curious murmur ran through the crowd. Beth's smile faded as she saw the looks on the faces of the people in front of her. From smiling good humour they had moved to uncertainty and even sullenness. Some were muttering to each other and a few were watching her with undisguised hostility. Even Salome Trevithick looked stern. Beth bit her lip, conscious of their resentment but taken aback by the suddenness with which it had sprung up.

There was an awkward pause, then a woman who had been standing a little apart from the crowd bent down to murmur in the ear of the small blonde child beside her. A moment later, the girl had trotted forward and held out a wilting posy to Beth.

'Welcome to the island, my lady,' she whispered.

Beth forgot about the strange hostility of the crowd and her own dishevelled state. She smiled at the child, then crouched down to take the flowers and give her small admirer a kiss. The little girl looked at her with huge, considering blue eyes for a moment, then smiled back, stuck her thumb in her mouth and ran back to her mother. Another murmur ran through the crowd, this time of guarded approval.

'Prettily done,' Salome Trevithick said gruffly, grasping Beth's elbow and helping her to her feet. 'Suffer the little children to come unto me! Matthew nineteen, verse fourteen! Let me show you to your room, Lady Allerton. You look in sore need of some refreshment!' She linked her arm through Beth's and steered her up the castle steps. 'Some of the islanders have long memories, I fear, Lady Allerton. But ashes to ashes, I always say, and never speak ill of the dead!'

Before Beth could ask her to explain this strange pronouncement she found herself inside the castle and forgot everything in admiration of the sheer splendour of it all. Saintonge Castle had originally been built in the thirteenth century, but within the huge, windowless walls, a more modern dwelling had been fashioned. The stone-flagged entrance hall was neither as shabby nor as bare as Beth had imagined it, but was hung with rich tapestries and decorated with polished silver. Salome ushered her upstairs, to an opulent suite of rooms set into the southern wall of the castle. There was a huge bedroom with a wide window that looked out over the sea, a sitting room with a most comforting fire, and a modern bathroom with the biggest bath Beth had ever seen. She went back into the bedroom and walked over to the stone casement, standing by the window to look at the huge sweeping panorama of the sea. She gave a little sigh.

'Oh, how beautiful!'

'Bless you, my child!' Lady Salome said, moist-eyed. 'It is indeed a lovely place! Now, I shall send Martha McCrae to you in a little while to see if you need anything. She is the mother of that delightful child who greeted you outside!' She paused. 'Martha will bring you dinner in your room tonight, for we do not eat *en famille* until tomorrow. I thought you might be too tired for company!'

'Thank you!' Beth said gratefully. She did indeed feel worn out with travelling and trying to absorb new experiences. Lady Salome smiled and went out, red cloak flying, and Beth sank down on to the window seat to look out, entranced, across the bay.

She was still sitting there half an hour later, when Martha McCrae knocked at the door and came timidly into the room, bearing a supper tray.

'Is everything to your liking, my lady?' The housekeeper sounded a little strained.

Beth turned to her with a smile. 'Oh, of course! It is entirely delightful! I am just so taken aback by the beauty of the whole island!'

Martha McCrae smiled shyly. Unlike her blonde daughter, she had soft brown hair and kind brown eyes. Her complexion was very pale and freckled, and her face wore an unmistakably worried air. Beth wondered what could be making her so nervous.

'Have you lived on Fairhaven for long, Mrs McCrae?' she asked, anxious to put the woman at her ease.

The housekeeper nodded. 'A little while, Lady Allerton, but not as long as Lady Salome and the vicar. I came here as a bride six years ago, when the old Earl took Colin on as his estate manager here.' She wiped her hands down her apron in a sudden, nervous gesture. 'It has not always been easy—the winters are hard and the Earl—well, I believe that he forgot about us being here sometimes.' She sighed. 'That is why we thought...

When we heard that the new Earl was finally coming here, we hoped—' she broke off and resumed '—we hoped he might have the good of the island at heart. But it seems he intends to give Fairhaven away—'

She broke off and her pale face flushed bright red. 'Forgive me, my lady. I was thinking aloud! Excuse me. I will send a maid up with some water...'

And before Beth could say another word, she had turned and fled.

Beth sat down a little heavily on the edge of the big tester bed and pecked half-heartedly at the food on the tray. Now she understood—in part, at least—the hostility of the villagers. Like the McCraes, they had believed that Marcus's arrival on Fairhaven must herald a better time ahead. They had flocked to welcome him, buoyed up by hope and expectation. And almost the first thing that he had done was tell them that he was giving Fairhaven over to her. Worse, her arrival threatened the future of St John and Salome, the only members of the Trevithick family who had ever shown any loyalty to the island and its inhabitants...

The water arrived. Beth stripped off her sodden clothes and washed the sticky salt from her skin. She felt tired and light-headed. The seasickness had gone now, although the floor still showed a disturbing tendency to rock beneath her feet. She donned a fresh petticoat and was about to lie down when she heard the echo of a door closing below and footsteps ascending the stairs.

'All I am saying, my lord, is that the Fairhaven estate is no plaything for a girl—'

The voice was that of Colin McCrae, pitched somewhat louder than his customary soft burr because of the passion with which he spoke. Marcus replied, but Beth could not hear his quieter tones.

'And with the current threat from the sea, it would be the greatest folly—'

'That will be short-lived.' Marcus's voice was clipped. 'We land Marchant's cargo tomorrow night.'

Beth's curiosity was caught. Where previously she had tried not to overhear, now she strained closer. The men had paused on the landing, a little away from her room. They were speaking quietly, but she caught the odd phrase here and there and pressed against the door to try to hear more.

'Will you tell Lady Salome?' Colin McCrae was asking now, his voice amused. 'I can imagine her reaction…'

'Oh, Aunt Sal is up to all the rigs!' Marcus laughed. 'There can be no harm in telling her about the business with Marchant!'

'And Lady Allerton?'

Marcus's voice had sobered. 'No. There is no need for that. Now, Colin, you were telling me about the need to build a new barn up at Longhouses…'

Their footsteps and their voices blurred as they passed Beth's door and moved on. She expelled a sharp breath and leant against the panels, pushing the door closed. Her head was spinning.

The threat from the sea…Marchant's cargo…and the fact that Marcus did not intend to tell her… Her imagination raced. Could it be—was it possible—that Marcus was using Fairhaven Island for smuggling, as his grandfather had done before him? Certainly the island was perfectly placed for such a venture and she knew that Marcus needed to make money.

Beth lay down on the bed and stared fixedly up at the

vast canopy. It all seemed to hang together. She had
suspected from the first that Marcus intended to travel
to Fairhaven. Her presence had provided the perfect excuse and the perfect camouflage. His ship had been ready
and waiting in Bridgwater, so clearly his men must have
received their instructions some days before. Lady
Salome and all the villagers had been expecting their
arrival. There was evidently a plan.

And who knew what cargo the *Marie Louise* had been
carrying today. Marchant's cargo, Marcus had said.
Perhaps Marchant was the free trader with whom Marcus
was in business... Beth turned over restlessly, wondering if she should confront Marcus straight away or wait
until she had some evidence. Her instinct was to challenge him at once, to demand an interview now and have
it out with him, but she reluctantly decided to wait. It
went against her nature but Marcus had been so sparing
of the truth up until now that Beth had no doubt he
would think of some plausible excuse. Better to keep
quiet and watch what happened. And she would not have
long to wait, for if Marcus was correct, tomorrow night
would reveal the truth.

Dinner the following day was an entertaining meal.
Beth had spent much of the day resting and felt quite
restored by the time she joined Marcus and his aunt in
the castle's impressive dining room. Lady Salome was
resplendent in purple satin, orange turban and pearls, and
Beth felt supremely dowdy in her practical grey gown.
She remained quiet whilst Marcus and his aunt covered
all the family gossip, but then Salome moved on to ply
her with eager questions about London, the fashions, the
scandals and the entertainments, and Beth soon forgot
her reserve. They chatted through to dessert, when Lady

Salome started on a series of outrageous anecdotes about her own Season some thirty years before, looking from Beth to Marcus with sparkling brown eyes.

'I did not *take*, my dears. The style was for plump girls with fluffy blonde hair—rather like those little dogs that Lady Caroline Lamb is said to favour—so I was utterly unfashionable! I was in despair of ever finding a rich husband and even considered running off with my piano teacher, but he always smelled of mothballs and that was quite quelling to passion!' She popped a sugared plum into her mouth and pushed the dish in Beth's direction. 'Where was I? Oh, yes… Well Papa was a man of little patience and when I had not caught a husband after a few months he decided to despatch me to Fairhaven! St John had lost his housekeeper here—she fell from the cliffs in strange circumstances—and so Papa thought to save some money by sending me in her place!'

Beth smiled. 'Have you lived here ever since, Lady Salome? It is a very long time!'

'Oh, yes, my dear, but then it is my home. Home is where the heart is. Now is that St Mark's Gospel or the Book of Proverbs?'

'Neither, I believe.' Marcus laughed. He stood up. 'Excuse me, ladies. I will take my port and rejoin you in the drawing room shortly.'

'Take your time, dear,' Salome said absently. 'Lady Allerton and I have much to talk about! Ah, the sweetness of a friend!' She looked triumphant. 'Now, *that* is the Book of Proverbs!'

Marcus bowed and went out, a twinkle in his eye, and Beth sighed unconsciously. For all the relaxed atmosphere of the meal and the entertaining company of Lady Salome, she did not delude herself that she was forgiven.

Marcus had barely spoken to her directly during the evening, except to ask if her room was comfortable and if she had everything she required, and she felt uncomfortable in his presence. Once or twice she had caught his gaze upon her, expressionless or stern, but when she had looked up at him he had not smiled in return. There was so much that needed to be said between them, yet she did not know where to start. Last night he had been too angry to listen to her. Now she hardly dared approach him, particularly if it were only to stir up more trouble on the matter of smuggling.

'You look sad, my dear,' Lady Salome said comfortingly, when they were ensconced in front of the drawing-room fire and had a big pot of tea between them. 'I suppose you must be tired from your travels and all the excitement of reaching Fairhaven at last! Marcus tells me that it has long been an ambition of yours to regain the island for your family!'

'Yes, I suppose so.' Beth said dolefully. Suddenly, sitting here under Lady Salome's bright gaze, it did not seem such a worthy thing to want to reclaim Fairhaven. 'Ever since I was a little girl I wanted to come here, but...' she looked up, troubled '...I did not think... What will you do, ma'am, if you leave the island?'

'Oh, I shall travel to the fleshpots of Exeter!' Salome said enthusiastically, ladling three spoonfuls of sugar into her tea. 'Or perhaps to London itself—Sodom and Gomorrah rolled into one! You have no idea, my love, how frustrating it is to receive six-month-old copies of the *Ladies' Magazine* and never to have the fashionable clothes to wear when one goes out! And then there is the food—salted, pickled but seldom fresh! Unless one likes turnips, of course, but I never have! Indeed, I am *aux anges* to be thinking of escape!'

Beth smiled, but she was not convinced. She knew that Lady Salome thought of Fairhaven as home and suspected that the redoubtable spinster was just putting a brave face on things. Besides, there was St John to think of as well—how would an elderly cleric cope with a new parish when he had become so attached to his eccentric islanders, and they to him?

'Besides—' Lady Salome leant forward a little arthritically to put another log on the fire and Beth hurried to help her '—you are so rich, my dear! You may give the island all the things it needs!'

'Materially, perhaps,' Beth murmured. She smiled at Lady Salome. 'Surely there are other things more important? The love of money is the root of all evil, after all! The Book of Timothy, I think!'

'Very good!' Lady Salome clapped her hands. 'But, oh, to be the one camel that passes through the eye of the needle! Matthew nineteen, verse twenty-four!' She happily capped Beth's quotation, then fixed her with her perceptive dark gaze. 'Tell me, do you like Marcus, Lady Allerton?'

The abrupt change of subject took Beth aback a little. Normally she would have prevaricated, particularly on so short an acquaintance. Yet there was something about Lady Salome's open friendliness that made her reply truthfully.

'Yes. Yes, I do. I like the Earl of Trevithick a lot, but...' A tiny frown wrinkled her brow.

'But!' Lady Salome said sonorously. 'There is always a but!'

Beth laughed. 'Oh, Lady Salome, there are difficulties. We do not know each other very well—'

'Love conquers all!' Lady Salome said grandly. 'The Book of Kings—'

'Quite,' Beth said, thinking it unlikely. She saw that Marcus had come in and hastily changed the subject. 'Are there many tales of smuggling in these parts, Lady Salome?'

Lady Salome gave her a penetrating look. 'Not since the time of your grandfather, my dear! There's no money in the trade these days and little interest in it!'

Beth could feel Marcus's gaze resting on her thoughtfully. She gave him a dazzling smile. 'I was asking your aunt about smugglers' tales, my lord—'

'I heard you.' Marcus took a cup of tea from Lady Salome and sat back, stretching his long legs out to the fire. 'The profession has almost died out, has it not, Aunt Sal?'

'Along with piracy and wrecking!' Lady Salome agreed. 'Life on Fairhaven is nowhere near as exciting as one might imagine, my dear! Why, even the American War scarce touches us here!'

'That reminds me,' Marcus said. 'McCrae has given me the direction of one of the islanders who knew your grandfather, Lady Allerton. I am sure he will be pleased to talk to you! Jack Cade, I believe his name is, up at Halfway Cottage. Perhaps you may choose to walk up in the morning?'

'Perhaps I shall,' Beth agreed. 'Thank you, my lord.' She was not sure why she did not feel more exhilarated at the news, but for some reason she could summon up little enthusiasm. It was all very odd. She had been wanting to come to Fairhaven for years, with an intensity that had eclipsed all else, yet now she was here it was all falling oddly flat. Beth wondered if she was one of those tiresome people who, once they had achieved something, had no use for it any more. She hoped not.

She stood up and smiled at Lady Salome. 'Pray excuse me, ma'am, Lord Trevithick…' she gave Marcus a distant nod '…I am tired and would like to retire. There is no need to accompany me,' she added sharply, as Marcus rose from his chair with some reluctance, 'I can find my own way. Goodnight!'

As she went up the stairs, Beth reflected that there was nothing more insulting than Marcus's pretence of courtesy towards her, no doubt assumed for Lady Salome's benefit. She hated this coldness between them that threatened to harden into indifference, then plain dislike. Already she felt absurdly distanced from Marcus, as though their earlier intimacy had never been. It seemed almost impossible to believe that Marcus had once held her in his arms, had kissed her, had evoked a response from her that she had not even known could exist. Yet all that was in the past. From now on a slightly bored courtesy was probably all that she could expect.

Beth sat on the window seat in her bedroom and looked out at the moonlight skipping across the black water. The poor weather that had dogged their crossing the day before had vanished and it was a clear night with the stars showing bright and hard in the heavens. Somewhere in the depths of the castle, a clock struck one. The chimes echoed through the stone walls and died away. Beth shivered a little. She had been waiting for four hours and was thoroughly tired and chilled, but she had been determined not to miss whatever it was that Marcus and Colin McCrae were up to that night.

The sound of stone on stone far below cut through her boredom. Someone had opened the door of the castle and was even now setting off down the twisting track to the beach. Beth pressed her nose to the cold window glass. Her bedroom looked out on a short stretch of grass that ended abruptly where the track began its descent of the cliff. She could hear nothing, but she could just see the dancing flame of a torch as someone picked their way down towards the harbour. Beth slid off the window seat, reached for her cloak, and made for the door.

She drew back the bolt, turned the huge knob and pushed. The door did not move. Beth pushed again but it remained shut fast. She stood back, frowning.

The door had not stuck earlier in the evening. Then, it had swung smoothly on oiled hinges. Which meant that now it could only be locked—on the far side. She pushed the door again, sharply. Nothing happened.

Kneeling down, Beth peered through the keyhole. She could see the key still in the lock on the other side of the door. Indignation swelled in her, confirming her suspicions. Marcus had locked her in, and she knew why.

Beth went to her trunk and took out the enamelled box that held her hairpins. Near the window stood an old wooden writing desk and she was almost certain she had seen some thick blotting paper there earlier. She whipped it up and hurried back to the door. There was a gap of at least an inch between the smooth stone step and the bottom of the door and Beth bent down, stealthily inserting the paper into the space. The first hairpin bent when she pushed it into the lock but the second loosened the key and after a little jiggling, it fell to the floor. The blotting paper muffled the sound and all Beth heard was a soft thud.

Holding her breath, she drew the paper towards her. The key caught on the bottom of the door and she bit her lip, trying to manoeuvre the paper through the gap without making any noise. After a few nerve-racking seconds, it slid smoothly into her grasp.

Dusting her skirts down, Beth turned the key and

opened the door a crack. The corridor outside was faintly lit by lamplight and was quite empty. She pulled the door closed behind her and tiptoed to the top of the stairs.

It took her several minutes to negotiate Saintonge Castle's dark corridors and stairs, for she was anxious to make no noise and draw no attention. At one point she was obliged to dodge into the Great Hall when a servant came out of the kitchens with a pile of clean crockery, and she had almost reached the front door when Martha McCrae came hurrying down the nursery stairs, a candle in her hand. By the time that Beth slipped out into the night, her heart was in her mouth and she had to stop to rest for a moment in the lee of the castle wall.

It was a fine night, but there as a strong wind blowing. Beth quickly realised that it would be the utmost folly to try to descend the cliff path without the aid of a light, for even in the daytime the track was treacherous. It was also the perfect way to walk directly into the smugglers' path before she had realised it. She had just resigned herself to another long wait out in the cold dark when she saw the glint of torchlight below and heard the crunch of footsteps on shingle. They were already coming back. She dived for shelter behind the nearest wall.

She was just in time and the sight that met her eyes was a curious one. A torch-lit procession of men was coming up the cliff path, but where Beth's imagination had supplied all the trappings of a smuggling operation—the donkeys, the panniers full of bottles, the packets of lace—they were carrying two coffins high on their shoulders. Beth recognised the crew of the *Marie Louise* and some of the village men she had seen earlier in the day. Amongst them, Marcus was carrying the corner of one coffin and Colin McCrae another. Beth crouched behind the wall and watched them pass by, and stared after them into the darkness.

She had not been aware that the *Marie Louise* was carrying any men home for burial, but then she supposed that Marcus would not necessarily want to distress her with the fact. Perhaps this was what McCrae had been referring to when he had asked Marcus if he would tell her, and Marcus had said that there was no need. Perhaps so, perhaps not. The whole thing was odd in the extreme.

The more Beth thought about it, the odder it became. The men had been smiling and chatting amongst themselves and there had been none of the grim-faced respect that she would have expected on such an occasion. She pulled her cloak about her and tried to huddle more closely into the shelter of the wall. Where did Marcus's reference to 'Marchant's cargo' fit in? Were the coffins the cargo, and if so, were the deaths suspicious? Why not wait until daylight to bring the coffins home to rest? And why lock her in her room to ensure that she knew nothing of the night's activities?

Beth scrambled out onto the track and set off towards the village in the direction that the men had taken. She could just see the flickering of the lanterns up ahead and the moon cast enough light on the track for her to pick her way. All the same it was an uncomfortable walk and she almost slipped and fell several times. She resolved that the road was the first thing that she would spend money improving when once she was the official owner of Fairhaven.

By the time that Beth reached the first cottages, the pallbearers were entering the church, which, Beth thought, was entirely appropriate if they had a couple of dead men for burial. She felt cold, stiff and rather silly to have become so wrapped up in her own imaginings, and she was about to turn back when she heard a crash in the church porch and Marcus's voice carried to her on the wind.

'Careful there! Marchant will not be pleased if the goods are damaged…'

Curiosity aroused once more, Beth picked her way across the graveyard and peeked around the church door. She knew she was taking a big risk, but it was dark and the men were safely inside the church, so it seemed safe to take a look.

Fairhaven's chapel was small and ill lit and though she could just make out the shapes of the coffins laid out before the altar, a huge pillar obscured the rest of her view. The smell of musty cloth and dust hung in the air. Taking care to remain unseen, Beth slipped behind one of the Mostyn family memorials and peered round.

Two lanterns had been placed at either end of the altar and in their flickering light Beth could see the men from the ship busy with the coffin lids. They were showing little respect for the dead now. One man had a crowbar that he was wedging under one corner. There was a creak of protest from the wood and then a splintering noise as the lid came free. Beth smothered a gasp.

'Fine workmanship on these,' she heard one of the sailors say appreciatively as he leant over the coffin.

'Aye…nothing but the best…' One of his colleagues was lifting something from inside. The lantern light glinted on steel. Beth drew back sharply as she saw the rifle in his hands and the pile of guns spilling over the top of the coffin.

Suddenly there was a prickling feeling on the back of her neck, a warning instinct that was as ancient as it was inexplicable. Beth froze, her eyes still on the scene before her. Several of the crew had guns in their hands now and were inspecting them with admiration. Colin McCrae was exchanging a few words with one of the sailors as they fastened the lids back down. But of Marcus there was no sign.

Beth turned slowly. The empty ranks of pews and the rows of memorials stared back at her, cobwebby and dark. There was nobody there. She started to back towards the door, stepping silently, pausing to check every few seconds that she was unobserved. She could see no one at all but the feeling of being watched persisted. And then someone moved.

Beth caught her breath on a gasp that seemed to echo around the chapel's rafters. She saw the sailors put down the guns and look in her direction and then Marcus Trevithick stepped from the porch directly into her path.

'Good evening, Lady Allerton,' he said politely. 'What an unexpected pleasure to find you here!'

For a moment Beth seriously considered trying to push past him and run, but then Marcus put out one hand and took her arm in a grip that was not tight but that she could not have broken without a struggle.

'Do you know,' he said conversationally, 'that you are forever running away from me, Lady Allerton? On this occasion I do beg you to reconsider. I would be put to the trouble of trying to catch you and you would probably go straight over the side of a cliff in the dark!'

They stood staring at each other, then Beth let go of the breath she had been holding. 'Oh! I might have known that you would find me here! Though why you did nothing to prevent me seeing the rifles—' She broke off as she tried to work out what was going on. She saw Marcus grin.

'Why should I prevent you? There is nothing illegal

to hide and if you wish to wander about Fairhaven in the middle of the night, that is your choice!'

'Nothing illegal?' Beth's voice had warmed into indignation. 'You smuggle munitions in here, no doubt intending to sell them on—' Once again she stopped, this time as he laughed.

'Is that what you think? My dear Lady Allerton, I am always astounded by your fertile imagination! This is no Gothic romance!' His voice changed, became grimmer. 'I am less flattered by the fact that you always suspect the worst of me!'

Beth felt suddenly ashamed. She freed herself from his grip and stepped back, smoothing her cloak down with a self-conscious gesture.

'Yes, well you must admit that your actions were of the most suspicious! If I have been mistrustful of you it is only because I found myself a prisoner in my own room!'

'Let us discuss this back at the castle,' Marcus suggested. He drew her through the doorway and into the porch, picking up his lantern as they went. The light skipped over the gravestones and illuminated the uneven stone path to the lych-gate. Marcus took Beth's arm again, this time in a gentler grip as he guided her back to the road.

'Stay close to me,' he said abruptly. 'I am amazed that you did not break an ankle creeping about in the dark!'

They walked back to the castle in silence. The moon was high and the combination of that and the torch lit the way well enough, but by now Beth was shaking with cold and reaction. She was glad when they reached the huge oak front door and Marcus ushered her into the hall.

'Please join me in the drawing room, Lady Allerton.'

Beth, who had been nursing a craven desire to run upstairs and hide in her room, realised that this was not an invitation so much as an order. She reluctantly allowed Marcus to take her cloak from her, noting that the once-smart black velvet was now crushed and stained from its travels and would never be the same again. Marcus held the drawing-room door open and Beth went in. She watched as he kicked the embers of the fire into life before moving over to the silver tray on the sideboard.

'A nightcap, Lady Allerton, to accompany our discussions? The brandy will warm you.'

He put what looked like a huge quantity of amber liquid into the glass before passing it to her. Beth risked a taste and felt the spirit burn her stomach. But Marcus was right. It was warming and in a little while she had stopped shivering.

Marcus gestured her to a chair by the fire and sat down opposite her. In the faint light his face looked brooding, severe. He looked up and their eyes met, and Beth's heart skipped a beat. Marcus smiled faintly.

'I see that the small matter of a locked door cannot stand in your way, Lady Allerton! I have seldom met anyone so indomitable!'

Beth shrugged, avoiding his gaze. ''Tis simple to open a locked door, my lord, when the key is still on the other side!'

Marcus laughed, a laugh that turned into a yawn. He slid down in the chair and stretched his legs towards the fire. 'Excuse me. It has been a long night. I blame Colin McCrae for leaving the key in the lock. I warned him to make sure that all was secure but, unlike me, he underestimated you!' He looked at her and his smile faded. 'Believe me, Lady Allerton, it was for your own good.'

Beth took a mouthful of brandy. 'I do so detest it when people say that,' she confided, 'for generally it is not true at all! From what were you protecting me, my lord? My own curiosity?'

Marcus inclined his head. 'That, and the vivid imagination that has already led you to invent wild stories this night!' He grimaced. 'But your reproof is fair, Lady Allerton. I should not have had you constrained in your room. Indeed, I should have trusted you with the truth and I apologise that I did not.'

Beth took another sip of brandy. The fiery taste was growing on her and the warm feeling it engendered even more so. She could feel the colour coming back into her face, the relaxation stealing through her limbs.

'And the truth is—what, precisely, my lord?'

Marcus shifted in his chair. 'The truth is that there is a certain Dutch privateer by the name of Godard, who has been taking advantage of the hostilities between our nation and America to prey on the ships trading from Bristol.' He leant forward and threw another log on the fire. 'The guns that you saw were entrusted to me by Captain Marchant of his Majesty's navy. Marchant wanted an arsenal for the navy to draw on locally if they find themselves within striking distance of the enemy. There is more to unload from the *Marie Louise* tomorrow.'

He looked across at her and smiled. 'That is the explanation for tonight's activities, Lady Allerton!'

Beth frowned. 'Do you think this privateer is likely to threaten Fairhaven, my lord?' she asked after a moment.

'It is most unlikely.' Marcus stood up to refill her glass. 'Godard would gain little from taking Fairhaven, for then he would have to defend it. It is more likely that he would stage a raid in order to gain fresh supplies, but even that is improbable. I confess that it was that aspect of the case that held me silent, however, for I did not wish to disturb you with the knowledge unless the threat became real.'

Beth drained her glass. 'I see. But Lady Salome has a stout enough constitution to be told the truth?'

Marcus grinned. 'You heard that, did you? McCrae and I should be more careful of speaking behind peoples' backs!' He shrugged. 'The truth is that Aunt Sal, for all her disclaimers, has dealt with everything from smugglers to pirates in her time here on Fairhaven and is quite up to snuff! Whereas you, Lady Allerton...' his smile robbed the words of any sting '...you are young and have led a more sheltered life!'

Beth decided to let this go. It was indisputable; anyway, there were other matters she wanted to pursue.

'Why go to such an elaborate charade with the coffins, my lord?'

'It was all for show.' Marcus laughed. 'It is, in fact, a convenient way of carrying a large quantity of guns and Marchant and I thought it might confuse any spies...'

'Such as myself,' Beth said ruefully. She had begun to realise just how much she had built up on so little. What was it that Marcus had said—that she always suspected the worst of him? That, and the fact that she was always running away from him. She bit her lip. Perhaps both charges were true and the thought made her feel uncomfortable. She put her empty glass down carefully on the walnut table, suddenly aware that she was feeling rather light-headed from unaccustomed liquor.

'I am sorry, my lord...'

'For what, Lady Allerton?'

Marcus was sitting forward, his own glass held between his two hands. His dark eyes were fixed on her face. 'Are you apologising for suspecting me unjustly, or for running away from me or even for locking me in a cellar?'

Beth looked up at him, then away quickly. There was something in that intent gaze that disturbed her and though his tone was light she had the oddest feeling that he had been hurt by her behaviour.

'For all of those, I suppose, my lord. I did try to apologise to you before about the cellar incident...' Beth groped for words. 'It was...very bad of me and I truly regret it...'

'Do you?' Marcus's face was unyielding. Beth, who had hoped that time would have softened his anger towards her, felt her heart sink. She had not thought him a man who bore grudges, but perhaps she deserved it.

'It is just that I thought I had to do it in order to reach Fairhaven first!' she burst out. 'That had been my intention all along and I did not think I could expect you to help me.'

'You mean you did not think you could trust me to keep my word even though I told you I would give Fairhaven to you.' Marcus's quiet tones cut through her excuses and silenced her. He looked at her, a hint of amusement coming into his eyes. 'Well, perhaps you had good reason, my lady. I had broken my word to you twice and you have no reason to suppose I would not do it a third time.'

'No, I...' Beth frowned. That seemed all wrong, but she was tired and light-headed and unable to frame her thoughts properly. She knitted her fingers together in her lap and stared fixedly at them.

'I do not think that is fair, my lord.' She spoke very quickly, before her courage deserted her. 'I do trust you and it was very wrong of me to behave as I have and, if I have hurt—offended—you in any way, I am truly sorry.' She looked up swiftly and gave him a watery smile. 'At least we are speaking to each other again!'

Marcus moved so that one of his hands was covering her clenched fingers. 'Did it trouble you that we were at odds?'

Beth stared at him, unable to tear her gaze away. There was warmth and tenderness in his eyes and she felt such a rush of relief that the tears came into her eyes and she almost cried.

'Oh…' She cleared her throat, embarrassed. 'Well, it was decidedly uncomfortable…'

Marcus smiled. He raised his hand and turned one of her curls absent-mindedly about his fingers, but his eyes never left her face. 'I thought so too.'

'Then—' Beth held her breath '—are we to be… friends…again, my lord?'

'Friends?' Marcus's gaze became thoughtful. 'I do not think so, Lady Allerton. Of all the things we are or could be, that is far too tepid a description! Passionate enemies or equally passionate lovers, perhaps, but nothing less than that!'

His fingers brushed her cheek and he took her chin in his hand. His gaze dropped to her lips. 'Are you sure that you trust me?'

'Yes,' Beth whispered.

Marcus laughed. He bent his head and kissed her, a brief, hard kiss, before allowing his hand to fall to his side.

'What a way you have of taking the wind from a fellow's sails, Lady Allerton!' His tone was rueful as he pulled Beth to her feet and steered her out into the hall. 'If you could see yourself, ever-so-slightly drunk and more than a little tempting...' He shook his head. 'And for the first time, you are looking at me with utter trust in your eyes! Your sense of timing is immaculate!'

He lit a candle for her and handed it over with a quizzical lift of his brows. 'I hope that you can find your own way to your room? It would be a mistake to trust me to deliver you there safely!'

Beth took the candle and scurried away up the stairs. She was aware that she was indeed more than a little tipsy, although the blame for that could be laid squarely at Marcus's door for giving her so much brandy. She was more concerned, however, about that casual kiss and the promise behind it. For although Marcus had behaved as a perfect gentleman, there had been an assurance in his tone that Beth was certain would be fulfilled. Enemies or lovers; she knew which she would secretly prefer and it was not just the brandy in her blood that was speaking. She closed her bedroom door behind her and locked it carefully. For now it was enough to know that she and Marcus were reconciled as friends, but for the future... Beth undressed quickly, lay down and blew out her candle flame.

Chapter Eight

It was in fact a little over a week before Beth found the time to visit Jack Cade and ask about her grandfather. Salome Trevithick had seen it as her duty to show Beth the island and had bundled her into the gig every day, taking her to meet the farmers and cottagers, and to view all the places that Salome whimsically referred to as 'the sights'. By the end of the week Beth's head was spinning with names and faces, but her overriding impression was how deeply Salome was involved in the life of the community and how much the islanders loved her. Beth they greeted with a guarded respect that was cold in comparison, but she knew that love and loyalty had to be earned and were not given for nothing. She set about following Salome's lead and spent hours at the school or in the different houses, chatting to the villagers, reading to the children or playing outside with them when the weather was fine. In the rare moments when she was left to her own devices, Beth would wander for hours along the cliff tops, admiring the view or just watching the clouds chase across the sea.

Meanwhile, Beth could not help but notice that Marcus was setting out to make a particularly good impression on his tenants. Not only did he spend a great deal of time with Colin McCrae, discussing his plans for the farms and the harbour, but he did not scruple to get his hands dirty. A new barn was being built alongside the five-acre field, and Marcus could be seen there every morning, stripped to the waist and lending a hand.

When Salome had stopped the gig by the gate one day and called Marcus over to tease him about his industry, Beth had tried to look away—the sight of Marcus's bare brown torso and firm muscles had been curiously disturbing. But instead of fixing her gaze on a nearby flock of sheep, she had found herself staring, until Marcus had looked at her with raised eyebrows and asked if she was feeling quite the thing. And certainly Beth had *not* been feeling at all well. Her face was flushed and her pulse was racing and she wondered if she had contracted a fever. Salome had taken one look at her, smiled, and said that she thought Beth was suffering from a certain affliction, but had not said which.

Marcus had sought Beth out one evening and explained that he did not wish to leave Fairhaven until he had had the chance to discuss the future with his uncle St John as well as with Salome. This was clearly impossible with St John in Exeter, and Beth, anxious not to appear to be pushing the Trevithicks from their home, made no demur about extending her time on Fairhaven. She sent a letter to Charlotte, explaining what was happening and saying that she intended to be back at Mostyn Hall for Christmas, then, when she finally had a spare morning, she set off to find Jack Cade.

Jack Cade's cottage sat about a mile away from the main village, on a small hill that looked out westward across the harbour to the coast of Devon. Marcus had said that Cade had been a fisherman all his life, but that he was too old to go to sea any more and had retired to live alone. The other villagers considered him something of an oddity, but as one of the longest-lived inhabitants of Fairhaven he was given grudging respect.

Beth trod up the shell-lined path to the cottage door. A few straggling plants huddled in the shelter of its white-painted wall and there was a collection of floats and old rope tumbled amidst the grass of the headland, with a sheep grazing placidly nearby. Beth knocked tentatively at the door. Now that the moment had come for her to meet one of her grandfather's contemporaries, she was almost sick with nerves.

The door creaked open to reveal a bent old figure in the aperture. Beth's smile faltered a little.

'Mr Cade? I am Beth Allerton. I heard that you knew my grandfather, Charles Mostyn, and I wondered if you would be able to tell me about him, please?'

The old fisherman looked at her. His eyes were as sharp and bright as a hawk's in a face of old leather. He smiled, showing the stumps of blackened teeth. 'I thought you'd be a'coming, my lady. Yes, I knew Charles Mostyn. I could tell you about him.'

A trickle of anticipation crept down Beth's spine, making her shiver. She was shaking at the prospect of being so close to the truth at last and hearing directly what had happened to Lord Mostyn on the night he had died.

'Take a seat, ma'am,' the old man said courteously, stepping back to allow her to precede him into the cottage. He swept a pile of floats and nets from the armchair nearest the fire and Beth sat down, looking about her with interest.

There was only the one room but it was snug and

wood-lined, with a roaring fire in the grate. Various bits of flotsam and jetsam adorned the walls: a set of antlers, a brown glass bottle, a twisted piece of bleached wood— all the bits and pieces that Cade must have picked up throughout his life at sea.

The old man sat down on the settle opposite Beth, groaning and creaking like the old wood as he found a comfortable position. He pulled a bottle of whisky towards him, knocked his pipe out on the arm of the chair and stuffed it full of fresh tobacco. He did not speak until it was lit and he was puffing away, with several clouds of evil-smelling smoke adding to the alcoholic fug in the room.

'Charles Mostyn…' he said, thoughtfully. 'He was the one before the old Earl. The Evil Earl.' He cackled suddenly. 'Not like this young 'un, for all his London ways. Seems like some good can come out of the old stock after all!'

Beth held her tongue and kept her patience. There was no point in hurrying the old man and she had heard plenty of people sing Marcus's praises over the past week.

'The Old Earl,' Jack Cade said again. 'Aye, he were a bad 'un and no mistake. And Mostyn too—as alike as two brothers, with nothing to choose between them!'

Beth sat up straight in her chair, frowning slightly. This did not sound right. 'Nothing to choose? But, Mr Cade—'

Jack Cade puffed hard on the pipe. 'Trevithick had a violent temper, but Mostyn was cruel hard—cold and vicious where Trevithick was loud and brutal. But Mostyn was clever, see?' His sharp gaze pinned Beth to her chair. 'He brought the trade in here, though we said as we wanted no trouble. But he wouldn't listen. Needed the money, I reckon, and the silly lads with him.'

'The…trade?'

'Smuggling!' Cade said triumphantly. 'Smuggling, m'lady! Big business here in the straits it was in them days. Trevithick and Mostyn at each other's throats, allus a struggle to control the trade along the coast. That's all! No more to it. But Mostyn held Fairhaven, see, so he had the advantage and a hard landlord he was, into the bargain.'

Beth swallowed hard. This was not at all as she had imagined it, nor indeed how the old stories had been spun to her in the nursery at Mostyn Hall all those years ago. She cleared her throat.

'Mr Cade, are you sure? I mean—' she saw his piercing gaze resting on her '—it is simply that I was told a vastly different story.'

'Bound to tell you something different, weren't they!' Cade said simply. 'Little lass wi' no family to speak of! Who'd want to tell the truth? Plenty to hide, that family, plenty to hide!'

Beth took a deep breath. She was shaking so much that she had to lock her fingers together to still them, but it was not with anticipation now. There was a pain lodged somewhere in her chest and another that blocked her throat until she could barely speak. But she had to know the truth now.

'What happened?' She whispered. 'In the end, I mean.'

There was pity in Cade's face. She could see it there and it struck another blow to her heart.

'In the end there was so much rivalry for the trade in these waters that Trevithick and Mostyn came to blows.' The old man coughed. 'Trevithick won and he took the island, and no Mostyn has been here since. 'Til now, my lady.'

'How did Trevithick take Fairhaven?' Beth asked. She stared as the old man took a deep swig from his whisky bottle, wiped his mouth on his sleeve and smacked his lips.

'Ah! The last quarrel. It was all over a load of brandy Mostyn was waiting for, see? The free traders brought it in, but Mostyn was late for the meet and Trevithick got here first. Offered to double the payment for the men if they traded with him, not Mostyn, and helped him take the island into the bargain.' Cade shook his head. 'Didn't need much persuasion. Everyone hated Mostyn. Trevithick was little better, but at least he was paying well. So when Mostyn came they ambushed him and cut him to pieces—saving your presence, my lady.'

'But I thought—' Beth stopped, swallowed hard, and started again. 'I had heard that he was ambushed by the Earl of Trevithick's men, and the Earl stole the family silver.'

Cade cackled with laughter. 'Weren't no silver, m'lady. Mostyn was too mean to pay his dues! There was just the sword and the ring.' He got to his feet and hobbled over to an old sea chest in the corner, rummaging about inside. 'I've never worn this. Didn't seem right, somehow, after Trevithick had cut it from his finger! Best for you to have it now, perhaps, seeing as he was your grandfather!'

Beth held out her hand automatically and Cade dropped the signet ring into it. Through the blur of her tears, she saw the arms of Mostyn cut deep into the gold, the motto that was barely legible after all these years: *Remember*. She closed her fist tightly about it.

'What happened to the Sword of Saintonge?' she

asked, marvelling at the steadiness of her own voice. 'Did Trevithick take that too?'

Cade was shaking his head. 'The sword broke in the fight, my lady. I have the stump of it here, but it's nothing but rust now—'

Beth was suddenly, devastatingly aware that she was about to cry and she had absolutely no wish to do so in Cade's cottage. She stood up abruptly.

'Excuse me. You have been more than kind, Mr Cade, but I fear I must go.'

The old man patted her arm clumsily. 'Forgive me, my lady. I did not know what to do for the best, but his lordship said that it was important I tell you the truth.'

Beth paused, her tears suddenly forgotten. A ray of sunlight struck across her eyes from the open door and she moved impatiently into the shade. 'His lordship said so? Lord Trevithick? When?'

Cade shifted awkwardly. 'When he came to see me, ma'am. Said you were looking for someone who knew your grandfather and that I was to tell you everything, honestly. Imperative, he said it was—'

Beth wheeled round and ran out of the cottage door, scaring the sheep that had been calmly grazing by the gate. She plunged down the village street, conscious that people were looking at her curiously, and practically crashed into the farm gate where she had last seen Marcus helping to stack some hay. He was still there. The last of the bales had been moved into the barn and he was standing nearby, talking to Colin McCrae.

'Lord Trevithick!' Beth had intended to sound imperious, but her voice came out with a desperate wobble in it. She tried to steel herself. 'Lord Trevithick, I require to speak with you! At once!'

Marcus exchanged a few quick words with Colin

McCrae, then came across to her, vaulting over the gate and taking her arm. His gaze was searching.

'You have seen Cade, then, Lady Allerton? Are you all right?'

'No, I am not all right!' Beth said stormily. Two bright spots of angry colour shone in her cheeks. Despite the chill of the day, she felt feverishly hot. 'How dare you, Lord Trevithick!' Her voice rose. 'How dare you let me go to speak to that old man when you knew the truth about my grandfather and could have told me yourself and spared me the pain!'

'Not here,' Marcus said. His grip tightened on her arm. He was looking over her shoulder at the crowd of farmworkers and villagers who were now providing an embarrassed but none the less interested audience. Beth shook herself free. At that moment she would not have cared if the entire island had gathered for the entertainment.

'Let go of me!' she hissed. 'I detest your behaviour, sir.'

There was the flash of something elemental and angry in Marcus's eyes. This time his grip bruised her skin. 'And would you have believed me if I had told you that your grandfather was nothing but a common free trader, Lady Allerton? I think not! Your trust in me has been notable for its absence up until now! You had to hear the truth from someone else!'

Beth stared into his angry eyes for what seemed like hours. Behind her the crowd shifted and murmured and even through her preoccupation she heard one buxom lady saying to another: 'Cade has told her all about Charles Mostyn... They'd told her he was a good man, poor lamb...'

It was the pity that broke Beth. She could see it on

the faces of all those about her as they witnessed her
terrible distress. It was the same sympathy that had been
reflected in Jack Cade's eyes at the end. Probably they
had all known the truth about Charles Mostyn, but no
one had wanted to mention it to her. At first they might
even have imagined her to be a chip off the Mostyn
block, come to take them back to the bad times. She and
Marcus both. Trevithick and Mostyn, at each other's
throats, dragging their people down with them when they
should have been defending them.

There was no sympathy on Marcus's face. He looked
at her and his expression was carved from stone. With
a cry, Beth tore herself from his grip and turned her back
on all of them, running down the hill towards the castle
until her legs were going so fast that she was almost
falling over herself. The wind roared in her ears and her
hair whipped about her face, blinding her. She slammed
the castle gate open and raced across the greensward to
the cliff edge.

'Beth! For God's sake! Stop before you fall!'

Marcus caught her from behind, knocking all the
breath from her body as he pulled her to the ground. She
was crying now, struggling and pummelling him in her
efforts to get away from him, gasping for breath until he
had quite simply to lean the whole of his weight on her
to subdue her. Beth lay still, trying to calm her sobs,
feeling the cold grass beneath her cheek and the warm
tears that ran down her face and splashed onto the
springy turf.

'Oh, Beth…'

There was a world of pity in Marcus's voice now and
she did not resist him when he pulled her into his arms,
half-cradling her as she cried as though her heart was
breaking.

For what seemed like endless hours she wept into his jacket and felt his hands stroking her and his voice murmuring words that made no sense but sounded inexpressibly comforting. And at length she sat up a little, wiped her hand across her wet cheeks and said, in a small voice, 'I never cry!'

Marcus smiled, brushing the hair back from her face. 'No, indeed. I had noticed.' He got to his feet, pulling her with him. 'Come, we must get you inside. Sitting on the damp grass will not make you feel any better...'

Beth clung to him. 'Marcus...'

'I know.' For a moment Marcus's arms tightened about her in a hug before he slid one arm about her waist and guided her back towards the castle. Lady Salome met them at the door, her gardening trug over her arm, a look of distress on her face.

'I heard,' she said, patting Beth's shoulder consolingly. 'My poor girl, to have all your memories dashed in such a cruel way! Oh, the betrayal of innocent blood! Matthew twenty-six, verse twenty-seven!'

Beth hiccuped a little and smothered a giggle. 'Oh, Lady Salome, you are a very present help in trouble!'

'A glass of madeira and a hot brick are what we need!' Lady Salome said bracingly. 'Come upstairs, my dear, and I will give you rest!'

'Exodus thirty-three, verse sixteen,' Marcus said, with a sigh.

'Matthew eleven, verse twenty-eight!' Lady Salome called, over her shoulder. 'Marcus, pray ask Mrs McCrae to bring some hot soup and some physick—'

'I am not ill!' Beth objected, borne irresistibly upwards on Lady Salome's arm.

'Nonsense! You have sustained a shock and require food, drink and rest,' Lady Salome said decisively. She opened the bedroom door and pushed Beth inside. 'You mark my words—within half an hour you will be asleep!'

The sound of the sea was in Beth's ears and it was very soothing. She opened her eyes reluctantly. The room was bathed in candlelight and the long curtains were drawn. Martha McCrae was sitting beside the bed, reading a book. She looked up as Beth opened her eyes and her face broke into a smile.

'Oh, my lady! How are you feeling now?'

Beth frowned slightly. 'Have I been asleep, Martha? Good gracious! Lady Salome gave me a glass of ratafia and the next thing I remember... Why, I do believe I feel hungry!'

Martha jumped up. 'There is some fresh broth made this afternoon, my lady, the very thing! I will go and fetch some for you—'

'Stay a moment, please!' Beth put out her hand and caught the girl's sleeve. 'Martha, will you answer something for me?'

'If I can, my lady.' Martha looked apprehensive.

'Does everyone on the island know the truth of my grandfather's dishonour?'

Martha fidgeted, avoiding Beth's gaze. 'Oh, my lady! Everyone knows the old stories, of course, though it was only Jack Cade and one or two others actually remember...' She twisted her hands together. 'I'm sorry, my lady. We thought you knew, you see, until his lordship told Colin that you had been told quite a different tale! Then we were afraid, for we knew you would find out...' Her unhappy brown eyes met Beth's and there was apology in their depths. 'It has all been so difficult, my lady, what with thinking his lordship was showing an interest in the place, then hearing that you would be taking Fairhaven over, and worrying for Lady Salome, and not knowing what was really going on.'

Beth nodded. 'I understand. But Lord Trevithick *has* shown a genuine interest in Fairhaven and has done so much for the island—'

Martha smiled and it was like the sun breaking through clouds. 'Oh, my lady! Now we don't know what to think! We know you care about Fairhaven, but Lord Trevithick is a good man and has already helped us so much! If only you could both keep Fairhaven—' She broke off, getting to her feet. 'Excuse me, my lady. I will go to fetch that soup.'

Beth turned her head against the pillow. Now she fully understood the hostility of the villagers when first she had come to Fairhaven. They had either remembered the bad old days of the Mostyns or remembered hearing stories of that time. Her grandfather's legacy had gone deep and in ways that she had not even imagined. Beth sat up, reached for her wrap and propped herself up on her pillows. She had seldom had a day's illness in her life, but just for now it felt pleasantly indulgent to stay in bed and let Martha wait on her. She no longer felt tearful, but she did feel tired.

'Entirely respectable, alas!' The voice from the doorway made her jump and she turned to see Marcus strolling forward into the room. He grinned at her in the old way that she remembered and gestured to the edge of the bed.

'May I?'

'Well…' Beth frowned. 'You should not be here, my lord! Whatever would Lady Salome say?'

'I know!' Marcus looked unabashed. 'But Martha left

the door open and I was anxious to see if you were really better!'

Beth dropped her gaze. She felt curiously shy, aware of the thinness of her nightgown and wrap, even if Marcus seemed oblivious to it. Which was in itself rather disappointing... Annoyed at the direction of her thoughts, she forced herself to meet his gaze.

'Please, my lord, before you say anything else I must apologise—'

Marcus touched her hand. He shook his head. 'Beth, do not. You had sustained a huge shock and anything you said was entirely understandable.'

Beth gave him a slight smile. 'Thank you.' She hesitated. 'I do understand why you did not tell me. I had to hear it from someone who had been there, someone who had seen with their own eyes—'

'Believe me—' Marcus voice was a little rough '—if I had thought that there could be any other way...'

Beth felt her face grow warm. She was glad that there was no light but the glow of the fire. She felt a constraint between them, a tension that was due to all the emotions that were present but unspoken.

'I confess I feel rather foolish,' she said, after a moment. 'For so long, the history of the Mostyns has been like...' she hesitated '...almost like a talisman to me, I suppose. The romantic history, the feud, good vanquished by evil, or so I thought, when really...' Her voice trailed away.

'When really there were two warring families, neither of whom deserved your good opinion,' Marcus finished drily.

Beth sighed. 'The whole quest for Fairhaven was based on a false dream. I can scarce believe it! Ever since I was a child I have longed for it!'

Marcus let go of her hand and stood up a little abruptly. She could not read his expression but his voice was once more his own. 'It is not surprising. Children are most tenacious of dreams, after all, and you were orphaned young and needed something on which to hang your hopes.' He smiled down at her. 'Now I must go. Martha will be back soon with the soup and would be scandalised to find me here!'

He went out, leaving Beth staring blindly into the fire. Something in Marcus's tone had pierced her, stripping away the remaining illusions from before her eyes. Somewhere in the past few weeks she had become so intent on gaining Fairhaven and achieving her dream that she had been prepared to sacrifice anything to win it. That feeling had possessed her when she had met Marcus in London, it had prompted her to start the chase down to Devon, it had even driven her to lock him in Theo March's wine cellar just so that she could get ahead. The obsession with Fairhaven had always been slumbering, but once the island had seemed almost within her grasp, it had taken over.

Beth slid down under the blankets. It seemed extraordinary now, for she no longer felt that way. She could see clearly for the first time in years, and what she saw was that her quest had exacted a higher price than any wild goose chase. There was Charlotte, who had loyally accompanied her from London on what she had surely known was a fool's errand, only to be abandoned at Theo's vicarage for her pains. Beth had regretted her behaviour to her cousin before, but now she saw its full magnitude.

And there was Marcus... Weeks ago—it seemed like years to Beth now—she had realised that she was in danger of falling in love with Marcus too quickly, too soon. She had distracted herself by the race for Fairhaven, pretending that they were in opposition when, in fact, their conflict had only masked the growing attraction between them. An attraction that Beth now realised, with a dreadful sinking feeling, had developed on her part at least into a hopelessly deep love…

With a groan, Beth rolled over and buried her face in the pillow.

'My lady, are you feeling poorly again?'

Beth raised her head to see Martha McCrae standing by the bed with a steaming pot of soup on a tray. 'Oh, Martha! I did not see you there! No, I am very well…'

After she had finished the chicken broth, she slipped out of bed and trod across the room. Her cloak was still hanging over a chair before the fire. Beth put a hand in the pocket. Her grandfather's signet ring was still in there. She took it out and held it up to the firelight, reading the inscription once more. *Remember*. There had been too much of that. Beth opened the casement window and a flurry of snow blew in on the cutting edge of the wind. Beth gave her grandfather's ring one last glance and flung it out into the darkness.

'You look very beautiful, my lady,' Martha McCrae said with a smile, twisting the last lock of hair into Beth's chignon.

Beth looked at her reflection and smiled. 'Certainly no one would know that you had fashioned my dress out of some old curtains, Martha! You have done a splendid job!'

Martha giggled. 'But they were the best drawing-room curtains, ma'am, and you have the figure to carry anything off!' She gave Beth a sly look. 'I'll wager his lordship will think so too!'

Beth could feel herself colouring up. Now that she was so aware of her feelings for Marcus she was hopelessly self-conscious. She had done everything she could to avoid him over the past week and had been practically tongue-tied in his presence, feeling like a green girl scarcely out of the schoolroom. Fortunately Marcus did not seem to have noticed, for he was so involved in various projects of Colin's devising that Bath barely saw him. He had gone about the estate and she had helped out in Lady Salome's garden and another week had slipped by, bringing them to the date of the annual Fairhaven dance.

'I imagine that there will be plenty of young ladies vying for Lord Trevithick's attention tonight,' Beth said lightly. 'I shall not expect to monopolise him!'

Martha looked disappointed. It had amused Beth that the villagers, who had started by assuming that she was Marcus's mistress, had swiftly learned of their error and had actually seemed disappointed that she and Marcus were not in fact lovers. Beth had wondered if this was because they wanted a neat solution to the future ownership of the island. It would certainly solve the problem if she and Marcus were to share ownership of Fairhaven, but she knew this was not to be. For several days, watching him about the estate, she had felt a growing conviction that it would be wrong to take Fairhaven away from Marcus. Soon she would have to tell him so.

Beth saw that Martha was still watching her and gave her a quick smile. 'Besides, I shall want at least one dance with your Colin tonight, Martha! Now, should you not run along and get ready yourself? You have spent so much time helping me that it is almost time to go down!'

After Martha had hurried away to her own toilette,

Beth picked up her reticule and stood up to admire the clinging cherry-red velvet dress. With her black hair and silver eyes it did indeed look striking and appropriately festive since this was the island's annual dance. Beth sighed unconsciously. She felt as gauche as a debutante and hoped that the young ladies of Fairhaven would distract Marcus's attention. With his strong physique and dark good looks she knew that he was much admired, for she had seen the village girls watching him and giggling together in corners. But perhaps the good people of Fairhaven had had enough of a lord with a wandering eye. The stories of the Evil Earl's philandering had been enough to shock even Beth's strong constitution.

She realised that she could hear music playing below, the pluck of the violins and the thump of drums. That meant that the musicians had already arrived and with them, no doubt, most of the other villagers. It was time to go down and she just hoped that Marcus would be too occupied to notice her.

That vain hope died as she went slowly down the stairs. Marcus was standing in the hall, dressed in evening clothes that had certainly not been fashioned from some cast-off furnishings. He was talking to Lady Salome, who looked glorious in a dress of yellow satin with an overskirt of green sewn with lots of tiny diamonds. Her hair was dressed with pheasant and seagull feathers. Beth hoped that the birds of Fairhaven had not died in vain.

Marcus looked up as Beth came down the final flight and watched her all the way, with a disconcertingly direct gaze that made her feel totally flustered. As she reached the hall, he took her hand and raised it to his lips.

'You look very beautiful, Lady Allerton. I particularly like your necklace! It matches your eyes!'

Beth laughed, fingering the beads a little self-consciously. She had brought no jewellery with her on her journey, but the low-cut dress had cried out for something and Martha had tentatively pressed on her a necklace made of tiny grey pebbles from the beach. Beth had thought it quite as beautiful as the expensive pearls and diamonds she had locked away in London and had been touched by Martha's gesture.

'Sheba dressed to greet Solomon!' Lady Salome said expansively, enveloping Beth in a scented hug. 'I hear that the dancing has started. Excuse me, my dears, I am off to tread a measure!'

Marcus offered Beth his arm and they followed slowly. A lively country dance was striking up as they came into the Great Hall. 'It is remarkable that there are so many musicians on the island, my lord,' Beth observed, looking at the motley orchestra, 'especially with the ruinous effect of the sea air in warping their instruments!'

Marcus laughed. 'A resourceful lot, our islanders! If one asks why there are so many young children on the island or why there are so many musicians, one receives the same answer—that there is nothing else to do during the long winter!'

'My lord!' Beth laughed in spite of herself.

'Come and dance with me,' Marcus said persuasively, smiling down at her. 'I have been saving the first dance for you!'

'In the face of much temptation from other young ladies, no doubt,' Beth said, arching her brows.

Marcus gave her an expressive look. 'There is only

one lady who throws temptation in my path, Lady
Allerton, and sooner or later I will fall!'

Beth had always considered the Great Hall to be a
cold and bare room, but tonight it looked as she imagined it might have done for some masque centuries before. A huge fire roared in the grate and the light from
a score of torches reflected off the polished shields and
swords on the walls. The tapestries glowed with rich
colour and between them were draped boughs of ever-
green as a reminder of the approaching Christmas
season. It seemed that all eighty-six inhabitants of
Fairhaven were present, resplendent in their best party
clothes.

As all the servants had been invited to the dance, the
food and drink was very much a matter of helping one-
self. A large table almost bowed under the weight of
Christmas pies made of minced beef and spices and
everyone was dipping into a large cauldron that held a
brew that Marcus informed Beth was called Puffin
Punch.

'The bird does not form the chief ingredient, however,' he added, when Beth drew back, wrinkling her
nose up. 'I believe you will find it quite appetising.'

He was right. The mixture of wine, spices, oranges
and lemon was thoroughly delicious and put Beth in
mind of the soothing mulled wine that Marcus had sent
up for her and Charlotte that night at the inn in
Marlborough. The memory brought a strange lump to
her throat, for it seemed that so much had happened
since that night and not all of it as she had planned.
Marcus was watching her, his eyes narrowed on her face.

'What is it, Beth? You look as though you've seen
a ghost!'

Beth raised her eyebrows haughtily. 'My name, my lord?'

Marcus laughed. 'You think me inappropriate? After all that we have…been through together? You have called me by name before!'

'You are certainly inappropriate to remind me, my lord,' Beth said pertly, looking at him over the rim of her drinking cup.

'Yet on such an evening as this we could dispense with formality, perhaps?'

Beth finished her punch. 'Very well then, Marcus. But we must not let Lady Salome hear us, for I am sure she is a stickler for formality—' She broke off as Lady Salome whirled past them clasped in the arms of one of the sheep farmers. His face was flushed with drink and excitement and Lady Salome was roaring with laughter at whatever tale he was telling her.

'Well, perhaps not!' Beth finished.

'I hope that the Fairhaven festivities will not shock you, Beth,' Marcus said, grinning. 'They are rumoured to be quite outrageous!'

Beth tried to look cool and unshakable but it was difficult under Marcus's mocking gaze. She looked down the table, seeking distraction.

'Good gracious, what is that?' She pointed to an orange studded with cloves and decorated with a sprig of holly that stood in the centre of the table on a little tripod of twigs.

'The Calennig,' Marcus said indulgently. 'I believe it is a Welsh tradition, for here the customs of Wales and England merge sometimes. It is a symbol to bring a fertile harvest.'

Beth looked around. 'And are there any other traditional decorations here tonight?'

'There is the mistletoe,' Marcus said, a wicked gleam suddenly in his eye. He pointed to the beams above her head. 'If you would care to glance up, my lady…'

Beth evaded the snare deftly. 'Hmm. I think not, my lord. I would prefer to dance!'

The country dance was ending and the impromptu orchestra swung straight into the next tune. Beth clapped her hands.

'Oh! The Furry Dance! I have not danced this since I was a child!'

The dancing was fast and furious, and bore little resemblance to the sedate entertainment of a London ballroom. Beth managed one country dance with Marcus before he was snatched away from her and she was whirled into a jig by one of the village lads. They had no shyness in approaching her and she barely had any rest during the evening as the old folk dances of her childhood and familiar country airs intermingled. The dancing became progressively less decorous as the evening went on and finally she was swept into the lilting rhythm of something called the Brawl, and ended up face to face with Marcus, as she had begun. Dark eyes blazing, he swept her into his arms.

'A kiss under the mistletoe!' one of the village lads shouted, energetically setting the example with his own partner.

Beth saw Marcus grin. 'It is customary,' he murmured, and before she could reply he bent his head and kissed her. His lips were gentle at first, but Beth could not conceal her instinctive response and he crushed her to him, unleashing a passion in both of them that could not be denied. When he let her go and steadied her with a hand on her arm, Beth felt dizzy and confused, aware of the curiosity and approval on the faces all about her.

Marcus kept a protective arm about her as he steered her towards the refreshments and someone pressed another glass of Puffin Punch into her hands.

'This is probably a mistake,' Beth said hopelessly, aware that she was already more than a little inebriated. 'If you do not wish me to be drunk, my lord—'

'Marcus, remember?' Marcus was smiling down at her in a way that made Beth feel distinctly unsteady. 'My dear Beth, I should be delighted to see you a little foxed if it makes you more receptive to my advances! Would you care to see the castle gardens by moonlight?'

'Marcus, it has been snowing these five days past!' Beth said severely. 'If it is your wish that we catch our deaths—'

'Then perhaps we could watch the snow falling from Lady Salome's orangery?' Marcus suggested, a glint of amusement in his eyes. 'That would be most romantic and so very pretty...'

'Lady Salome would scarce approve!' Beth said lightly. The idea held much appeal but she was no green girl to fall for such a suggestion. She knew exactly what would happen once the orangery doors were closed behind them.

'Marcus, why do you not take Beth to see the view from the orangery?' Lady Salome said, appearing beside them with a huge glass of Puffin Punch clasped in her hands. 'It would be so very pretty with all the snow!'

'Exactly what I have been saying, ma'am!' Marcus agreed, whilst Beth smothered her giggles. 'Come now, Lady Allerton, surely you cannot resist such a recommendation!'

'She is matchmaking,' Beth said, as Marcus tucked her arm through his and steered her firmly out of the hall and along the corridor to the orangery. 'Or making an alliance to save Fairhaven, perhaps!'

'I imagine all the villagers are behind her!' Marcus agreed. He held open the orangery doors. 'There…and is that not as pretty as I promised it would be?'

Beth moved forward to the big windows, feeling the cold coming from the glass in contrast to the warmth of the room behind. The bare branches of the orange and lemon trees struck spiky shadows across the floor. The snow brushed softly against the windows, melting as it ran down the glass. Outside, nothing could be seen but the soft darkness and the falling flakes.

Beth turned. Marcus was standing just inside the door, his face shadowed, but a faint smile on his lips. She felt puzzled. She had been certain that he would kiss her as soon as they were alone and she had been ready, waiting even. Such sweet pleasure could not be denied even if she was uncertain where it was leading. Yet now he made no move towards her and she felt confused—and more than a little disappointed.

'It is very pretty, my lord.' Her tone was cool as she struggled to master her feelings. 'However, I think I should retire now, if you will excuse me—'

'I will escort you to your room,' Marcus murmured.

Beth looked him in the eye. 'I am not likely to become lost, my lord.'

'No, but you are a little intoxicated—'

'I am not foxed!' Beth said indignantly, clutching the nearest orange tree for support and belying her words. 'I may be a little merry—'

'More than a little,' Marcus said, lips twitching.

'But it is a most pleasant feeling…'

'Not to be recommended on a daily basis, however.'

'Dear me…' Beth wavered a little '…you have become most censorious, my lord!' She had reached the orangery door and looked up into his face. 'Yet it seems to me that, for all your severity, you are not above taking advantage!'

'It is well-nigh impossible,' Marcus said solemnly, 'and I swear you are deliberately tempting me...'

He took a step forward and drew her into his arms. His lips touched her cheek. 'Dear Lady Allerton, have I told you how much I esteem and admire you?'

'No,' Beth said, determined to be prosaic despite the excitement racing through her blood, 'you have not.'

'Well, I do.' Marcus's mouth grazed the corner of hers. Beth stood quite still repressing the urge to press closer to him. He took her chin in his hand and brushed his thumb across her lower lip. Beth felt a shudder go straight through her. Desire swept over her in a crashing wave, leaving her thoroughly shaken.

'My lord—'

'Marcus, remember...' Marcus's voice was husky. He kissed her lightly, slowly, his lips just touching hers. Beth made a small, inarticulate sound deep in her throat and melted against him.

'Marcus...'

'Mmm...no.' Marcus drew back slightly. 'Beth, there is something I must ask you. Will you marry me?'

For a moment Beth clung to him, her senses still adrift, then her mind focused on what he had said.

'Marry you? I don't think... What...? Why...?'

She lost the thread as Marcus took her earlobe between his teeth and bit gently. 'I want to marry you, Beth. I want you very much.'

Beth's eyes, a cloudy silver grey, searched his face. 'Marcus, I cannot think properly if you keep kissing me.'

'Fortunately, there is no necessity to think. Will you marry me? Here on Fairhaven? Say yes.'

'Because of Fairhaven?'

'Devil take Fairhaven! I want you, not the island!'

Marcus was kissing her again fiercely, robbing her of breath. Beth realised that he had abandoned the idea of a gentle approach, abandoned restraint. Her whole body shook with the force of his passion—and of her own, for she was wrapping her arms round his neck to pull him to her with an urgent need that matched his own. Her body was besieged by heat and desire, desperate to be closer to his.

There was an insistent tapping on the orangery window behind them. Beth spun round.

'Marcus!' Lady Salome was peering at them through the glass. 'How much longer do you need? We are all waiting for an announcement!'

Beth laughed shakily. 'My guardian angel!'

'With the devil's own timing,' Marcus said ruefully. 'Very well, Aunt Salome. We will be with you shortly.' He took both of Beth's hands in his. In the pale, white light of the snowbound conservatory, Beth saw him smile faintly.

'So what do you think, my love? If you do not like the idea you need only say!'

Beth smiled shyly. 'I do quite like the idea—' she confessed, and got no further as Marcus swept her back into his arms again.

Chapter Nine

'I fear I must be leaving you for a trip to the mainland,' Lady Salome said dolefully to Beth, leaning on her hoe and tucking the ends of her orange and purple scarf more firmly inside her green velvet coat. They were standing in the castle garden, where Lady Salome had been using the hoe to break the ice on the fishpond, so that the golden carp could breathe. Beth could see the faint flash of a fin deep in the gloom at the bottom of the pond. She hoped that the carp were warmer than she was, or at least more able to withstand the cold.

'Drat this frost!' Lady Salome proclaimed. 'We cannot be doing with a hard winter! Not when there is so much to do about the island!'

'Why are you leaving, Lady Salome?' Beth asked, as they crunched across the fresh snow to the castle door.

'A letter from St John!' Lady Salome said. 'He has been delayed in Exeter and asks that I join him. He is worried that we may be away for Christmas and what our poor, benighted islanders will do for pastoral care in the meantime is not to be imagined! I suspect that there will be any number of christenings to attend to next autumn!'

Beth giggled. 'Surely the Bishop will send a curate to take care of your flock here?'

Lady Salome humphed. 'Very likely, but it will not be the same! And indeed, my dear—' she fixed Beth with a stern gaze '—I cannot like leaving you alone here with Marcus, for all that you are betrothed! It is most irregular!'

Beth blushed and made a little business of wiping all the snow from her boots before she followed Lady Salome into the warmth of the hall.

'You know that we intend to leave Fairhaven in a few weeks, Lady Salome!' she said. 'I have promised to join my cousins at Mostyn for Christmas and Marcus is going to Trevithick, and the wedding will probably be in the spring—'

'It is what happens in the next week that concerns me,' Lady Salome said darkly. 'It is easy to stray from the path of righteousness! And without me here to act as chaperon—well, the descent into hell is easy, but there is no turning back!'

Beth tried not to smile. To her mind, being seduced by Marcus would be heaven rather than hell, but she could scarcely express such inappropriate remarks to Lady Salome.

'I really do not think that you need to worry, Lady Salome!' she said wistfully. 'Marcus has been a very pattern of propriety these last three days since the dance!'

Lady Salome looked unconvinced. 'You mark my words, child—once a rake! Still...' her face softened '...I do believe that Marcus truly loves you! It is a blessing to see it!'

Beth was not so convinced. Although she did not think that Marcus had proposed merely to reach a compromise over Fairhaven, she was not certain that he loved her. She was even beginning to doubt that he desired her for, although he had been ardent in his pursuit of her before their betrothal, since the dance he had been positively distant. Beth knew that Marcus was deeply engrossed in the plans for the estate, even more so now that he knew there would be her money to back his projects. Even so, she thought he might have been a little more attentive as they were so newly engaged.

The week following Lady Salome's departure did nothing to change this view. Marcus either worked in his study with Colin McCrae or was out and about the island. He and Beth dined together in the evenings, took a pot of tea like any old married couple and sat chatting, reading or playing cards. When it was time for Beth to retire, Marcus would escort her to the bottom of the stairs, light her candle for her and give her a chaste peck on the cheek. It was becoming so frustrating that Beth swore to herself that she would cast herself into Marcus's arms the next night just to see how he reacted. She was tolerably certain that he would simply disentangle himself and ask her if she was feeling unwell. It was as though the passion that had flared between them had never existed at all.

Now that Lady Salome had gone to the mainland, Beth found herself taking over many of that redoubtable spinster's responsibilities towards the islanders. She would visit the sick or call in at the school and she kept a keen eye on Lady Salome's garden, knowing that her future aunt-in-law would never forgive her if the orange trees died or the fish perished. On days when the weather was crisp and fine she would sometimes walk along the shore or over the hills, delighting in the beauty of the island and the freedom of the open air. Once, when she had returned to her room at the castle after a scramble over a rocky beach, Beth had looked at her reflection in the mirror and wondered what on earth Charlotte would say if only she could see her now; her hair was all tumbled and windblown and her cheeks flushed from the cold air. There was a long rent in her skirt where it had snagged on the rocks and her petticoat was stained equally with mud and seawater. Decidedly she did not look like a lady, or at least not the sort of lady who flourished on the rarefied air of a London drawing room. Charlotte would despair of her.

November slid into December. It was a full two weeks since Lady Salome had left for Exeter and still they had had no word of whether she and St John would be returning for Christmas or whether a curate would be sent in their place. Beth knew that Marcus was delaying his departure from Fairhaven until he had word, but she had reluctantly started to think that she needed to make her own plans to rejoin Charlotte at Mostyn. She was thinking about it as she walked along the seashore that afternoon, idly tossing pebbles into the water. Martha McCrae was also on the beach; she had brought Annie, baby Jamie and some of the village children down to the shore to see if they could find any driftwood to fashion into decorations for Christmas. Martha had explained that there were so few trees on the island that had to improvise with other ideas and a fine, imaginative time they had of it.

The tide was coming in. The water sucked at the pebbles about Beth's feet, splashing on to the hem of her dress. Beth turned and looked back down the beach. Martha and the children had walked a long way now and were examining some shells that one of the girls had picked up from the sand. The children's cries mingled with the call of the seabirds, tossed on the wind. There was another cry too, thin and faint, but closer at hand. Beth stared. Martha had put the reed basket with the baby in it on the rocks some twenty yards away, but with the incoming tide it had slid into the water and was bobbing about in the waves, already several yards from the shore. Martha, engrossed in keeping her flock together, had not yet noticed.

Beth started to run. The wind was cold on her cheeks and the pebbles slid from beneath her shoes, hampering her. By the time she reached the rocks where Martha had left Jamie she could hardly see the reed basket in the dips between the waves.

Beth waded out to the rocks, feeling the tug of the tide seize her. Even here, so close to the shore, there was a strong tidal race out to sea. A rowing boat was tied up there, dipping on the rising waves. Beth was already up to her waist and her soaking skirts wrapped about her legs so that she almost fell. The basket was bobbing further away all the time and she knew she could not swim out to it, knew that the tide race was pulling too fast for her to catch up. She heard Jamie wail again as a wave splashed over the side of the basket and it threatened to tip over. In desperation she grabbed the rowing boat and tumbled over the side. The rope burned her palms as she pulled it free of its mooring, then she had grabbed the oars clumsily and turned it out to sea.

Beth had never rowed a boat before and whilst she soon realised that the tide was carrying her in the right direction, she had no skill to direct her course. Out of the corner of her eye she saw the shoreline receding with frightening speed. The children had realised now that something was wrong; one of them had grabbed

Martha's skirts and started to cry. Several were screaming whilst one little girl, more resourceful than the rest, was running in the direction of the harbour and help, as fast as her small legs could carry her.

Beth was within a few feet of the basket. She could see Jamie's crumpled little face and hear his screams above the splash of the waves. She leant out, almost overturning the boat in her desperation. A wave hit her in the face and she gasped, shaking the blinding water from her eyes. Then her fingers grazed the edge of the wicker and she clung on and pulled, regardless of the cold that numbed her hands and the force of the waves that threatened to pull her arms from their sockets.

When she finally heaved the basket aboard, Jamie was soaking and screaming and Beth was exhausted and her clothes stiff and face sore with salt spray. She had paid no attention to the shore for several minutes and was horrified to discover that they were now at least a hundred yards out, with the strong tide pulling them towards Rat Island. One of her oars was gone and she had not even noticed. The prospects for both herself and Jamie were looking increasingly bleak.

'Hold on!'

The shout came from behind her and she squirmed around, collapsing back in the boat with relief as she saw another small craft drawing close. Colin McCrae was in the bows, his face a tight mask of tension as the men behind him rowed like the devil to reach her side. The two boats bumped together and Colin grabbed the bulwark, pulling them alongside. Beth reached for Jamie and thrust the screaming bundle into his father's arms.

Strong hands grasped her and half-lifted, half-pulled her into the other boat. She felt Marcus's arms close around her—she knew it was Marcus even though her eyes were closed—and she turned her face into his neck, breathing in the warm and reassuring scent of his skin. Then she burst into tears. She could feel Marcus's mouth pressed against the salty coldness of her cheek and heard him say, 'Oh, Beth,' as he held on to her as though he would never let her go. The feeling soothed her and she lay still, paying no more attention to their rescue.

Things became even more confused when they reached the jetty. Quite a crowd had gathered, with other people coming running as word went around about the accident. Colin jumped ashore and handed Jamie to Martha. She was crying as well and squeezed the baby to her so tightly that he promptly started to scream again.

'Nothing wrong with his lungs,' Colin commented with a grin, giving his wife a hug. 'I think he has survived the ordeal with no harm done!'

Beth had stopped crying, but when she tried to step ashore her legs buckled beneath her and Marcus was obliged to pick her up into his arms. A ragged cheer went up as the crowd saw her and started to push forward to shake her hand and pat her on the back. Beth, who wanted nothing more than a hot bath and peace and quiet to recover from the shock, found it unnerving. Martha pushed close, trying to thank her, and she could see the tears in Colin's eyes now as he started to relate the details of the rescue to the eager crowd.

In the end Marcus was obliged to force his way through them all to reach the horse and cart, and she, Martha, Jamie, Colin and Marcus piled aboard. Marcus held her firmly cradled on his knee, regardless of propriety. He did not speak, however, and stealing a look at his face, Beth saw that it was set and grim, his previous tenderness replaced by what looked like anger. Her heart sank. She did not feel she could bear him to ring a peal over her just now.

'Mustard baths, steaming gruel and physic,' Martha was saying, having recovered her self-possession now that she was certain baby Jamie was safe. 'Oh, Lady Allerton, how can we ever thank you? You were unconscionably brave!'

'Unconscionably foolish!' Marcus said shortly, earning himself an indignant exclamation from Martha before she fell silent under her husband's meaningful glare.

Marcus put Beth down at last when they reached the castle entrance. She was feeling much recovered, although the wind had flattened her wet clothes against her body in a manner that was unpleasantly clinging. She could feel the water dripping from her hair and splashing on the stone floor. Martha started to fuss about her, but Beth interrupted.

'Martha, why do you not go to the nursery and tend to Jamie? All I need is a hot bath and some rest. I have taken no hurt—'

'Which is less than you deserve!' Marcus snapped. 'I shall see you to your room, Lady Allerton, lest you fall into some foolish scrape on the way!'

Beth heard both Colin and Martha gasp at his tone. At the back of her mind she knew that his short temper was probably only the product of relief, but indignation flooded through her and with it an anger that was warming.

'You shall not escort me, Lord Trevithick!' she said smartly, striding away towards the stair. 'I have no need of your further censure! I did what I thought was right—'

'Almost drowning yourself in the process!' Marcus finished curtly. 'When will you learn, Lady Allerton, that such impulsive actions lead only to trouble? There were plenty of men there eminently more capable than you of handling a rowing boat—'

'My lord—' Colin McCrae objected, only to fall back under Marcus's withering glare.

'Do not mistake me, Colin,' he said, more gently, 'I am more than glad that Jamie is safe and would have done anything to see him so.' He swung back to look at Beth, who was dripping quietly onto the stairs. 'What I object to is those who are not qualified wilfully rushing towards danger and causing more difficulties for themselves and other people—'

Beth did not wait to hear any more. She stalked off up the stairs, aware that she was making an undignified squelching noise and that there was a wet footprint on every step.

She felt cold and unpleasantly damp, and wanted nothing more than to strip off her clothes and rub herself dry. She devoutly hoped that Marcus would leave her alone, for she was in no mood to endure his condemnation. She was still shaking from a combination of shock and reaction. She slammed her bedroom door behind her. How dared Marcus! How dared he condemn her when she had been doing her best to save Jamie. Perhaps he was right in that there had been others more capable, but she could not stand by and simply watch the basket float out to sea!

She peeled off her soaking clothes, dropping them on the floor and hurrying into the closet to find a towel. Once she was dry she felt much better, although her hair had been blown into a hopeless tangle by the wind and would take hours to comb out. Beth wrapped herself in her brocade robe, picked up her comb and hurried back to the fire. She had just sat down and started to tease the tangles from her silky black hair, when there was a knock at the door.

'Come in!' Beth called. She had expected to see one of the maids there and her eyes widened in shock as Marcus strode into the room. He had evidently had time to change, for although his hair looked damp, his clothes were dry. Beth looked at him dubiously.

'Oh! Lord Trevithick! I did not think... You should not be here—'

'I wanted to talk to you,' Marcus said abruptly, closing the door behind him.

Beth fired up. 'Well, I do not want to hear any more! Ringing a peal over me when all I was trying to do was help—'

'I am aware of that,' Marcus said tightly. Beth saw that his hands were clenched at his side. 'What you do not seem to understand, Beth, is that the sea is treacherous around here and that you could so easily have been drowned yourself! Sometimes I think that you have no more sense than a child!'

Beth's eyes filled with easy tears. She had had a nasty shock and now she felt decidedly humiliated. 'Well, if I am lacking in sense, you are surely lacking in sensibility, my lord!' She made a wild gesture with the hand that held the comb. 'It is the cruellest thing to censure me when I am so upset—' She broke off as she saw that Marcus's attention had shifted from her white face to somewhere considerably lower. The brocade robe had loosened at her dramatic wave of the hand and was now falling open. Suddenly Beth was devastatingly aware that she was naked beneath its slippery folds. She gathered the material closely at her neck with a defensive gesture and fell silent. Her throat was dry and she could only watch as Marcus, eyebrows slightly raised, allowed his gaze to travel up again to rest thoughtfully on her now flushed face.

'You are correct, Beth.' His voice was husky now as he took a step towards her. 'It is quite wrong of me to reproach you. My anger arose only from a desire to protect you, for it seems to me that you plunge headlong towards danger without any thought of self-preservation...'

It seemed to Beth that she was racing towards danger at that very moment. The warmth of the fire could not account for the sudden heat that suffused her skin from her bare toes to the top of her head. The soft material of the robe seemed unbearably stimulating against her naked flesh. She cleared her throat, intending to ask Marcus to leave, but some inexplicable impulse kept her silent. Instead she just watched as he took the final step towards her. His eyes were very dark, reflecting his desire for her, but overlaid with an expression of tenderness that held her still. He took hold of her upper arms and drew her very gently towards him, and as his own arms closed about her, his mouth came down on hers.

An involuntary shudder went through Beth's body as her lips parted under his. His skin smelled clean and fresh, and without conscious thought her hands unclenched their hold on her gown so that she could tangle her fingers in the thick darkness of his hair. Marcus deepened the kiss and Beth moved closer into his arms with a tiny moan. She blinked dizzily as he lifted his mouth from hers and touched her lips with the tip of his tongue. Conventional behaviour, the dictates of society, had ceased to exist for her as soon as Marcus had started to kiss her; all Beth knew was that her pent-up fear and anger had fused into something exquisitely tender and sweet.

Her head fell back against Marcus's supporting arm, allowing his mouth to drift down the taut line of her throat to the hollow at its base. She felt his tongue flick over her skin, tasting her, and shivered beneath the caress. Her legs were trembling so much that she was afraid that she might fall, and Marcus evidently thought the same, for he picked her up and placed her gently on the big bed. Beth felt the cold air against her legs and realised with a faint shock that the brocade robe was almost completely undone; as soon as it came to her the knowledge seemed almost irrelevant, for Marcus was beside her and the warmth of his body kept out the cold.

She felt his fingers at her waist, loosening the robe so that it fell back completely. A moment later, Marcus's palm brushed the slope of her breast and his mouth closed over the tight peak of her nipple, the gentle caress becoming firmer and stronger as Beth gave a soft moan of satisfaction. She was adrift with pleasure, unaware of anything except her need for him. She reached out to him blindly, digging her fingers into his back, tugging at his shirt so that she could run her hands over the hard, bare skin beneath.

It felt cold as soon as Marcus left her side. Beth rolled over, the brocade robe crushed beneath her, and opened her eyes. There was the most extraordinary ache inside her and she had never experienced anything like it, nor the violent desire for that ache to be satisfied.

'Marcus...' She realised that he had only left her in order to remove his clothes and smiled a little. She was still smiling when he came back to her side a moment later.

'Beth...' There was a fierce desire in his face, but she could see that he was frowning. 'Beth, if you do not wish for this, you must say so—now...'

Beth opened her eyes very wide. 'I wish it more than anything...'

There was a moment of stillness and then Marcus smiled too and lay down to take her in his arms again. He kissed her gently, but not so gently that the effect did not vibrate all the way through Beth's body. He was stroking her back, a soft sweep of a caress from her shoulder to the curve of her buttocks, with a touch so sensual that Beth was almost melting. She rolled over helplessly on to her back, then squirmed with renewed pleasure as Marcus's mouth closed over her breast again.

'Oh, please...'

She felt his hand dip between her trembling thighs, parting her legs. He was still kissing her when he entered her and Beth was engulfed immediately in a violent surge of pleasure that made her cry out against his mouth. A second later Marcus followed and he gasped her name, pressing his face to her throat until the pleasure died away.

Beth lay quite still, her body quiescent, her mind floating. She could not even begin to think, nor did she feel that there was any immediate necessity to do so, for Marcus had pulled the covers over them and had drawn her close to his side. She turned her head against his shoulder and drifted into sleep.

When Beth woke again it was almost dark outside. Marcus was lying beside her, deeply asleep. She looked at him, marvelling at the black sweep of his eyelashes against his cheek, the faint shadow of the stubble that darkened his chin, the hard lines of his face that were soft in sleep. She wanted to touch them all. A piercing stab of love washed over her, so intense and poignant that it almost hurt. Smiling a little sadly, she picked up her robe and went over to the window embrasure, curling up so that she could look out at the pewter sea.

Charlotte had always said that she was too impulsive, but her impulses had never led her to such a point before. She and Marcus were lovers now and the whole castle, the whole island, must surely know it, for he had been alone with her in her room for hours. Beth frowned. She did not feel like a fallen woman, for her mind was so full of love for Marcus that it seemed to transcend everything else.

Beth supposed that she was now only one of a great number of rich widows who had taken a lover, yet that seemed too shabby, too unemotional a description for what had happened between herself and Marcus. She knew that society's rules, whilst allowing no latitude for unmarried girls, were far more understanding of ladies in her position. Widows and married women were given a certain freedom, one might even say laxity, to behave as they pleased. And after all, she and Marcus were already betrothed. So, provided that they were discreet... Beth frowned again. She knew she had never been very good at being discreet. Her temperament was too open and now she wanted to shout from the rooftops that she loved Marcus to distraction.

Beth drew her knees up to her chin. She felt warm and happy and satisfied in a way that she had never felt with Frank Allerton. He had shown her none of the physical pleasure or the tenderness that Marcus had. She smiled wryly, remembering that she had previously thought herself physically cold. She had started to discover her mistake when she had first encountered Marcus in London and the explosive nature of their attraction had made her realise there was a whole side of her character that she had not known existed. Now she realised that to the full.

'Beth?' Marcus had stirred and was leaning on one elbow, watching her. Her heart swelled with love for him. She went across to the bed and sat on the edge, looking at him. A faint smile touched his mouth.

'Are you quite well, my love?'

Beth dropped her gaze. It was very nice to be called that and perhaps it might even be taken to imply that he loved her… She waited, hoping he would say so, but he did not.

'I am well,' she said, a little shyly.

'What were you thinking?' Marcus asked. His dark gaze was very direct. Beth plucked at the bedcovers.

'I was thinking that…oh, that Lady Salome and Charlotte and everyone else would not approve, and that I am indeed a shameless creature…'

She saw Marcus smile, but his gaze remained grave. 'So you regret what has happened?'

'No,' Beth said, hampered by her honesty. 'I cannot. But Marcus—do you…I mean, do you think me—?'

Marcus raised a hand and touched her cheek. 'I think that you are lovely, Beth. We are to be married and I do not think the opinions of others matter.'

A strange feeling took Beth, part triumphant and part forlorn. Whilst reassured that Marcus thought no less of her, she could not help feeling that he could afford to be hardy about the opinions of others whereas she was more vulnerable. She watched as he sat up and wrapped the sheet about him. He was still watching her, but with a speculation now that made her skin prickle with excitement.

'I wondered if you would care to take a bath,' Marcus

said. 'After your ordeal in the sea it would perhaps be efficacious for your health…'

Beth looked at him. There was a spark of teasing in his eye, a hint of mischief and something more. The prickle of excitement turned into a tingle of unmistakable anticipation.

'Well, if you think I should—'

'I am certain.' Marcus swung his legs over the side of the bed and reached for his shirt. 'But only if you share it with me.'

Beth's eyes opened to their widest extent. 'Oh! But…could we?'

Marcus grinned. 'I do not see why not!'

He wandered over to the fireplace and rang the bell. Beth gave a squeak. 'Marcus, the servants—'

Marcus only grinned at her again. He sauntered back to her side and slipped his arms about her, dropping a light kiss on her lips. 'So shy, my love? I fear it is a little late for that…'

Beth knew this was true but, all the same, it seemed sensible for Marcus to go to his own rooms and for her to wait discreetly alone whilst the water was drawn.

It was Martha McCrae who delivered it herself, in company with two maids, and their faces were so blank that Beth almost had a fit of the giggles. Tellingly Martha did not enquire after Beth's health, but her gaze did rest for a moment on the tumbled bedsheets and Beth thought that she almost smiled.

'Martha,' she said quickly, as they were leaving, 'how does baby Jamie? I hope that he is fully recovered?'

Martha did smile then, and a wicked dimple appeared in her cheek. 'Yes, thank you, milady.' She dropped a curtsey. 'He has taken no hurt, as indeed I hope you have not…'

Beth blushed, flustered. Martha gave her an innocent smile and closed the door softly.

Beth went through to the bathroom. The water had been scented with lavender and smelled delicious. She slipped out of her robe and into the hot water, closing her eyes with a sigh.

A moment later she opened them wide with a little shriek as Marcus slid into the bath behind her. She felt the press of his body against hers and almost squeaked again when he pulled her back against him. The water rose dangerously, threatening to slop over the sides of the bath on to the floor.

'Stop wriggling,' Marcus instructed, laughing softly. 'Just keep still, or you will drown us both! We are fortunate that there is so much room in here…'

Beth complied, holding her breath as she felt his hands start to massage her shoulders gently. It felt delicious. The scent of the water, the hot, rising steam, the smell of lavender and the soapy slipperiness of Marcus's hands against her skin provoked the most delightful sensations within her. When he bent his head to kiss the side of her neck, where the damp black curls stuck to her skin, she leant back against his chest and closed her eyes. When his hands slipped lower to caress her breasts, she was certain she was about to dissolve with sheer pleasure.

So rapt was she in the desire he was invoking that Beth barely noticed when Marcus scooped her out of the bath and swept her up into his arms. He wrapped her in a huge towel and carried her through to the bedroom. They tumbled down on to the big bed together, Marcus pulling her under him. His mouth took the place of his hands at her breast and the exquisite surge of pleasure almost pushed Beth over the edge. She reached for him, gasping his name. Then all thought was lost as her mind was swamped in pure delight.

'You have been very quiet tonight, my dear,' Marcus observed, as he and Beth sat over the chessboard the following evening. 'Are you too tired to play? Do you wish to go to bed?'

They had taken dinner together and had now retired to the green drawing room, as had become their habit during the past two weeks. Although they usually played cards or talked, tonight Beth had chosen to play chess instead and had promptly lost the first game. She had been totally preoccupied because she had been wondering what was going to happen between herself and Marcus that night.

Marcus had stayed the previous night with her but when she had woken that morning he had been gone and she had not seen him for the whole of the day. The servants had told her that he was out with Colin McCrae on estate business, which was only natural, but Beth had been unable to settle all day. She had gone on a long walk to Admiral's Point, had done some unnecessary gardening and probably killed some of Lady Salome's wintering bulbs, and had undertaken any number of tasks to distract her thoughts from the night before. She wondered if their lovemaking had perhaps been an aberration, a night borne out of the indisputable tension that had built up between herself and Marcus. Perhaps neither of them would ever speak of it again and pretend that it had never happened, and she was not sure how she would feel if that was the case. Her emotions felt too raw and new for too much soul-searching.

Beth's pulse jumped as she saw Marcus's dark gaze resting on her, wickedly assessing, and she suddenly thought that perhaps the previous night had not been an aberration after all. Her face warmed as she thought about it. The room was intimately dark, shadowed and fire lit, with only one additional branch of candles.

Beth realised that Marcus was still awaiting her reply. She looked up, met his eyes and smiled demurely. 'No, I am not tired. Perhaps I do not have the right kind of calculating mind for chess.'

'But you always respond to a challenge,' Marcus murmured. 'How if we were to make the stakes higher? If you lose a pawn…' he paused, his gaze considering her '…then you also lose…a garment?'

Beth almost choked on her tea. 'Marcus! No, really! Surely you are in jest?'

'What, too afraid to take the challenge?' Marcus laughed, leaning back in his chair. 'That is not like you, my love, and this way the game is so much more enjoyable…'

Beth bit her lip. It was difficult to decide, to think clearly, for her mind was dizzy with anticipation and remembered desire. She admitted to herself that the challenge was well nigh irresistible and that she might as well be hung for a sheep as a lamb…

Marcus was still watching her with speculative amusement. She met his gaze directly. 'What if I should win, my lord? Once before I won a wager against you.'

'That's true…' Marcus started to set up the chessboard again. 'Well, sweetheart, we shall see!'

Beth stared at the checkerboard squares, concentrating hard. Frank had taught her chess, but he had never made it as interesting as this. On the other hand, he had taught her a sound strategy and she was determined to use it. The trouble was that Marcus was a very good player and she found she could not concentrate for long…

Even so, it was several minutes before she lost her first pawn. She paused, considering, then removed her spencer and folded it neatly over the arm of the chair. She did not dare look at Marcus for she knew that he would be watching her and that would put her off even more. The room was warm and from that point of view she scarcely noticed the loss of the spencer, and a quick mental inventory of her remaining clothes reassured her that there were plenty left. All the same, there were seven pawns left on the board...

Marcus lost two pawns in quick succession and shrugged out of his jacket and untied his stock. Beth glanced at him and looked quickly away. He was still wearing his blue embroidered waistcoat and beneath that, his linen shirt, but he already looked slightly dishevelled. His shirt was now open, revealing the strong brown column of his neck and the sight of the bronze sheen of his skin was wholly disturbing to Beth's senses. It certainly would not help her concentration to keep looking at him. She gazed fixedly at the chessboard and moved her castle, a little tentatively. A moment later she realised that she had made a mistake. A bad one.

She saw Marcus move a pawn and his hand close over the castle to take it off the board. He was watching her with a look of amusement.

'That counts as three items of clothing, I fear, my love. I forgot to tell you that there was a...sliding scale.'

Beth sighed. 'My slippers? That must be two items...'

Marcus sat back in his chair. 'I rather think that they should count as only one.'

Beth frowned at him. 'It seems to me that you are making up the rules as you go along, my lord!'

'Perhaps so.' Marcus smiled. 'That is part of the fun.'

Beth kicked off her slippers under the table, then after

a moment, put a hand up to unpin her lace cap. She was very conscious of Marcus watching her every move, his dark eyes never leaving her face. She tossed the cap aside. Now she had something of a dilemma. Unless she chose to unroll her stockings, it had to be her dress.

'You will have to help me, my lord…' Her voice was husky. She stood up and turned around. Marcus came round the table and a moment later she felt his fingers on the buttons of her gown, moving methodically downwards. Then his hands skimmed her bare shoulders, sliding the dress down.

Beth discovered that the potent effect of his touch on her skin, so explosive the previous night, had not lessened. With a little sigh, she let the dress fall to the ground. Anticipation was hammering through her body with each beat of her pulse, its dizzy stroke making her feel utterly light-headed. And she still had a game to complete. She had thought that the wager at the Cyprians' Ball had been perilous enough. Now she had an entirely new sense of danger. Danger and excitement, inextricably linked. She slid from under Marcus's hands and resumed her seat, focusing on the board.

When she captured his bishop she looked at him triumphantly. 'If the castle counts for three items of clothing, my lord, surely the bishop is two? Can you deny it?'

Marcus grinned. 'Absolutely right, sweetheart! What would you like me to remove?'

Beth swallowed hard. Her throat was suddenly dry. 'Your waistcoat and…your shirt?'

Marcus smiled with devilish pleasure. 'Certainly…'

The rustle of starched linen filled Beth's ears. She was not yet accustomed to seeing Marcus naked and knew perfectly well that the sight of his bare brown torso would destroy any remaining chance she had of concentrating. When Marcus sat down again she deliberately averted her gaze from him, despite the almost overwhelming temptation to stare. But it was already too late. Her attention had been fatally distracted and her next move was disastrous.

Marcus moved a pawn across the board and captured her queen. 'Check,' he said contentedly.

'Is that the end?' Beth whispered.

'Not yet,' Marcus said thoughtfully. 'That is, you need not necessarily lose the chess game, but I suspect you have insufficient clothing left to cover your debt—amongst other things…'

When Beth looked at him she saw that the devilish light in his eyes had deepened and he was watching her with undisguised desire. He got up and came round the table again, taking her hand and drawing her to her feet. Beth shivered a little, suddenly aware that she was already wearing little more than her chemise.

'I protest,' she said huskily, 'that you have changed the rules shamelessly, my lord—'

'I always play by my own rules,' Marcus pointed out.

He bent his head and kissed her. His mouth was soft and seductive, spinning a snare of delight. His fingers moved to unpin her hair.

Beth's mind cleared briefly. 'Marcus, we are in the drawing room! The servants—'

'—will not come in. They are too discreet.'

He kissed her again, moulding her yielding body against the hard lines of his. Beth ran her hands over the hard muscles of his chest and felt herself tremble, faint with the taste, touch and smell of him. She felt his hands move, deft and warm. Something gave, and she realised that her stays were gone, discarded. Marcus pulled her down with him on the rug in front of the fire.

The light was pale, bathing them both in its gentle glow. The fire felt warm through the thinness of Beth's chemise. Marcus pulled the tapes and undid the bodice, exposing her breasts. She saw desire distilled in his face as he bent his head to take one rosy tip in his mouth. Beth squirmed then, shivers of pleasure coursing through her. She could not believe that this was happening, not here, not now. She opened dazed grey eyes as she felt Marcus move to kneel between her thighs.

'Marcus…you still have your clothes on—'

'Barely.' She heard the laughter in his voice. She knew he still had his boots on and his pantaloons, and he was now undoing the fastening in a feverish hurry. There was something inexpressibly exciting in the urgency of the need that ran between them.

Marcus's hands slid under the hem of the chemise, pulled it up to her hips and lingered on the bare flesh at the tops of her silk stockings. She heard him give a rough groan against her throat.

'Oh, Beth, my love…'

She felt him shudder convulsively as soon as he came into her and she dug her fingernails into his back, exulting in the power she had over him. But it was too soon to feel triumphant, for the same conflagration swept over her, leaving her breathless and shaking. They lay still in the warm glow of the fire, then Marcus rolled away from her and for a moment Beth felt cold and bereft. Then he propped himself on one elbow and leant over to kiss her, tiny, teasing kisses that were very sweet.

'Such haste is not always a good thing, however…'

Beth felt his hand brush her thigh, moving intimately to part her flesh again, and groaned aloud.

'Marcus, I do not think I can—'

'Yes, you can.' His breath was soft against her face. His fingers caressed her. 'I have won this wager, remember…'

This time he took his time, spinning out the pleasure for both of them. Beth was so lost in her feelings that she did not even realise that she cried aloud as her body shook again in exquisite torment. When she finally opened her eyes, it was to see Marcus pushing the tumbled hair away from her brow as he bent to kiss her once more.

'Checkmate,' he said.

Marcus pushed the pile of papers away from him with an exclamation of disgust and rose to his feet, stretching vigorously in an attempt to shake off some of the lethargy that seemed to possess him every time he tried to study the maps. McCrae had explained it all to him several times and yet he appeared to be utterly incapable of concentrating on the plans for the new harbour. On one sheet were the scale drawings of the building work required and on the other were neat columns of costs, timings and the manpower needed. Yet more pages gave a detailed plan of how the project would be managed and supplied. McCrae was nothing if not thorough.

Marcus poured himself a glass of whisky and wandered moodily over to the window. He knew the reason for his preoccupation, of course—Beth. All the time that he was trying to concentrate on the business of the estate, she seemed to insinuate herself into his thoughts, easily clouding out every other consideration. It was not simply her physical attributes that obsessed him, although he had to admit that he had spent as much time thinking about them as any infatuated boy. Marcus laughed with self-deprecation. It was a new experience for him to be so besotted, but not an unpleasant one. He knew that Beth was revelling in her newly found sensuality and so was he. There was no likelihood that she would consider herself physically cold ever again.

However, he had to acknowledge that there was far more to his feelings than that. He loved Beth. He loved her for her openness and her lack of artifice and pretence. He loved the innocence of character that made her give so generously of herself. He had watched her with the servants and villagers, seen her genuine interest in their lives and their concerns, and it had made him want to crush her to him and never let her go.

Marcus wandered back to his desk and picked up the letter that lay a little apart from the rest of the papers. It had come that day from Lady Salome, and related that she and St John would not be returning to Fairhaven until the spring. Church business was keeping St John occupied, Lady Salome explained, and in the meantime she was visiting old friends and making the most of a sojourn on the mainland. She finished off with many expressions of affection for him and especially for Beth, and had included a paragraph about expecting him to behave with honour, which she had underlined several times.

Marcus frowned, tossing the letter down onto the table. He had been desperately hoping that St John and Salome would be back imminently, bringing a special licence from the Bishop with them. It had always been his intention to ask his cousin to marry him to Beth on Fairhaven and he had been severely disappointed to find St John away when they had arrived. Now his final hope had been dashed with the news that St John would not return before Christmas.

Marcus took a mouthful of whisky and sat back in his chair, considering his options. Suddenly it all seemed damnably difficult and he felt a keen pang of guilt at ever getting into the situation. Lady Salome's letter, with its underlined paragraph, reproached him. He had compromised Beth and now he could not put the matter right as he had intended. The only thing that he could do was marry her as soon as possible once they had returned to the mainland, and such a hasty match seemed furtive and not good enough for her when he had intended matters to be so different. The best compromise that he could think of was that they might marry at Mostyn just after Christmas, which would give time for the banns to be read and would also be an appropriate place. Beth would probably like that but he could not be sure. After all, her first marriage had taken place there.

With a groan, he pushed the glass away before he was tempted to top it up and turned back to the map of the harbour with a mixture of irritation and grim determination. McCrae would be back to ask him for his decision within the hour and he did not want his estate manager to think he had been wasting his time. And once he had dealt with business he would turn to the pressing and more important matter of his marriage. He wanted it resolved.

Beth stood by her bed, folding her clothes and tucking them neatly into her trunk in preparation for her journey to the mainland. She had considered taking the ball gown made from the drawing-room curtains because it had special sentimental value since she had been wearing it when Marcus proposed. However, she did not have enough room, so she had hung the gown up in the closet, hoping she would return to Fairhaven before too long and wear it once again.

The previous week had passed in a whirl. During the day, Marcus was still spending some of his time out and about on the estate or talking to Colin McCrae about his plans for the island. It pleased Beth to see just how involved Marcus had become in the future of Fairhaven and how much he cared that the farm would prosper and succeed. Sometimes she rode with him about the island, exploring the rocky crags and the secluded bays with their stretches of pure white sand. Once she had been tempted to paddle in the winter sea, charmed into thinking it would not be too cold because the sun was shining and the water gleamed blue in the light. She had been frozen within a few seconds, and Marcus had laughed and pulled her to him and kissed her, and she could taste the salt on his lips and would almost have sworn that it was love that she saw reflected in his eyes. Perhaps it had only been a reflection of her own feelings, for she loved Marcus and her love for him seemed to deepen every day.

She sighed. It was that love that led her to be free and unguarded, with her feelings as well as her body. And that was another story... Beth shifted a little as she thought about it. The foolish pretence that she was nothing more than a friend to Marcus had been thoroughly disproved on the very first afternoon that he had spent in bed with her, and since then there had been several others. What the servants thought when they disappeared after lunch was anyone's guess and at first Beth had been appalled. It had never occurred to her that people might make love during the day rather than wait for the night, nor had she realised the infinite variations that might apply. Marcus had seemed amused at her naïveté and quite evidently delighted to extend her education. And there was no doubt that she had been an apt pupil.

Now, however, all that might change. Being on Fairhaven had been unreal in some ways, a paradise cut off from the rest of the world where society's rules need not apply and she and Marcus had been protected from censure. Now they were to return to the mainland, to marry and to resume their place in society. There would be their estates to visit and the London Season and the Dowager Countess of Trevithick to contend with... Beth sighed. No, matters could not be the same.

In bed in the following dawn, Beth awoke and lay still, watching the grey light filter from behind the curtains and hearing the faint rhythmic roar of the sea on the rocks far below. She knew that it would be the last time she would wake like this and she was imprinting it on her memory. When she moved a little, Marcus pulled her into his arms, his mouth against her hair.

'Why are you not asleep, sweetheart?'

'I was thinking,' Beth said. She rolled on to her stomach and lay looking down into his face.

'Marcus, I was thinking that my dreams of Fairhaven were not real at all...'

She saw that he was wide awake and watching her. A tender smile was curving his lips. 'Oh, Beth. Was it so hard to find out the truth about your grandfather?'

'Yes,' Beth said softly. She bent her head. 'At the time it was hard. But now it is not so bad after all. But, Marcus, I am afraid that everything will change once we leave here—'

Marcus pulled her into the crook of his arm. 'Do not be afraid, sweetheart. This is just the start.' He paused.

His fingers were tracing the path of her spine and it was most distracting.

'We are to be married straight after Christmas—and at Mostyn. What could be better than that?'

Beth smiled. 'I know. It will be lovely.' Despite her words, a tiny qualm of disquiet remained and she did not understand it. She wriggled a little as Marcus's fingers drifted lower and his caresses became more insistent. Her melancholy thoughts faded. The urgent touch of Marcus's hands on her body was enough to send all other thoughts spinning out of her head. He made love to her slowly, with a tender intensity that left them both trembling. And when it was over he wrapped her in his arms and pulled her close to him. Beth was just drifting off to sleep again when she heard him whisper:

'Beth, I love you.'

Beth's whole body felt soft and satisfied. A little smile curled her lips. Yet at the back of her mind the doubt returned, faint but disturbing. She tried to push it away but it would not go, not completely. With a sigh she fell asleep again, but her worries pursued her, nameless and threatening, through her dreams.

When she woke in the morning, Marcus had already gone. That was not unusual in itself. At the start of their affair he had always been sure to be back in his own rooms before the other inhabitants of the castle started to stir, then Beth had pointed out to him what an unnecessary fiction this was and he had gladly stayed by her side. This morning, however, his absence left her feeling somewhat lonely and she was at a loss to explain why.

She had barely finished dressing when there was a knock at the door and Martha McCrae stuck her head round.

'Oh, my lady, I am sorry to disturb you but an urgent letter has come from London! His lordship is about to depart—'

Beth's eyebrows shot up. 'Good God, whatever can be so pressing—?'

Marcus and Colin McCrae were in the study when she hurried down. Marcus was already dressed for travelling, booted and cloaked, and when he saw Beth his face lightened for a moment before a frown returned. Colin glanced from one to the other and withdrew softly.

'Beth.' Marcus came across and took both her hands in his. 'I am so sorry. I have to leave for London at once. A letter has come—' He gestured to the desk behind him. 'Well, you may read for yourself. My mother is in despair. She writes that my sister Eleanor has been seduced and abandoned, and begs me to return to help her.'

Beth stared up at him, shocked. 'Good God, how dreadful! But who can possibly—?' She was not sure whether her own heart provided the answer or whether she read it in Marcus's face. She drew her hands away.

'Oh, no, not Kit…'

'It seems so.' Marcus's face was grim. 'I cannot be sure of the precise situation, for the letter is somewhat incoherent. But I must go, Beth. You must see…'

'Yes, of course…' Beth stared at the sheets of paper on the desk. She knew that Kit had had a *tendre* for Eleanor Trevithick. She had observed it herself and had even teased him about it, but to ruin the girl was another matter…

'I cannot believe it!' she burst out. 'Kit would never behave so! It cannot be true!'

Marcus's face was set. 'Well, I shall find out. I am

sorry, Beth, but I must go.' He came back to her side. 'Go back to Mostyn Hall—'

'I shall not!' Beth screwed up her face, trying to think straight. 'If you are for London, I shall go too! Charlotte will be distressed and all alone—'

Marcus was controlling his impatience with difficulty. 'There is no time to talk now. I have to catch the tide. Beth, you must see that this changes all our plans! I fear our wedding cannot go ahead as we had intended, but if you go to Mostyn—'

'No!' Beth said again. 'I cannot stay quiet in the country whilst this is happening!'

Marcus pulled on his gloves. 'Then contact me as soon as you reach London. And take great care on the journey.' He took her hands in an urgent grip. 'Promise me!'

'I promise,' Beth said.

'This was not how I wanted it to be for us,' Marcus said, in a hard, angry voice. 'To have everything spoiled—' He broke off, gave her a fierce kiss and straightened up. For a moment, Beth thought that he was about to say something else, then he turned on his heel and she heard his footsteps fading away across the hall.

Beth picked the Dowager Viscountess's letter from the desk and sat down in the armchair. Five minutes later, when she had perused the contents twice, she let the letter fall to her lap and stared into the fire.

The letter had been written a week before and it was evident that its author had been in a tearing hurry as well as great distress. Amidst the invective against the Mostyn family was the core of the tale: how Kit Mostyn had tricked and seduced Eleanor, then promptly abandoned her and disappeared.

Beth frowned. She knew Kit had a rake's reputation,

but he had never stooped to seducing innocent young girls. He had never needed or wanted to. Besides, Beth was certain that his feelings for Eleanor had been sincere and he would never act dishonourably. Nevertheless, the facts appeared damning. She would have to go to London herself and find out.

She crossed to the window and looked out. It was a beautiful sunny morning and she could already see the speck that was Marcus's boat, growing smaller all the time, as it tacked across the strait to Bideford. Her heart felt heavy. She knew Marcus had not had the time to wait for her and that if the two of them had travelled together it would have slowed his journey down. Nevertheless, she felt an irrational disappointment that he had not suggested it. It felt as though he did not want her with him.

Standing there, she went over the conversation that she had just had with Marcus. Of course their wedding would have to be postponed, but... She felt suddenly chill. What was it that he had said? *You must see that this changes all our plans! I fear our wedding cannot go ahead...*

But she had not seen what he was trying to say, not immediately. She had assumed that he meant only to delay rather than to call it off. It was only now, as she watched him leave without her, that the true implication of his words hit her.

This was not how I wanted it to be for us. To have everything spoiled...

She had thought that he had been going to say something else—something more final, but at the last moment he had not. Had that, perhaps, been when he was about to end everything between them, but had decided to spare her feelings until he had time to soften the blow—when they met in London, perhaps?

Beth watched the boat until the sun on the water made her eyes ache, then she turned back to the room. It seemed darker now, depressing. She hurried out into the hall and up the stairs, determined to press on with her own departure. It was the only way to keep her fears at bay. And deepest and most unacknowledged was the growing fear that Kit's actions had ruined them all and damned forever the relationship between her and Marcus. Their engagement had not been officially announced and now, surely, the marriage would not take place. For how could Marcus wish to associate with her after her cousin had apparently brought such dishonour on the Trevithick family by ruining his sister? His parting words had confirmed as much. Kit had caused the most immense scandal and all relations between the Mostyns and Trevithicks must, by necessity, be severed once again.

Chapter Ten

'You are looking very sickly, my love,' Charlotte said, holding her cousin at arm's length and looking her over critically. 'It is all this worry over Kit and Miss Trevithick, I suppose! And travelling in winter, of course. That is never to be recommended.'

There was a certain strange hush about the house in Upper Grosvenor Street, a gloominess that mirrored Beth's own feelings most accurately. She had been travelling for four long weeks in the most dreadful conditions and had finally reached London ten days after Christmas. The capital was shuttered and silent, for everyone had left Town to celebrate the twelve days of Christmas in the country. The streets were empty and cold, the skies a dull grey and the joyful Christmas spirit most noticeably lacking, particularly in their townhouse where everyone looked pinched and fearful, waiting for information about Kit and yet dreading that it might be bad. Charlotte had been relieved to see her, but the first piece of news that she had imparted was that Kit had not reappeared and there had been no progress in finding him.

'I am sorry that you had to chase all the way to

Mostyn Hall only to find that I had come up to London,'
Charlotte said, leading Beth into the drawing room. 'My
letter must have passed you on the road. How was everyone at home?'

'Well enough.' Beth gave her cousin a watery smile.
She stripped off her gloves and cloak, and hurried gratefully over to the fire. 'They are all very worried, of
course, but there is no news from Mostyn either. Kit
certainly did not go there after he disappeared.'

Charlotte wrinkled up her face. 'It was the first place
that I thought he might go to if there was trouble—' She
broke off. 'I am sorry! You are barely through the door
and here I am regaling you with nothing but bad news!
Let us at least wait until the tea is served!'

Beth laughed. 'Or let us speak of more pleasant matters! Despite our troubles you look radiant, Charlotte! I
believe you must have some good news for me!'

Charlotte's worried expression immediately dissolved
into a glowing smile. 'Oh, Beth, it seems all wrong to
be so happy when Kit has caused so much trouble,
but…yes, that is…Mr Trevithick and I are betrothed!'

Although the news was not unexpected, Beth had to
fight hard to crush down an unworthy feeling of jealousy. She gave Charlotte a tight hug that left her cousin
breathless. 'Charlotte, I am so happy for you! You see,
travelling in the winter *can* be beneficial!'

Charlotte blushed. 'Indeed, it was all settled by the
time that Justin—Mr Trevithick—had escorted me back
to Mostyn Hall…'

'Just as I had thought it would!'

'And we are to be married in the spring!' Charlotte
hugged her back hard. 'Oh, Beth, how can I be so fortunate when Kit…'

'You deserve your good fortune,' Beth said staunchly,

'if that is what it is! Personally, I feel that Mr Trevithick is the lucky one!'

Charlotte blushed and disclaimed, 'Of course, I was concerned that this dreadful behaviour of Kit's might put an end to our engagement, but Justin—' she blushed harder '—assured me that it did not weigh with him. He has no position to uphold within the family, of course. If it had been his cousin the Earl it would have been a different matter—' She broke off. 'All the same, it is decidedly awkward!'

Beth nodded sadly. Charlotte's words had only confirmed her own conviction that Marcus could not possibly have anything to do with her in the future. Once again his parting words came back into her mind. But perhaps it was for the best. Their relationship on Fairhaven had been decidedly irregular. Beth shuddered to think what would be said in the *ton* if it all came out—the callous seduction and abandonment of Eleanor was bad enough and the scandalous affair between herself and Marcus could only be grist to the gossips' mill. She had had plenty of time to think about it on her journey up from Devon—and plenty of time to tell herself that she had to try to learn to live without Marcus. Her heart was not listening to her head; she had missed him dreadfully and her love had not weakened but her hope had, with each hour that passed.

She sat down a little heavily.

'Let us have tea at once,' Charlotte said, ringing the bell. 'Indeed, dearest Beth, you look worn to a thread! Tell me what has happened to you! I have been so selfishly full of my good news—'

'Nonsense!' Beth said. She was finding it very difficult to remain bright when she found that all she wanted to do was to cry. 'Besides, I have nothing to tell you! I have agreed that Fairhaven Island should remain the property of the Earl of Trevithick and that is the end of the tale!'

Charlotte looked startled. 'But, Beth... After you were so anxious to claim the place—'

'I know!' Beth clasped her hands together. 'Well, now I have been there I realise how different from my imaginings was the reality! I will tell you about it all some time, Charlotte, but not now if you will forgive me. I am a little tired.'

'Of course.' Charlotte frowned a little as she watched Beth's face. 'But, Beth, I thought that Lord Trevithick was intending to ask you—'

'Let us not speak of that now,' Beth said hastily. She had no desire to explain the complexities of her stay on Fairhaven to Charlotte. 'The matter of Kit and Eleanor is surely more pressing...'

The tea arrived at that moment and Beth was relieved when Charlotte appeared distracted, although sorry to bring the frown back to her cousin's face with thoughts of Kit's disappearance. Charlotte pressed her hands together distressfully.

'Oh, Beth, is it not terrible? I came up from Mostyn Hall as soon as Gough informed me, although I do not know what good I can do here! How could Kit ruin and abandon the poor child? I can scarcely believe it of him!'

'But is it certain?' Beth enquired, accepting the cup of tea Charlotte handed her. She was glad to be speaking of someone else's affairs rather than her own, even if they were so bleak. 'I simply cannot believe that Kit would seduce and desert an innocent girl!'

Charlotte looked dubious. 'Oh, but it is worse than that apparently! Eleanor claims that they are married!'

'Is that worse?' Beth asked, a little bitterly. She saw

Charlotte give her a curious look and said hastily, 'At least Miss Trevithick does not have the shame of being ruined—'

'No, but such a scandalous marriage!' Charlotte looked as though she was about to cry. 'And then to desert her and disappear only a day later! I cannot believe he could be so dishonourable!'

Beth put down her teacup and came across to take Charlotte's cold hands in hers. 'He is not! Something must have happened to him that we do not yet know—'

'That could be even worse!' Charlotte clutched Beth's hands. 'Needless to say, I have had Gough look everywhere, but to no avail! Oh, Beth!'

Beth sat down beside her. 'You had best tell me the whole story,' she said. 'I may not be able to think of anything new, but at least I can try!'

The tea had gone cold and a fresh pot had been delivered before Charlotte had finished the tale. Much of it was third-hand from Justin, who had apparently heard the whole from Marcus, who had in turn spoken to his sister. It seemed that six weeks before, Eleanor Trevithick had taken exception to the man that her mother had indicated she should marry and had foolishly fled to Kit for help. According to Eleanor, they had been married by special licence and Kit had abandoned her the very next day. Since then there had been no word from him and Eleanor had returned to Trevithick House, heartbroken and disgraced.

'The Viscountess has been most intemperate in her condemnation,' Charlotte said, with a little sniff. Her tragic blue eyes met Beth's. 'I cannot believe that she has helped her daughter's cause by speaking as she has done! Why, the entire *ton* is aware of all the intimate details, even down to why there can be no annulment!'

Beth raised her eyebrows expressively. 'Oh, dear, poor Eleanor! I suppose we must be grateful that most people are out of town now, and the scandal must surely die down through lack of interest!'

Charlotte smoothed her dress with nervous fingers. 'Justin feels that matters will improve now that the Earl has returned, for he and his sister are close. But if we cannot find Kit I cannot see what else can be done—' Her voice broke on a sob. Beth pressed her hands.

'Oh, Charlotte, do not! All will be well, I am convinced of it!'

She was not, but she knew that it would do her cousin no good to sink into a fit of the dismals.

'Excuse me, my lady.' Carrick was in the doorway. 'Mr Justin Trevithick has called.'

Beth jumped, terror coursing through her. On no account could she face seeing Justin, for he would undoubtedly bring news of Marcus and just at the moment Beth did not feel strong enough to hear it. She saw Charlotte's face brighten immediately and knew her own had lost what little colour it had. She got to her feet.

'Oh, excuse me, Charlotte! I have not yet washed the journey off and am in sore need of a rest! Please give Mr Trevithick my best wishes.'

She saw Charlotte's look of amazement as she sped from the room with just a whisper of time to spare before Justin came in. Once in her bedroom, she collapsed on the bed and tried to still her trembling. It was going to be decidedly difficult if Justin persisted in calling on Charlotte every day, as her cousin had intimated he did. Even now he would be aware that she had returned from Fairhaven and he would certainly tell Marcus.

Beth lay back against her pillows. On the journey up from Devon she had decided that she must not see

Marcus again. There were a hundred good reasons that said that this was the best course of action. Firstly there was Kit's behaviour, which had destroyed even the remote possibility of an alliance between the two families. Unlike Justin, Marcus *did* have a position to uphold within the Trevithick family and that made any link he might have with the Mostyns quite untenable. Once Beth had accepted the truth of this, any remaining hope she had harboured of marrying Marcus had died a swift death. She had only to remind herself of what he had said that last morning on Fairhaven, to know that there was no hope. Yet the irony was that there was now a reason why marriage might be even more desirable...

Beth closed her eyes. She loved Marcus too much to torture herself with seeing him when she could not have him. The thought of meeting him, talking to him and agreeing that they must part was exquisitely painful to her. She had already decided that once she had done the best she could to help with the search for Kit, and had given Charlotte the moral support she needed, she would return to Mostyn Hall. It would be a strange and lonely January without either of her cousins, but at least Charlotte had Justin to look after her now... Beth impatiently dashed away a tear that persisted in squeezing from under her eyelids. She had never felt sorry for herself in all her life and she did not intend to start now.

The following morning, rather than feeling an improvement from having a good night's rest, Beth felt so sick that she could scarcely raise her head from the pillow. Charlotte came to see her, most concerned, and Beth felt quite angry with herself for adding to her cousin's troubles.

'It is nothing serious,' she croaked, in answer to

Charlotte's anxious enquiry. 'I shall rest here today and be as right as rain by the evening!'

Charlotte was wearing a smart walking dress and confessed shyly that she had started to venture out a little with Justin as her escort. London was quiet and the crowds were small and not too frightening. Beth watched her go with pleasure and not a little envy, then turned over and fell asleep immediately.

She awoke in the middle of the afternoon, uncertain just what had disturbed her, until she heard a familiar voice down in the hall.

'I understand that Lady Allerton has returned to town?'

Marcus! Beth struggled to sit up, then changed her mind and lay very still, as though her immobility might actually convince him that she was not in the house at all. She knew Marcus was perfectly capable of walking right into her bedroom—he had done so often enough, after all, albeit in Fairhaven, not London. She held her breath as the butler replied.

'Lady Allerton is resting after her journey and has asked not to be disturbed, my lord. I will tell her that you called.'

'Please do so.' Beth could read a wealth of displeasure in Marcus's tone. 'Pray tell her that I will call on her tomorrow.'

She did not relax until the door had closed behind him, when she slid supine beneath the covers and lay trembling. So Marcus had come to find her, as she might have imagined he would do. Beth knew Marcus was not the sort of man to ignore a difficult situation and hope it would just go away. He was far too honourable for that. He would deem it his duty to see her and tell her that their betrothal must end. It was a private matter between the two of them, for the engagement had never been officially announced, or at least only on Fairhaven. She could leave the island in Marcus's care, could write to Lady Salome explaining that family circumstances prevented the marriage, and could then return to Mostyn Hall and forget the whole thing. Except that she could not. For in addition to her feelings for Marcus, which would not simply go away, there would soon be a very real reminder of what had happened between them…

Beth groaned and rolled over in the bed. In her heart she knew it was going to be hopeless to try to avoid Marcus but just at the moment she did not feel she had the strength to face him, and certainly not to keep secrets from him.

In the evening Beth managed to struggle from her bed but as soon as she joined Charlotte for dinner she realised that she could not bear to eat a mouthful and promptly retired to the drawing room. Charlotte reported that Gough had no further news of Kit's whereabouts; he had sent word to all the ports but to no avail and none of Kit's friends claimed to have seen him for well over two months. It appeared that he had vanished into thin air.

'Justin says that his cousin the Earl is most anxious to see you, Beth,' Charlotte said, when they had fruitlessly discussed Kit's disappearance for half an hour. 'Apparently Lord Trevithick called here earlier—'

'I heard him,' Beth said hurriedly. 'Unfortunately, I did not feel well enough to receive visitors.'

Charlotte was looking at her thoughtfully. 'Well, perhaps tomorrow? It may help in the hunt for Kit if we share our information.'

Beth shook her head stubbornly. 'I do not wish to see Lord Trevithick, Charlotte. I will not be at home.'

A frown furrowed Charlotte's brow. 'But, Beth, why—?'

'Please...' To her horror, Beth felt the weak tears rise in her throat. 'I do not wish to speak of Lord Trevithick!' And once again she hurried from the room before Charlotte could remonstrate with her.

On the next day she was as good as her word. When Marcus called she refused to see him and had the satisfaction if hearing him storm from the house, slamming the door behind him. Beth knew she was being cowardly in avoiding him, and when Charlotte returned from her walk with Justin, she told Beth so in no uncertain terms.

'As though things were not difficult enough as they are,' Charlotte scolded. 'Really, Beth, have you quarrelled with Trevithick again? Because, if so—'

'Please!' Beth said quickly. 'Charlotte, please do not!'

In desperation she put on her coat, hat and gloves and called the carriage to take her to Gough's chambers in Holborn. The man of business had nothing new to impart, but at least Beth felt that she was doing something useful and it took her away from Charlotte's too-perceptive questioning.

It was as she was leaving the building that she saw the Earl of Trevithick across the street, with Eleanor by his side. Beth's heart began to race. Just seeing him again was dreadful. He looked tired and worn and Beth wanted to rush across the street and fling herself into his arms.

They were taking a farewell of a gentleman whom Beth took to be the Earl's man of business, Gower. She had forgotten that he and Gough had rooms so close to one another and cursed herself for not thinking of it. Even as she made to turn away, Marcus saw her, exchanged a quick word with Eleanor and then set off across the street towards her. Quick as a flash, Beth jumped into her coach, without even pausing to thank Gough for his help. She was aware of similar looks of astonishment on the faces of both Gough and Marcus, though Marcus's look was decidedly more threatening. Before she could give the order to drive off, he had swung open the carriage door.

'Lady Allerton!'

Beth adopted her most haughty tone. It was the only way she could keep her voice from shaking.

'Lord Trevithick?'

Marcus was looking puzzled and annoyed. It made Beth want to cry.

'Will you step down and speak with me, ma'am?'

'No!' Beth snapped. 'I do not wish to, my lord!'

She saw Marcus flinch and it gave her a pain inside. He still looked more bewildered than angry, which only made Beth feel worse about the way she was treating him.

'Is this because of what has happened, ma'am?' he asked with constraint. 'Your cousin's behaviour—'

'It has nothing to do with that!' Beth said stonily. She wished that he would not persevere in questioning her, for she was sure that she would burst into tears in a moment.

'Then it must be the change in our own circumstances,' Marcus persisted, running a hand through his tumbled dark hair. He looked cross and confused. 'You have every right to be angry at the changes this has necessitated, Beth, but at the least let us discuss the matter.'

Although it was only what Beth had expected, the confirmation hit her like a blow. She tried to tell herself that it was no surprise, that she had known since Fairhaven that Marcus no longer wished them to marry, but she could not be reasonable about it. She felt herself shake with the shock and misery.

'I do not believe that we can speak with each other again, Lord Trevithick,' she said, as firmly as she could. She avoided Marcus's eye. 'It would not be appropriate!'

She saw his gaze narrow furiously on her. 'Inappropriate, ma'am? I never heard such nonsense! Shall I remind you just how inappropriate your behaviour has been with me?'

Beth shrank back. 'I would be obliged if you would leave me alone, sir! We have nothing more to say to each other!'

For what seemed like an age Marcus's gaze searched her face, then he stood back abruptly. 'Very well! You always were very attached to the idea of the feud between our families, were you not? If you are determined to pursue it, then I shall not oppose you! Good day to you, ma'am!'

The door swung closed. Beth leant back against the cushions and closed her eyes, but the tears slid out from beneath her lids. She had burned her boats now and, although she knew there was no alternative, she felt more desolate than she had ever done before.

Beth was down early for breakfast the next day, for she was intending to tell Charlotte of her plan to return to Mostyn Hall. It was the second week of January and seemed an appropriate enough time for a new start, except that it was not always possible to leave the past behind entirely. Beth needed no reminder that she would

be taking a substantial keepsake of the past few months
with her.

Her cousin was already at the table, looking fresh and
pretty in a yellow and white striped dress, her hair confined in a matching bandeau. Her face was radiant and
Beth felt decidedly wan in comparison. She slid into the
seat opposite.

'Charlotte,' she began, 'I have decided to go back to
Mostyn tomorrow—' She broke off as Charlotte lifted
the lid off one if the serving dishes and placed it carefully on the sideboard behind. Beth stared at the devilled
kidneys with fascinated repulsion.

'It always was Kit's favourite,' Charlotte was saying
despondently, 'and I had no heart to tell Cook that I
could not eat it. I believe that the servants are as upset
as we are over Kit's unaccountable disappearance—'

Feeling an uprush of nausea, Beth pressed a hand over
her mouth and got hastily to her feet. 'Excuse me,
Charlotte!'

She only just managed to gain the shelter of her room
in time; after she had been sick, she washed her face
and peered dispiritedly at her reflection in the mirror.
She looked dreadful, her face as pasty as parchment and
her hair hanging damp and lifeless about her face. She
still felt sick and dizzy, and went over to the bed to lie
down.

There was a knock at the door.

'Beth?'

Beth closed her eyes in despair. She felt too wretched
to curse the kind nature that prompted Charlotte to check
up on her, but she would have given anything for her
cousin not to see her just now. But it was too late.
Charlotte had opened the bedroom door and was ad-

vancing towards the bed with a determined expression.
She sat down next to Beth with a soft hush of silk skirts.

'Beth, how long have you been sick like this?'

Beth looked at her cousin and swiftly away. There was
a knowledge in Charlotte's eyes that meant that she
needed no explanations. With a sinking heart Beth acknowledged that she would never lie to her anyway, not
to Charlotte, her dearest friend.

'Only a few days,' Beth said weakly. 'I feel
wretched.' A tear squeezed from the corner of each eye
and slid down her cheeks. Charlotte took her hand.

'You will feel better soon,' Charlotte said, in a practical voice. 'After twelve weeks the sickness generally
improves—'

'Charlotte—'

Charlotte shook her head slightly. 'Oh, Beth, I may
not have had any children of my own yet, but I saw
many born on campaign! I know about all sorts of
things, from how to deliver a baby to the best cures for
the morning sickness—'

'Not just the morning!' Beth said dolefully.

Charlotte smiled. 'No, well, it takes some people that
way, unfortunately! But there are remedies.' She leant
forward and gave her cousin a gentle hug. 'Thank you
for not trying to pretend that you had travel sickness, or
had eaten something disagreeable...'

Beth burst into tears. 'Oh, Charlotte...'

'I know.' Her cousin gentled her.

'I'm so unhappy and confused! I cry all the time and
I hate it!'

Charlotte laughed a little shakily. 'Yes, it is so unlike
you! It was one of the first things that alerted me—that
and your persistent refusal to speak of Lord Trevithick!

Beth…' she put her cousin away from her a little '…what happened?'

Beth sniffed, reaching for a handkerchief. 'I would have thought that that was obvious, Charlotte!'

'Yes, well…I mean…' Charlotte hesitated. 'But how…?'

Beth sighed. 'I am sorry, Charlotte. I did not mean to be flippant! Marcus did not seduce me, if that is what you mean.' A shade of colour came into her pale face. 'It just happened. I became his mistress… I chose to do so, there was no coercion! Quite the reverse…'

Charlotte frowned. 'But I thought—we all thought— that Lord Trevithick intended marriage! Justin was quite certain of it.'

Beth winced. 'Well, we are betrothed, or at least we were—' She stopped and started again. 'Marcus always intended that we should be married on Fairhaven, but then his cousin the vicar was absent, so it could not be. So then we planned to marry at Mostyn after Christmas—' she swallowed a sob '—but now this business with Kit and Eleanor has ruined our plans and we are not to marry after all and I certainly did not intend—' She gestured vaguely.

'Your planning does not seem very good all round!' Charlotte said drily. 'And I would venture that you have not even told Trevithick that you are increasing! *That* is why you keep avoiding him.'

Beth clutched at the bedspread. 'You will not tell him—'

'No,' Charlotte said, sounding sterner than Beth had heard her in a long time. 'You will tell him yourself!'

Beth shook her head. Her eyes sought Charlotte's. 'Oh, Lottie, I cannot. Not because I am afraid—' she spoke quickly as she saw Charlotte was about to interrupt '—but because I know he will insist on marrying me! He is too honourable to do otherwise!'

'So I should hope—'

'No, please!' Beth twitched the material between her fingers. 'I could not bear to be married to Marcus simply because of the baby! I love him so much and I would always be thinking that he had only proposed to save my reputation!'

Charlotte frowned. 'Beth, you are not thinking straight! Marcus has already proposed to you—why, you were betrothed on Fairhaven! Of course he wants to marry you! There is no difficulty—'

Beth shook her head. 'Yes, there is! The matter of Kit's dishonour—'

'Oh, fie!' Charlotte was starting to look really cross now. 'Are you to martyr yourself because of my foolish brother? I know it is the most monstrous scandal, but it is not your fault!'

Beth turned her face away. 'You said yourself that someone in Trevithick's position, with the honour of his family to uphold, could not possibly even speak with us any more, let alone consider a marriage alliance!'

'I…' Charlotte hesitated. 'I know that I said that before, but this puts a different complexion on the matter…' She fell silent.

Beth turned her head tiredly on the pillow. 'No, you were correct, Charlotte. Before he left Fairhaven, Marcus told me that the marriage could not go ahead. There is no more to be said!'

Charlotte put her hands on her hips. 'Have you discussed this properly with him, Beth? I thought that you had not even done the Earl the courtesy of seeing him!'

'I have told Marcus that I do not want to see him ever again—' Beth's voice broke on the words. 'It is better this way! I cannot see him again, for I would not be able to keep the secret of my condition from him!'

Charlotte looked stubborn, but she did not argue. 'So what will you do?' she asked quietly, after a moment.

Beth looked at her defiantly. 'I shall go back to Devon just as soon as I can manage it. Tomorrow, perhaps, if I am well enough to travel! There is nothing I can do to help find Kit, and should Marcus discover my situation…'

'Beth, he find out soon enough! You cannot hope to give birth to Marcus Trevithick's child without the most immense scandal!'

Beth looked mulish. 'I shall deal with that as and when it happens!'

Charlotte got to her feet. 'Well, we shall see. For myself, I think you are speaking a deal of nonsense, but we shall not quarrel now! I will go to fetch you some dry toast. It may sound odd, but it will make you feel better!'

Charlotte had been down to the kitchen, fetched the toast and was about to knock on the door of Beth's room again when she heard a sound from within. She paused. It sounded as though Beth was crying again, and in an intense, heartbreaking way that suggested that to disturb her would be too cruel. With a heavy heart, Charlotte retraced her steps and went to sit in the drawing room whilst she tried to think.

She sat down in an armchair with a heavy sigh. She did not doubt that Beth loved Marcus deeply, for her cousin had never shown any interest in casual love affairs. Charlotte had always thought Beth too impulsive, too unguarded, and had wanted to protect her cousin. Now she could see that Beth had given her heart and herself where she loved, and was set to be dreadfully hurt because she believed that her marriage to Marcus could not go ahead.

Charlotte sighed again. She was utterly convinced that her cousin would do exactly as she had said, and would run away to Devon without seeing the Earl of Trevithick again. Obstinate, headstrong and in this situation just plain wrong... Charlotte smiled sadly. She loved Beth for all her faults and she was determined not to allow her to make so terrible a mistake. The issue of Kit's dishonour was a powerful one, but surely not enough to keep Marcus from Beth's side once he knew the truth.

Charlotte frowned as she thought it over. Beth's obstinacy was clear, but what was Marcus's view? Surely if he had become concerned to sever all connections between the Mostyns and Trevithicks, Justin would have told her. Yet not only was Justin as ardent in his attentions as ever, but he had also brought messages from his cousin, the Earl, showing that Marcus was anxious to see Beth as soon as possible. To Charlotte's mind, that was not the behaviour of a man who wished to break his engagement.

She drummed her fingers on the arm of the chair. Beth had said that Marcus had told her the wedding would not take place, but Charlotte wondered if Beth had misunderstood. In the rush and distress of their parting it would have been all too easy to misconstrue his words, and after that they had never discussed the matter properly. And now Beth had told Marcus some cock-and-bull story about not wishing to see him again and his pride had no doubt prevented him from persisting. They were apart and unhappy. Charlotte tutted to herself. Really, they deserved each other! But she could not let them suffer...

She got up and went to fetch her cloak, bonnet and

gloves. Her conscience was troubling her a little. It was really Beth's place to tell Marcus that she was in a delicate condition and strictly none of her business at all, but she knew that Beth was too stubborn to be persuaded. That being the case, she was acting in Beth's best interests...

Charlotte had never been out on her own in London, for her agoraphobia had made her shy away from the busy streets and crush of passers-by. When she had had Justin by her side she was reassured, but now she was alone. She almost gave up on the steps and went back into the house, but the memory of Beth's white face and desperate sobs was enough to drive her on. Even so, she was shaking by the time she reached Trevithick House and could barely tell the impassive butler that she wished to see the Earl of Trevithick. It was inevitable that she should be told that the Earl was not at home.

Charlotte was trembling like a leaf. Tears of fear and abject misery were not far away, but she drew herself up and said:

'Indeed? Tell Lord Trevithick that Mrs Cavendish wishes to speak to him on a matter of the highest importance—'

One of the doors to the entrance hall opened and Marcus Trevithick came out, deep in conversation with another man. Charlotte noticed that there was a deep frown on his forehead and he looked as though he was in an exceptionally bad mood. Her heart sank.

'We have tried the Port of London and sent runners to Southampton—' The other man was saying. Both of them broke off when they saw Charlotte and after a moment, to her inexpressible relief, Charlotte saw Trevithick's expression lighten.

'Mrs Cavendish! Pray forgive me for not receiving

you sooner, ma'am! Gower…' he turned courteously to the other man '…excuse me. We will talk again later and I thank you for your help.'

Charlotte came forward a little shakily as Marcus held the door of the study open for her. 'Let me send for a glass of wine for you, Mrs Cavendish,' he said solicitously. 'You look somewhat done up! What can have put you to so much trouble as to come here in person? Has there been some news of your brother?'

Charlotte smiled a little shakily. 'No, sir, I am afraid not. This is far more important. This is to do with my cousin…with Beth—Lady Allerton.'

She saw Marcus's expression harden, felt him withdraw from her, and put a pleading hand out.

'Please…'

She was not sure what was showing in her face but, whatever it was, Marcus's own expression softened and he took her arm and guided her to a chair. 'I am sorry, ma'am. Pray do not be distressed. Now, what is it that you wished to tell me?'

Some ten minutes later, Justin Trevithick called at Trevithick House and was astounded to hear from the butler that a Mrs Cavendish was with his cousin the Earl. Another moment, and the door of the study was flung open and Marcus strode out across the hall, his face set and intent. He checked on seeing his cousin.

'Justin! The very man! Mrs Cavendish is here and I fear I must desert both of you! Pressing business! If you could escort the lady home I should be most grateful, old fellow, but pray leave it for at least a half-hour! I rely upon you to think of a way to pass the time!' And, without another word, he was gone.

On gaining the study, Justin found his betrothed sitting calmly sipping a glass of madeira and looking quite pleased with herself. There was a twinkle in her eye as she gave her hand to him.

'Good morning, Mr Trevithick! How do you do?'

'I should be considerably better if someone could explain to me just what the devil is going on!' Justin said feelingly. 'How comes it that you are here, Charlotte, and what have you said to Trevithick, to send him off in such a confounded hurry?'

He thought that Charlotte looked positively mischievous as she replied. 'I have struck a light,' she said contentedly, 'and I am certain it is about to explode into flames!'

Beth had found the plate of dry toast waiting outside the door and was astonished to discover that it had indeed made her feel better—so much restored, in fact, that she decided there was no point in delaying her preparations to remove to Mostyn. Happily, her trunk was still out since she had not bothered to unpack it from her last journey. She did not think of Charlotte's reaction to her hasty departure, nor of Kit's mysterious disappearance, and especially not of Marcus Trevithick. She knew that she would only become odiously miserable if she dwelled on any of them and she was running for home out of simple instinct.

At first she did not hear the fuss in the entrance hall and then assumed that Gough had called to see Charlotte. After a moment, however, she heard an unmistakable male voice.

'Don't be so bloody foolish, man! Of course Lady Allerton is at home!'

Then there was a step on the stair, and the door was thrown open.

'Running away again, my dear?' the Earl of Trevithick said with silky politeness. 'It is become quite a habit!'

To Beth's eyes he looked both devastatingly handsome and frighteningly unyielding. With her hands full of underwear and the half-open trunk giving her away, she decided to hold her ground. Her heart was beating uncomfortably fast, but she raised her chin defiantly to stare him out.

'Good day, Lord Trevithick! I fear that you find me on the point of departing for Devon—'

'Again?' Marcus lounged in the doorway, making it quite clear that she was unable to go anywhere. 'You rocket about the countryside like a dangerously loose cannon, my dear!' He came forward into the room. 'I fear I cannot allow it. Not in your condition!'

Beth lowered her hands slowly. She could feel what little colour she had fading from her face.

'You know!' she whispered.

'I know,' Marcus confirmed grimly. 'Your cousin had the grace to tell me, Lady Allerton, where you did not.'

'She had no right,' Beth said stiffly.

Marcus strode over to the window. There was so much suppressed violence in his movements that Beth shrank away. 'Maybe not,' he said evenly, 'but when were you going to tell me, Lady Allerton? Ever? Or was I to hear about my own child from some gossip at a *ton* party?'

Beth's eyes filled with the infuriating tears that beset her all the time. 'Oh, do not! I did not intend…I just thought that you would insist on marrying me.'

Marcus raised his eyebrows. He took a deep, impatient breath. 'Beth, I have been wanting to marry you this past age—'

Beth's tears overflowed. 'You said that we could not

be married!' she contradicted him crossly. 'You know it is impossible because of Kit's behaviour to Eleanor! You have only changed your mind because of the baby—' She broke off, crying too hard to carry on.

Marcus sat down on the bed and pulled her on to his knee. He took a clean handkerchief out of his pocket and carefully wiped her face, kissing her gently when he was done.

'This is foolish. I *never* said that we could not be married—'

'Yes, you did!' Beth burst out. 'When you were leaving Fairhaven you said that all our plans were changed and our wedding could not go ahead! You said that everything was spoiled for us…' She gave a huge gulp and fell silent.

Marcus was frowning. 'I remember. We did not really have time to talk properly, did we? I only meant that our Christmas wedding could not take place, but I had every intention of rearranging it as soon as I could! I never meant for the engagement to end!'

Beth gave a doleful sniff. Another tear slid down her cheek. 'But—'

Marcus gave her a little shake. 'Listen to me, my darling. I have had a special licence for the past four weeks—you may check the date if you wish!—and all because I wanted to marry you so much that I obtained one as soon as I arrived in London!' His arm tightened about her. 'I did that before all else—before seeing Eleanor, or enquiring into your cousin's whereabouts, or discussing matters with Gower. It was always the most important thing to me and the fact that your cousin has ruined my sister is irrelevant to our marriage! I do not intend to let him ruin my happiness as well as Eleanor's!'

Beth was so astounded that she stopped crying altogether. She borrowed the handkerchief and blew her nose hard. 'But I thought—Marcus, it is impossible for you to associate with the Mostyn family, with me—'

Marcus started to laugh. 'I have already associated with you and I intend to continue to do so at every available opportunity! I love you, Beth! You know that I always wanted to marry you—I was in a fever of impatience for St John to return to Fairhaven, and it was not because I simply wished to see him! When he did not return in time to marry us, and then all my plans were dashed again, I was frustrated and most disappointed!'

Beth looked at him. Marcus was smiling at her with a gentleness that somehow made her feel quite weak inside. She squashed the treacherous warmth and frowned at him.

'Promise me that this is not simply because I am increasing…'

Marcus pulled her into his arms again. 'Oh, Beth, do you doubt me still? I blame myself more than you could know, my darling, for damaging your reputation and exposing you to gossip through what happened on Fairhaven…' He hesitated. 'I wanted to marry you almost from the first time we met, when you challenged me to that ridiculous wager.' He brushed his mouth against her hair. 'Beth, I am more happy than I can say about the child, but I wanted to marry you long before I knew. I love you…'

Later, when she had stopped kissing him long enough to draw breath, Beth said a little diffidently, 'I thought perhaps that you would not wish to marry me because I was not suitable…'

Marcus kissed her again. 'It seems to me that you

have imagined every possible or impossible reason to keep us apart! How could you not be suitable?'

Beth fidgeted. 'Well, because I…because we—did things together that were not at all respectable—'

Marcus started to laugh. 'Oh, Beth, I can see I need to change your view of how married people behave! And you must never think I believe you unsuitable. I love you for your openness and your lack of artifice!'

This seemed to warrant another kiss. Then Beth drew back again.

'I have been so miserable without you, Marcus! It has been the most unhappy Christmas—'

'We shall make up for it, I promise you!' Marcus kissed her again.

'But what are we to do about this dreadful situation of Kit and Eleanor?' Beth frowned. 'I could not blame you if you damned the name of Mostyn forever!'

Marcus's face hardened. 'My love, I wish your cousin to the devil for what he has done but, as I told you, I refuse to let it ruin my happiness! Justin is in the right of it—we shall end the Mostyn and Trevithick feud and damn the gossips!'

'Passionate enemies and passionate lovers?' Beth asked mischievously and smiled as Marcus started to kiss her again. She freed herself for a moment. 'My lord, you mentioned the wager and, strictly speaking, I have still won Fairhaven—'

Marcus pulled her back firmly into his arms. 'Wager be damned!' he said.

* * * * *

The Notorious Marriage

Prologue

December 1813

When Kit Mostyn stepped through the doors of Almacks Assembly Rooms that night, it was difficult to tell who was the more surprised, the chaperones of the hopeful débutantes assembled there, or Kit himself. Certainly Almacks was not a place where Kit normally sought entertainment, and this evening he had struggled rather incredulously with the compulsion that drove him there. It, or rather *she*, had so strong a hold on him that he could not resist, and being a man who chose not to struggle against fate, he resolved to meet his with a certain equanimity.

He saw her as soon as he entered the room. Miss Eleanor Trevithick, daughter of the late Viscount Trevithick and younger sister to the current Earl. She was dancing with an elderly roué, Lord Kemble, if Kit did not miss his guess, and just the sight of the two of them together made his temper soar dangerously. As he sought to keep a grip on it he was forced to acknowledge that it mattered little who was partnering Eleanor—the fact that it was someone other than himself was all that counted.

Slender, sweet and impossibly innocent, Eleanor Trevithick was the most demure of débutantes, yet there had been something between them from the beginning, a startling attraction that both she and Kit recognised—and knew they had to ignore. It had caught Kit by surprise, and although they had never spoken of it, he instinctively knew that the strength of the attraction both frightened and fascinated Eleanor. As for himself, he had cynically dismissed his feelings at first—a man of his age and considerable experience with the opposite sex was hardly likely to fall in love with an innocent in her first Season. The feelings she stirred in him could be no more than desire—admittedly strong, undeniably surprising, but no doubt of short duration.

He had been wrong. Kit had wanted Eleanor Trevithick for the whole of the past year, ever since they had shared an illicit dance at her eighteenth birthday ball, and his desire showed no sign of waning. Indeed the reverse was true. He was very close to admitting now that he loved her, but he did not wish to be that honest with himself at the moment. It would only undermine him still further. One could not always have what one wanted, and he could not have Eleanor.

Kit, whose title and position would have made him a more than acceptable suitor for any number of young ladies, was the one man whose addresses could never be welcomed by Eleanor's family. There was a feud between the Trevithick and Mostyn families that went back hundreds of years, and the Dowager Viscountess, Eleanor's mother, would cut him dead whenever she saw him. The fact that his cousin Beth was currently engaged in a dispute with the current Earl of Trevithick over the ownership of part of his estate only made matters worse. Kit had had no intention of being drawn any further into the Mostyn and Trevithick feud. Nor was he hanging out for a wife anyway. At the moment he had other responsibilities.

Even so…

He approached Eleanor as soon as he was able, cutting out the young Viscount who had thought this set of country dances belonged to him. Kit knew that all eyes were upon them, knew that Lady Trevithick was swelling like a turkey-cock in a temper and that her rout chair looked set fair to break under the weight. He ignored her, ignored the speculative looks of the other chaperones and the envious, spiteful glances of some of the débutantes, and smiled down into Eleanor's eyes.

'Miss Trevithick… It is a great pleasure to see you tonight.'

Eleanor met his gaze listlessly for a brief second. She did not smile. There was none of her usual vivacity in those dark Trevithick eyes. She avoided his gaze, looking over his shoulder to where her mother and Lord Kemble sat huddled at the side of the floor.

'Thank you, my lord.'

Kit frowned slightly. It was not that he expected her to show her partiality for him, for Eleanor was far too well-bred to make a display of her feelings in public. He was perceptive enough, however, to see that there was something wrong—something dreadfully wrong. Eleanor's face was pale and pinched, all light quenched. She steadfastly refused to look at him.

Kit tightened his grip on her hands. 'Eleanor...' he said urgently.

She looked up. For a fleeting second, Kit saw all the misery and hopeless longing reflected in her eyes and his heart skipped a beat. Then her lashes came down, veiling her expression.

'I believe you must wish me happy, my lord,' she said, softly but clearly. 'I am betrothed to Lord Kemble.'

'No!' The word was out of his mouth before Kit could help himself. His grip tightened murderously on her hands. He saw her wince, and had to force himself to let her go. 'No,' he said again, very politely. 'That cannot be so.'

'I assure you that it is.' Eleanor's dark lashes flickered again. 'The notice will be in the *Morning Post* tomorrow. It is all arranged.'

'It cannot be.'

For a moment her eyes searched his face and this time there was entreaty there. 'Why not? It is not as though you can offer me an alternative, my lord!'

They had been speaking in edged whispers until

that point, but now Eleanor's voice rose as though she could not control her anguish. She bit her lip, a wave of colour coming into her pale face then receding to leave her even paler.

'I beg your pardon,' she said, regaining a faltering control. 'I should not have said that.'

Kit's heart turned over. He could see the hopelessness beneath her fragile dignity and it touched him deeply. He felt a rush of protective desire, stronger than anything he had ever experienced before.

'If I could help you—'

'Eleanor!' Lord Kemble's unctuous voice cut across his words. 'I believe that this next is my waltz.'

He bowed to Kit, his hooded gaze watchful. 'Your servant, Mostyn. Ain't you going to congratulate me? This little honey-pot is all mine!'

Kit's own bow was so slight as to be barely there. 'I pray that you will not take your good fortune for granted, Kemble. Miss Trevithick...' He smiled at Eleanor. 'I must bid you good night.'

He watched as Kemble took Eleanor away. The man oozed a self-satisfied lasciviousness that was deeply offensive. The thought of Eleanor's slight figure crushed beneath him, subject to his lusts, was almost too much for Kit to stand. He wanted to call the man out and put a bullet through him. In fact he was not sure if he would bother with the formality of calling him out, just shoot him where he stood.

Or he could take Kemble's neck-cloth and use it to
strangle him...

He saw Eleanor smile stiffly at her betrothed as
Kemble took her in his arms for the waltz. Kit turned
away and threaded his way to the door, trying to
keep his expression impassive as he passed through
the knots of chattering débutantes. The cold night air
helped to clear his anger a little. He had to think,
had to decide what to do. If only it were not so
damnably complicated... By the time he had reached
the house in Upper Grosvenor Street his anger had
once again been subdued to cool reason but he was
no clearer on his course of action. All he knew was
that Eleanor Trevithick was his and as such could
never be permitted to marry Lord Kemble.

It was later—much later—when the butler came
to him to tell him that there was a young lady on
the doorstep who was begging to speak with him.
By that time Kit had consumed half a bottle of
brandy and he simply laughed.

'I don't think that would be a particularly good
idea, would it, Carrick?' He murmured. 'In the first
instance I am three parts cut and in the second,
young ladies...' he stressed the words '...are pre-
sumably tucked up in bed...alone...at this time of
night, not walking the streets of London!'

Carrick, who was enough of a butler of the world
to know that this was true, nevertheless stood his
ground.

'Begging your pardon, my lord, but this is very

definitely a lady. A young lady, my lord, and in considerable distress...'

Kit sighed with irritation. His first thought—that Eleanor Trevithick had come to seek him out—had been quickly dismissed as wishful thinking. Eleanor was so very proper, so entirely well brought up, that she never put a foot wrong. Certainly she would not even think of entering a gentleman's house alone, especially not in the middle of the night. Respectable young ladies simply did not behave in such a way.

Therefore it must be another sort of lady. An enterprising Cyprian, perhaps, or even a débutante with fewer scruples than Eleanor, intent on catching him. Kit had learned to be cynical. Several young ladies had twisted their ankles outside the house in Upper Grosvenor Street in the last week or two. He had even found a girl in the drawing-room one evening and she had sworn that she had simply mistaken the house for that of a friend. When Kit's housekeeper had ushered her off the premises she had been distinctly annoyed.

Kit's gaze swept around the firelit study, taking in the tumbled pile of papers on the desk, the empty bottle of brandy and the glass of the same amber liquid that stood by his armchair. To entertain a lady here would be the greatest folly. Besides, he had other preoccupations that night, plans that needed serious consideration. Plans that had suffered because of his preoccupation with Eleanor. He shook his head.

'I am sorry, Carrick, but you must turn this so-

called young lady away. I am certain that it can only
be a trap and I am scarce going to walk straight into
it…'

The words had barely left his lips when he heard
the sound of running feet on the hall tiles and the
scandalised voice of one of the footmen:

'Pardon, madam, but you cannot go in there…'

Both Kit and the butler swung round towards the
doorway.

'Kit!'

Kit smothered a curse. He turned to the butler.
'Very well, Carrick, you may leave us.'

Carrick inclined his head. 'Yes, my lord,' he said
expressionlessly. He went out and closed the door,
softly but firmly, behind him.

'I know I shouldn't be here!' Eleanor said defiantly, immediately the door had closed and they
were alone. She was wearing a black velvet cloak
over the same dress of pale white gold she had worn
earlier in the evening. It was the demure, expensive
raiment of the débutante. Her dark brown eyes, huge
in her elfin face, were fixed on him. Her hair had
come out of it's chignon and rich, chestnut brown
curls tumbled about her shoulders, spilling over the
cloak and down her back. She looked delectable—
and terrified. Kit saw her lock her fingers together
tightly to still their trembling. He deliberately looked
away from her.

'You are correct. You should not be here. It is
madness.' Kit spoke curtly to mask a variety of emotions. He came towards her, keeping his hands very

firmly in his pockets. 'Miss Trevithick, I suggest that for the sake of your reputation you should turn around and go directly home—'

Eleanor shook her head.

'Kit, I cannot! You must help me! I cannot bear to be married off to Kemble! That disgusting old man—why, he speaks of nothing but his horses and his gaming, and wheezes and snores his way through every play and concert we have ever attended! And then he paws at me in the most revolting manner imaginable!'

Kit took a deep breath, maintaining a scrupulous distance away from her. Miss Eleanor Trevithick, temptation personified. His mind was telling him to show her the door and his body was telling him to take her in his arms.

'The correct thing to do in this situation is to apply to your brother,' he heard himself say sternly. 'He is the head of the family and could easily prevent such a match…'

'You know that Marcus is away in Devon, and Justin too!' Kit saw tears squeeze from the corner of Eleanor's eyes and she rubbed them impatiently away with her fingers. 'Mama means to marry me off before they return—she is hot for the match! And I have no one to apply to for help! Please, Kit—' she broke off. 'I thought when we spoke earlier that you might save me…' Her gaze touched his face and moved away at what it saw there. 'Perhaps I was wrong…'

'You were.' Again, Kit ruthlessly repressed the

urge to take her in his arms. He took a sharp turn away from her and moved over to the fireplace, leaning against the marble chimney-breast. 'Your mama cannot force the match, Eleanor, and certainly not before Trevithick returns—'

'Kemble has a special licence!' Eleanor burst out. 'Oh Kit...' she spread her hands in a pleading gesture and Kit felt himself flinch inside '...you do not understand! I was so sure that you would help me...'

Kit took a deep breath. Every instinct that he possessed was urging him to crush her to him, promise her that he would look after her, swear that all would be well. Yet in the morning she might well regret the whole escapade. In the cold light of day she might realise that she had ruined herself—and the only way to save her from that was to make her turn round now and go home, before anyone was the wiser. Besides, even had there not been such a violent feud between their families, Kit knew he was in no position to marry. He had other commitments, matters that might take him away at any moment. He was not free...

'There is no need for such drama,' Kit said, powerless to prevent the harsh tone of his voice, cursing himself that he could not help her. 'In the morning everything will seem better and you will realise that the situation is far from desperate...'

He saw Eleanor's chin come up as she heard the repudiation in his words. She squared her shoulders. Her dark eyes flashed.

'Very well, Lord Mostyn. I see that I misunderstood you! I will leave now! There is no need to say any more!'

Oddly, Kit found that her pride angered him, got under his defences. He had been able to guard himself against her distress—only just, but he had managed it by telling himself that he simply had to withstand her for her good as well as his own. He would have to deal with his own feelings of helplessness and self-disgust—he did not intend to explain to Eleanor. In the cool light of day he might think of a solution, find a way to help her. But now her danger was intense and she did not even appear to understand that...

She was drawing on her cloak, preparing to leave and looking at him with a mixture of desperation and contempt in her eyes that provoked him beyond reason.

'I thought you a gentleman,' she said, softly but with biting sarcasm, 'but it seems I was mistaken...'

Kit tried to clamp down on his frustration. 'It is precisely because I am a gentleman that I am concerned for your reputation, Eleanor—'

She made a little noise indicative of her disgust. Kit straightened up and came across to her. He told himself that it would do no harm to make her think about what she was doing, frighten her a little so that she would never do it again. The thought of Eleanor throwing herself on someone else's mercy in this trusting and foolish fashion made his anger burn almost out of control.

She was looking down her nose at him as though

she expected him to hold the door open for her, as though he were some kind of damned butler. Instead, Kit leant one hand against the door panels and leaned over her. Now there was a flash of puzzlement in her eyes, puzzlement mixed with something more potent. Her lashes flickered down, veiling her expression.

'Excuse me, Lord Mostyn,' her voice trembled very slightly. 'As you have pointed out to me, I should be leaving now...'

'What exactly did you expect of me tonight, Eleanor?' Kit's tone was rough.

She looked up again. Her eyes were very dark brown sprinkled with gold and framed by thick black lashes that the blonde débutantes would give half their fortunes to possess. Her gaze was candid. She had more courage than he had thought and he admired her for it.

'I thought that you would agree to marry me,' she said.

Kit started to smile, despite himself. 'Is that a proposal, Miss Trevithick?'

Eleanor glared. She might be young but she had all the Trevithick pride. Her chin came up and she gave him a haughty glance.

'I think you flatter yourself, Lord Mostyn! The offer is withdrawn!'

Kit laughed. 'A little late for that, Miss Trevithick! You are alone with me in my house—'

'Your cousin's house—'

'A fine distinction! The material point is that neither my cousin nor my sister is here to give you countenance! You are alone with me—'

'That situation can be addressed immediately!' Eleanor said, in arctic tone, 'if you will stand aside, my lord!'

Kit shrugged. 'But I may have changed my mind!'

Eleanor's shrug was a perfect echo of his own. 'Too late, alas, my lord!' She wrinkled up her nose. 'I should have known better than to approach a gentleman in his cups! I see that everything they say about you is true!'

Kit turned so that his shoulders were against the door panels. He folded his arms and looked at her. Her face was flushed, her delectable mouth set in a tight line. He had noticed her mouth before; it was pink and soft and made for smiling, not for disapproval. Or made for kissing... Kit shifted a little.

'And what do they say, Miss Trevithick?'

'Why, that you are a rogue and a scoundrel!' Eleanor's gaze swept from his face to the brandy bottle and back again with contempt. 'There are those who say that your business dealings are none too scrupulous and your morals even less so!'

Kit's eyes narrowed. 'Yet you are still here?' he said softly.

He saw Eleanor's fingers clench tightly on her reticule. 'I thought...' Her voice faltered. 'I did not truly believe it of you...' Their eyes met. Kit could see the entreaty in hers; she was begging him to live up to her good opinion, prove himself a gentleman.

It made him feel sick with self-loathing that he could not help her.

'I thought that you liked me,' she finished softly.

Kit caught his breath. Liking was far too pale a word to describe the feelings he had for her. He felt his self-control slip perilously.

'Eleanor, I more than like you, but there are reasons—' he began, only to break off as she made a slight gesture and moved away.

'I am sure that there always are, my lord. Forgive my importunity and pray let me go now.'

Kit opened the study door for her with immaculate politeness. The hall was dark and empty—one stand of candles cast shadows across the tiled floor. The long case clock struck one.

Eleanor was halfway through the door when Kit put his hand on her arm.

'Eleanor, I cannot let you go like this. I truly wish I could help you, but—'

'Don't!' She shook him off with sudden, shocking violence. He saw the candlelight shimmer on the tears in her eyes, before she dashed them away. 'Do not try to excuse your behaviour, Lord Mostyn! You are not what I thought you and I made a mistake in coming here. That is all!'

Kit could smell her scent, the softest of rose fragrance mingled with nursery soap. Her innocence hit him like a blow in the stomach; her desirability dried his mouth.

'It is not all,' Kit said roughly, knowing he should

agree, let it go, let her go. 'Eleanor, you know I care for you…'

She looked him straight in the eye. 'I thought you wanted me,' she said.

Kit was never be sure which of them had moved first but the next minute she was in his arms, her slender body pressed close to his, her mouth beneath his own. Her lips parted slightly and he took ruthless advantage, touching his tongue to hers, deepening the kiss when her instinctive gasp offered him the opportunity. There was a moment when he felt her resist and he was about to pull back, but before his mind had caught up with his body she had softened, melted against him, pliant in his arms. He covered her mouth with his again, drinking deep, until she was as breathless as he. Desire washed through him, hot and sweet. He thrust one hand into her tousled hair, scattering the pins, feeling the silky softness against his fingers. He had so wanted to do that… His other arm was about her waist, the velvet of her cloak slippery beneath his hand. He pushed it aside so that he could hold her closer still, feel the warmth of her body. The cloak fell to the ground with a soft swish of velvet.

'Eleanor,' he said again, though this time it came out as a whisper. He watched as she opened her eyes. They were so dark they were almost black, cloudy, bemused with passion. Her mouth, bee-stung with kisses, curved into a smile.

Kit held on to the last rags of his self-control. 'Eleanor, if you are not certain…'

The smile lit her eyes. She raised one hand to Kit's cheek and he almost flinched beneath the touch, so sharp was his desire for her.

'I am certain,' she said.

And after that there were no more words between them for a long time.

Kit Mostyn woke up with a headache. It was certainly not brandy-induced but it was, without a doubt, the worst headache that he had experienced in a very long time. The room was moving around him, rising and falling with a sickening regularity that wrenched a groan from him before he could help himself.

'How are you, old chap?' a voice asked, solicitously. 'Been out cold for almost two days, y'know—unnecessary force, if you ask me…'

Kit rested his arm across his eyes and tried not to be sick. Then he tried to think, but the effort was monstrously difficult. His head felt as though it were two sizes too large and stuffed with paper into the bargain. And there was something troubling him, a memory at the edge of his mind…

'Eleanor!' He sat up bolt upright, and then sank back with a groan.

'Steady, old fellow,' the same voice said. 'No cause for alarm.'

Kit opened his eyes and surveyed his companion with a distinct lack of enthusiasm.

'Hello, Harry. What the devil are you doing here?'

Captain Henry Luttrell grinned. 'That's the spirit! Knew you'd feel more the thing shortly!'

Kit sat up again, gingerly this time. The room was still swaying, but he realised that that was because he was on a ship. It was a pleasant cabin, well appointed, comfortable. The *HMS Gresham*, out of Southampton, just as arranged. Something had gone spectacularly wrong. He rubbed his hand across his forehead.

'Harry. Where are we?'

Henry Luttrell's handsome face creased into a slight frown. 'Two days out, on the way to Ireland. I thought you knew...'

Kit shook his head slowly. 'I went to the meet at the Feathers, but it was to pass a message to Castlereagh that I could not go...'

Now it was Luttrell's turn to shake his head. 'Don't you remember, Kit? It was agreed to stage it all—the fight, the press gang...'

Kit looked at him. 'I don't remember a thing. What happened?'

Luttrell shifted against the bulkhead. 'You walked in, Benson hit you, we carted you off here... It was all arranged...'

Kit groaned again. 'Harry, I went there to tell Benson it was all off...'

'You never got the chance, old chap,' Luttrell pointed out. 'Benson hit you first, no questions asked.'

Kit rubbed his head ruefully. 'Yes, I can tell! And yes, I do remember we had agreed to stage it that way, but... devil take it, what about Nell! I only got married the day before...'

Luttrell's eyebrows shot up into his hair. 'Married! Thought you were keeping away from the petticoats, Kit!'

'Well of course I was, but it just...happened!' Kit said furiously. His head was aching more than ever now. 'I married Eleanor the day before I went to the meet—that was why I was going to tell Benson I couldn't make this trip!' He put his head in his hands. 'For God's sake, Harry, do you hear me? I've just got married! I've left my bride all alone with no idea where I am...'

Luttrell put a calming hand on his shoulder. 'Deuced bad luck, old fellow, but how was Benson to know? Besides, that was three days ago now...'

Kit raised his head and stared at him, his eyes wild. 'Eleanor's been alone with no word for three days now? Hell and the devil...'

'You can send word when we get to Dublin,' Luttrell suggested. 'Besides, we'll only be gone a few weeks, Kit. All over before you know it and no harm done. Surely your bride will understand when you explain...'

Kit shook his head, but he did not reply. There were two distinct sorts of sickness, he discovered. He had never been a good sailor but could deal with seasickness. It was purely physical. But the second... His heart ached. He remembered Eleanor, smiling at him and begging him prettily not to be gone too long... He groaned aloud. Three days ago!

Luttrell was getting to his feet. 'I'll bring you some hot water and something to drink,' he said. 'There's food, too, if you feel up to it, though you still look a bit green, old fellow...'

Kit gave him a half-smile. 'My thanks, Harry. Much appreciated. Is there pen and paper here?'

Luttrell gestured towards the desk. 'Over there.' He went out.

Kit stood up and stretched. He felt bruised all over. It must have been a hell of a blow to the head, but then he had always suspected that Benson did not like him. For all that they had worked together on various operations, he had never quite trusted the other man. Harry was a different matter, of course, dashing, devil may care, but utterly trustworthy. A true friend. If anyone could help him out of this mess...

Kit sat down at the writing desk and drew the paper slowly towards him. This was probably not the best time to write to Eleanor, when his head felt the size of a stuffed marrow, but he had to try. He would never forgive himself otherwise. Probably he would never forgive himself anyway and as for asking her pardon... Kit grimaced, momentarily wishing for a return to oblivion. It was a true nightmare and it had only just begun.

Chapter One

May 1814

Eleanor Mostyn knew that she was in trouble even before the landlord told her, with a sideways wink and a leer, that there was only one bedchamber and there would be no coaches calling until the next morning. Eleanor, following him into the tiny inn parlour, thoughtfully concluded that the signs were all there: they were miles from the nearest village, it was pouring with rain and the carriage had mysteriously lost a spar when only yards from this isolated inn. What had started out as a simple journey from Richmond to London looked set fair to turn into a tiresome attempted seduction.

It had happened to her before, of course—it was one of the penalties of having a shady reputation and no husband to protect her. However, she had never misjudged the situation as badly as this. This time, the relative youth and apparent innocence of her suitor had taken her in. Sir Charles Paulet was only two-and-twenty, and a poet. Though why poets should be considered more honourable than other men was open to question. Eleanor realised that her first mistake had been in assuming it must be so.

She knew that Sir Charles had been trying to charm his way into her bed with his bad poetry for at least a month. The baronet was a long, lanky and intense young man who laboured under the misapprehension that he was as talented as Lord Byron. Still, she had thought his attentions were a great deal more acceptable than those paid to her by some other men during the Season. He might be trying to seduce her but she had believed that the only real danger she was in was of being bored to death by his verse. That had to be mistake number two.

Eleanor removed her sodden bonnet and decided against unpinning her hair, even though it would dry more quickly that way. She had no wish to inflame Sir Charles's desires by any actions of her own, and she knew that her long, dark brown hair was one of her best features. No doubt her hopeful seducer had written a sonnet to it already. At the moment he was out in the yard, giving instructions to his groom and coachman, but she knew that she had very little time before he joined her in the parlour, and then she would need to be quick-witted indeed. The lonely inn, the unfortunate accident, the single bedroom... And he had been dancing attendance on her for the past four weeks and she had been vain enough to be flattered...

Here Eleanor sighed as she looked at her damp reflection in the mirror. Eleanor, Lady Mostyn, passably good-looking, only nineteen years old and already infamous, having been both married and deserted within the space of a week. She could remember her come-out vividly, for it had only been the Season before. Then, she had been accorded the scrupulous courtesy due to all innocent débutantes; now she was a prey to every dubious roué and rake in town.

Her re-emergence into the *Ton* this Season had set all the tongues wagging once again about her notorious marriage, just as Eleanor had known it would. Not enough time had passed for the scandal to die down, but she had been foolishly determined to confront the gossips, to prove that though her husband were gone, squiring opera dancers around the Continent if the stories were true, she was not repining. She had the Trevithick pride—plenty of it—and at first it had prompted her to defiance. Let them talk—she would not regard it.

Eleanor stripped off her cloak and hung it over the back of a chair. Needless to say, she had underestimated the power of rumour. One salacious story had led to another, each more deliciously dreadful than the last. The gossips said that she had eloped with Kit Mostyn to avoid a forced match; that he had deserted her on her wedding day because he had discovered her to be no virgin; that she had told him to leave because she had discovered he was a brute and a satyr who indulged in perverted practices...

Eleanor sighed. The gossip had caused a scent of disrepute that hung about her and had the rakes sniffing around and the respectable ladies withdrawing their skirts for fear of contamination. Worse, she was not blameless.

Despite her mama's strictures that a lady always behaved with decorum, Eleanor had decided to scorn the gossips and fulfil their expectations. Just a little. At the start of the Season her off-white reputation had actually seemed rather amusing, much more entertaining than being a deadly dull débutante or a devoted wife. And in a complicated way it was a means of revenge on Kit, and she did so desperately want revenge. So she had flirted a little, encouraged some disreputable roués, even allowed a few rakes to steal a kiss or two. She had planned on taking a lover, or even two, perhaps both at the same time. The possibilities seemed endless for an abandoned bride whose husband clearly preferred to take his pleasures elsewhere.

The idea had soon palled. Eleanor had known all along that she was not cut out to be a fast matron. The liberties were disgusting, the kisses even more so. All the gentlemen who buzzed around her had the self-importance to assume that she would find them attractive and did not bother to check first. Their attentions had become immensely tedious, their invitations increasingly salacious and their attempted seductions, such as the present one, most trying. In the space of only six weeks Eleanor had had to slap several faces, place a few well-aimed

kicks in the ankle or higher and even hit one persistent gentleman with the family Bible when he had
tried to seduce her in the library. And she was miserably aware that it was her own fault.

Eleanor sat down by the meagre fire and tried to
get warm. Now she had to deal with Sir Charles's
importunities. If she had found it difficult to decide
whether to live up or down to her reputation previously, she knew now beyond a shadow of doubt that
she was not cut out for some sordid intrigue. There
was enough scandal already attached to her name
without some indiscreet dalliance in a low tavern
with a man she found boring. Besides, she inevitably
compared every man she met to Kit and found them
wanting. It was curious but true—he had left her
alone to face the scandal of their marriage and she
had not heard a word from him since, yet still she
found other men lacking.

In the five months since Kit's defection, Eleanor's
childish infatuation had turned to anger and misery.
When her mother delighted in passing on another
snippet of gossip about Kit that had been garnered
from her acquaintance, Eleanor hardened her heart a
little more each time. However, it did not prevent
the memory of her husband from overshadowing
every other man she knew.

But that was nothing to the purpose. Eleanor
smoothed her dress thoughtfully as she tried to decide what to do. She could appeal to Sir Charles's
better nature but that was probably a waste of time
as she suspected that he did not possess one. She

would not be here if he did. She could play the innocent and scream the house down if matters turned nasty, or she could act the sophisticate, then run away when she had lulled Sir Charles into a false sense of security. Eleanor frowned. She was not entirely happy with either option. There was plenty of room for error.

She could hear voices getting closer—Sir Charles was quoting Shakespeare in the corridor. Oh dear, this was going to be very tiresome. The door opened. Sir Charles came in, followed by the innkeeper bearing a tray with two enormous glasses of wine. Eleanor raised her brows. That was not in the least subtle and somehow she had expected better of a poet. She really must rid herself of these false expectations.

'There you are, my love!' Sir Charles's voice had already slipped from the respectful courtesy of their previous exchanges to an odious intimacy that made Eleanor's hackles rise. 'I hope that you are warm enough—although I shall soon have you wrapped up as cosy as can be, upstairs with me!'

The innkeeper smirked meaningfully and Eleanor looked down her nose haughtily at him. No doubt *he* was warmed by the size of the bribe Sir Charles must have slipped him to connive in so dubious an enterprise. She wondered whether Sir Charles had always spoken in rhyme and why on earth she had not noticed it before. It was intensely irritating.

'The inn is adequate, I suppose,' she said coldly, 'but I do not anticipate staying here long, sir. Surely there is someone who could carry a message to Trevithick House? The others will be almost back by now and will be concerned to find me missing...'

'Oh, I do not believe that you need trouble your pretty little head about that, my love,' Sir Charles said airily. He struck a pose. 'Why, I sense a verse coming over me!' He smiled at her. 'My heart leads me to wed when I spy your pretty head, as you lie in my bed...'

'Pray, sir, restrain your imagination!' Eleanor snapped. 'I do not believe that an inclination to *wed* forms any part of your plans! As for the rest of your verse, I like it not! A work of folly and vivid imagination!'

Sir Charles did not appear one whit put out. Evidently it would take more than plain speaking to deter him. He came close to the fire, rubbing his hands together. Eleanor found herself hoping uncharitably that his ruffled sleeves would catch alight. His dress was very close to that of a macaroni, with yards of ribbons, ruffles and lace, and she was sure he would go up like a house on fire.

'Alas, my dear Lady Mostyn, that you are married already, otherwise I would show you my affections were steady!'

Sir Charles fixed her with his plaintive dark eyes, behind which Eleanor could see more than a glimpse of calculation. 'You must know that my love and esteem for you know no bounds—'

'As does your effrontery, sir!' Eleanor interrupted, before he could finish the rhyme.

Sir Charles pressed a glass of wine into her hand and downed half of his own in one gulp.

'You know that your relatives will not reach home for a half hour at least, sweet Eleanor, and will not start to worry about you for another hour after that, by which time it will be dark...' His eyes met Eleanor's again, carrying the implicit message that no one would be coming to help her. Eleanor noted wryly that he could speak plainly enough when he chose. 'But have no fear! You are safe with me here!'

Eleanor bit her lip and turned her head away, hearing the innkeeper's laugh as he went out and closed the door behind him. There would be no help from that quarter.

Sir Charles nodded towards her wine. 'Drink up, my love. It will fortify you.' He suited actions to words, gulping the second half of his wine in one go, wiping the excess from his chin. 'This is a charming opportunity for us to get to know each other a little better. Most opportune, my rose in bloom!'

'Or most contrived!' Eleanor said coldly. She looked straight at him, noting that he was nowhere near as good-looking as she had once imagined him to be. His pale brown eyes were too close set to look trustworthy, and taken with his long and pointed nose they gave him the appearance of a wolfhound. Who was it had told her never to trust a man who looked like a hunting dog? It could only have been her aunt, Lady Salome Trevithick, and Eleanor wished she had paid more attention.

She took a sip of her wine, if only to give herself breathing space. Damnation! How could she have been so unconscionably foolish? She had been set up like a green girl and now had very limited options. The poet was nowhere near as harmless as he pretended and her dénouement looked to be only a matter of time. She shuddered at the thought.

Sir Charles smiled at her. It was not reassuring. His lips were thin and wet-looking. Eleanor, realising suddenly that staring at his face might give quite the wrong impression of her feelings, looked hastily away.

'How far are we from London, sir?' she asked casually.

Sir Charles's smile became positively vulpine. 'At least ten miles, my lovely Lady Mostyn. We are benighted, I fear. You must simply…accept…your fate, my love, my dove.'

Eleanor's eyes narrowed. 'The carriage—'

'Will not be ready until tomorrow, alas.' Sir Charles spoke contentedly. 'Tomorrow will be soon enough. Here we shall stay in our pastoral heaven with only our love, the darkness to leaven…'

Eleanor, privately reflecting that Sir Charles's poetry was the hardest thing to tolerate so far, nevertheless thought that it could be useful. If she could but flatter him…

'Pray treat me to some more of your verse, sir,' she gushed, with what she knew to be ghastly arch-ness. She hoped that his vanity was greater than his intellect, or he would know at once precisely what she was doing.

Sir Charles wagged a roguish finger at her. 'Ah, not yet, my pet! I believe our landlord is waiting to serve us a feast fit for a king...'

'Well, let us see what he can bring,' Eleanor finished a little grimly.

Sir Charles looked affronted. 'No, no, my love, it does not scan!'

The door opened to admit the landlord with the dinner tray. Eleanor, who considered him a most unpleasant character, was nevertheless pleased to see him, for his arrival afforded her time to think—and time when the odious Sir Charles could not press his attentions for a space, unless he was inclined to do so over the dinner plates and with an audience. Eleanor thought this entirely possible. It seemed that Sir Charles was so in love with himself and his pretty poetry that he could not envisage rejection, and probably an audience would add to his enjoyment.

While the landlord laid out the dishes, she measured the distance to the door with her eyes, then reluctantly abandoned the idea of trying to run away. They would catch her, she was in the middle of nowhere and it was getting dark. How had she ever got herself into this situation? Her foolish idea of taking a lover, or even two, mocked her. Here was Sir Charles, proving another of Lady Salome's adages, which was that reality was seldom as exciting as imagination. What folly had possessed her to accept his escort on the journey from Richmond back to London, when only five minutes before, her sister-in-law, Beth Trevithick, had looked her in the eye and told her that Sir Charles was an ill-bred philanderer who would try his luck if only given the chance? Eleanor had tossed her head in the air and allowed the baronet to hand her up into his curricle, and had not even noticed as they had fallen behind the other carriages and finally become separated altogether.

But this was not helping her to effect an escape. She allowed Sir Charles to hold a chair for her, watching under her lashes as he took the seat opposite and pressed her to accept a slice of beef, for all the world as though this were some *Ton* dinner rather than a squalid seduction. Eleanor accepted the beef, and some potato, wondering if either would be useful as a weapon. Probably not. The beef was too floppy and the potato too wet, though she supposed she could thrust it in his face and try to blind him with it. Her first plan, to hit Sir Charles over the head with the fire irons, had been crushed when she realised that there were none. The dinner plate would be a better option but it would probably crack, leaving him undamaged.

Eleanor sighed and tried to force down a little food. Even if she were able to escape Sir Charles for a time, she still had the landlord to contend with and she was alone and benighted in the middle of the country. All the same, there was little time for finesse in her planning. She had to come up with an idea, and quickly, and in the meantime she had to lull her seducer's suspicions by flattering his diabolical poetry.

'I remember a poem you wrote for me but a few days ago,' she began, fluttering her eyelashes. 'Something to do with beauty and the night...'

'Ah yes!' Sir Charles beamed, waving a piece of speared beef around on the end of his fork.

'Oh she doth teach the torches to burn bright, She walks in beauty, like the night, And brightens up my lonely sight...'

'Yes...' Eleanor said slowly, bending her head to hide her smile as she calculated how much the poem owed to Lord Byron and William Shakespeare. 'How many other words rhyme with bright, Sir Charles? There must be so many to inspire you!'

'You are so right, my brightest light!' Sir Charles proclaimed fervently. He seized her hand. 'Lovely Lady Mostyn, your instinctive understanding of my work persuades me that we should be as one! I know that you have your scruples, virtuous lady that you are, but if you could be persuaded to smile upon me...'

Eleanor, tolerably certain that she was being spared the second verse so that Sir Charles could get down to the real business in hand, modestly cast her eyes down.

'Alas, Sir Charles, your sentiments flatter me, but I cannot comply. You must know that I am devoted to my absent spouse...'

Sir Charles let loose a cackle of laughter. 'So devoted that you let Probyn and Darke and Ferris dance attendance upon you! I know your devotion, Lady Mostyn! Aye, and your reputation!'

Eleanor resisted the impulse to stick her fork into the back of his hand. Despite his ridiculous habit of talking in verse and his overweening vanity, Sir Charles would not prove easy to overcome. And all this talk of love was a hollow fiction, to dress up his lust. He was filling his wineglass for a third time now and his face had flushed an unbecoming puce.

'Eat up, my little filly! The night is becoming chilly and I need you to warm my—'

'Sir Charles!' Eleanor said sharply.

The inebriated baronet had come round the table to her now. His hand was resting on her shoulder in a gesture that could have been comforting and paternalistic—for all that he was only two years her senior—but it was neither of those things. His fingers edged towards the lace that lined the neck of Eleanor's modest dress. Her temper, subdued for so long and with difficulty, triumphed over her caution. She pushed his hand away, repulsed.

'Kindly stand further off, sir, and avoid any inclination towards intimacy! I may be marooned here with you but I have no intention of using the occasion to further our acquaintance! Now, is that clear enough for you or must I express myself in rhyming couplets?'

The angry, dark red colour came into Sir Charles's face. He leant over Eleanor's chair, putting a hand on either armrest to hold her in place. His breath stank of wine and meat and his person smelled of mothballs. Eleanor flinched and tried not to sneeze.

'Very proper, Lady Mostyn!' Sir Charles was still smiling, his teeth bared yellow in his flushed face. 'I suppose I should expect a show of decorum at least from one who was raised a lady but has never managed to behave as such!'

He moved suddenly, grabbing Eleanor's upper arms, and she was sure he was about to try to kiss her. It was disgusting. She pulled herself away, pressing the back of her hand to her mouth. She was shaking now. It was no more or less than she had expected but the reality made her realise how hopelessly out of her depth she had become.

Into this charade walked the landlord, the pudding held high on a covered dish. There were footsteps in the corridor behind him but Eleanor did not notice, for she was too intent on a plan of escape. As the landlord came in, Sir Charles straightened up with an oath and in the same moment Eleanor stood up, swept the silver cover from the dish and swung it in an arc towards his head. It clanged and bounced off, throwing the startled baronet to the floor where he lay stunned amongst the remains of the blancmange. Eleanor staggered back, almost fell over her chair, and was steadied, astoundingly, by arms that closed around her and held her tight.

There was a moment of frozen silence. Sir Charles had sat up, the blancmange dripping down his forehead, a hunted look suddenly in his eye. Eleanor freed herself and spun around. Then the world started to spin around her. She grasped a chair back to steady herself.

'Kit?'

It was undoubtedly her husband who was standing before her, but a strangely different Kit from the one that she remembered. His height dominated the small room and his expression made her insides quail. His fair hair had darkened to tawny bronze and his face was tanned darker still, which made the sapphire blue of his eyes gleam as hard and bright as the stones themselves. There were lines about his eyes and mouth that Eleanor did not remember and he looked older, more worn somehow, as though he had been ill. Eleanor stared, bemused, disbelieving, and unable to accept that he had appeared literally out of nowhere. She swayed again. The chair back was slippery beneath her fingers and she shivered with shock and cold.

'Kit...' she said, trying to quell her shaking. 'Whatever are you doing here? I had no notion... I had quite given you up for lost...'

'So it would seem,' Kit Mostyn said to his wife, very coolly. His hard blue gaze went from her to the lovelorn baronet, who was showing all the spine of an earthworm and was still cowering on the floor, on the assumption that a gentleman would not hit him when he was already down. A smile curled Kit's mouth, and it was not pleasant. Sir Charles whimpered.

'So it would seem,' Kit repeated softly. 'I see that you have indeed all but forgotten me, Eleanor.'

Eleanor barely heard him. Darkness was curling in from the edges of the room now, claiming her, and she gave herself up to it gladly. She heard Kit mutter an oath, then his arm was hard about her and she closed her eyes and knew no more.

'This is all most unfortunate.' Eleanor had not realised that she had spoken aloud until a dry voice in her ear said: 'Indeed it is.'

Eleanor turned her head. It was resting against a broad masculine chest, which she devoutly hoped was Kit's since for it to belong to anyone else would no doubt cause even more trouble. His arm was around her, holding her with a gentleness that belied the coldness of his tone.

'Drink this, Eleanor—it will revive you.'

Eleanor sniffed the proffered glass and recoiled. 'Is it brandy? I detest the stuff—'

'Drink it!' Kit said, this time in a tone that brooked no refusal, and Eleanor sipped a little and sat up. Kit disentangled himself from her and moved over to where Sir Charles Paulet was standing near the door, brushing the remaining blancmange from his person.

Eleanor watched, hands pressed to her mouth, as Kit grasped the baronet by the collar and positively threw him out of the door, dessert and all.

'Get back to London, or to hell, or wherever you choose,' Kit said coldly, 'and do not trouble my wife again!'

The door shuddered as he slammed it closed. Then

he turned to Eleanor. She shrank back before the sardonic light in his eyes.

'My apologies for removing your…ah…admirer in so precipitate a manner, my love,' he drawled, 'but I fear I have the greatest dislike of another man paying such attentions to my wife! Perhaps I never told you?'

'Perhaps you did not have the time, my lord!' Eleanor said thinly. She put the brandy glass down with a shaking hand and swung her feet off the sofa and on to the floor. She glared at him. 'We scarce had the chance to come to such an understanding in the few days that we spent together! You were gone before we had exchanged more than a few words and I do not believe that any of them were goodbye!'

Kit drove his hands into his pockets. 'I realise that it must have surprised you for me to appear in this manner…'

'No,' Eleanor said politely, 'it is not a surprise, my lord, rather an enormous shock! To disappear and reappear at will! Such lack of consideration in your behaviour is monstrous rude—'

'And I can scarcely be taken aback to find my wife in flagrante as a result?' Kit questioned, with dangerous calm. His glittering blue gaze raked her from head to toe. 'As you say, we meet again in unfortunate circumstances, my dear.'

Eleanor's temper soared dangerously. Matters, she thought savagely, were definitely not falling out as they should. Her errant husband, instead of demonstrating the remorse and regret suitable for their reunion, was exhibiting a misplaced arrogance that she had always suspected was part of the Mostyn character. It made her want to scream with frustration. Except that ladies did not scream like Billingsgate fishwives. They endured.

'Surely the point at issue is your want of conduct rather than mine, my lord,' she said sharply. 'I am not the one who has been absent for five months without so much courtesy as a letter to explain!'

Kit sighed heavily. 'Eleanor, I sent you a letter— several letters, in fact—'

'Well, I did not receive them!' Eleanor knew she was starting to sound pettish but her nerves were on edge. 'As for finding me in flagrante, surely you cannot believe that I am in this poky little inn by choice!'

'Then you should arrange for your lovers to find somewhere more acceptable, my dear,' Kit observed, his tone mocking. 'I have searched for you in hostelries from Richmond to London, and there are plenty more that could offer you greater comfort!'

Eleanor felt the tears prick the back of her eyes. This was all going horribly wrong, yet she did not understand how to stop it. The anguished questions that she had wanted to ask ever since he had left her—*why did you go, where have you been*—remained locked inside her head, torturing her. She had been told that ladies did not question their husbands' actions in such an unbridled manner and since Kit had not volunteered the information of his own free will she could scarcely shake it out of him. Eleanor struggled to master her anger and misery.

'You misunderstand the situation, my lord,' she said coldly. 'If there have been others who have paid me attention during your absence, that was because you were not here to discourage them—'

'And because *you* did not choose to!' Kit said, between his teeth. His face darkened and Eleanor realised with a pang just how angry he was. 'Do you know that all I have heard since I set foot back in England is that Eleanor, Lady Mostyn, is the Talk of the Town? The lovely Lady Mostyn, so free with her favours!' His voice was savage. 'They are taking bets in the Clubs, my lady—should Probyn be next, or Paulet? The wager is a monkey against Darke being your current lover!'

His fist smashed down on the table, making the brandy bottle jump. 'Mayhap I am at fault for leaving you for all this time, but you have scarcely been pining in my absence!'

Eleanor turned her back on him. She could feel the fury bubbling up in her like a witches' cauldron after a particularly uncontrollable spell. Here was Kit, firmly, demonstrably and absolutely in the wrong after deserting her with no word for five months, and here was she, being hauled over the coals for something that was not even her fault! She had already found herself trying to justify her presence in the inn with Sir Charles whereas Kit had barely mentioned his disappearance. Apologies, explanations... Clearly they were foreign to his nature.

She sighed sharply and moved away from the window. 'How did you find me here, my lord? If you are but recently returned to England...'

Kit looked up. He raised an eyebrow. 'I am sorry—did you not wish to be found? I must have misunderstood! I thought that you had just been strenuously explaining that you were not here by choice!'

Eleanor gritted her teeth with exasperation, wavering on the edge of abandoning the polite manners bred in her bones and upbraiding him as he deserved. She wanted to shriek at him, to beat at him with her fists and pour out all the hurt and misery of the past five months. Except that ladies did not—could not—behave like that, no matter the provocation. Self-possession was all. She screwed her eyes up tight and took a deep breath.

'I dislike your double standards, my lord, but I suppose that a husband may do as he pleases, appearing and disappearing if he so chooses!' The words came out with a kind of haughty desperation. She stole a look at Kit. He was pouring himself a glass of brandy and his face was quite expressionless. The misery that was squeezing Eleanor's heart tightened its grip. She stared blindly out into the dusk, where Sir Charles's carriage, its broken wheel spar miraculously restored, was just setting off down the road to London.

'You may have been debauching yourself in all the bordellos from here to Constantinople for all that

I care, sir,' she added untruthfully, 'but you could at least have warned me of your return!'

Kit stretched his legs out before the fire and took a long draught of brandy. 'I am sorry if I have spoiled your fun, my dear!' he drawled. 'I had no notion that you had set up as a demi-rep!'

Eleanor made a sound of repressed fury. 'All you can reproach me for, my lord, is indiscretion, whereas you...' Her voice failed her. She could not even begin to put into words all the things that Kit had done wrong.

'What was I supposed to do?' she burst out. 'Sit and wait for you? You might never have returned! At one point we even thought you dead!'

Kit's expression was bleak. 'And better off that way so that you could carry on a merry widow? You honour me, my dear!'

It was the last straw. With an infuriated squeak, Eleanor picked up the ugly clock from the mantelpiece and threw it at him. Kit fielded it with ease.

'Glaringly abroad, my dear! One wonders why you did not use it against Sir Charles if his attentions were so repugnant to you!'

There was a heavy silence. Eleanor pressed both hands hard to her mouth to prevent herself from crying. She could not believe how close she had come to losing her self-control, nor how furious and unhappy Kit was making her. She could not see beyond the wicked coil that had enveloped her. Kit's return had solved no problems for her; in fact it had generated nothing but trouble.

Kit rubbed his hand across the back of his neck. For the first time, Eleanor noticed that he looked weary.

'Maybe we are both in the wrong, Eleanor.' Kit's tone was heavy. 'May we not just sit down and discuss this sensibly? I know that I have been away for a space, but I sent you a letter as soon as I could, explaining what had happened. And then several more, after that. Surely you cannot deny it?'

The very patience of Kit's tone grated on Eleanor's nerves now, when all she wanted was to give way to impassioned recriminations. Perhaps if he had shown such calm forbearance when he had come in, matters might have been different. But he had not. And now...

She looked at him and wondered if she really knew him at all. Once, a year ago perhaps, she would have said that she knew Kit instinctively. There had been a recognition between them, sharp and exciting, as they had circled each other at *Ton* balls and snatched a dance or a conversation when her mother's back was turned. Kit Mostyn was the type of man that all the chaperones warned against and under the veneer of well-bred sophistication, Eleanor had sensed a certain degree of ruthlessness in him that had made her feel in danger yet protected at one and the same time. She had not understood it but it had been desperately romantic—or so she had thought.

Now, though, she realised that she was married to a stranger. A very good-looking stranger, she al-

lowed, as she studied him. The Mostyns, like the
Trevithicks, were generally accounted to be a good-
looking family and Eleanor saw little to argue with
in that assessment. Like his twin sister Charlotte, Kit
was tall and fair, but where Charlotte's classical features were pleasingly feminine, Kit's face was strong
and unforgettable, aristocratic arrogance softened
only by a rakish smile that had made her heart beat
faster. But he was not smiling now. The arrogance,
Eleanor thought furiously, and not the charm, was
decidedly to the fore.

She walked over to the fire and made a business
of checking her cloak and gloves to see if they were
yet dry. The steam was still rising from her dress.
Eleanor felt as though she was going through the
washing process still inside it. And strangely she was
suddenly aware of how every damp fold clung to her
figure, yet when she had been intent on preventing
Sir Charles's seduction she had not even noticed it.
But it was Kit who was watching her now, his smoky
blue gaze appraising as it rested on her. Eleanor's
nerves tightened with misery and anger.

She swallowed hard. 'Several letters!' she said incredulously. 'Thank you, my lord. I fear I never received them.'

Kit sighed again. It was clear that he simply did
not believe her. Eleanor felt another hot layer of anger add to the volcano inside.

'Very well,' he said wearily. 'I am quite willing
to explain what happened and where I have been…'

Eleanor clenched her fists to prevent herself from

screaming. So now he wanted to explain—when it was too late! If he had arrived at Trevithick House one evening rather than catching her in flagrante in such a ridiculous situation, if he had been remorseful rather than accusatory, if she had not felt so wholly in the wrong and yet so furious with him... Eleanor shook her head. It was impossible to sit down and discuss matters quietly now.

Visions of opera singers flitted before her eyes and she tried to swallow the tears that threatened to close her throat. She did not want the humiliation of hearing Kit justify that a man was permitted to come and go as he pleased, to take his pleasure where and when he chose, whilst expecting a different standard of behaviour from his wife. She had heard all of that from her mother when she had been a débutante and had thought it so much nonsense—except that now it appeared to be true. She had had such romantic notions of marriage, whereas her husband evidently did not expect it to interfere with his existing way of life.

Eleanor pressed her hands together. Her pride would never permit her to tell Kit her true feelings—how she had waited for him, heartbroken; how her mother had made matters irredeemably worse by broadcasting intimate details of her situation to the *Ton*; how she had been reviled and made a laughing-stock, her hasty marriage and even swifter abandonment the *on dit* on everyone's lips. It was Kit who had left her at the mercy of every rake in London then made matters worse by apparently parading his amours elsewhere. And deeper than all of these things was the secret suffering that made it impossible for her ever to forgive him his desertion.

Explanations... There were some that she would never make to him. And Kit was clearly incapable of expressing any kind of remorse. He had not apologised, not at all, and with every minute that went by Eleanor resolved that she would not, *could not*, move to make matters right when he clearly did not care. She turned away and hunched a shoulder against him.

'You do not need to explain yourself to me, my lord! You may do as you please!'

Kit was now looking positively thunderous. A little thrill of pleasure went through Eleanor at her ability to provoke him. She knew it was childish but just at the moment it was all she had.

'Eleanor, I *want* to explain...'

Eleanor smiled. Even thwarting him in this small matter made her feel perversely better. It might be contrary but it was satisfying.

'There is no need for explanations, my lord,' she said coolly. 'I think it would be better if we pretended that it had never happened!'

'Confound it, Eleanor, do you simply not care?' Kit sounded exasperated now. 'Not ten minutes ago you were castigating me for leaving you! I thought you would at least wish to know the reason why!'

Eleanor fabricated a delicate shrug. 'It was the suddenness of your reappearance that shocked me, my lord, rather than anything else. I have no particular desire for us to become drawn into descriptions of what each has been doing. That would be most tiresome! Far better to let the matter drop!'

There was a pause. She saw a strange expression steal across Kit's face but she did not understand it. He ran a hand through his dishevelled fair hair and sighed heavily.

'I understand you, I suppose! And for all my anger earlier I shall ask no questions of you. Truth to tell, I really do not want to know.'

Eleanor frowned a little. She was not quite sure what he meant.

'Oh, I was not intending to tell you anything of my exploits anyway, my lord!' she said brightly. 'I have managed quite well on my own! I have had the status of a married lady after all, without all the tedious responsibilities of tending to a husband!' She paused as she heard Kit swear, and finished sweetly: 'Now that you are back we shall be a thoroughly modern couple—you have your interests and I have mine—'

'And plenty of them—'

Eleanor ignored him. 'And we may present a charming façade to the *Ton*—'

'It sounds delightful,' Kit said, with an edge to his voice.

Eleanor essayed a bright smile, though in fact she knew the tears were not far away. For all that she had manoeuvred the conversation in this direction, it was not what she truly wanted. If only he had swept her into his arms and told her he loved her, everything else, even apologies and explanations, could have waited. She had imagined a reunion with Kit a hundred times, and it had never been like this. This cold stranger, with an angry light in his dark blue eyes, was not a man she could reach.

She told herself sternly that she had been brought up to understand the concept of duty in marriage and so did not expect a husband to show her an unsuitable affection, the way that her brother Marcus did so unfashionably with his wife Beth. Her parents had preserved just such a chilly outward show, and whilst she had sometimes thought that love might be more fun, she had learned that that was not so. Nevertheless, something was hurting her and she did not intend to give Kit the satisfaction of knowing it.

'After all, I hardly expect you to hang on my sleeve in a tediously slavish way!' she finished lightly. 'You shall go your way—indeed, you already have done!—and I shall go mine—'

'As you also appear to have done,' Kit concluded dryly.

They looked at each other in silence, and then Eleanor shrugged. 'So there we have it, my lord! What happens now?'

'We go up to our chamber, I believe,' Kit said slowly. A mocking smile touched his mouth. 'As you are so determined to maintain a pretence of normality, my lady wife, I do believe we should start practising straight away!'

Chapter Two

'This is ridiculous, my lord,' Eleanor said in an outraged whisper as Kit, the candle clasped in one hand and his other firmly gripping her elbow, steered them up the rickety stairs to the bedchamber above. 'Why can we not simply go back to London tonight?'

'I do not care to do so,' her husband said coolly. 'It is dark and I cannot risk an accident to the wife I have so recently found again...'

Eleanor made a humphing sound. 'I cannot believe that such matters can weigh with you, my lord! And if you think that I will get one minute of sleep in this flea pit—'

She broke off. It was not the fleas that were troubling her but the thought of sharing a chamber with Kit. She glanced at him apprehensively. His face was set, dark and brooding, and he did not look at her. Eleanor's stomach did a little flip.

'You may stay awake if you please,' Kit said in-

differently. 'I assure you that I am tired from gal-
loping across country to find you and will no doubt
sleep as soon as my head touches the pillow. Ah, a
charming room...' He pushed the bedroom door
open.

'The scene of your seduction, I imagine!'

Eleanor wrenched her arm free of his grip.
'Enough, sir! I do not wish to hear another word
from you on that subject! If you think that it has
been pleasant for me to suffer Sir Charles's attentions and then to be subject to your scorn as well...'
She stopped, sniffed hard and pressed a hand to her
mouth. Now she was going to cry. She knew she
should not have said anything.

Kit was watching her. He passed her a handkerchief as she angrily dashed her tears away.

'I beg your pardon,' he said expressionlessly.
'You will perhaps feel better once you have had
some rest.'

Eleanor glared at him. 'If you think that I will
have a moment's rest whilst you are here you are far
and far out! Can you not sleep in the parlour or
somewhere?'

'Or somewhere?' Kit raised his brows. 'Somewhere away from you, I infer?'

'Precisely!' Eleanor scrunched the handkerchief
into an angry ball.

Kit shook his head. 'I fear I cannot leave you unprotected, my love...'

'Fiddle!' Eleanor marched across to the bed and
looked at it unfavourably. The curtains were full of

dust and the bedclothes none to clean. 'There is no one here to be a danger to me...'

Except for you. Scarcely had the thought formed when she realised that Kit had read her mind and she blushed to the roots of her hair. He smiled gently, coming across to take the crumpled handkerchief from her hand. His touch was warm.

'There is the landlord. He looks a villainous fellow...'

'You are absurd.' Eleanor found that her voice came out as a whisper. Kit was standing close now, his hand resting in hers. She found herself unable to move away, unable to look away from that shadowed blue gaze.

'Your dress is still damp.' Kit's voice was as husky as hers. 'You should not catch a chill...'

Suddenly Eleanor was back in the house in Upper Grosvenor Street, remembering with exquisite pain the only occasion on which they had made love. The night before their marriage. And the morning... She ached at the sweetness of the memories and recoiled at the naïve trust of the girl she had been.

'I can manage very well on my own, my lord,' she said, almost steadily, taking her hand from his and stepping back. 'You will oblige me by sleeping in the armchair if the parlour does not suit.'

Kit looked at her in silence for a long moment, then he inclined his head. 'As you wish, Eleanor. Good night.'

Before she realised what he intended he had raised a hand and touched her cheek. The feather-light touch shivered down her spine and made her tremble.

'Good night, my lord,' she said, with constraint.

After Kit had gone out she locked the door, removed her damp dress and lay down on the bed, curled into a ball. She did not cry, but lay staring dry-eyed into the darkness. And she tried to tell herself that she was glad he had left her alone.

Kit Mostyn closed the parlour door, moved over to the sofa and sat down. The fire was dying down now and the room was chill. The dinner plates had not been removed and sat on the table, the food congealing, and the smell of beef still in the air. There was also a slippery patch of blancmange just inside the parlour door.

Kit reached for the brandy bottle, poured a generous measure into a glass, and then paused. Truth to tell, he did not really want a drink, but the temptation to drown his sorrows was very strong.

The springs of the sofa dug into him. It was going to be an uncomfortable night, hard on the body but even harder on the mind. Which was why the brandy was so tempting. He could simply forget it all. Except it would all be waiting for him when he awoke...

Kit pushed the glass away and lay down, wincing as a spring burst and stabbed him in the ribs. Eleanor. His mind winced in much the same way as his body had just done, but he forced himself to think about her. It was only five months, yet she had changed so much. Previously she had had an artless self-confidence that had been the product of a privileged and sheltered upbringing. She had been bright and innocent and sweet. Now... Kit sighed. Now Eleanor had a shell of brittle sophistication and he was not entirely sure what was hidden beneath.

Kit shifted on the sofa as he tried to get more comfortable. The candles were burning down now and the old inn creaked. He wondered if Eleanor was asleep yet.

He thought about her and about the rumours that had assaulted him ever since he had returned to England, and about finding her in a cheap inn taking dinner with Sir Charles Paulet. He had been so angry to see all the rumours apparently confirmed. Angry and jealous. His innocent Eleanor, who had evidently not spent the waiting time alone.

Yet she had insisted that she was there under duress and there was the evidence of the blancmange... Kit turned his head and the arm of the sofa dug painfully into his neck. Perhaps it was true—but then what of the others; what of Grosvenor and Probyn and Darke?

Most telling of all was Eleanor's fearful reaction when he had suggested that they should sit down and discuss matters calmly. Kit frowned. He knew that he should have explained himself much sooner, that he would have done so had his jealous anger not intervened. Yet when he had tried she had shied away from it. What had she said—'*I have no particular desire for us to become drawn into descriptions*

of what each has been doing'. He was all too afraid
that he knew the reason why. There must be compelling reasons why Eleanor did not wish him to enquire too closely into what she had been doing in
the past five months.

A huge, heavy sadness filled Kit's heart. She need
not worry—he would never force explanations from
her, put her to the blush. Nor would he press her to
accept his account of what had happened to him and
thereby risk prompting any unfortunate disclosures
from her. It seemed they were trapped within the
modern marriage that Eleanor had decreed, each going their separate ways. It was not at all what he had
hoped for when he had returned.

By the time that the carriage rolled into Montague
Street the next day, Eleanor's nerves were at screaming point. She had slept very little the previous night,
had rejoined Kit for a poor breakfast of stale rolls
and weak tea and had spent the journey mainly in
silence, pretending to an interest in the countryside
that she simply did not possess. It was raining again,
and it seemed only appropriate. Kit had been as silent as she on the journey—Eleanor thought that he
looked tired and he had seemed withdrawn. All in
all it was enough to make her retreat even further
into herself and to reflect that her life from now on
would be a pattern card of superficial contentment.
She and Kit would preserve a surface calm, and no
one would know that underneath it her feelings were

still aching. Least of all her husband. And one day, perhaps, she would feel better.

Eleanor could well remember her mother, the Dowager Viscountess of Trevithick, instilling in her day after day that a lady never gave way to any vulgar display of feeling and particularly not in public, but when the carriage steps were lowered and Kit helped her down, her composure was put to the test almost immediately.

'But this is not Trevithick House!'

She saw Kit smile. 'No. Naturally I would expect my wife to live with me in the house that I have rented for the Season!'

Eleanor stared. 'But my clothes—all my possessions…'

Kit took her arm, urging her up the steps, out of the rain. 'They were sent round from Trevithick House yesterday.'

Eleanor was outraged at this apparent conspiracy. 'But I don't want to stay here with you! Surely Marcus—'

'Your brother,' Kit said, with a certain grim humour, 'whilst disapproving heartily of the whole matter, was not prepared to come between husband and wife! Come now, my dear, we are getting wet and achieving very little standing here…'

Eleanor allowed him to help her up the steps and through the door of the neat town house. The butler came to meet them; Eleanor recognised his face and flinched away. How could she fail to recognise Carrick, whom she had last seen fetching a hansom to take her back to Trevithick House five months before? She had been pale and exhausted from crying over Kit's disappearance and Carrick's face had mirrored the pity and concern he felt for her. Now, however, he was smiling.

'Welcome home, my lady. I will show you to your room.'

Eleanor raised her chin, horrified to realise that she was almost crying again, uncertain if it was because of the unlooked-for warmth of his welcome or for other reasons. This was ridiculous. She was turning into a watering-pot and could not bear to be so feeble. This rented house, comfortable and welcoming as it looked, was not her home and she did not want to be here, especially not with Kit. She managed a shaky smile—for the benefit of the servants.

'Thank you, Carrick.'

The butler looked gratified that she had remembered his name. Eleanor felt even worse. She followed him across the hall and up the staircase, very aware that Kit was bringing up the rear. She wanted to tell him to go away. Instead she ignored him. It was the best that she could do.

The house was small but extremely well appointed. Eleanor could not fail to notice that the carpet was a thick, rich red, the banisters polished to a deep mahogany gleam. There were fresh flowers on the windowsill and the smell of beeswax in the air. It was charming and she could not fault it. It was simply that she did not want to be there.

Her suite of rooms consisted of a large, airy bedroom and an adjoining dressing room decorated in cream, gold and palest pink. A small fire burned cheerfully in the grate though the May morning was promising to be warm.

Carrick bowed. 'I will send your maid to you, my lady—'

'In a little while, Carrick.' It was Kit who answered, before Eleanor could even thank the butler. 'There are some matters that Lady Mostyn and I have to discuss first.'

The butler bowed silently and withdrew. Eleanor straightened up, marshalling her forces. She looked at her husband as he lounged in the doorway.

'Must we speak now, my lord?' she asked, just managing to achieve the bored tone she strove for. 'I am unconscionably tired and want nothing more than some hot water and a luncheon tray. Then I think I shall sleep. I fear that I had very little rest last night.'

Kit strolled forward into the room, swinging the door carelessly closed behind him.

'It will not take long, my dear,' he said, effortlessly matching her *sang-froid*. 'I simply wanted to mention that I understand there is to be a ball at Trevithick House in a couple of days and we shall attend.' His smile deepened. 'It will be the perfect occasion to demonstrate our reconciliation!'

Eleanor grimaced. The Trevithick ball had been planned for some months but now it threatened to turn into more of an ordeal than ever.

'I am not sure that I wish to attend…'

Kit wandered over to the window. 'If you are as intent on presenting a good face to the *Ton* as you implied last night, you will have to be there.' His tone was sardonic. 'People will talk otherwise. Moreover, we shall have to be seen to pay at least a little attention to each other!'

Eleanor sighed. 'This is all very difficult...'

'It is indeed.' Kit's voice betrayed his tension. 'But I am tolerably certain that we shall pull through—provided that we do not ask each other any difficult questions, of course!' He looked at her thoughtfully. 'Do you think that is sufficient understanding between us?'

Eleanor clutched her reticule to her as though it was a lifeline. Her heart was beating fast and she felt panic course through her.

'Lud, my lord, we do not need an understanding!' she said, in a brittle tone. 'We are married, after all! That should be understanding enough.'

Kit's expression closed. 'Very well. In that case I will just add that I do not expect to have to fight my way past every rake in the *Ton* in order to claim a dance with my wife! It may be unfashionable in me to expect it, but you will behave with circumspection, my dear. Is that understood?'

Eleanor narrowed her eyes. 'I shall behave precisely as well as you do, my lord.'

Their gazes, dark blue and dark brown, met and locked, then Kit inclined his head. 'Capital! Then we may preserve that excellent pretence that you alluded to so charmingly last night. Neither too warm, nor too cold! Delightfully mediocre, in fact.'

Just for a moment Eleanor thought that she had detected something else in his voice other than a bland lack of concern, a hint of bitterness, perhaps, which was gone so swiftly that she decided she must have been mistaken. She looked at him uncertainly. He was still looking at her, with a mixture of speculation and amusement.

'Was there anything else, my lord?'

'Just one more thing,' Kit murmured. His gaze drifted from her face, which was becoming pinker all the while under his prolonged scrutiny, down her slender figure and back again. His eyes lingered, disturbingly, on her mouth. Eleanor stiffened.

'I wished to disabuse you of any notion you might have of a marriage of convenience,' Kit said slowly. 'All this talk of going your own way and I going mine might lead you to imagine…erroneously…that ours would be a marriage in name only.'

Eleanor stared at him. Her face, so flushed a moment previously, was now drained of colour. Her heart fluttered and she felt a little faint.

'But I… You… We cannot…'

'No?' Kit had come closer to her, unsettlingly close. 'It would not be the first time.'

'No,' Eleanor snapped, moving away abruptly in order to conceal her nervousness, 'only the third! It is out of the question, my lord! *You* may disabuse yourself that there is any likelihood of our marriage becoming a true one! I married you for your name and your protection, and just because I made a bad bargain I need not pay any more for it!'

Kit nodded thoughtfully. Eleanor was disconcerted to see that he did not look remotely convinced.

'It is a point of view, certainly. But not one that I can share. Maybe it is old-fashioned in me to wish for a true marriage—and a family. However, that is how I feel.'

A family! Eleanor shivered convulsively. She walked across the room to her pretty little dressing-table, simply to put some distance between them. Kit's proximity was too disturbing and his words even more so. She started to fiddle with some of the pots on the tabletop and kept her face averted.

'I believe we are at an impasse, my lord,' she said. 'I cannot agree with you.'

Kit smiled a little mockingly. 'I dare say it will take you a little time to grow used to the idea, Eleanor. And since I have no wish to force my attentions on an unwilling woman, you are quite safe—for the time being.'

Eleanor doubted it—not the truth of his words but the strength of her own determination. Already he had come dangerously close to undermining her resolve, or rather, she had been in danger from herself. It seemed that she could dislike Kit intensely—hate him for the way he had behaved to her, she told herself fiercely—and yet feel a confusing mixture of emotions that owed nothing to hatred. She shivered.

Kit raised her hand to his lips and she snatched it

away, but not before his touch had sent a curious shiver along her nerve endings. Eleanor flushed with annoyance. She did not intend to give him the impression that he still had any power over her feelings.

'I will send your maid to you, my dear,' he said, and sauntered out of the room leaving Eleanor to let her breath out on a long sigh.

She heard his voice in the corridor, speaking to Carrick, then his footsteps died away and she was alone.

Two minutes later she was sitting on the end of the bed, staring into space, when the door opened and Lucy, her maid from Trevithick House, came in with an ewer of water. Eleanor thought that the girl looked excited. Goodness only knew the stories that were circulating in the servants' quarters.

'Oh milady! Is this not grand! The master returned and the two of you together again…'

Eleanor sighed. So that was the story—some highly coloured romance, no doubt encouraged by Kit to give the impression of a happy reunion! She knew that she should be grateful, appearance mattering above all, but it felt hollow and a sham.

Lucy was still chattering as she emptied the water into the bowl for Eleanor to wash her face.

'They say that his lordship has been abroad for a space, ma'am…'

Eleanor nodded listlessly, not troubling to reply. What could she add? *He was on the Continent with his opera singers.* She started to unfasten her spencer.

'In Ireland, ma'am...'

Eleanor frowned, her fingers stilling on the buttons.

'On government business, I understand...' Lucy nodded importantly. 'Bromidge the first footman said that his lordship has done such work before, in France, for the War, ma'am...'

'Nonsense!' Eleanor said sharply, slipping the damp spencer from her shoulders and sighing with relief. She started to unpin her hair and Lucy came to help her. 'I am sure that Lord Mostyn has been doing no such thing, and if he had it would be a secret...'

In the mirror her eyes met those of the maid. Lucy's eyes were as round as saucers. She gave a little conspiratorial nod.

'Oh no, of course he hasn't been abroad or...or doing any such thing, ma'am!'

Eleanor sighed again. So now they were both involved in some imaginary conspiracy of silence to do with Kit's absence. This was getting foolish. She really must tell him not to spin such tales to the servants.

To distract Lucy's attention, she pointed to a door at the opposite end of the bedroom. 'This is really a very pleasant house, but what is through that door, Lucy?'

'That's his lordship's dressing-room, ma'am,' the maid said, picking up the hairbrush again. 'His suite of rooms is next door, and then the guest suite. It's ever so pretty, ma'am, furnished in blue and gold...'

Eleanor was not listening. She had hurried across to the connecting door, only just managing to stop herself opening it through a sudden, belated realisation that she was now in her shift and Kit might well be on the other side.

'His lordship's dressing-room! But I had no idea he was so close...'

The maid smiled. Indeed it looked to Eleanor as though she almost winked, but thought better of it at the last moment.

'Oh yes, ma'am! This is a most convenient house, if you take my meaning! Well-situated rooms—' She broke off as she caught Eleanor's quelling look. 'Yes, ma'am, and may I fetch you anything else?'

'Just a carpenter to fix a large bolt upon the door!' Eleanor said brightly, happy to see that she had wiped the complacent smile from the girl's face at last. 'And if you cannot find one, Lucy, bring me a hammer and nails! I will do the job myself!'

'Truly, Kit, what do you expect? A hero's welcome?'

It was seldom that Lord Mostyn had to face the combined disapprobation of both his sister and his cousin, who were the only people on the face of the earth who could make him feel as though he were back in the nursery. He now reflected wryly that he had rather face Marshal Soult in the Peninsula again than take on the combined forces of his relatives.

Not that anyone knew he had been in the Peninsula. That had been when he was supposed to be working for the East India Company, and before that... Kit sighed, and sat back, accepting the cup of tea that Charlotte passed him. She gave him a severe frown at the same time. Kit offered her a weak smile in return.

'You look radiant now that you are a married woman again, sis—'

'Gammon!'

'And Beth...' Kit manfully braved the glare that his cousin was directing his way '...increasing already! You are to be congratulated...'

'Pray spare us, Kit!' Beth said shortly. 'You cannot be glad to see either of us married into the Trevithick family, but since you were not here to advise us you must just accept the consequences!'

Kit raised his brows. 'Would you have accepted my advice, Beth?'

'Certainly not! Especially with the example that you have set us!'

It showed all the signs of degenerating into a nursery tea party. Kit sipped his tea and wished he were at his club. He had hoped that his sister and cousin would be pleased to see him, fall on his neck with tears of joy, and provide the welcome that Eleanor had so singularly failed to do. He shifted uncomfortably. He was already grimly aware that he had no right to expect a warm reception from his wife and the fact that her coldness had hurt him was just too bad. He would learn to live with it.

To be fair to Charlotte and Beth, they had greeted him very warmly when he had first arrived at Charlotte's town house that morning. Now, however, they were over their initial relief and pleasure and were full of questions—and recriminations.

'How could you do that to poor Eleanor!' Charlotte was saying, strongly for her. 'To marry her and leave her all in the one day! To marry her in the first place so precipitately…'

'To *seduce* her in the first place!' Beth put in, eyes flashing. 'Yes, Kit, I know that Eleanor ran away to you, but you could have exercised some restraint…'

Kit gave her a speaking look. Beth looked at him, looked down at her own swelling figure and after a moment, burst into a peal of laughter.

'Oh, very well, I know I cannot upbraid you when my own behaviour has not been above reproach, but what an odious wretch you are to remind me, Kit! And I shall have you know that I am most respectably married now, and even if the tabbies count the months they can go hang—'

'Beth!' Charlotte said warningly. 'You become ever more unbridled in your speech!' She passed her brother a biscuit. 'As for you, Kit, you know you have no defence. Your treatment of Eleanor has been truly dreadful!'

Kit sighed. He dipped the biscuit into his tea—it immediately broke off and sank to the bottom of the cup. It seemed all too apt.

'I never intended to treat Eleanor so shabbily but

matters fell out that way. I am not at liberty to explain...'

He shifted uncomfortably. They were watching him with scepticism and it made Kit feel both guilty and annoyed. He did not like the sensation of feeling in the wrong—and he felt it most strongly.

'It was a difficulty relating to business that kept me away so long...'

'Oh, please...' Beth murmured, putting her teacup down with a disgusted clink of china.

'I am sorry that I cannot be more precise...'

He thought he heard Beth say something that sounded like: 'Pshaw!'

'It is not important for you to explain to us, Kit,' Charlotte said gently. 'Eleanor is the one who requires an explanation—and an apology. I feel sure that you are able to take her into your confidence.'

Kit shrugged, hiding his frustration beneath a nonchalance he was far from feeling. 'I have tried to offer Eleanor an explanation, sis! She would not let me speak. She has decreed a marriage of convenience and she says that she has been enjoying herself hugely as a married woman without the constraints of a husband!'

Kit cleared his throat and looked away from his sister's penetrating eye. He had no wish to allude any more precisely to his wife's disgrace and he hoped that he had not given away too much already. But perhaps Charlotte and Beth already knew all about Eleanor's behaviour. It seemed that the whole of the *Ton* knew.

Charlotte and Beth exchanged glances over the teacups.

'Oh dear,' Beth said. 'Eleanor has taken this every whit as badly as I would have expected.'

'She is very young and has all the Trevithick pride,' Charlotte agreed. 'Besides, she has suffered a great deal. It is no wonder she is so adamant.'

Kit looked at them, mystified. They appeared to him to be speaking in riddles.

'It seems quite simple to me. Eleanor is not interested in explanations…'

'Nonsense!' Beth said robustly. 'She is hiding her hurt behind that confounded pride, Kit! I'll wager she is positively expiring to know! If Marcus disappeared for five months without a word, the *first* thing that I would wish to know is where he had been—'

'And the *second* would be who he had been with!' Charlotte finished, nodding. 'That would be after he had apologised, of course! Kit, I hope that the very first thing that you said to Eleanor was how sorry you were and how much you had missed her…'

Kit could feel the guilty expression spreading across his face. 'Well… There was the matter of Paulet to deal with first…'

Charlotte sighed heavily. 'Oh Kit—no! Tell me you did not blame Eleanor for her situation!'

Kit made a hopeless gesture. 'I tried to explain matters to her later when my temper had cooled, but—'

'Too late!' Beth said, in a disgusted tone. 'How like a man!'

There was a heavy silence.

'There have been rumours about you, you know, Kit,' Charlotte ventured. 'It has been most distressing for Eleanor.'

Kit looked up, his attention arrested. 'Rumours of what?'

'Rumours of actresses—or was it opera singers?' Charlotte looked vague. 'You know how these tales spring up! People were forever claiming to have sighted you abroad and Eleanor has heard every one of the stories! The gossips made sure of that!'

Kit scowled. This was getting worse and worse. His guilt settled into a lump in his stomach. So Eleanor had heard rumours about him and he had heard scandal about her... And if he was unsure whether *she* had been unfaithful, she must believe the same of him... What a confounded mess they had got themselves into!

'Those stories are not true!' he said coldly. 'And I have heard plenty of stories about Eleanor, if it comes to that! Muse to Sir Charles Paulet, mistress to Lord George Darke—'

'Poppycock! Club scandal!' Beth's silver eyes flashed. 'Eleanor is as virtuous as on the day you married her!'

Kit frowned at her. 'Beth, I admire you for defending Eleanor, but...' he shifted his shoulders uncomfortably '...she practically admitted to me that she had encouraged the attentions of other men! Oh, not in so many words...' he had heard Beth's exasperated sigh '...but why else would she refuse to discuss what had happened during the last few months? She is afraid to tell me the whole truth!'

He thought that his cousin looked as though she would explode and he almost backed away. Beth could be awesome when her anger was roused.

'Kit,' Beth said, with reasonable restraint, 'you are speaking nonsense!' She took a deep breath. 'We were not going to tell you this since we both agreed that it was Eleanor's place to speak to you, but...' she broke off at Charlotte's murmured objection '...no, Lottie, I cannot keep quiet! For some extraordinary reason Kit thinks himself the injured party, when poor Eleanor is only nineteen and has been reviled and laughed at and *ruined* through the careless way in which he abandoned her—' She ran out of breath and started again. 'And now Kit adds his own voice to the chorus of disapproval! Oh, it makes me so cross!'

'Yes,' Charlotte said, in her customary, more measured tones. 'Beth is correct, you know, Kit!'

Kit held a hand up in surrender. 'Perhaps I have misjudged the situation...'

Beth glared at him. 'You have, Kit! Indeed you have!'

'I am sorry.'

There was a startled silence.

'I beg your pardon?' Beth said faintly.

Kit gave her a glimmer of a smile. 'I know you think I can never apologise...'

'No, I know it…'

'Whatever the case…' Kit grimaced. 'I had no notion of any of this.' He looked away. 'I do not understand. How could Eleanor have been reviled when I was the one who deserted her?'

Beth raised her eyes to heaven.

Charlotte tutted. 'For all your supposed experience of the world, Kit, I sometimes think you the veriest babe in arms! Do you not know that it is always the woman's reputation that suffers? If you left her there must have been a reason—so goes the reckoning. In this case the favourite explanation is that you found her not to be virtuous… Which is where the rumours started!'

Kit groaned. 'I did not think… Was it so very bad for her?'

'Yes,' Beth said baldly. 'However, I believe she might have borne it with fortitude had she but heard one word from you!'

Kit put his head in his hands. 'I sent her letters…'

'They never arrived.' Charlotte was definite. 'And though I agree with what Beth has said, what good a letter when it was you that Eleanor needed, Kit!'

'It might at least have made a small difference to how she felt.' Kit remembered the words he had written with something like pain. He had never penned a love letter before but his anguish had lent finesse to his words:

My dear love
Forgive me for leaving you so suddenly and

without a word. I had no intention of this...
Pray seek my sister's help until I may return
and I swear it will not be for long... Forgive
me, my love...

But it had been long, far longer than he had intended. Each day away from her had been purgatory,
hoping that she had received his letters, that she
would understand. And then he had come back,
found his wife in a compromising situation with another man and had heard all the scandalous tales
about her. He had been blinded by an astonishing
jealousy that had swept all other thoughts from his
head. She had not been pining without him. She had
had the effrontery to stick her proud little nose in
the air and declaim that thcy should have a thoroughly modern marriage. Well, that was one idea of
which he would just have to disabuse her!

He stood up. 'I believe that I must speak with my
wife. We must untangle this muddle. I will *make* her
listen to me!'

Charlotte smiled. 'No, Kit, I believe that would be
disastrous! You should handle the situation with delicacy rather than go rushing in like a bull at a gate.
You must set out to court your wife again and only
when you have her trust can you embark on the necessary explanations.'

'Yes,' Beth added, with a mischievous grin, 'and
then you must *seduce* your wife, Kit! Slowly and
subtly. For a man of your reputation it should not be
too difficult a matter!'

Kit gave her a rueful smile. 'With a lady of Eleanor's strength of mind I believe I shall have my work cut out. She will not forgive me easily.'

'Good!' Beth said severely.

When Kit had gone out, the two Trevithick ladies looked at each other in silence for a moment.

'I hope, Lottie, that you did not think me too harsh with your brother?' Beth asked, hesitantly for her. 'I am afraid that I did lose my temper a little.'

Charlotte smiled ruefully. 'No, no, Beth, you said nothing Kit did not deserve! Indeed, I believe he got away lightly and we certainly gave him something to think on. I was only afraid that you were going to say something about…'

'About the baby?' Beth said slowly. 'No. Only Eleanor can tell him about that.'

'Do you think she will?' Charlotte asked.

Beth looked sad. 'I do not know, Lottie. I do not know.'

Had Kit but known it, his wife was having no easier an interview that he was himself. On discovering that her husband had gone to take tea with his sister in Upper Grosvenor Street, Eleanor had decided that she also had some calls to make. It would not do to be seen to be sitting around at home waiting for him. The difficulty was where to go. During the Season she had been taken under Beth and Marcus's wing and depended very much upon them for society. Though they had not been able to prevent the outrageous gossip about her amongst the

Ton, they had been steadfast in their support and Eleanor had even felt comfortable enough to joke that Marcus would have called out every man who insulted her, except that he did not have enough time to deal with them all.

Now, however, she felt a reluctance to go to Trevithick House. Beth would probably be with Charlotte and Kit, and even if she were not... Eleanor sighed. Beth was Kit's cousin, after all, and Eleanor did not wish to put her in an awkward conflict of loyalties. She also shrank from sharing her feelings with anyone when she felt so sore and confused.

Instead she went to Bedford Square, where the Dowager Viscountess of Trevithick had taken a small mews house and was happily ensconced in ripping to shreds the character of her family and acquaintance, much to the enjoyment of her small audience of like-minded matrons. They were all assembled: Lady Pomfret, sharp and fat, Mrs Belton with a thin face like vinegar, and sundry other ladies large and small, with the common interest of malice and scandal. Eleanor had always secretly called her mother's gossiping friends the Trevithick Tabbies and had given them a wide berth during the Season. Now she came forward into the circle, already regretting the impulse that had driven her into their company and almost half-inclined to flee.

'Eleanor, my dear!' Lady Pomfret, her mother's bosom bow, edged along the sofa to make room for her. 'How lovely to see you again! You have been avoiding us, you naughty puss! Squeeze in here, my love, and tell us all about that *wicked* husband of yours! He has not left you again, I presume?'

Someone else tittered. The Dowager Viscountess grunted her approval of the sally and leant forward to drain her glass of laudanum, her massive figure creaking like a ship in a storm. Her bonnet was awry on her greying curls and her face was curiously flushed, her eyes sunken and bloodshot in the folds of her face. Eleanor wondered, with a stab of pity, whether her mother realised quite the figure she cut.

Lady Trevithick gestured impatiently to Eleanor to refill the glass before she sat down, and after a moment Eleanor moved across to the sideboard and poured from the bottle concealed in the corner. She made sure the glass was full—Lady Trevithick would only send her back to top it up if it was not. Eleanor sighed. Her mother had become increasing dependent on her laudanum in the last few years, taking it to mitigate the pains of bad headaches, or so she said. She handed the glass to her mother, who swallowed most of it immediately.

'Bad blood in the Mostyn family,' the Dowager said, glaring malevolently at her daughter from under her heavy brows. 'Bad *Ton*. Always were a bunch of pirates and scoundrels!'

The group murmured its agreement. Eleanor shifted slightly on the sofa. She accepted a cup of tea and picked at a piece of fruit cake.

'Is Lord Mostyn happy to be back, my dear?' Mrs Belton enquired, picking biscuit crumbs from her dress and watching Eleanor covertly under the guise of the manoeuvre. 'I had heard that he was having such a high time of it abroad!'

'He has been kept occupied with business these past five months, ma'am,' Eleanor said, wondering why she was bothering to defend Kit when she was so cross with him herself.

'Business was it?' Lady Pomfret cackled. 'I hear he is very adept at that sort of business!'

Eleanor flushed. These harpies, who considered themselves so very well bred, were more vulgar than anyone she knew.

'Kit has been in Ireland,' she said coldly. 'He has told me all about it!'

Mrs Belton's painted eyebrows swooped up. 'Ireland, was it? I heard it was the Continent! I could positively swear that he was seen in Italy...'

'They seek him here, they seek him there,' Lady Pomfret murmured. 'Dearest Eleanor sought him quite everywhere, did you not, my love? But then, you do not seem to be repining! I heard that Sir Charles Paulet has written an ode to your ankles!'

'Oh!' The ladies plied their fans.

'Sir Charles does indeed have a vivid imagination,' Eleanor agreed frostily. She turned to her mother.

'Pray, Mama, has my Aunt Trevithick written to say when she will be arriving in town?'

Lady Trevithick nodded, and paused from stuffing bonbons into her mouth. 'She arrives in a couple of weeks.' Her gaze swept around the circle of curious faces. 'My late husband, God rest his soul, has an eccentric sister who sees fit to come up to London. I am sure we shall make her most welcome, for all that she is quite unpresentable!'

'We shall show her how to go on.' Lady Pomfret nodded condescendingly.

'Explain to her the ways of town.' Mrs Belton simpered.

Eleanor felt a sudden lift of spirits. The prospect of this group of cats attempting to give Lady Salome Trevithick some town bronze was enough to cheer anyone who knew that eccentric spinster. She rose to her feet.

'Well, I must be going home. We are engaged to dine with the Fanshawes tonight and there is the Trevithick ball the day after tomorrow...'

'Oh indeed!' Lady Pomfret beamed. 'I can scarce wait...'

'And you need to make sure that your husband is still with us,' Mrs Belton observed, smiling sweetly. 'How terrible if he had disappeared again. Dear Eleanor, such a pleasure to see you! I am so glad that you are not in the least cast down by that dreadful man.'

'Dreadful man—dreadful behaviour!' Lady Pomfret echoed. 'All men are beasts, dear Eleanor!'

Eleanor bent dutifully to kiss her mother's cheek. 'Goodbye, Mama. I will see you this evening.'

Lady Trevithick grunted. She pressed the sticky glass into Eleanor's hand. 'Fetch me another before you go, girl. And make sure that no one sees you.'

This was clearly impossible, for all eyes were upon her. Eleanor refilled the laudanum again, noting that Mrs Belton dug Lady Pomfret in the ribs as the Dowager Viscountess reached greedily for the glass.

'We will see you at the ball, Eleanor dear!' carolled Lady Pomfret. 'Be sure to hold on to that wicked husband of yours when he tries to stray away! Or at least persuade him to be more circumspect next time. Discretion, my dear. Discretion is all!'

Chapter Three

Eleanor had lied. There was no dinner engagement for that night, and as the coach clattered home she remembered that Lord and Lady Fanshawe were in fact out of town, and thought that no doubt Lady Pomfret would discover this for herself and would quiz her about it. The time stretched emptily before her. Would Kit be home for dinner or would he dine at his club? Would he return at all that night? If he did so, would they have anything to say to each other or would they sit staring into space, occasionally making desperate remarks on the decoration of the room or the flavour of the food? Eleanor had observed that many married couples, of long standing or otherwise, had absolutely no conversation with one another and spent their entire time seeking more congenial company. She had not wanted that to happen to her.

The house was quiet and Carrick respectfully informed her that Lord Mostyn was out but was expected back for dinner. There were two posies of flowers waiting for her in the hall; the first were pink rosebuds tied with ribbon, and the second were huge stripy orange lilies, their stamens covered in thick pollen, lolling open in a way that Eleanor could only consider most vulgar. She looked at the rosebud posy and her heart lifted slightly. Perhaps that was from Kit—tasteful, understated, a small token of admiration that might grow into something more meaningful, were she to permit it... There was a note nestling between the stems. Eleanor felt a sudden rush of anticipation and pulled it out, scratching her fingers on the thorns on the process.

The sweetest rose
That ever grows
Amidst the snows
Is mine to...

The final word was scored through, as though the poet had had some difficulty with his rhyme and could not be bothered to rewrite his message. Beneath was scrawled:

'I live in hope, sweet Eleanor, that you will still be mine,' followed by the flourish of Sir Charles Paulet's signature.

Eleanor felt a vicious stab of disappointment, stronger by far than the irritation engendered by Sir Charles's obtuse persistence. Of course Kit would not be sending her flowers—how could she have been so foolish? She was cross with herself for even wanting it.

The rosebuds had no scent and she was tempted

to ask Carrick to throw them away, but she loved flowers and could not bear to waste them. Sending Lucy to put them in water, she turned her attention to the lilies. They really were dreadfully brash, like a Cyprian tricked out to catch a new protector. Again there was a card. Eleanor opened it with some trepidation. There were only five words:

'The night of the ball?'

Eleanor clutched the card to her chest as though she had already been caught out in an illicit act. She did not recognise the writing but in her heart she knew these could only be from the man who had been pursuing her for some time, the most notorious rakehell in London...

'Oh, ma'am!' Lucy had reappeared and was eyeing the lolling lilies with a mixture of admiration and doubt. 'How...um...striking! Are they from his lordship?'

'No!' Eleanor snapped, still heart sore. 'Married people do not send each other flowers, Lucy!'

Lucy's eyes opened wide. 'Flowers of another sort! Oh ma'am, they look very common...'

'Excessively!' Eleanor said crossly. 'I cannot conceive what sort of man would think these appropriate to me...'

'Well, there is Lord George Darke, ma'am,' Lucy said obligingly. 'He is forever pestering you and I have heard tell that he is the most dreadful rake! Indeed, before his lordship returned I did wonder if you would succumb to his charms, but what the master would say now...'

'Be quiet, you foolish girl!' Eleanor frowned ferociously at her. 'Take those ugly flowers and put them in the darkest corner of the house! No, put them in the cellar—'

She broke off as the street door opened and Kit came in. It was raining a little outside and she saw that his hair was dusted with tiny drops that sparkled in the light like diamonds. He stripped off his gloves and handed them with his coat to Carrick, with a quick word of thanks. He came across to her and gave her a cool kiss on the cheek. Eleanor jumped away. She knew it was only for the benefit of the servants but it threw her into confusion.

'Good evening, my love,' Kit said casually. His gaze fell on the lilies. 'Dear me, what ugly flowers! One would hope for better taste from your admirers!'

Eleanor knew it was true but she was still furious that Kit would not wish to send her flowers himself, yet still criticised those who did. She turned to Lucy.

'Bring the flowers up to my bedroom once they are in water please, Lucy…'

Lucy dropped a flustered curtsey. 'But ma'am, I thought you wished them to be placed in the cellar…'

Eleanor saw a twinkle come into Kit's eyes. She sighed sharply. 'Just do as I ask, please, Lucy! And quickly! I need you to help me dress for dinner!'

'You will surely be sneezing all night with those flowers in your room,' Kit observed. 'The pollen is most potent!' His keen blue gaze travelled over her and stopped at chest level. Eleanor started to blush, then realised that she was still clutching the card in her hand.

'And who is this admirer with so sound a taste in some things and not in others?' Kit enquired gently.

It was a moment of some delicacy. Eleanor clutched the card all the harder.

'I do not know,' she stuttered, knowing that she was reddening to the roots of her hair. 'The card does not say...'

Kit raised a disbelieving eyebrow. Lucy bobbed another curtsey.

'Oh ma'am, I thought it was Lord George—'

'Lucy!' Eleanor almost screeched. 'Get you gone with those lilies! Now! Throw them out of the house for all I care!'

As Lucy sped away, Kit started to laugh. 'If you are to indulge your penchant for romantic intrigue, my love, you will have to change your maid! That girl is incapable of artifice! I will see you at dinner.'

He raised a hand in casual farewell and started up the stairs.

Eleanor glared after him. She was mortified to feel in the wrong again but worse than that was the evidence that Kit did not care one way or the other. If he had rung a peal over her for encouraging other admirers... She sighed. If he had rung a peal over her, that would have been wrong as well but at least it would have showed he cared. But perhaps that was not true anyway. Last night he had been furious, but with the fury of a man whose pride did not wish him to be seen to be cuckolded.

She traipsed slowly after him up the stairs. Well, if Kit did not care, there were others who would. She told herself that the admiration of a man such as Lord George Darke was balm in the face of such apparent indifference. And immediately her heart whispered that Lord George's feelings for her were counterfeit and not really what she wanted at all.

'Atishoo! Atishoo! Atishoo!' Eleanor sneezed three times, reached for her scrap of lace cambric, realised that it was not up to the task and gratefully accepted the handkerchief that Kit proffered.

The lilies had indeed been banished but their legacy still lingered. Eleanor felt as though her nose was twice the size it should be and her eyes had been watering for a full half hour.

She put her spoon down as a tear dropped into her soup bowl and looked at Kit through streaming eyes.

'If you so much as smile, my lord…'

Kit gave her a look of injured innocence from his very blue eyes. 'I would not dream of it, my dear, when you are suffering so! Are you sure that it is not that charming posy of rosebuds that is causing the problem?'

Eleanor's head snapped round. She had forgotten Sir Charles's gift, which had paled into insignificance beside its more florid cousin. Now, however, she saw with a sinking heart that Lucy had chosen the dining-table as a suitable place to display the flowers, and not just that but the foolish girl had left the card amongst the stems so that Sir Charles's hopeless ditty was displayed for all the world to see. She really would have to speak to the maid.

Kit gestured to the footman to take the soup away.

'Did you have a pleasant day today, my dear?' he enquired.

Eleanor stifled a yawn. 'Yes, thank you. Did you?'

'Yes, thank you.'

The next course arrived, an overcooked turbot with boiled potatoes. Eleanor suppressed a shudder. Kit raised his wineglass to her.

'Your good health, my love.'

Eleanor nodded politely. 'Thank you.'

The conversation languished.

Roast pheasant with cauliflower succeeded the turbot. After a few minutes of silent, valiant chewing, Eleanor put her fork down.

'Oh dear, I think I need to speak to cook about menus. I did not wish to interfere before I knew the standard of servants you had engaged, my lord, but...' she looked at her plate and wrinkled up her nose '...I think perhaps this might be improved...'

'As you wish, my dear,' Kit responded. 'The ordering of the household is, of course, your domain now that you are here...'

Eleanor bit her lip. She was tempted to send the footman for Kit's newspaper, so bored did he sound. When she had specified a modern marriage she had not thought that it might be quite so tedious. To have nothing in common with one's life partner, to exchange only the most banal of observations... She would be fit for bedlam within a week if she could not find something more interesting to say to Kit.

'Perhaps we might give a dinner party in a week or so,' she ventured.

Kit looked at his plate of food and looked at her quizzically. 'Perhaps we should leave it a little while longer, my love.'

Eleanor's shoulders slumped. 'Of course.'

'Though I do hear that the dinner party is the ideal way to conceal the fact that a husband and wife have so little to say to each other,' Kit continued. 'There are so many other people to talk to, after all. And then there are the balls and the concerts and the other entertainments... No wonder the Season is so popular! One need scarcely see one's spouse at all!'

Eleanor sighed. This echoed her own thoughts precisely—except that Kit did not seem to mind. He continued to chew his way through the pheasant, a bland smile on his face. Eleanor, piqued by his indifference, picked up her side plate, turned it over and examined the base.

'I see they have furnished us with the latest Wedgwood china, my lord. It is in very good taste. One can never be sure with a rented house...'

Kit looked around him vaguely. 'Yes indeed. I think the house has been furnished very well, though I do wonder if this room needs decorating. What do you think, my love? A colour scheme in pink and gold perhaps?'

Eleanor put her knife and fork down with a sharp snap and revised her view that she would be bored to death within the week. Two days would do the trick. She was tolerably certain that soon they would be addressing each other as Lord Mostyn and Lady Mostyn, in that odiously coy manner that she had observed being adopted to hide a lack of affection. She mentally surveyed her social diary. She had no engagements other than the Trevithick ball the night after next, but she would have to find something else to do or she would run quite mad in this stifling nothingness. She stood up.

'If you will excuse me, my lord, I think that I shall forgo the pleasure of a pudding. Pray do not hurry your port. I shall see you tomorrow.'

Kit stood up politely. 'Good night then, my dear. Sleep well.'

An hour later, Eleanor was sitting on her bed, a sheet of paper in front of her and an inkpot and candle resting on the table nearby. She put her pen down and held the paper up to the light, contemplating the list of activities that she had just finished.

It started with balls, routs, picnics, concerts and the like. Eleanor frowned a little. She had put them first because they were the most obvious of the Season's entertainments but even these were not without problem. She could not attend unescorted and, more to the point, she could not arrive uninvited. Previously all her invitations had come via Marcus and Beth, but now the mantelpiece was bare. Perhaps it would start to display those coveted cards once word of Kit's return spread. And then he would have to be prepared to escort her...

Eleanor moved on down the list. Exhibitions and talks. She was not sure about these, mostly because she did not know anything about them other than that there were a lot of them about. She could attend alone, but it would probably label her an eccentric. Perhaps that did not matter. It was better than sitting at home alone, or taking tea with the Trevithick Tabbies. She remembered that during her come-out, her mother had denounced such entertainments as the last resort of the uninvited, full of cits and mushrooms who could not gain entrance to more sought-after events.

So… Eleanor sighed. The circulating library. Eminently respectable, but she had never been a great reader. Which left the park—walking, driving or riding. She could not ride. She crossed that out.

Eleanor stared into space. When she had been a débutante there had been no difficulty in filling her days. In fact it seemed that she had the delightful problem of not having enough time for all the activities. There had been dancing lessons, of course, although she had not really needed them, and music lessons, and so many débutante balls and parties… It had been delightful… Well, it had not always been enjoyable because some of the other girls had been quite cattish, but it had mostly been fun. Whereas now she had a house to run and a stranger for a husband, and no fun unless she availed herself of the dubious and dangerous offers of the rakes of the *Ton*…

Shopping. That was fun and she could still do that.

Eleanor picked up the pen, then put it down again. Shopping involved money, which meant an allowance and she did not have that any more. Marcus had settled some money on her at the start of the Season but that was almost gone and it would not be appropriate for her to apply to him for more. Which meant that she had to ask Kit... Eleanor sighed again. Still, there was always credit...

Feeling more restless than ever, Eleanor got up and walked over to the window. The street outside was busy with carriages and couples strolling, for the evening was still young. There would be balls and masquerades going on, and she was sitting in her bedroom like a child banished to the nursery. It was intolerable.

She ran down the stairs. The dining-room door was open but the room was empty. A half-eaten marasquino jelly was sliding off the plate. Eleanor could not help giggling. No doubt Kit had given up and gone out to his club. Which meant that his study was empty...

It was. Up until that moment Eleanor would have sworn that she had no intention of rummaging about in Kit's office to see if she could find any evidence of where he had spent the previous five months. In fact she would probably not have admitted, even to herself, that she wanted to know. Now that the opportunity was upon her she barely hesitated. She pulled the door closed behind her and went across to the desk.

At first her search turned up a disappointing lack

of information. There were two or three letters relating to the renting of the house, plus a couple of bills from Schultz the tailors. Two of the drawers were empty. Another held only candles. Eleanor frowned. There was a day-old newspaper lying discarded by the armchair, a book on the table by the fire and pen and ink on the top of the desk. It seemed that her husband led an utterly blameless life.

There were no scented notes from opera singers or actresses, smelling of rose water and tied with pink ribbon. Eleanor was uncertain whether she had hoped to find one or not. In fact there were no personal notes of any kind, which was suspicious. Decidedly that was suspicious. Eleanor was sure this was unnatural and that these missives would be found elsewhere. Except that there was nowhere else…

Caught in a crack in the wood at the back of the very bottom drawer was a piece of paper. Eleanor had to kneel on the floor and peer right to the back of the drawer to see it, then work her fingers into the gap to pull it out. It was only a scrap, written in a flowing hand. Eleanor sat back on her heels and let her breath out on a sigh. That was definitely a woman's writing.

'St John at seven tonight. With all thanks—'

Eleanor came round the desk, trying to decipher the next line. It looked like a signature, but the paper was torn and frustratingly difficult to read. In the top right hand corner was another scribble that looked like the date but again she needed to scrutinise it in a good light...

There was a stealthy click as the study door closed. Eleanor spun round. She dropped the piece of paper and put her foot firmly on it, sweeping her skirts over the top.

'Can I help you, my dear?' Kit enquired. 'Are you looking for anything in particular?'

'Oh! No...' Eleanor knew that she sounded flustered and the realisation made her blush all the more. What mischance had prompted Kit to return from Whites so soon when she would have laid odds he would be there all evening? It was most unhelpful of him.

She made an airy gesture. 'Oh, I was just looking for pen and...and ink. I wished to write a letter to...' She stopped, utterly unable to think of anyone she might wish to correspond with.

Kit waited. After a second he said:

'No doubt the servants could have brought you all you needed to avoid you having to hunt around here in the dark. But now that you are here, my love, perhaps you would like to join me in a nightcap? Shall we go into the drawing-room?'

'Oh no!' Eleanor could not think up a way of picking up the scrap of paper without Kit seeing and she was determined that she was going to read it properly. St John at seven tonight... Could that have been an assignation? She looked up, suddenly remembering that Kit had asked her a question.

'Oh, let us sit here!' she said gaily. 'This room is

so cosy, my lord, and I so seldom venture in here!'
She edged over to the nearest armchair, pushing the
paper a little with her foot and sweeping her skirt
along as though it were a broom. Fortunately it was
only a couple of steps to the armchair. If Kit would
only turn his back...

Unfortunately Kit did not. He came over to help
her sit down and then poured her a glass of Madeira,
all without taking his eyes off her. Eleanor found it
disconcerting and even more so because of her guilty
secret. She could feel the piece of paper smooth beneath the sole of her slipper.

'Have you had a pleasant evening, my love?' Kit
asked. His blue eyes twinkled. 'I hope that you have
not been bored. No doubt we shall receive plenty
more invitations soon.'

'I expect so,' Eleanor said half-heartedly. A few
more evenings like this and she would be fit for
Bedlam. She took a sip of Madeira and tried to concentrate.

'Of course, it is the way of things for a husband
to go out to his club and a wife to sit in at home,'
Kit said, straight-faced. 'I do hope that you were not
expecting more in the way of excitement, my dear.
A few dinner parties and a ball or two—those are
the kind of entertainments suitable for you now that
you are no longer a débutante.'

'I suppose so,' Eleanor said. Her débutante days
did indeed seem far away. 'Though surely I may be
able to go visiting sometimes...'

'Not alone in the evenings,' Kit said sharply. 'You

would be a prey to every rake in town—again!' He got up to refill his glass. Eleanor started to bend down surreptitiously to retrieve the paper. Kit turned back. Eleanor straightened up quickly.

'No indeed…' Kit continued '…a little needlework or reading, perhaps… It will do you no harm to give the impression of virtue!'

Eleanor bristled. For all her quarrel with Kit she had never previously considered him a self-important man, yet here he was showing all the signs of turning into the most odiously pompous of husbands!

'I am sure it is not a question of an *impression* of virtue, my lord—' She began hotly, but Kit held up his hand.

'My dear…' His tone was condescending, 'the whole *Ton* will have seen your somewhat questionable behaviour in the past, so I venture to suggest that an impression of virtue is precisely what you wish to cultivate! The likes of Darke and Paulet must learn not to send their pathetic little floral tributes to this house—'

Eleanor made an infuriated noise. Under most circumstances she would have agreed with him but this irritatingly patronising tone was too much to bear.

'Upon my word, my lord, I had no idea that you were such a killjoy!' she said furiously. 'I may not go out, I may not entertain, I may do nothing more amusing than embroidery—why, I declare I shall be dead of boredom within a week!'

'Not if you learn a little decorum, my dear,' Kit commented.

Eleanor leaped to her feet. 'I have heard enough! I may be lacking in decorum but at least I am not pompous and arrogant! Allow me to say, my lord, that living with you is the most tiresome thing imaginable—boring, tedious and utterly without enjoyment! Good night!'

'Good night, my love,' Kit murmured as she shot past him out of the room. His smile lingered as he heard her angry footsteps beating a quick pit-a-pat across the tiles of the hall. He got up, stretched lazily and moved across to where Eleanor had been sitting. The small scrap of paper was still there by the leg of the chair. Kit bent to pick it up, read it and smiled again. He tucked it into his waistcoat pocket.

He sat down again and reached for his book, glancing at the clock as he did so. If he knew Eleanor at all he would wager that she would come back when she realised. He did not believe that she had the temperament for a long game. He gave it ten minutes.

It took only seven.

There was a flicker of movement outside the study door and Kit put the book down again, opened the door quickly and caught his wife's arm before she could hurry away again.

'Whatever is the matter, my dear Eleanor? Did you forget something earlier?'

He saw her gaze flash to the carpet before it returned to his face with what she no doubt thought was a guileless expression. Kit tried not to laugh. To see Eleanor try to dissemble was highly amusing. She evidently had no talent for deceit at all. The thought warmed him.

'No... Yes... I...'

'This perhaps?' Kit reached into his pocket and extracted the scrap of paper. He was rewarded by a vivid blush. Eleanor's eyes widened.

'Oh, no! But...' She peeked at him. 'Did you know I was hiding that all the time we were talking?'

Kit's lips twitched. At least she had not underestimated him. 'I knew you were hiding something! You are not good at deception, my dear!'

Eleanor's blush deepened. 'And did you deliberately set out to make me cross so that I would forget it?'

'That too!'

'Well, I call that very cruel of you, Kit.' Eleanor sounded piteous. 'I just saw the little piece of paper on the carpet when I came in for the...er...the pen and ink! I confess I was curious...'

'Spinning me another tale, my love?' Kit said cheerfully. 'Why not confess you have been rummaging through my drawers? Would you care to tell me why?'

Eleanor's lips pursed. 'Oh...well...'

'Perhaps you were trying to discover what I had been doing during my time away? Would you like me to tell you?'

A stormy look came into Eleanor's eyes. 'No! I have told you that it is of no interest to me, sir!'

'Very well.' Kit smiled to himself. That was manifestly untrue but it seemed he would have to give her more time. That was no hardship, for he was starting to enjoy himself.

'Good night then, my lord.' Eleanor was looking at him hesitantly, surprised, perhaps that he was about to let her go so easily. Kit put out a hand.

'A moment, Eleanor...'

'My lord?'

She was standing close enough for him to smell her perfume. It was a very subtle mix of rose and jasmine, faint but sweet as Eleanor herself. Kit felt his senses tighten.

'Do you truly think me pompous and boring?'

She cast her eyes down in maidenly confusion. 'Oh no! But you were deliberately saying those things to provoke me, my lord!'

'Very true. And is our life together very tedious and lacking in excitement? I imagine it could be much different...'

This time she did not look away, but held his gaze with her own. He saw innocence and confusion in her eyes and it was unbearably tempting. He leant closer and touched his lips to hers. Her eyelashes fluttered as she closed her eyes, her lips softened, full and sweet. Every predatory instinct Kit possessed was pushing him to take her in his arms and plunder her mouth with the ravenous hunger that had possessed him ever since he had seen her again.

He drew back.

He heard her sigh quietly and could have sworn that it was with frustration. He hoped so.

'Good night, Eleanor.' He held the door open for her and after a moment she went out of the room, pausing to look back at him as she crossed the hall. He watched her all the way up the stairs and she looked back at least twice more.

Kit smiled as he closed the study door softly. So Eleanor was curious about his absence even though she was denying it. That augured well. And she had not pulled away when he had kissed her. And she had addressed him by his given name. Only once, perhaps, but entirely naturally. Kit picked up his unfinished drink and took a swallow. It would take time to win back her trust but he was confident that he could do it.

Chapter Four

The following day was fine. Eleanor woke to sunlight, the sounds of the birds and the faint calls of the vendors who were already setting up their stalls in the street outside. For a moment she lay still, feeling vaguely happy. Last night… Last night Kit had kissed her—if that tiniest touch of the lips could really be called a kiss—and it had been very pleasant. Very pleasant indeed. Eleanor frowned. That was not what she had intended. That would not do at all. She was angry with Kit and wished to keep him at arm's length. The happy feeling drained away.

When she went down to breakfast she discovered that Kit had already left the house for some unspecified destination. The remaining scraps of Eleanor's cheerfulness now disappeared in a manner she could not but admit was contrary. She had wanted to avoid Kit rather than seek him out. Yet…

She called Lucy, put on her bonnet and went out. From the extensive list of entertainments that she had put together the previous night she chose the circulating library. It did not hold her interest for long, though she chose two books, one Miss Burney's *Evelina* and the other a well-worn copy of a book called *Tristram Shandy*.

From the library she went to look at the shops, with Lucy still respectably in tow. This proved to be a mistake, however. With her nose pressed to the window and no money in her reticule, Eleanor felt deprived and cross, though she struggled hard with herself against the feeling.

No one called in the afternoon. Eleanor sat in the garden and read *Tristram Shandy* and rather enjoyed it. As the day wore on she went in to speak to Cook about menus for the rest of the week and was happy to approve the list for dinner that night. She went up to change early, filled with a happy anticipation of Kit's company, which she assured herself was only because she had been alone all day. In the event she could have saved herself the excitement, for Kit sent an apology explaining that he was dining with a business acquaintance and did not know when he would be back. Eleanor sat alone at the big table with her book propped in front of her, pushed the food around her plate and retired early.

She had been reading in her room for another hour when she started to feel restless again and decided to go back downstairs. This time she had no intention of rummaging through Kit's drawers but decided to play the piano. The music-room was cold, for no fire had been laid and this was the north side of the house. Shivering a little, Eleanor opened the piano lid and sat down on the stool, placing her candles on the piano lid. Then she realised the next problem—there was no music. But in fact that was not a problem. She had not excelled in many things—her needlework was no more than adequate, her watercolour painting very poor and her singing painful to the ear of a listener—but she loved music and dancing. She resolved to play from memory.

At first her fingers stumbled a little over the notes, for she had not played for over five months and was out of practice. She chose a couple of Bach cantatas to help her regain her skill, and the smooth, slow cadences were soothing to her spirit. Then she tried something a little more lively—a minuet by Louis Boccherini that she had heard at a concert the previous year and had committed to memory. Finally she picked a haunting tune by Beethoven that had been popular with the débutantes because of its romantic overtones and poured all her feelings into it.

The candlelight guttered as the last notes died away and Eleanor shivered in the draught from the doorway. She had been playing from memory, eyes closed, but now she opened them and blinked a little. Kit was standing by the empty fireplace, his tall figure casting a long shadow. He did not speak at once.

Eleanor got clumsily to her feet and closed the piano lid with an abrupt click, almost trapping her fingers in her haste to go. She felt obscurely as though she had been caught doing something wrong—again.

'I did not realise that you had returned—' She began, then stopped because that made her sound even more guilty although she had nothing to be guilty for.

Kit came forward into the circle of light thrown by the candles. His voice was low. 'That was beautiful, Eleanor. I had no idea you played so well.'

Eleanor looked at him, then away swiftly. 'Thank you.' She knew she sounded stilted. All her frustrations came rushing back. 'It is not surprising that you did not know. I never had the opportunity to play for you, did I?'

'No,' Kit said slowly. 'I imagine that there is a great deal that we do not know about each other.'

They looked at each other very steadily. 'Almost everything,' Eleanor said. She shivered. 'Excuse me, I must go. It is cold in here.'

Kit took her hand in his, which was not precisely what she had intended.

'You are frozen! Come into the study and have a glass of wine to warm you.'

He picked up the candlestick and offered his other arm to Eleanor, who accepted reluctantly. After the chill of the music-room the study was warm, with a welcome fire glowing in the grate. A glass of port stood on the table beside Kit's chair; a book was turned spine up on the seat. Evidently Kit had been reading and had got up when he had heard her playing.

Eleanor took the other chair before the fire.

'Sherry, ratafia?' Kit raised his brows.

Eleanor smiled. 'Thank you. I will have a glass of port with you.'

Kit smiled and inclined his head, filling a glass for her and topping up his own. He put the book aside and sat down.

'So how did you learn to play without music?'

Eleanor took a sip of port and savoured the taste. She knew it was not a lady's drink, at least not a drink that respectable ladies took, but it was extremely nice.

'I just found that I possessed the talent,' she said candidly. 'I had been playing the pianoforte for years, but one evening when I was about fifteen my parents held a concert and I heard a piece that I did not recognise. I tried to commit it to memory and the next morning I went down and played it.' She laughed. 'Everyone was so surprised! Oh, I made a few mistakes, but I soon mastered it. And of course I practised and practised.' She saw that Kit was watching her with a disturbingly intent look in his eye. 'All débutantes must have an accomplishment, be it singing, or playing, or drawing,' she finished brightly.

Kit nodded. 'I suppose so. Only yours is rather unusual.'

Eleanor shifted a little uncomfortably. She downed the rest of her port in a single draught.

'Thank you, I am warm now. I will leave you to your book.'

'A moment.' Kit put out a hand and touched the back of her wrist lightly. Eleanor tried not to flinch.

The slight touch felt as though it had burned her, making her catch her breath. The study was warm, small, intimate.

'You said earlier that we knew so little of each other and you were right,' Kit said slowly. 'How would it be if we spent a little time—like this—just talking on innocuous topics. There could be no harm in that, surely?'

Eleanor sat and looked at him. It sounded harmless. In fact, it sounded very pleasant. Here was a way to avoid the loneliness that had frightened her earlier, whilst in no way threatening the comfortable surface calm of their marriage. She gave a tentative nod.

'Well... I suppose...that sounds quite enjoyable...'

Kit smiled slightly. 'I think so too. Perhaps tomorrow you could tell me of your other interests?'

'Tomorrow it will be your turn!' Eleanor said pertly. Her face fell a little. 'But there is the ball, and we shall have no time...'

'I am sure we can make time,' Kit said gently.

Eleanor got up. She suddenly felt quite tired. Then she remembered about the allowance, and lingered.

'Kit...' she could feel herself blushing a little '...there are some items that I need to buy, a few trifling purchases...'

Kit nodded. 'We shall go shopping tomorrow.'

'Oh!' Eleanor frowned a little. 'But there is no need for you to come! They are only small things, underwear...'

Kit looked at her quizzically and somehow it made her feel even more self-conscious. 'Of course if you wish to come that would be very pleasant, but...I only wanted to save you the trouble, and if you were to make me an allowance instead, then you could go to your club instead of squiring me about town...'

'Eleanor,' Kit said softly, 'I should be delighted to accompany you.'

There seemed little else to say. Eleanor looked at him, a little at a loss. 'Then that would be most agreeable...'

Kit got up to hold the door for her. 'In the morning?'

Eleanor glanced up at him. 'Um... Yes, thank you.'

Kit took her hand and pressed a kiss on the back. Eleanor felt it all the way down to her toes. When she reached the bottom of the stairs she glanced back and saw that Kit was still standing in the doorway watching her. It made her feel strange. She imagined that she could feel his gaze following her all the way up the stairs, raising a little tingle of awareness on the nape of her neck. Once in her bedroom, she called for Lucy to help her undress and endured her chatter with far more patience than before. She did not expect to sleep well and would have been astonished to discover that she had fallen asleep as soon as her head touched the pillow.

'The amber scarf would become you exceedingly, my love, and the rose pink too,' Kit said judiciously.

They were seated on the striped satin sofa in one of Bond Street's most elegant—and prodigiously expensive—mantua-makers, and Eleanor was bewildered by the fact that she had just purchased a walking-dress in bronze, a ball-gown in gold and a dashing pelisse in a deep crimson velvet, despite the fact that she had set out requiring one pair of gloves, some silk stockings and possibly, just possibly, a new bonnet. It was Kit's bad influence, she told herself—he had suggested purchases with a prodigality that had made her eyes open wide and had made the shop's proprietor, a lady who was as well-upholstered as her gilt sofa, beam with pleasure. And Eleanor was forced to admit that shopping with her husband had been so very much more pleasant that going out with her maid.

'I will take the amber,' Eleanor said cautiously, 'and perhaps a pair of gloves in the pink—'

She broke off as she saw Kit exchange a nod of complicity with the proprietor. No doubt both scarves would find their way into her wardrobe and she could scarce complain, for they were excessively pretty.

'That really was quite unnecessarily generous of you, my lord,' she said, once they were out on the street, sped on their way by the heartfelt good wishes of the shop owner. 'I have no need of additional dresses and as for the scarves, I can hardly wear two at once! It really was quite unwarranted extravagance—' She broke off at the spark of amusement in Kit's eye.

'Why, what is it?'

'I do believe that you are a secret puritan, my love,' Kit said ruefully. 'It is another aspect of your character that I would never have guessed! How many gentlemen have to *force* their wives to buy dresses...' He gave her a droll look. 'I can see I shall have to watch you to prevent you sending them back!'

Eleanor laughed. 'Oh, I am not so much a puritan as that, my lord, and they are all very pretty.' She sighed. 'I only required some stockings, however...'

Kit looked down at her. There was a wicked smile curving his lips. 'Then by all means let us go and buy you some, my love...'

'However, I think that I shall send Lucy to purchase them for me!' Eleanor finished swiftly. The thought of Kit sorting through silk stockings with her made her feel quite faint. 'I am a little fatigued and would like to go home now.'

Kit shot her an amused look but he did not demur. They strolled along the pavement, through the crush of shoppers. It was a fine morning and Bond Street was busy.

'So now I know you are a secret puritan who plays the piano like an angel,' Kit said thoughtfully. 'What a curious mixture you are, my dear, and I wonder what else there is to learn?'

Eleanor smiled up at him. 'It is your turn,' she reminded him.

Kit looked thoughtful. 'Well... I prefer living in the country to living in town, I detest mock turtle soup and I was bullied shamelessly by my cousin and sister when I was a boy!'

'Oh for shame!' Eleanor burst out laughing. 'That cannot be true! Charlotte and Beth would do no such thing!'

Kit grinned. 'I assure you that being the only boy at the mercy of those two girls was no pleasure. Charlotte, being the elder twin, would order me about, and Beth, being younger than the two of us, would whine to join in. But since you do not like my disclosures, tell me what you already know of me instead.'

Eleanor's eyes sparkled. This was much easier than she had thought, for once she started to think of it there were plenty of things she remembered about Kit from her come-out Season. Perhaps he was not so much of a stranger as she had thought.

'You like the plays of Mr Sheridan but not those of Mr Shakespeare,' she began. 'As a boy you used to steal apples for cider—I am sorry I do not recall the correct term...'

'Scrumping,' Kit said obligingly.

'Yes—you would go out with the village boys to raid the orchards!' Eleanor laughed. 'I remember you telling me about it one evening when we sat out a dance together. And speaking of dancing, I also know that you are very kind, for when Lord Grey scorned poor little Miss Harvey at Almacks that time and referred to her as a cit, you asked her to dance—'

'When I would have preferred to stand up with

you!' Kit finished. He grimaced. 'I suppose that was kind…'

'Excessively so, and you know it. You did it to spare her blushes.' Eleanor paused, head on one side. 'Unless I mistake, of course, and you were cherishing a secret *tendre* for her!'

Kit smiled down at her. 'I think not! I had room in my heart for only one secret passion…'

There was an odd pause. They looked at each other. Eleanor was silent, utterly unaware of the crowds that ebbed and flowed around them. Suddenly she was aware of Kit in the most curious detail; the sheen of his skin in the sunlight and the tawny gold of his hair, the smooth material of his sleeve beneath her fingers and the strength of his arm beneath that, the fresh air scent of him and the warmth of the smile that was creeping into those blue eyes as he looked down at her…

'Eleanor! And Kit! I am so glad to see you! I was hoping to call on you soon—'

Eleanor jumped and tore her gaze away from Kit, knowing instinctively that he too had been snatched from whatever intense preoccupation had captured them. She blinked a little in the sunshine.

'Beth! Marcus! How lovely! Are you—' Eleanor broke off. Her brother had given her a brief smile, but when Kit had held his hand out, Marcus had ignored it as though Kit simply were not there. Now Eleanor watched as her brother turned to Beth a little abruptly.

'If you are ready, my dear…'

The colour flamed to Eleanor's face. Although Marcus had acknowledged her, she was as indignant as if he had cut her dead. How dared he ignore Kit in such a public manner! She felt Kit stiffen beside her and shot a quick look at him. She could tell that he was furious. His expression was set, his blue eyes hard. Eleanor saw his hand fall back to his side, saw Marcus cast him a look of comprehensive dislike. She was mortified—this was all on her account and she could not bear it. Eleanor trembled, thinking that in another moment her husband would be calling her brother out and they would all be engrossed in the most appalling scandal imaginable.

It was Beth who rescued the situation whilst the rest of them stood about like waxworks. She reached up to kiss Kit's cheek, then turned to Eleanor as though there was nothing wrong in the world.

'I was hoping to catch you for a quiet coze, my love! Were you returning home? I confess I have been shopping and am quite done up!'

'Oh yes!' Eleanor said hastily, not daring to look at Kit's unyielding face. 'By all means let us return to Montague Street! Kit, dearest…' she put a hand on her husband's arm '…you do not mind if I go back with Beth? I know that you have business at the gunsmith's…'

'Of course.' Kit covered her fingers with his own and Eleanor was inexpressibly relieved. He gave her a glimmer of a smile. 'I will see you later, my love. Good day, cos…' He bowed to Eleanor and Beth, ignored Marcus pointedly, and strode away.

'Marcus—' Beth began indignantly, but her husband merely sketched them a bow, turned on his heel and strode away—in the opposite direction to Kit.

'Men!' Beth said furiously. 'Of all the silly, childish behaviour...'

'And we are left to procure ourselves a hackney carriage!' Eleanor said mournfully. 'One or other of them could have had the chivalry to call one for us before they left!'

'Of course, it's all of a piece!' Beth said half an hour later, as she and Eleanor sat in the drawing-room of the house in Montague Street taking tea together. 'You know as well as I, my love, that Marcus can be the most tiresomely obstinate creature when he chooses. Goodness knows, I love him to distraction, but sometimes...' She broke off, stirring sugar vigorously into her cup. 'Well, I shall have to speak to him about it!'

Eleanor shuddered slightly. When it came to obstinacy, Beth could win prizes herself and Eleanor was sure the results of such a confrontation would be spectacular.

'It is all a little difficult,' she said carefully. 'I had no notion that Marcus would disapprove so...'

'It is not his place to approve or disapprove,' Beth said sharply, reaching for a piece of cake. 'It is a matter between yourself and Kit only. Oh, I am so cross! And so hungry! I am always hungry!'

'I expect that is because you are in a delicate condition,' Eleanor commiserated. 'Indeed, Beth, you should not allow Marcus to annoy you so. It will be bad for the baby!'

Beth sat back with a sigh. 'Let us hope the child is of a less stubborn disposition that its father. But never mind about that! What about you, dearest?' She fixed Eleanor with her perceptive silver gaze. 'I so wondered how you were getting on but thought that you might not wish to see me.'

'Because Kit is your cousin and you felt you had to defend him?' Eleanor asked. She gave a rueful laugh. 'Oh, Beth, this is getting so complicated!'

Beth patted her hand. 'It need not be. We are friends, Eleanor, as well as sisters-in-law and,' she laughed, 'cousins-in-law if you will. If you wish to talk to me I should be pleased but if you wish me to attend to my own affairs then pray tell me so!'

Eleanor laughed too. Deep down she had known that Beth would stand her friend whatever the situation, but it was reassuring to have the matter confirmed.

'To be frank, I should be glad of a confidante,' she said, 'but I do not wish to make matters awkward for you, Beth...'

Beth shrugged, scattering cake crumbs. 'Oh, do not regard it. I know I am a sad rattle and I rush in where angels fear to tread, but if you do not wish me to tell anyone your secrets, dear Eleanor, then of course—I shall not!'

Eleanor only just managed to restrain herself from hugging her. 'I know! I trust you. After all, you hold the biggest secret of them all.'

Beth's smile faded. 'You have not told Kit, then? Perhaps it is too soon…'

Eleanor pressed her hands together. Despite the warmth of the day, she felt the chill steal over her. It was always the same when she remembered those miserable months in Devon. She looked up and met Beth's gaze.

'I don't intend to tell Kit, Beth. Not ever! Oh…' she hurried on as she saw Beth's look deepen into concern '…I know we have spoken of this and you think that Kit should know about the baby, but…' she shook her head '…I could not bear to tell him! It would be too painful!'

'I see,' Beth said slowly. She leant forward and picked up her teacup. 'Of course you may change your mind. Trust takes time to grow…'

'I do not wish to trust Kit ever again!' Eleanor said, in a rush. Now that she had started to talk it felt as though all her feelings were rushing out in an unstoppable flood. She looked at her sister-in-law. 'Did Kit tell you that I had refused to listen to his excuses?'

'Well…' Beth said carefully.

'Oh do not scruple to be kind to me!' Eleanor said, feeling as though she wanted to burst into tears. 'Truth to tell, I know I am being contrary but I am doing it deliberately because it is the only way to defend myself! I have to keep Kit at arm's length, Beth, for once I start to let him even a little closer, where will it end?' She made a gesture of despair. 'First he will apologise and then he will tell me

where he was for those five months and then I will
forgive him and tell him what befell me and...' she
gulped '...before I know it I will be in danger of
falling in love with him all over again!'

'Well...' Beth said again. She looked up and fixed
Eleanor with a serious look, the sort of look that
made her sister-in-law's heart sink. 'Would that be
so bad, Nell? I know that Kit deserted you but he is
a good man and there were reasons...'

Eleanor put her hands over her ears. She remembered the affinity that she and Kit had achieved only
hours earlier. She did not want that to happen again.
'I do not wish to hear!'

Beth smiled ruefully. 'Very well!'

There was a silence. Eleanor peeked at her. She
knew her sister-in-law was exercising almost super-
human powers of self-control in order to keep quiet,
and somehow that made Eleanor feel even fonder of
her than before because she knew Beth found it so
difficult. After a moment she said cautiously:

'Did Kit tell you where he had been, Beth?'

Beth gave her an old-fashioned look. 'I am not
telling!'

Eleanor sighed. 'Please?'

Beth reached for another piece of cake. 'Oh, very
well. No, he did not tell me! Charlotte and I felt that
Kit should speak to you first, Eleanor, before the rest
of us hear his tale. So if you persistently refuse to
hear him then I suppose we shall all just have to go
in ignorance!'

Eleanor hesitated. Beth looked at her shrewdly. 'Do you truly not want to know, Nell?'

Eleanor sighed. 'Of course I want to know! I am consumed with curiosity!'

They both laughed, Eleanor with a little embarrassment.

'Then...' Beth said meaningfully.

'But I shall *not* ask!' Eleanor said, with spirit. 'I have told you, Beth—I do not wish to like Kit any more...'

'What, any more than you do already?'

Eleanor sighed again. There went another of her secrets. 'Beth...'

Beth clapped her hands together. 'I knew it! You cannot help yourself!'

Eleanor blushed a little. 'I do like Kit, I admit it! I cannot seem to help it! Yet...' she sobered '...I am also so very angry with him, Beth! I cannot just forgive and forget!'

'Then speak to him!' Beth urged, leaning forward. 'Oh Nell, you cannot bottle it all up and pretend it never happened! Your resentment will fester and turn sour and...' she made a slight gesture '...what sort of existence is that? Please...'

Eleanor's heart was beating fast. She had to make Beth understand. She put her teacup down carefully.

'Beth, I cannot allow Kit too close,' she said baldly. 'He wants a family and will expect—in time—that we will resume...that things will be...oh, you know what I mean!' She made a gesture of exasperation. 'He does not want a marriage in name only…'

'I imagine not!'

'So…' Eleanor looked at her pleadingly. 'Surely you understand? I cannot go through that again! The thought of making love…' She shuddered. 'Oh, a part of me wishes reconciliation with Kit more than anything, for safety, for security… But then I remember…'

Beth sighed. 'Eleanor, because it happened once, it need not be the same again. And with Kit's love and support—'

'No!' Eleanor could feel a pain starting in her throat, the pain she always got when she remembered the horror of losing her child. 'I know there is no good reason for how I feel…'

'Of course there is!' Beth caught both her hands. 'The best reason! You were young and alone and you miscarried your baby! No wonder you are angry and upset…'

Eleanor clung to her. 'Then say you understand! If I allow myself to like Kit even a little, I am afraid of what will happen!' She freed herself and put her hands over her face.

She felt Beth's arms go around her as her sister-in-law hugged her tight. It was inexpressibly comforting. Eleanor gave a little sigh.

'Damnation! I hate being such a watering-pot!' She sat up. 'You should know, Beth, that though I envy you the affection you have in your marriage to

Marcus, in mine I intend nothing more than a luke-warm respect...'

'Oh, Eleanor!' Eleanor heard the laughter in Beth's voice as her sister-in-law let her go and sat back. She looked at her enquiringly.

'Beth? What have I said?'

Beth was shaking her head. 'Have you thought about Kit at all in this, my love?'

Eleanor frowned. Was Beth being deliberately obtuse? 'Constantly! I thought that you realised that that was the problem...'

Beth shook her head again. 'No, I mean, have you thought what Kit will do whilst you try to achieve some sort of lukewarm, makeshift marriage?' She laughed. 'I have known my cousin all my life and I would say that he is no more patient than the next man! Well...' Beth shrugged '...a little more patient than Marcus, perhaps, but in general terms—' She broke off.

Eleanor watched her with foreboding. She had the sudden feeling that she had miscalculated and that Beth was about to put her finger on the flaw in her reasoning.

'All the time that you are laying your plans, Nell...' Beth expanded carefully '...Kit will be making his. And believe me, they will not involve a marriage of convenience, or a compromise where you never speak to each other except to request the butter! So you must be prepared to oppose him. And which of you will be the stronger? Especially...' Beth fixed her with a stern regard and Eleanor felt herself shrink a little '...when at least a part of you is on the same side as Kit!'

Eleanor felt her heart sink. She knew Beth was right but she also knew she had to try. It was the only compromise that she was prepared to accept. The idea of making love, the thought of another pregnancy, the horror of another miscarriage... She shuddered violently.

'It is the only thing that I can do,' she said sadly. 'I am sorry, Beth, but I have no choice.'

Chapter Five

'Damnation!'

Eleanor peered at her reflection in the mirror, dropped her reticule on the floor with a thud and sank down on to her bed in a heap. She was already dressed for the ball and now she had decided that she would not attend after all. She was feeling very cross-grained. In fact, she was blue-devilled.

'Whatever is the matter, milady?' Lucy enquired mildly. She had been helping her mistress to dress and only a moment before had told her how very pretty she looked. And indeed, Eleanor thought now, she did look her best in her favourite dress, a simple silk slip with gold gauze that flattered her colouring and emphasised the slenderness of her figure. She had chosen the dress for two reasons—one was to give her courage at the first social occasion since Kit's return and the second... Eleanor snapped her fan closed and drummed it against her fingers. The second reason also featured Kit and here Eleanor frowned ferociously. Her pride had demanded that she look her best so that Kit admired her and now she was disgusted with her own behaviour. Remembering her conversation with Beth earlier, Eleanor sighed heavily. Kit's admiration—or lack of it—should be nothing to her. If she wished to keep her distance from Kit she should do nothing to encourage him.

'I am not going,' she said baldly.

Lucy continued with her placid tidying of the room. She picked up several discarded dresses and hung them away.

'I expect you're feeling nervous, ma'am,' she sympathised. 'You'll feel better when you have his lordship by your side...'

'No I shan't!' Eleanor said pettishly. 'I shall feel much worse! In fact the thought of going to this ball with Lord Mostyn makes me feel quite monstrous ill...'

'May I come in?'

Eleanor broke off sharply at the sound of Kit's voice. He was standing in the doorway, not the door to his dressing-room, which was still firmly fastened on Eleanor's side with a shiny new bolt, but the door to the landing. Eleanor scrambled to her feet, feeling foolish and annoyed to have been found slouching on her bed in so undignified a position. Had Kit heard her words? She could not tell. His face was impassive. She felt ashamed of herself.

'I have something for you,' Kit continued, coming forward into the room. He was carrying a flat package in his hand. He nodded a dismissal to Lucy who tripped out, a smile of romantic satisfaction on her face. It only added to Eleanor's irritation that her maid persisted in thinking that she and Kit were involved in some passionate reconciliation—despite the ostentatious bolt on the door.

'What is it?' she asked, knowing she sounded ungracious.

Kit seemed unperturbed. 'It is a surprise,' he said. 'Turn around to face the mirror and close your eyes.'

It was on the tip of Eleanor's tongue to refuse, but something in Kit's face made her comply with his request. She closed her eyes, then almost jumped as she felt Kit's fingers lightly touch her neck, warm against her skin. The sensation was in no way unpleasant but suddenly her skin seemed peculiarly sensitive to the brush of his hand and she had to force herself not to move away. She felt confused and light-headed, and it was a relief when Kit said:

'Open your eyes!'

Eleanor did so, and saw that she was wearing a delicately worked pendant necklace of diamonds and emeralds set in white gold, the exact colour of her dress. She stared, entranced.

'Oh, it is so pretty! But...' she turned her head to look at Kit '...surely these are the Mostyn diamonds? I have seen Beth wearing them...'

Kit was smiling at her in a way that only served to increase her confusion. 'They suit you very well,' he said slowly. 'I thought that they would.'

Eleanor stroked the stones of the necklace gently.

The metal had felt cold at first but was starting to warm now as it lay against her skin. It was a beautiful necklace and Kit was right, its delicacy suited her well. Not for her the enormous parures of some of the matrons, the stiff encrustations of jewels that looked as though they were some sort of armour. She was so slender that she needed something equally light and ethereal.

'Beth wanted you to have them,' Kit said now, smiling at her reassuringly as Eleanor continued to look uncertain. 'They are family jewels intended to be worn by each Lady Mostyn. They are rightfully yours. Besides,' he grinned, 'maybe it is ungentlemanly of me to mention it, but Beth felt that she needed something slightly more…robust… to suit her figure!'

Eleanor was betrayed into a giggle. 'Well, she could carry off something more magnificent, whereas I do not have the…er…appropriate proportions…'

She glanced down at her own, small bust, looked up and realised that Kit was looking in the same direction. He raised a lazy eyebrow, the smile still on his lips.

'I have no complaint, Eleanor!'

Eleanor felt a huge wave of colour start at her feet and envelop her up to her hairline. She felt hot and embarrassed and, worse, she felt dizzy and confused. If Kit was always going to be able to make her feel such a troubling awareness, she was not sure that she could bear to live in such close proximity with him. To cover her embarrassment, she reached for her evening cloak and started to chatter brightly.

'Perhaps if Mama could be persuaded to give up the Trevithick rubies, Beth would have a necklace worthy of her. They are not really Mama's to wear anyway, given that Papa was never the Earl. Have you seen the necklace, Kit? It is a magnificent piece but huge and barbaric and needs to be set off by an appropriate…' She stopped and waved her hands about mutely, realising that she was back on the same subject again.

'An appropriate décolletage?' Kit murmured. He had taken the cloak from her and was setting it about her, and Eleanor was aware of his hands on her shoulders, firm and strong. She pulled the cloak together to hide her own décolletage, which once again appeared to have become the focus of his eyes.

'Well, shall we go?' she enquired, a shade too brightly. 'We do not wish to miss any of the ball!'

'No indeed,' Kit said, a little wryly. 'It should be an occasion to remember!'

Eleanor eyed him a little warily. It had not occurred to her that Kit might have any concerns about the evening, yet when she thought about it she realised that his position was as awkward as her own. Not only was there the difficult water of family relationships to negotiate, but there was the unknown element of the reaction of the *Ton*. Society was so fickle and could outlaw one of their own at a stroke.

'I am sure you need have no concerns about your welcome from the family,' she said, as they seated themselves in the carriage. 'No matter what anyone is thinking, I am persuaded that their behaviour will be quite proper on the surface.'

'As your brother did this morning?' Kit enquired with sarcasm. 'You may feel it important to maintain a superficial façade, my dear, but I fear that Trevithick does not share your values!' There was such an undertone of bitterness in his voice that Eleanor put out an instinctive hand to him, then snatched it back, hoping that Kit had not seen. They completed the rest of the short journey to Trevithick House in silence.

'Marcus!' Eleanor hissed in her brother's ear two hours later, 'can you not behave with a little more discretion? Everyone is looking at us and if you persist in cutting Kit dead every time that you pass him they will have plenty more to gossip about! It was bad enough for you to behave so disgracefully earlier, but now it is outrageous!'

They were standing in the entrance to the main ballroom and were ostensibly watching the press of visitors who were pushing their way into the room with the eagerness, Marcus had said distastefully, of a crowd at a public hanging. Eleanor supposed that the popularity of the event was no great surprise—the Trevithick ball was one of the major events of the Season and in addition, society wished to indulge its curiosity. One family could provide a great deal of entertainment, after all, and just at the moment the Trevithicks were good value. There was the handsome Earl of Trevithick and his beautiful wife who would, it was whispered, produce a child after only *seven months* of marriage. Since no one knew exactly when the marriage had taken place they could not be completely sure, but they were counting. Then there was the bride's cousin Charlotte, a beautiful widow who had lived retired but had been snapped up by the Earl's cousin, Justin Trevithick, who had fallen in love with her at first sight. Justin himself was quite scandalous because he had been born out of wedlock. It was all a long time ago, but some of the dowagers had very long memories. And then there was Eleanor herself and the titillating tale of her desertion and apparent reconciliation... Eleanor sighed. Until that morning, she had not thought that Marcus would make a gift of things to the gossips.

'If you could just speak to Kit without looking as though you would like to hit him across the room...'

The Earl of Trevithick gave his sister a derisive look. 'Eleanor, that is precisely what I wish to do to your husband and I never saw fit to hide my feelings on the matter! Whether you wish to effect a reconciliation with Mostyn or tell him to go to hell, that is your concern and I will support you whatever you choose! However, you cannot expect me to *like* him after what he did...'

Eleanor clutched his sleeve, trying to smile at the same time at Lady Pomfret, who was hovering a short distance away. 'But Marcus, the scandal! Everyone will see...'

Marcus shrugged. 'Who cares? You refine too much upon such things, Eleanor!' A smile softened his face as he looked down at her. 'I only agreed to you staying with Mostyn because Beth persuaded me I should not stand between you. Do not ask any more of me than that, I beg you!'

Eleanor sighed. She knew that Marcus, ever the protective elder brother, only wanted what was best for her, but he was making matters very difficult, whilst Beth and Charlotte, with connections on both sides, were trying to make peace. It was as though the Mostyn and Trevithick feud, so virulent for centuries and only recently laid to rest, had somehow reasserted itself. Except that it was not that simple any more.

She tried one last time. 'Marcus, I am trying to put a good face on this and you and Justin are undoing all my good work...'

Marcus quirked a brow. 'So Justin is shunning Mostyn as well, is he? Excellent!'

Eleanor sighed in exasperation. 'I believe you have put him up to it!' she said wrathfully. 'And Charlotte is deeply upset... Oh, it is too bad of the two of you! Why must you be so stubborn?'

Marcus grinned. 'It is the Trevithick pride, my dear Eleanor! Surely you know of it, for you possess it too!'

'Well, I do not see why you should be so proud of being proud!' Eleanor said, trying not to stamp her foot with frustration. 'It is childish and conceited and rude! Really, Marcus! I shall not stand up with you for the boulanger now!'

Marcus sketched her a bow, giving her an unrepentant grin. Eleanor found it was surprisingly difficult not to smile back. She was very fond of him for all that he infuriated her.

'Very well, dear sis, withdraw your promise to dance—if you wish to make a scandal!'

He strolled off and Eleanor could almost swear he was whistling softly under his breath.

Feeling irritated in the extreme, she sought the quiet of the conservatory, which had been decorated with little coloured lanterns and furnished with rustic benches to provide a restful place away from the noise of the ballroom. She had arranged to dance the next with Kit, but for the moment he was dancing a stately minuet with Beth and Eleanor was glad to see that despite Marcus's poor example there were plenty of people who were prepared to acknowledge him.

Eleanor sat down. It was most infuriating that she, with the greatest grievance, was the one who was defending Kit against Marcus's intransigence. She hoped that Beth might exert some influence but she thought it unlikely. Marcus could be damnably stubborn. The whole family suffered from the trait.

A movement caught her eye in the most deeply shadowed part of the conservatory and for a moment Eleanor wondered if she had disturbed a tryst. It was not unlikely, for people would snatch whatever moment of privacy they were afforded. Then she real-

ised that the lovers—if that was what they were—
had not even noticed her presence, for they were
continuing to talk in low, urgent whispers. She could
overhear a very little:

'Do you have some for me? Oh please…'

There was a laugh. 'Not if you cannot pay for it,
my lady…'

There was more pleading, even, Eleanor thought,
the sound of a suppressed sob. She tried to keep still
and quiet, hoping that the others would go out of the
long doors at the other end of the conservatory without realising that she was there. It was impossible
for her to escape without being noticed and she had
no wish to move now and give away the fact that
she had been there a little while—she was in a most
difficult position.

'Here, take this then…' She heard a scrabbling
sound, then a sigh of satisfaction. 'Ah, at last…'

'Thank you, my lady.' The man spoke a little
louder now. Eleanor knew somehow that this was
not a pair of lovers—the woman's desperation was
of another sort and the man's tone more mocking
than affectionate. She heard a step, fortunately away
at the other end of the room, then the creak of one
of the rustic benches as the woman moved into the
lantern light and sat down. Eleanor could see that
she was alone now, tilting a glass to her lips, closing
her eyes. Eleanor stared, and felt the cold freeze her
to the marrow. No young lover, this. It was the
Dowager Lady Trevithick.

Eleanor leapt to her feet and hurried down the

conservatory without pausing to think. Ever since her mother had made such a terrible fuss over her elopement, she had kept away from her as much as was practical, allowing the Dowager's anger to cool, avoiding the worst of her diatribes. They had never been on intimate terms, for Lady Trevithick was too cold and distant to have endeared herself to any of her children, but now Eleanor could think of nothing but that her mother must be ill, or in trouble, and needed her help. She reached Lady Trevithick just as the Dowager, with a little, furtive gesture, slipped something into her reticule and hauled herself to her feet, smiling at her daughter with a type of cunning triumph that was as puzzling as it was unpleasant. In the pale light of the coloured lanterns her eyes seemed unnaturally bright and her bonnet was askew. She was panting slightly.

'Mama?' Eleanor looked at her closely. 'What are you doing here? Are you feeling unwell? Are you fatigued?'

Lady Trevithick beamed at her daughter. 'Not at all! I am in plump currant! Never better! Delightful evening, is it not? Lend me your arm, girl, for I think I shall go to the card room for a round of vingt-et-un…'

Eleanor automatically extended her arm and the Dowager leant heavily on it as they walked with painful slowness towards the conservatory door and out into the ballroom. The crowd was thinning a little now but it was too late for Eleanor to identify her mother's companion of a few moments before.

She hesitated to ask, knowing it was inviting a crushing set down, but her curiosity was strong.

'That gentleman, mama—the one who was just leaving…'

Lady Trevithick's claw-like hand dug into Eleanor's arm with bruising force. Eleanor winced.

'Mama! You're hurting me…'

'Did you see him?' Lady Trevithick hissed. 'Did you hear?'

Eleanor looked at her in puzzled incomprehension. 'No… That is, I was just coming in as he left you…'

'Ah…' The cruel grip on her arm relaxed just a little. Eleanor looked down, where the Dowager's hand still clutched her. Her mother's fingers were encrusted with diamonds and rubies, and round her throat hung the Trevithick rubies, the gleaming stones almost lost amongst the deep lines and folds of the Dowager's neck. Rings, necklace… Eleanor frowned. There was something missing. The ruby bracelet that matched the magnificent necklace had gone. Her mother's wrist was quite bare. In an instant Eleanor remembered the mysterious conversation in the conservatory, the payment… She bit her lip.

'I was talking to Kemble, my dear,' her mother said sweetly, smiling. 'You must remember Lord Kemble—you jilted him! He helped me to a seat so that I could rest. So thoughtful a man! I know that you have no taste for him, my dear, but I have always rather liked him!' She blinked at her daughter gently, her dark eyes unfocused. 'It would have been so much better had you married him, Eleanor, so much easier... My debts...'

'Mama,' Eleanor said again, deeply worried now. 'Are you sure you are quite well? Indeed you look most ill...'

The Dowager swayed like a giant tree in the wind. Eleanor tightened her grip on her mother's arm to help her stay upright and felt something sharp press against her—the bottle in her mother's reticule.

'I feel just the thing,' the Dowager murmured vaguely. 'I shall go and play a hand of cards and who knows, I may win! Money to pay my debts— now there's the thing!'

She loosened her grip on Eleanor's arm and raised a hand in unsteady salutation. 'Good night, my dear!'

Eleanor watched the Dowager wend her unsteady way towards the door of the card-room and did not know whether to feel glad or sorry when she saw the joint cohorts of Lady Pomfret and Mrs Belton converge on her from either side and carry her over the threshold. No doubt they would fleece her and then her mother would be in even greater debt. But to whom did she owe money? Lord Kemble? And if so, for what? Eleanor looked at her mother's voluminous figure as the Trevithick Tabbies carried her off and in her mind's eye could still see the tell-tale bulge of the bottle in the reticule and the tell-tale absence of the ruby bracelet from her wrist.

'Eleanor? Is anything wrong?'

Eleanor turned sharply to see that Kit had come

up to her, unnoticed. He gave her a searching look. 'You seem a little discomposed, my dear. Is aught amiss?'

Eleanor painted a bright smile on her face. 'Why no, my lord, not precisely.' She took his proffered arm and they started to walk slowly around the edge of the floor. 'Everything is quite perfect if one discounts Mama's peculiar behaviour, and Marcus's bad manners...'

Kit's expression hardened. 'As far as your brother is concerned, he is only behaving as I would do if someone had acted so shabbily to Charlotte. In my heart I find I cannot blame him!'

This was not what Eleanor had expected to hear. She looked at him, a little taken aback. 'Oh, well—but that does not excuse him! Of all the childish things...'

Kit shrugged. He drew her a little closer to him. It felt very pleasant and Eleanor allowed herself to relax.

'I fear Marcus is too stubborn...'

'It is good of you to take my part against him but it is a trait that I understand,' Kit said with a smile. 'Is it not a charge that could be levelled at the Mostyns as much as the Trevithicks?'

'Yes, but Marcus should learn when it is appropriate to be more tolerant! Surely if I can behave with dignity...'

'Ah, but that is all for show, is it not?' Kit's expression, as it rested on her face, was quizzical. Eleanor flushed.

'Yes, but… No, not precisely. I mean I would be pleased if we could be friends…'

'Friends,' Kit smiled suddenly at her. 'That sounds most pleasant, albeit a little colourless. But perhaps we could start with that. Yes, I should like that too.'

Eleanor looked at him uncertainly. 'Are you teasing me, Kit?'

'Not at all. I am happy to accept whatever you are prepared to give.'

Eleanor looked up into his face. Behind the light tone she could hear something more serious and it made her pulse jump. She tore her gaze away from his and spoke quickly.

'Then that is settled. It would be more comfortable, I think, and a friendship need make no unnecessary demands upon us…'

She risked a look at his face and saw that he was smiling, saw the leap of something in his eyes that made her own body leap in response. This was moving a little too quickly for her. She found that she was breathless.

'My lord…'

'Evening, Mostyn. I wish I could say that I am glad to see you back! Lady Mostyn, I have come to claim our cotillion…'

Eleanor jumped again and the colour flooded her face. 'Lord George…'

Lord George Darke had come upon them whilst she had been quite intent on Kit and now she did not know whether to be glad or sorry. In a rush she remembered the pouting lilies and the card, heavy with promise. She was not at all sure she wished to go with him.

Kit bowed, not troubling to hide his dislike of the other man. 'I am no more pleased to see you, Darke, than you are to see me.'

The two men measured one another for a moment, then Darke gave Kit an insolent bow and turned to offer his hand to Eleanor, and Kit walked away. Eleanor saw him stop to ask another lady for a dance—Miss Eversleigh, the Toast of the Season. Kit was wasting no time. The sight of him taking the girl's hand gave Eleanor a curious pang. She turned away.

Lord George was smiling at her. His grey eyes did not waver from her face, and his smile was intimate, charming, for her alone. He was reputed the most dangerous rake in London, fair as an angel but with a reputation so black Eleanor thought it could not possibly be true. Or so she hoped. She had heard tell that he wasted no time on the naïve débutantes of the *Ton*, that his interest was solely in widows or jaded married ladies whose boredom he alleviated with skill and finesse. Eleanor assumed that most of these ladies had experience to match Darke's own. She, on the other hand, had far more in common with the innocent débutantes and she was uncertain that she could cope. So far their skirmishes had been relatively harmless—a dance here and there, a few compliments that she should have repressed but had not, no doubt leading him to believe that she was fair game. Now she sensed that Darke meant business and oddly, it seemed that Kit's presence made him even more determined. He was pressing her hand in the most odiously familiar manner.

'Lady Mostyn, I have been waiting all evening for the pleasure of a dance with you...'

Despite herself, Eleanor could not repress a shiver of nervousness. Although she was in a crowded ballroom, she felt quite alone. Kit, having demanded that she show no favour to the rakes of the *Ton* had immediately abandoned her with the most dangerous one of all! And without a backward glance! Eleanor stole a look in his direction and saw that her husband was smiling down at Miss Eversleigh, bending close to her as he whispered something in her ear. The girl went into a peal of laughter and Eleanor felt out of proportion cross.

Darke saw her frown and his smile deepened, his fingers tightening on hers. Eleanor felt uncomfortable. She pulled her hand free and stepped away from him. He did not seem disconcerted, merely amused, as though he credited her with playing a game far cleverer than anything she had ever intended. She moved further away. He followed.

'Dear Lady Mostyn, do you care to dance or would you prefer to go somewhere more...private?'

Eleanor looked into those dissipated grey eyes and hesitated. It was imperative that she made it clear to him that she would not become one of his flirts, but it was difficult to see how to do this without drawing further attention. She had never been alone with him, except for the spurious privacy provided by a drive in the park, and knew better than to step aside with him now. She glanced around; plenty of people were watching them, which would make it even more foolish. Then she realised that Darke had interpreted this as calculation on her part and was smiling gently. He leant closer, taking her arm, his breath stirring the tendrils of hair about her face.

'Eleanor, if only you could be persuaded to look with kindness on me…'

Eleanor gave him a haughty glance. 'My name, sir?'

'Very well, Lady Mostyn. I understand that we must preserve the proprieties now that your husband is returned.' Darke's smile was predatory. Eleanor could tell that he thought she was still toying with him. She felt vaguely panicked.

'It is a pity,' Darke continued, 'that Mostyn chose to return when he did. But with discretion we can manage the situation…'

With a shock Eleanor realised just what it was he was suggesting. She raised her chin.

'I think that you mistake, my lord. My husband—'

'Yes, I understand,' Darke murmured. 'But it will be a greater challenge this way.'

Eleanor gave him a look of disgust. In a flash she saw herself as he did—a lady with a slightly soiled reputation who would be just another conquest, although her seduction would be sweeter for Darke because he would have taken her from under the nose of her husband. She felt sick.

'I repeat, you misunderstand me, my lord! There is no more to say!'

Darke's eyes swept over her with amused comprehension. 'You should not fear just because Mostyn is back! Nor suffer a belated bout of loyalty! What do you imagine that he has been doing whilst he was away, Eleanor? I hear that the winters are very pleasant in Italy, particularly if one has a little opera singer to warm one's bed!'

Eleanor pressed her hands together. 'I know all about my husband's absence, my lord,' she said steadily, looking him straight in the eye. 'He has told me all—'

Darke gave a crack of laughter. 'And you believed him? My dear, you are more foolish than I had thought!' His tone was spiteful. 'It is simply that you have no stomach for the game any more, is it not, sweet Eleanor? Assure you, you'd find me more than a match for Mostyn—'

'Excuse me if I wrest my wife away from you now, Darke. You should have enjoyed the dance while you could.'

Eleanor heard Kit's voice with inexpressible relief. She turned to him. 'There you are, my dear! Would you take me home now? I fear I am rather fatigued!'

'Certainly,' Kit said with aplomb. He offered her his arm and gave Darke the slightest and most insulting of bows.

'Do not even think about approaching my wife in future, Darke,' he said smoothly. 'She has made it

quite plain that she does not wish to speak to you
and I wish it even less. So unless you would care to
meet me over this…' He let the sentence fade away.
'No, I thought not. Eleanor my dear, if you are quite
ready…'

Eleanor swept past the curious guests as though
they were not present, but by the time they reached
the entrance hall she was shaking with shock and
reaction. Kit took her cloak from the hovering footman and wrapped it around her, and she drew its
folds closer for comfort. They went out to the carriage.

'A word of advice for future reference, my love.'
Kit's voice was light. 'When you choose to divest
yourself of your next admirer, pray do so in more
private circumstances! That is if it is your expressed
wish to present a façade to the *Ton* rather than make
yourself an entertainment for them! I imagine people
have not been so diverted by a public disagreement
in an age!'

Eleanor's temper gave way. 'If *you* had not left
me alone with Lord George the problem would not
have arisen, my lord! Upon my word, I cannot do
right for doing wrong!'

Kit laughed. He was sitting across from her and
in the shadowed interior of the carriage Eleanor
could not discern his expression. He sounded quite
indifferent, however, and somehow that made
Eleanor even more cross.

'I am sorry, my dear,' Kit said easily, 'but how
was I to know that you wished to discourage Darke?

I assumed that it was an indication of you going your own way, as mentioned the other night…'

'Piffle!' Eleanor said crossly. 'Nonsense, my lord! I was trying to get rid of Lord George just as I was trying to deter Sir Charles the other night! Why must you wilfully misunderstand me?'

'I am sorry,' Kit said mildly. Eleanor could hear the undertone of amusement still in his voice. 'You did indeed make it quite clear—to the entire room—that you wished to discourage Darke! So are there any other admirers whose pretensions you would like me to…er…depress, my love?'

Eleanor looked at him suspiciously. She was sure he was laughing at her and the matter did not seem in the least amusing to her.

'Yes, my lord! All of them!'

'Dear me,' Kit said gently, 'and will there be that many? You have been unconscionably popular, my dear!'

Eleanor gave an exasperated squeak. 'How many times must I tell you that it is none of my doing, my lord! If you will believe all the scandal you hear in the Clubs…'

'Yes, I do apologise,' Kit murmured. 'And as I was not here to protect you before, the least I can do is to look after you now. You will find me the most attentive of husbands, I promise you.'

Eleanor shifted on the seat. She felt a little mollified. 'Thank you, my lord. If you can pretend to a certain degree of possessiveness…'

'No indeed…' there was a smile in Kit's voice

'…I shall be quite genuinely protective, I assure you, my love. All in the interests of our…ah…friendship, of course!'

'Of course,' Eleanor echoed. She frowned a little, feeling slightly confused. Did that mean that Kit really cared or that he did not? She was not going to risk asking him. She wished it did not matter to her.

Chapter Six

The singer came to the end of her aria and Eleanor applauded politely, as did the rest of the company. Lady Seaton was so very proud to have persuaded so famous an opera singer as La Perla to perform at her musicale, but it was not to Eleanor's taste. She preferred country airs and slightly less rarefied songs—such heavy emotion seemed too much for the drawing-room, especially a drawing-room as crowded as Lady Seaton's.

'Are you enjoying the music, my love?' Kit asked, a twinkle in his eye. He was sitting beside her and Eleanor was tolerably sure that he had been asleep during the performance, if that were possible whilst La Perla was forcing out those top notes. She smiled at him prettily.

'La Perla is a consummate performer, I believe, my lord! It is my fault not hers that the music is not really to my taste!'

Kit laughed. 'I think we are all in need of something to revive us after that! Shall I fetch you a glass of lemonade, Eleanor?'

Eleanor nodded. 'Thank you, my lord. That would be most pleasant.'

She watched him go, a little mischievous smile on her lips. Despite protestations to the contrary, she had to admit that it was very pleasant to have her husband dance attendance upon her. They had spent the best part of the previous week together, driving in the park, attending the theatre, dancing together at all the balls... Eleanor sighed. It had been delightful. Better still, it had been safe. Certainly there was nothing for her to fear, for they had slipped into the easiest and most undemanding of friendships.

Eleanor wrinkled up her nose. And yet... Perhaps it was not entirely a simple friendship, for she had the oddest feeling that Kit was waiting for something, holding back, biding his time... She flicked her fan open. She felt as though she was being courted, but so gently that it was scarcely noticeable. But perhaps she was imagining it. With so much unspoken between them it would be impossible...

Beth was waving at her from across the aisle. Eleanor smiled back. That evening they had avoided the embarrassment of Marcus, Kit and Justin coming to blows by arriving at different times so that they sat as far away from each other as possible. Fortunately the Dowager Lady Trevithick was also present and made such a fuss of sitting down and fidgeting around after the music had started that she drew all attention. Eleanor acknowledged that it was hardly a permanent solution but it saved face in public. She made a mental note to speak to Beth about the feud as soon as she could. The whole business was becoming tiresome, like a schoolboys' game. She would almost swear that the men were enjoying it.

Eleanor waited until Kit had disappeared into the refreshment-room then made her way over to where Beth, Charlotte and the Dowager Lady Trevithick were sitting. After the flurry of greetings, Charlotte said mischievously:

'Do you think that one of us should go to keep and eye on matters in the refreshment-room? Marcus and Justin are in there and it would be most unfortunate if there were pistols over the lemonade!'

'Oh, let us both go!' Beth said hastily. She gave Eleanor a speaking look. 'I apologise for leaving you, dearest, but I am sure you will enjoy a comfortable coze with your mama. I will call on you tomorrow if I may.'

'Of course,' Eleanor murmured. She was not so sure that she would enjoy a tête-à-tête with Lady Trevithick, who had turned so strangely unpredictable of late. At the moment her mother was rocking backwards and forwards and humming a little under her breath, but as she caught Eleanor's eye she sat bolt upright and snapped: 'What are you staring at, girl? Didn't I teach you it was rude to stare? Never catch a husband if you look him straight in the eye!'

Eleanor blinked. It did not seem possible that her mother had forgotten she was already married. 'Yes,

Mama. I was only concerned because you did not seem quite yourself tonight. Are you enjoying the music?'

Lady Trevithick made a vague gesture that knocked her diamond tiara askew. 'Ridiculous wailing noise! Wish I'd stayed at home!' She took a deep swallow of her lemonade. 'Pooh! Insipid stuff! Get me a glass of ratafia, there's a good girl!'

Eleanor looked around, hoping that Kit would be coming back so that she could escape with him. Unfortunately he was nowhere in sight. Instead a smooth voice said:

'Ladies, a glass of wine? Allow me...'

Lord Kemble had paused beside them, proffering two glasses and his obsequious smile. Lady Trevithick grabbed a glass so hastily that she almost spilled it. 'Kemble! Good man!'

Eleanor took the other glass rather more reluctantly. She did not care for ratafia and she cared even less for Lord Kemble, who now showed every sign of lingering by her side, a look of unwholesome admiration in his eyes. Eleanor looked around again a little desperately for Kit. How long could it possibly take to fetch a glass of lemonade?

'If you are looking for your husband, my dear, I fear he has found metal more attractive in the refreshment-room,' Kemble murmured, bending close to her ear. 'La Perla, you know. Mostyn is... renewing their acquaintance, I suppose you could say...I hear that they were quite...intimate... in Italy this winter...'

Eleanor caught her breath as a sharp pain seemed to stab her just below her breastbone. So this was the opera singer whom rumour had so persistently linked to Kit, and he had the effrontery to escort her to a performance by his mistress! A consummate performer indeed! Eleanor blushed scarlet. She hardly needed to tell Kit what he must know already!

Kemble was looking odiously pleased with himself. 'You did not know? Oh, dear me...'

Eleanor looked him straight in the eye. 'You are speaking nonsense, my lord, and you know it! Furthermore it is nonsense that I do not care for—'

'Nonsense!' Lady Trevithick agreed, unexpectedly. 'Mostyn's been in Ireland, not Italy, don't you know! Heard it from the servants!' She thrust her wineglass at Eleanor. 'Hold my glass, there's a good girl. I need something from my reticule!'

Eleanor looked in some consternation from her mother to Lord Kemble, who was not smiling any more. 'There you are, my lord!' she said clearly. 'Ireland, not Italy. A simple mistake to make if one is not accomplished in geography...'

Kemble flushed. 'Very well, Lady Mostyn. I stand corrected...' He looked with ill-concealed contempt at the Dowager, who had grabbed her glass back and was gulping the ratafia down.

'I would watch Lady Trevithick most carefully, if I were you,' he added spitefully. 'She is making a fool of herself for the entertainment of the whole company! Good evening, Lady Mostyn.'

He straightened up and strolled off, and Eleanor

blushed bright red and drank several mouthfuls of her ratafia to try to steady herself. It was true—Lady Trevithick was becoming so very odd and unpredictable that one had to wonder just what she would do next. Eleanor could see any number of their acquaintance sniggering and watching with avid curiosity as her mother calmly took all her personal possessions out of her reticule, placed them on the chair beside her, then started to put them all back again. She was humming again and seemed quite happy. Eleanor felt an acute embarrassment mixed with a sudden protective loyalty that made her want to denounce them all for spiteful scandalmongers.

'Mama!' She hissed urgently, trying to help Lady Trevithick push her combs, handkerchiefs and laudanum bottle back into the reticule, 'are you sure that would not prefer to retire—'

Lady Trevithick carried on as though she had not heard.

'My bottle,' she murmured. 'It is empty of laudanum…'

A chill stole into Eleanor's heart. Surely her mother had not taken to dosing herself wherever she went?

'I believe you have some more at home, Mama,' she said calmly. 'Why not wait until you go back…'

'Ask Kemble for some more!' the Dowager said fretfully, clutching her purse to her breast. 'Tell him that I can pay this time!'

Eleanor took the purse gently from her mother's

hand and placed it in the reticule, snapping it closed and handing it back.

'No, Mama. Look, Marcus is returning now and the concert about to start again. If you are sure you are well enough to stay—' Once again she broke off in consternation. Lady Trevithick had fallen asleep.

Eleanor finished her ratafia and handed the glass back to a passing servant. No, she did not like the drink and lemonade would have been preferable. Which reminded her about Kit... She looked around, but he was still nowhere to be seen. With a sigh, Eleanor went back to her seat and wondered waspishly whether La Perla would resume her performance or whether she would not be able to drag herself away from Kit's side. Could Kemble have been correct? The rumours had been so very persistent.

Someone slid into the seat that Kit had vacated and Eleanor turned, startled. It was Sir Charles Paulet, a lascivious gleam in his eye. Eleanor sighed sharply. The evening was fast becoming most tiresome.

'Good evening, Lady Mostyn. You are looking quite, quite radiant tonight, truly a sight for delight.'

Eleanor inclined her head coldly. 'Good evening, Sir Charles.'

Sir Charles tittered. 'I see that Lord Mostyn is entranced with La Perla—the Pearl of great price, or should I say great vice...'

Eleanor snapped her fan together with a force that broke two of the struts. 'Excuse me, Sir Charles. I find your verse does not agree with me tonight. In fact it does not agree with me *at all* and I wish to hear no more of it!'

She saw that Kit was finally returning with a glass of lemonade and felt even more annoyed. La Perla was strolling back to her place at the top of the room, her silken skirts swaying suggestively, an arch little smile on her lips. Eleanor felt hot and flustered and frumpish.

'Good evening, my lord,' she snapped as Kit came to stand beside her chair. 'I thought you must have gone to Gunters to procure my lemonade—or possibly made it yourself!'

Kit raised a quizzical eyebrow at this display of bad humour.

'I beg your pardon, my love, for keeping you waiting!'

Eleanor hunched her shoulder against him and turned away. She saw that Sir Charles was smiling and it made her even angrier. The whole evening was degenerating into a farce in which her husband paid court to his mistress, her brother behaved like a stiff-necked fool, her mother displayed her bizarre antics for all to see and Eleanor herself was beset with the attentions of tiresome admirers.

Kit took charge of the situation.

'Paulet,' he drawled, 'you must be remarkably slow of understanding for a man of letters! I am sure that I warned you not to pester my wife with your attentions again!'

Sir Charles scooted away and Kit took his seat and handed Eleanor her glass.

'Something seems to have upset you, my love,' he said with commiseration. 'Can I help at all?'

'It is nothing, my lord!' Eleanor said crossly. She was watching as La Perla, the smile still on her red lips, held court amongst a group of five eager men. 'In your brief but eventful absence I have had to contend with Lord Kemble and Sir Charles as well as a host of other irritations! Whilst you...' her annoyance finally got the better of her '...have been renewing your acquaintance with La Perla—or so I understand!'

Kit's amused gaze went from her face to La Perla and back again.

'Acquainted with La Perla?' There was puzzlement in his tone. 'Indeed I am not! I apologise for my absence but I was speaking to Charlotte whilst Justin's back was turned. I barely addressed the diva—although I felt obliged to compliment her on her singing since she was standing next to me just now.'

'Don't seek to gammon me, sir,' Eleanor snapped. 'There are those who say you knew her in Italy...'

'I have not been to Italy recently,' Kit said. His gaze was very steady. 'What is this, Eleanor?'

Eleanor was starting to feel uncertain and a little silly. 'It was Sir Charles,' she admitted. 'And Lord Kemble. They were intimating that you... That the lady was a friend of yours...'

'Ah...' A smile curled Kit's lips. 'Our inestimable

friend, Sir Charles! Always stirring up trouble! And in rhyming couplets to boot!'

Eleanor smothered a giggle. 'I am sorry.' She looked up, met Kit's eyes and fell silent. There was a curious feeling inside her now that the indignation had gone. She felt foolish for rising to the provocation, and she knew she had made it easy for those who had deliberately tried to upset her. But that was because she lacked confidence in Kit's affection and also...

'The rumours have been very persistent,' she said, blushing a little, 'and I did not know... You had not told me...'

Kit held her gaze very deliberately. 'I thought that we had agreed that you did not want to know?'

'Yes...' Eleanor fidgeted with the beading on her evening bag. She looked up unhappily and saw that Kit was still watching her. It made her feel curiously breathless.

'I was jealous!' She blurted out. The colour rushed to her face and she dropped her gaze at once, unable to believe what she had done. To confess such a thing, and in public! Why, anyone could have heard and now Kit only needed to laugh at her to shrivel her confidence completely.

He took one of her hands in his. His touch was casual but warm and it filled her with a curious tingling.

'Eleanor...' his voice was low, in her ear '...you have no cause for jealousy. Upon my honour, you never did.'

Their eyes met again, the deep blue of Kit's capturing and trapping hers. Eleanor took a shaky breath. 'Oh... Why did I say that?'

She saw Kit smile and it did strange things to her insides, making her dizzy.

'Friends can say anything to each other,' he said, tucking her hand through his arm. 'Old friends, good friends...'

Eleanor felt slightly disappointed but was not sure why. This friendship of theirs was becoming a little confusing and perhaps it was not exactly what she wanted after all. She struggled to sort out her feelings but was conscious of nothing but a rather peculiar languor coming over her. The room was full and very warm and now that the concert was starting again, La Perla was insisting on all the lights being doused because she preferred to sing by candlelight. Eleanor relaxed sleepily. They had been to a ball the night before and it had been a long day, but that hardly accounted for this strange feeling, which was a mixture of acute awareness and lassitude. She was very conscious of Kit next to her; her skin seemed to prickle where his arm brushed hers, and she imagined that she could feel the warmth of his body and told herself that she was becoming foolish.

She was, however, feeling very heated and was not at all sure why. At first she tried to fan herself but her hot cheeks seemed to radiate ever more heat. Then the room started to spin around very slowly. Eleanor sat up straighter, puzzled and alarmed. These were surely not the effects of thwarted love,

nor did she feel particularly unwell, but she did feel
rather giddy…

Her head brushed Kit's shoulder and she left it
there. That was nice. That felt very comfortable after
all the upsets of the evening. She closed her eyes
briefly.

'Eleanor!'

Kit's whisper stirred the tendrils of hair by her ear.
Eleanor opened her eyes reluctantly.

'What is it?'

'Are you ill?' Kit's face was very close, his expression concerned. Eleanor made an effort and
turned her head. The room seemed very dark, the
candlelight fluttering. The diva was still wailing, but
her voice appeared to come from a long way away.
Eleanor smiled.

'No indeed, I am quite comfortable, thank you.'

She saw Kit frown. 'Then why are you sleeping
in the middle of a recital? People will see…'

'Let them.' Eleanor remembered Marcus's words
when she had taken him to task at the ball. She
smiled slightly to herself. Marcus knew a thing or
two! Why worry what other people thought… She
yawned and allowed her head to sink back on to
Kit's shoulder. She felt as though she was sliding
very gently down. Soon she would be resting in his
lap but really it did not matter. She felt just as she
had done five years ago, when she had tasted her
mother's laudanum to see what it was like and had
not realised that a small dose was all that was

needed. Then she had slept for a whole day, but the initial feeling had been most pleasant.

'Excuse me, my wife is feeling unwell…'

'No I am not—'

Eleanor realised indignantly that she had been woken again. She struggled upright. She did not feel unwell—in fact she felt very happy. Kit had an arm around her and was steering her down the aisle between the chairs. Her feet seemed to be working independently of her mind. Fortunately. Behind them the opera singer's voice rose and fell like a peal of bells. Eleanor winced.

'She is giving me the headache…'

'Hush!' Kit spoke quickly, but there was an undertone of amusement in his voice that Eleanor could hear and it made her smile again. She could see quite well although the room was still revolving slowly and she could even keep her eyes open with an effort but it was pleasant to feel Kit's arm around her nevertheless. She leant against him a little more heavily and he obliged by tightening his grip.

They were in the entrance hall and Kit was requesting the carriage, quickly. He bundled her up the steps and sat down. Eleanor came to rest on his knee. She put her arms about his neck—to steady herself— and turned her face against his throat.

'Eleanor, you are foxed.' Kit's voice came sharply out of the darkness. 'What have you been drinking and how can you be in such state as this?'

Eleanor sat bolt upright. 'I am not drunk! I did not even have the lemonade if you recall…'

'No…' Kit still sounded sharp '…you evidently had something else! What were you doing whilst I was gone?'

Eleanor brightened. 'Well, there was the ratafia that Lord Kemble gave me, but I only had one glass. I have drunk it before, you know, and never felt like this! But do not worry, Kit! I am quite happy…'

The light from the carriage lanterns skipped across Kit's face. She could see that he was frowning heavily and she did so want to try to help him puzzle out the mystery.

'Laudanum!' she said helpfully, and winced as Kit took her by the shoulders in a grip that bruised. She slid off his knee and came to rest half-sitting, half-lying on the seat of the coach.

'Ouch! You are hurting me, Kit!'

Kit shook her slightly. Eleanor's head bounced. She almost giggled.

'Eleanor, have you been taking laudanum?'

'No!' Eleanor blinked owlishly at him. Really he could be quite slow sometimes. 'I meant that the only time I felt like this before was when I had sampled Mama's laudanum…'

'And have you been sampling it again this evening?' Kit demanded.

'No!' Eleanor felt most indignant. 'Mama was asking for some, but…'

She heard Kit sigh and snuggled closer to him. 'Unless it was in her glass of ratafia, of course! I do believe I may have given her the wrong glass after she had emptied her reticule…'

Kit took her chin in his hand and turned her face up to the faint light. Eleanor blinked, trying to focus on his face. It was difficult in the dark.

'Well, you have certainly had something!' Kit sounded decidedly snappish and Eleanor closed her eyes and put her head on his shoulder.

'I do not know why you are so very cross, Kit. I am not cross, I am happy.' She wriggled a little. 'Everything happened whilst I was waiting for you to disentangle yourself from La Perla. And although I am happy to hear that she is not your mistress...' Eleanor gave a little hiccup '...her singing gave me an earache...'

'A most remarkable *alter ego* seems to emerge at times like this,' Kit observed. He pulled her closer, so that she was resting again on his lap. 'It is as though you have partaken of several strong drinks! Have you much experience with alcohol, Eleanor?'

Eleanor smiled against his neck. 'Certainly not, for Mama never let me drink anything other than tea and lemonade during my Season.' She hesitated. 'I confess that at the start of this year I did try a few glasses of punch, for I thought it would be fun to become a fast matron...'

'Did you? Why was that?'

'Oh, because they were calling me the abandoned bride and I thought it would be so much more fun to be know as the *fast* Lady Mostyn!' She felt Kit's arms stiffen about her and said kindly: 'Do not worry, Kit, for I am quite over that now. It did not suit my nature to be promiscuous, you see, for I worry far too much about the opinion of the world!' She was struck by another thought. 'Also I suppose it would not have been the right thing to do, as I was married to you. And I know you believed me unchaste but that is quite untrue, which is why I was so very glad to find that La Perla was not your mistress...'

Eleanor struggled a little, feeling glad to have got that off her chest but aware that there was a little more for complete honesty. 'Of course, there were a few men who tried to snatch a kiss...'

Kit's arms tightened again and it felt wonderfully protective. 'Let them try now!'

Eleanor smiled. This was all very satisfactory. She liked being Kit's friend.

'I am sorry, Eleanor.' Kit's mouth was pressed against her hair. She was dimly aware that there was an odd wrench in his voice. 'I never intended for matters to go so awry...'

'That is perfectly all right, Kit,' Eleanor said magnanimously. She was feeling remarkably happy and full of generosity towards the entire world. She wriggled, and felt Kit shift beneath her. 'Oh, I am sorry if it is uncomfortable for you!'

'It is, but not in the way that you mean,' Kit said dryly. 'However, as we have such a excellent opportunity, perhaps we might continue to find out a little more about each other.'

'Mmm!' Eleanor nodded. It had been a little like a parlour game as she and Kit had discussed their likes and dislikes, their interests and their hopes a little more each day. She had enjoyed it and it had been quite innocent. Eleanor vaguely remembered that she was supposed to be keeping Kit at arm's length for some reason that escaped her just at the moment. She looked down. He was not precisely at arm's length now, but as he was so warm and safe and friendly she did not really mind.

'You start!' she said.

'Very well, then. I have a question for you.' Kit's voice was warm. 'Do you believe in love, Eleanor?'

Love! Eleanor wrinkled her brow. She knew she had all sorts of ideas about love normally but just at the moment she felt so extraordinarily sleepy that she could not remember them.

'That is a difficult question,' she said cautiously. 'What do you think, Kit?'

Kit laughed. 'A skilful answer... What do I think? Well yes, I believe in love!'

'Truly?' Eleanor was entranced. She rubbed her cheek against the smooth coolness of his shirtfront. 'That is nice!'

'Yes...' She thought that Kit was trying not to laugh. 'It would be even nicer if you were to agree with me!'

'Yes,' Eleanor said dreamily, 'and I do believe that there must be something in what you say, Kit! For there is Marcus and Beth and Charlotte and Justin to prove your case! And though it may not be fashionable to love one's spouse it is rather pleasant to see...'

'Pleasant!' Kit's lips brushed her cheek lightly and

Eleanor found herself shivering. 'That is one word for it, I suppose. A rather dull word—like friendship…'

'I do not think friendship dull!' Eleanor said, stung. 'It is the sweetest thing, for without Beth and Charlotte I should be quite lost…'

'And without me?'

'Oh well…' Eleanor smiled. 'You are quite different.'

'Better? Or worse?'

'Different!' Eleanor played with the intricate folds of his neck-cloth. 'I believe that you are fishing for compliments!'

'You may be right.' Kit sounded rueful. 'I doubt I shall receive any from you tonight though.'

Eleanor paused. She had succeeded in undoing the neck-cloth's starchy folds and felt quite inordinately pleased with herself. She also felt very light-headed, dizzy almost. This was an interesting experience but one she was not sure she wished to repeat.

'I do not know…' She put her head on one side. 'You are prodigious handsome, Kit, and it is pleasant to know that other ladies envy me your company. And you are really very kind to me and…'

'And?'

'And I think you quite an attractive man!' Eleanor finished triumphantly. 'There! So you see I can flatter you after all!'

'So you can.' Kit touched her cheek, very lightly, and Eleanor was perplexed to feel her dizziness increase. Something odd was happening, separating her mind from her increasingly wayward body. Whilst her thoughts were busily spinning off into space, her body appeared to be pressing itself closer to Kit, sweetly, confidingly wrapping itself around him...

'We are home,' Kit said dryly, and Eleanor realised that they were indeed turning into Montague Street and drawing up outside the house. She allowed Kit to help her down and the cool evening air outside the carriage doused her like a cold bath. She staggered a little and clutched Kit's arm.

'Oh! I beg your pardon. I shall not be taking any laudanum again, accidentally or not...'

'A wise decision,' Kit murmured. He swept her easily into his arms. 'Come along. I will take you upstairs.'

Carrick's jaw dropped when he saw Eleanor in Kit's arms, but he recovered himself quickly. Lucy, who had been stoking the fire in Eleanor's bedroom, and turning the bed down, was not so reticent.

'Oh sir, oh madam! How romantic!'

'No it is not!' Eleanor carolled, over Kit's shoulder. 'I am three parts disguised, I fear, Lucy, though from medicine and not strong drink!'

'Good night!' Kit said, shutting the door in the maid's startled face. 'I will call you if I need you!'

He placed Eleanor gently on the bed. She stretched luxuriously, arms above her head. It had been a most pleasant experience but she was aware that she was more than a little adrift and it would probably be better to go to sleep. She blinked sleepily at Kit. He was standing by the side of the bed looking down on her and in the pale light of the fire she could see that the lines of his face were tense. She wriggled a little and his gaze came up to her face and Eleanor saw the vivid flash of desire in his eyes before their expression was veiled again. She giggled.

'Oh dear, I am sorry! Am I behaving very badly? Do you wish to make love to me, Kit?'

She saw the flicker of a smile touch his mouth. 'Yes, but I believe I may be able to resist you! Although...' his gaze flickered over her face and rested on her lips for a second before he wrenched it away '...you are very lovely, Eleanor.'

Eleanor smiled sleepily. She felt warm and very happy. 'Thank you. If you would like to make love to me I do not mind...'

Kit smiled again. 'I would hope for slightly more enthusiasm on your part when the time does serve, my love. It would be better if you went to sleep now.'

There was no reply. Eleanor's eyelashes flickered, and then she gave a little sigh and turned her head against the pillow. She was still smiling.

Kit let out the breath that he had been holding and sat down gingerly on the side of the bed. There was a strange feeling in his stomach, similar to the guilt and pain he had felt when Beth had torn a strip off him—similar, but far more poignant. Eleanor looked so very young and vulnerable lying there, her dress just sliding from one shoulder to expose the slope of her breast, her hair tumbled across the pillow in strands of darkest mahogany and glossy black. Damn it, he had never meant to hurt her so. When she had confided about being the abandoned bride he had thought his heart would break.

Kit leant back against the bedpost and looked at her. Her face was untroubled in sleep, creamy pale, black lashes against the curve of her cheek.

'Do you wish to make love to me, Kit?'

Kit smiled despite himself. Of all the artless questions... They had made love only twice before he had gone away and it had been everything that he had always wanted and had told himself did not exist; sweetness, tenderness, intense pleasure. He had not experienced such a thing in any of his dealings with the bored wives of the *Ton* or the Cyprians whose legendary skill was supposed to grant such enjoyment. Eleanor's innocence had erased and supplanted all of that as though it had never existed. And she had cried a little in his arms and told him that she loved him...

But she did not remember that now. Tonight she was adrift with laudanum, and although it had shown a completely different side to her nature he was hardly ungentlemanly enough to take advantage. She would hate him for it in the morning and besides, there were too many matters unsettled between them...

Kit shifted, uncomfortable with both his thoughts and his state of arousal. He had ached to make love to Eleanor for the past week but this was scarcely the right time.

He put out a hand and brushed the hair away from Eleanor's face. It slid through his fingers, soft and silky. Her skin was warm to the touch. Kit stood up abruptly. Any more of this self-indulgence and he would be starting to undress her—whilst reassuring himself that it was only to make her more comfortable, to help her to sleep more easily. The idea was so appealing that he backed away hastily. Once he had started he would have to finish and disrobe her completely. It would not do to call the maid in when Eleanor was in her chemise—he did not wish to appear the sort of man who ogled his wife whist she was unconscious.

Bad-tempered and frustrated, Kit marched across to the door and flung it open. The corridor was suspiciously empty, although he suspected that Lucy would listen at doors if only to find out whether the longed-for reconciliation had been achieved. Not tonight, Kit thought grimly. Tonight the only union that would take place would be between himself and the brandy bottle at Whites. It was decidedly second best but it would just have to do.

Matters were not progressing happily between the Mostyn and Trevithick families elsewhere either. On returning from the musicale, Charlotte Trevithick had cornered her husband in the library. Her natural delicacy had prevented her from raising a personal issue in public but she wished to take Justin to task for his treatment of her twin. Charlotte's blue gaze, identical to her brother's, was stormy as she confronted him and she was twisting her hands together.

'Oh Justin, must you be so nonsensical? You cut Kit dead a dozen times tonight and you have no right to do so! You have been ignoring him ever since he returned! If Eleanor can be civil to her husband, who are you to criticise?'

Justin was looking mutinous. Fair-haired and green-eyed, he was different in appearance from the rest of his family but, as Charlotte had discovered, he had his own share of stubbornness. When she had first met him his easy-going nature had seemed in contrast to his cousin, the Earl—now she realised that they had certain infuriating characteristics the same.

'I am sorry, Charlotte…' Justin took her hands in his, which only served to make matters more difficult for his wife '…I understand that you feel a loyalty to Mostyn as your brother—indeed, it would be odd if you did not, but equally you must see that I have a loyalty to my family—'

'A loyalty to do what?' Charlotte snatched her hands away before Justin's touch could undermine her feelings of indignation. 'The decision is with Eleanor, and if she can stomach my brother as a husband then it is not for you or for Marcus to gainsay! This is pure folly and it only makes matters more difficult for Eleanor! People will talk—they are doing so already—and I have to say that you and your cousin are doing no more than making a cake of yourselves, yes, and making your family a laughing-stock!'

Justin ran a hand through his hair. His mouth was set in an obstinate line. 'I cannot approve of what Mostyn has done. Eleanor may choose to forgive him. I do not.'

'Oh!' Charlotte clenched her fists with aggravation. 'And does it matter nothing to you that you are making *me* unhappy? Does Marcus not care that Beth is made distraught by his behaviour?'

Justin put out a hand and pulled her resisting body close. '*Does* it make you unhappy, my love?'

Charlotte looked at him from beneath her lashes. 'Prodigiously!'

'Then I am sorry for it, but I cannot compromise my principles. Now, kiss me to show that there are no bad feelings between us...'

Charlotte wrenched herself from his grip and stood back. 'Kiss you! I think not, sir! Nor shall I speak to you again until this whole, wretched matter is resolved!'

Justin frowned. 'You will not speak to me at all?'

'No! Until you come to your senses!'

Justin scratched his head. 'Charlotte, this is foolish! Can we not simply talk about it?'

There was no reply. Charlotte gathered up the skirts of her dress, gave him a speaking look over her shoulder and swept out of the room and up to bed.

Beth, Countess of Trevithick, was sitting before her mirror in her shift and brushing out her hair. It had also been a most trying evening and she was prepared to lay the blame completely at Marcus's door. At this point in her thoughts, the connecting door to her husband's suite of rooms opened and Marcus came through. He was wearing a brocade dressing-gown with, Beth would wager, nothing underneath, and as always the sight of him made her catch her breath and caused her heart to beat a little faster. Tonight, however, she was in no mood to be nice to him.

She waited until he was standing behind her then met his eyes directly in the glass.

'Marcus, how long do you intend to persist in this ridiculous behaviour towards Kit? You put me quite out of patience with you!'

Marcus laughed. 'Why, as long as I please, my love! Your cousin should not think that he can return to be gathered into the bosom of the family! His behaviour has been inexcusable!'

'That is for Kit to resolve with Eleanor,' Beth said coldly, trying to ignore the shiver of pleasure that went through her as Marcus raised one hand and slowly stroked her bare arm beneath the short sleeve of the shift.

'I agree…' Marcus bent to kiss her neck. 'But as head of the family I have certain obligations and one is to make my disapproval plain…'

'Pompous poppycock!' Beth exclaimed, pulling her head away. 'Besides, Marcus, you are upsetting me…'

'Am I, my love…?' Marcus's lips moved to the soft skin of her throat. His hands were on her shoulders again, sliding the shift downwards. 'Let me make it up to you…'

Beth got to her feet, only to find that that brought her into even closer proximity with her husband. His arms went around her—she tried to pull away. The shift was already around her waist.

'Marcus, this is serious—'

'I know…' He had bent to kiss her breasts now and Beth almost groaned with frustration—and pleasure. It was becoming increasingly difficult to think.

'Marcus,' she whispered, 'if you do not end this ridiculous feud I shall not speak to you again!'

That caused him to pause for a whole five seconds. Beth held her breath. Marcus bent his head to hers, kissing her lips gently.

'We do not need to speak, love, at least not for now…'

Later, much later, cursing herself for her lack of determination, Beth looked at her sleeping husband and decided that something had to be done. Sterner steps should be taken to achieve her goal. And she had just had the very idea of how to do it.

Chapter Seven

'I am dreadfully sorry, my lord.' Eleanor tilted her parasol against the sunlight in an attempt to prevent herself from squinting. They were walking in the garden after breakfast and it seemed a very bright morning, unnaturally sunny, but perhaps that was merely because her head ached a little. When she had awoken she had had an imperfect memory of the night before, but she knew that it involved a mistaken dose of laudanum and that somewhere along the line she had made a complete cake of herself. She seemed to recall that Kit had been terribly kind to her, which somehow made her feel much worse. She peered at him from beneath the brim of her hat.

Kit was not squinting in the sunlight. He looked immaculately elegant to Eleanor's eyes, making her feel ever so slightly grubby. His hair was a tawny gold, ruffled by the slight wind, and his eyes a deep, dark blue. Eleanor gave an involuntary sigh.

'I am so very sorry, my lord,' she said again. 'I

did not intend to become unruly last night, or embarrass you in public...'

Kit's fingers, long and strong interlocked with hers. He was smiling.

'I confess it was a change to see you less...self-possessed,' he said. 'You need not apologise though, Eleanor. I found the whole experience highly instructive.'

Eleanor frowned. This sounded ominous, particularly as she could remember so little herself. She allowed Kit to take her arm and they walked down the terrace steps and on to the path that led across the lawn. The air was cool and refreshing.

'Instructive? Did you? But, surely...'

Kit smiled down at her. 'You said things that I am sure you would not have mentioned under normal circumstances. It was particularly interesting.'

Eleanor frowned a little harder. This sounded even worse than she had thought. 'I did? Such as...what, my lord?'

'Oh...' Kit's smile had a wicked edge '...that you wished to be a fast matron but that you found you did not care for it after all! That you had too much regard for the opinion of society but that in future you would not care so much...'

Eleanor pressed her hands to her cheeks. She had the dreadful suspicion that this was the least of the things that she had said. There had been something about stolen kisses...

'Did I mention...other men, my lord?'

'You did!' Kit eyed her blushing embarrassment

with good humour. 'I cannot tell you how glad I am that one small misunderstanding is resolved between us!'

Eleanor eyed him suspiciously. 'And that is...'

'That though we were apart from each other for too long, neither of us was tempted to avail ourselves of the charms of others. I confess I am glad that we may now both disregard the gossip!'

'Oh!' Eleanor let out a small breath of relief. 'It is a somewhat delicate topic...'

'But one that I am glad we have broached.' Kit smiled broadly. 'Now that that is taken care of, we may perhaps progress to resolving other matters—all in good time, of course, and in the interests of our friendship!'

Eleanor felt as though the ground was slipping from beneath her feet. On the surface Kit's suggestion seemed like a good idea—once they had resolved the past they might come to an easier understanding, and there were still plenty of issues between them that required resolution. Yet there was something treacherous lurking beneath the surface here. Each confidence brought them closer, inevitably, dangerously closer to each other. One thing led to another. Which reminded her of the previous night...

An image flashed through Eleanor's mind, a vivid picture of herself lying back on the big four poster bed—she could see the canopy above her head, and she could remember how she had stretched long and luxuriously and asked Kit... The colour rushed into her cheeks. She had asked Kit if he would like to make love to her, had invited him—twice! And he had turned her down...

'Ohhhh!'

'Are you feeling unwell this morning, my love?' Kit enquired solicitously, the twinkle still in his eye. 'It might have been expected. Come, sit down over here.' He led her to the garden seat that had been placed in the middle of the lawn, beneath a canopy of green. It was shadowed and cool and Eleanor sat down and folded her parasol, relieved to be out of the direct sun.

'Kit...' she spoke hesitantly, uncertain if she really wanted to know the answer '...is it true or did I just imagine asking you last night if you would make love to me?'

There was a pause whilst she waited for him to come to her rescue, to assure her that she had asked nothing of him at all. Kit grinned. He looked insufferably pleased with himself. 'No, you did not imagine it, Eleanor.'

Eleanor's blush deepened. 'Ohhhhh... But you did not...'

Kit sobered. 'No. It would scarcely have been the right occasion.'

Eleanor took a deep breath. 'I think that I must thank you, my lord. You could have taken advantage of me—and yet you did not.'

Their eyes met and held. Kit was still smiling very faintly and there was something else in his expression that made Eleanor's stomach drop away. She sat quite still, transfixed, and Kit leaned forward and kissed her very gently.

Eleanor's lips clung softly to his. She immediately knew that she did not want to pull away. The sensation was so very sweet, the touch of his lips so tender, demanding nothing but giving everything. Eleanor moved a little closer along the seat. She wanted more than this tentative caress and the knowledge of her own desires shocked her briefly. But there was no danger—the kiss was no more than the lightest of touches. It was up to her to make more of it if she wished.

She did wish. She found that she wished it quite desperately. She parted her lips beneath Kit's and was instantly gratified to feel the change in him, the demand that lay beneath his iron control. His tongue touched hers, exploring her mouth, slowly and sensuously, evoking a response that made her tremble. She felt languid and melting, yet unbearably excited at one and the same time. She knew that Kit was still exerting a frustrating self-control and suddenly it seemed imperative to make him lose it. She pressed closer to him and Kit broke off the kiss. Eleanor let out a sigh of pure annoyance.

'Oh!'

'I am sorry, my love.' Kit was breathing a little unevenly, the only sign that he had been disturbed at all. 'Charlotte and Beth are coming across the lawn, and with them—yes, Carrick with the morning tea tray!'

Eleanor spun around. Beth had said that she would

call, and on most occasions Eleanor would have been more than delighted to see her, but now… She shivered as the sensual warmth ebbed from her blood. To think that she had not been unduly concerned about her developing friendship with Kit! Had she been wilfully blind or just deluding herself…

Kit stood up, bending to brush his lips against her cheek in a gesture that sent another echo of passion fizzing along Eleanor's nerves.

'I will leave you with Beth and Charlotte now, but I will see you later, my love.'

'Very well,' Eleanor agreed shakily. She watched as he strolled across the lawn, pausing to kiss his sister and cousin and exchange a few words on the way. Carrick brought the tea over and Eleanor dragged her gaze away from Kit's tall figure. It was odd—she found it incredibly difficult to look away from him. She started to think about the kiss, then hastily sought to distract herself by rearranging the chairs and table and helping Carrick with the cups.

'Eleanor! How are you this morning?'

Beth, resplendent in a silver and white striped dress, bustled over and bent to hug her sister-in-law. 'I wondered what had happened to you at the musicale last night!' she reproached. 'I thought that you might not be feeling quite the thing, or it could just have been the caterwauling of the terrible singer…'

'It was dreadful, was it not,' Charlotte agreed, with a shudder. 'It gave me the most appalling headache…'

'You are both dreadfully uncultured!' Eleanor

scolded, tongue in cheek. She was feeling quite kindly disposed towards the diva now that she knew Kit had no interest in her. 'Why, everyone knows that La Perla is the most sought-after opera singer in Italy—in more than one sense!'

Eleanor saw Carrick blush to his ears and blink very rapidly, a sure sign that the butler was discomfited. Really, he was a dreadful old puritan.

'Thank you, Carrick,' she said hastily. 'We shall call you if we require anything else.'

'Poor Carrick,' Beth said as the butler withdrew, 'he is so easily shocked! Why, you would have thought that he was inured to such things after witnessing my behaviour...'

'And mine,' Eleanor said feelingly.

Charlotte touched her hand. 'So tell us what happened last night! Were you taken ill?'

'Oh!' Eleanor frowned a little. She felt strangely reluctant to admit to her mistake with the laudanum, more out of loyalty to her mother than because of her own shame. 'I had some ratafia and it did not agree with me.'

'Nasty stuff,' Beth commented. 'I tried the Negus...'

'Oh, you did not!'

'I did, and it was quite revolting! I shall stick to port in future!'

'For my part I had nothing but lemonade—' Charlotte said, drinking her tea.

'But then you are always so good!'

They all laughed.

'So Kit had to bring you home,' Beth said, wiping her eyes, 'and put you to bed, Eleanor?'

'Beth...' Eleanor said, blushing. 'Truth to tell, I remember very little of it! Kit and I are the best of friends, but it is just that—friendship!'

She did not miss the significant glance that flashed between her sister-in-law and cousin.

'I see,' Beth said slowly. 'And when we arrived just now you were kissing Kit goodbye—in a friendly manner?'

Eleanor blushed to the roots of her hair. Remembering the conversation she had had with Beth only a week ago, she thought suddenly how perspicacious her sister-in-law had been in thinking that Kit would not simply sit back and allow her to dictate their makeshift marriage.

'I did warn you!' Beth said shrewdly, eyeing the tell-tale rose-pink in Eleanor's cheeks.

'Pray do not put poor Nell to the blush, Beth!' Charlotte said, rescuing her. 'You are too inquisitive! I am sure it is nobody's business but their own...'

'Speaking of which...' Eleanor rushed in to change the subject '...what are we to do about this ridiculous feud that the men insist on indulging in? Why, it is Lady Knighton's rout tonight and I feel half-inclined to refuse just to avoid another foolish confrontation!'

'That is just what we were saying on the way here,' Charlotte said comfortably. She stirred sugar into her tea. 'I tried to reason with Justin after the musicale last night, but he was quite adamant. In the end I was obliged to tell him that I would not speak to him until he showed some sense!'

'Has it worked yet?' Beth enquired, leaning forward. She fanned herself. 'Goodness, but it is getting hot today! The rout will be a sad crush tonight.'

'No, it has not worked,' Charlotte said, a little disconsolately. 'I used to enjoy discussing matters with Justin—the papers, the politics, any matter that was worthy of debate, I suppose—but this morning he said that he may get sensible conversation at his club and if I choose to sulk that is my affair!'

Beth tutted.

'I hear that Marcus and Justin are speaking of having Kit blackballed from Whites,' Eleanor said hesitantly. 'I tried to speak to Kit of it last evening but he just said that it was a matter between the three of them.'

'Pshaw!' Charlotte took a piece of cake. 'Have you had any success in influencing Marcus, Beth? I know you mentioned you were planning to speak to him.'

Beth raised her eyebrows. 'Surely you jest, Lottie!' She went off into a peal of laughter. 'I too told Marcus last night that I would not speak to him if he persisted in such ridiculous behaviour and all he said was that we did not need to speak for what he had in mind!'

Charlotte spluttered into her tea. 'Fortunate that Carrick has gone, Beth! You would have shocked him to the core!'

'But what's to do?' Beth asked plaintively. 'If the men will not listen to reason we might be set with this foolish feud for months—or years—to come!'

'I agree that we need to take some action,' Eleanor said glumly. 'But what?'

The three of them looked at each other. Charlotte blushed. 'I did think of something...' she said, after a moment.

Eleanor and Beth waited.

'You are looking very furtive, Lottie!' Beth accused. 'Why, whatever can this be...'

Charlotte cast her eyes down modestly. 'I thought that if we were to refuse our husbands their... marital rights...they might come to heel a little more quickly than if we simply refuse to speak to them!' She looked at them. 'It was just an idea...'

There was a silence.

'Lottie!' Beth said, shocked. 'That is the sort of idea that I would have!' She sat back in her chair, looking thoughtful. 'Not that the scheme does not have merit! If we feel secure enough that our husbands will not seek solace elsewhere...'

'I do not think there is the least chance of either of your husbands considering such a course!' Eleanor said stoutly and truthfully. 'Why, anyone can see that Justin adores you, Charlotte, and as for Marcus, he has been known as the most attentive husband in the *Ton* for the past few months! Besides, you are both newly wed and I do not believe that it will take very long...'

Beth's eyes sparkled. 'No indeed! Oh, to see Marcus's face…'

Charlotte smiled. 'It is a piquant thought,' she agreed. 'I do believe we may have some success…'

Eleanor sighed. 'I am sorry that I cannot contribute to the plan. My friendship with Kit…' she blushed delicately '…is scarcely on such terms…'

'I'll wager he would wish it so though, Nell!' Beth said slyly. 'So you may find yourself called upon to participate! Remember—no giving in until the feud is laid to rest, no matter the temptation, no matter the blandishments…'

'When do we start?' Charlotte enquired, popping a sugared almond into her mouth.

'Tonight!' Beth said.

On returning from Whites, Marcus Trevithick was pleased to discover his wife alone in the drawing-room and apparently deeply engrossed in a book. There were a couple of hours before they were due to depart for Lady Knighton's rout and Marcus, contemplating the delicate line of Beth's shoulder and the delicious curve of her breast, was certain that he knew just how to pass the time.

'Good evening, my love,' he said, bending to kiss her lingeringly. 'I am so glad to find you here and alone…'

Beth returned the kiss in full measure but she did not put her book down and Marcus found himself ever so slightly piqued. Beth's pregnancy had led to certain changes in their lovemaking but she had never been anything other than wholehearted in her enjoyment. He kissed her again, allowing his lips to drift along the line of her neck to the soft skin above the lacy edge of her dress. He slid one hand inside her bodice and cupped her breast.

A moment later he felt Beth shift slightly and opened his eyes. She was reading her book over his shoulder.

Marcus was outraged. He straightened up and fixed his wife with a glacial look. 'I am sorry, my dear—was I boring you?'

There was a guilty expression in Beth's eye. 'Oh no, indeed! It is just that I had reached a particularly exciting bit…'

Marcus took the book from her and looked at the spine. '*A Vindication of the Rights of Woman!* Beth—'

He did not miss the flash of amusement deep in her eyes. 'Yes, my love?'

Marcus dropped to his knee beside the sofa, took his wife's chin in his hand and turned her lips up to his. This time he was really trying. After a moment he felt her lips soften and cling to his, a tell-tale quiver going through her. Marcus felt a surge of triumph. A particularly exciting bit indeed!

He stole a hand beneath her skirts and started to stroke her leg above the silken edge of her stocking. Beth shifted obligingly, sighing beneath his mouth. Marcus's fingers crept to the inside of her thigh. His own arousal was acute now and as he stroked he allowed himself to think about pulling up her skirts and...

Beth straightened up.

'No!'

Marcus froze. He hauled himself up on to the sofa and sat down heavily, only to feel the sharp edge of the book digging into a tender part of his anatomy. He picked the book up and threw it across the room.

'Beth, what the hell is going on?'

Beth's eyelashes fluttered modestly. She looked rumpled and pretty and very, very desirable. Marcus groaned.

'I am sorry, my love,' his spouse said sweetly, 'but everything has its price! Until you settle this ridiculous feud you have with my cousin...'

Marcus leant over and seized her shoulders. 'Are you telling me that you will refuse to sleep with me until I acknowledge Kit Mostyn?'

Beth nodded. Her eyes were bright with mischief. 'Exactly, my love.'

Marcus sat back and looked at her for a long moment, his dark eyes narrowing on her face. 'Beth, you will never succeed!'

'Oh, yes I shall!' Beth said. She smoothed her skirts down modestly, cast him one provocative look over her shoulder and got up to retrieve her book. She sat down again at the end of the sofa the furthest away from him.

Marcus sat irresolute for several moments. Beth turned the page. She seemed engrossed.

'God damn it!' Her husband said furiously. He got

up and went out of the room, slamming the door hard behind him. It was only when his footsteps had died away that Beth put the book down with a sigh of relief and went into a peal of laughter.

Eleanor had also fallen asleep that afternoon, her borrowed copy of *Tristram Shandy* sliding off her lap as she dozed against the sofa cushions. It was only when she heard voices in the hall that she roused herself, wondering if they had visitors. Then she recognised Kit's voice and wondered who was with him. She tiptoed to the drawing-room door and peered round, just in time to see Kit disappearing into the study with a gentleman that she did not recognise. Eleanor resumed her seat on the sofa and picked up the *Ladies' Magazine* but she barely glanced at it. She was curious to know to know the identity of her husband's mystery acquaintance.

Little more than a half hour later, the study door opened again and the gentlemen emerged. Eleanor wondered if Kit would bring the visitor in—he must know that she was at home, after all, and it would be courteous to introduce them. However Kit ushered the man to the door and saw him off personally. It was evident to Eleanor, watching through the half-open drawing-room door, that they were great good friends and further that the man was indeed a gentleman and a very good-looking one at that. She heard the front door close and at the same time a stray draught pulled the drawing-room door from her hand—she had been holding it steady so that she could see what was going on—and slammed it with enough force to bring the house down.

Eleanor whisked herself across the room and on to the sofa just as the door reopened to admit Kit. He was looking mildly concerned.

'Is everything all right, my dear?' he enquired. 'I heard the door slam and wondered if you had injured yourself.'

'Oh no!' Eleanor was feeling flustered and thought that it probably showed. 'I was asleep...'

'You are looking a little dishevelled, my love.' Kit's gaze, warm and ever-so-slightly disturbing, roamed over her and lingered on the curl of hair in the hollow of her neck. 'I was only concerned because I saw you standing behind the door and thought you might have trapped your fingers when it closed...'

'You saw me?' Eleanor was mortified. She felt herself colouring a deep rose-pink. 'Oh, Kit...'

'Do not worry!' Kit said cheerfully. 'I merely thought that you were curious about my visitor and were spying on me again! Really, my love, you have the most lively interest in my private affairs!'

Since this was exactly what Eleanor had been doing she found it difficult to demur, but she did her best.

'Yes, well, I was only wondering if you would bring your visitor to meet me, Kit, and I was worrying in case I looked untidy...'

'You look delightful, Eleanor,' Kit said, smiling. 'As for Harry, I would have introduced him but he had a pressing engagement elsewhere. You will meet him tonight at Lady Knighton's ball.'

'Harry?'

'Captain Henry Luttrell. He is an old comrade of mine with whom I was recently in Ireland, but of course…' Kit checked himself '…you do not wish to know about that!'

Eleanor was trapped. She wished to know quite desperately and had been feeling like that for the best part of two weeks. She looked at Kit, who looked back at her, brows raised quizzically.

'Perhaps I would like…' Eleanor began hesitantly. 'That is, perhaps we are now at that stage in our reacquaintance when I might ask… As we are friends again now…'

'Oh, of course,' Kit said courteously. He gestured to the sofa. 'Shall we sit down together, then?'

Eleanor sat down, clasping her hands tightly in her lap. Now that the moment of truth was upon her, she felt nervous and vulnerable and not at all sure that she wanted to know. Yet they could not continue as they had been doing, with so much lying unspoken between them. Perhaps it would be better to know everything and have done with it.

Kit did not hurry into speech. He sat looking at her with the same searching directness she had grown accustomed to seeing in his gaze. She shifted uncomfortably.

'Perhaps it would be best to start by saying that I spent the five months that we were apart in Ireland,' Kit said, at length. 'I was never in Italy, and certainly not consorting with any opera singers, whatever the rumours!'

'Oh, I know that!' Eleanor's nervousness made her loquacious. 'It is the least well-kept secret in London! Why, the servants have been telling me this age that you have been in Ireland *and* that you were about government business!'

Kit looked slightly winded. 'Have they? Good God! But how did they know?'

Eleanor almost giggled at his appalled expression. 'I do not know, Kit! Perhaps you are not as discreet as you think yourself!'

'Perhaps not!' Kit thrust a hand through his hair. 'It is a good job that the business is concluded and I am to take on no further work for Castlereagh, for it seems I am utterly incapable of keeping a secret!'

'That must mean that you were a spy, Kit.' Eleanor frowned. 'I confess that I do not like the idea!'

Kit laughed. 'Oh, I was no spy—never more than a glorified messenger boy, I assure you! It only came about in the first place because I travelled such a great deal! This last job was by way of a favour for Castlereagh, and a more mismanaged, farcical affair it could not have been!'

'Tell me!' Eleanor said, suddenly desperate to know.

Kit looked at her. She could read nothing in his face but a rather bleak unhappiness.

'The summons came on the very day that we were married,' he began. 'You may remember that I told

you I had to attend to a matter of business—I went
to the meeting place in the tavern, intending to explain that I had been married only that morning and
wished to delay my departure.' He sighed, sitting
back against the cushions. 'Unfortunately we had
previously agreed that I should be knocked on the
head in a tavern brawl—to cover my tracks, you understand! And I was, as soon as I walked in! By the
time I was in any fit state to explain anything, I was
ten miles out to sea in company with a gang of
pressed men...' He sighed. 'It would have been com-
ical had it not been so desperate.'

Eleanor stared at him. 'You mean that you never
had the opportunity to explain our situation...'

'Precisely.' Kit's expression was bitter. 'When I
finally woke up it was too late.'

There was a silence. Eleanor could feel Kit's gaze
upon her but he did not say anything else, and a part
of Eleanor recognised and appreciated the fact that
he chosen to tell her everything so plainly. He had
made no appeal to her emotions and she suspected
that this was not because he did not care but because
he felt it would be unfair to her. She shivered a little.
Now that she knew, she could see how simply such
an accident had occurred. How simple and how unlucky. She did not really know how to feel.

'I see. But you wrote to me to explain?'

Kit shifted slightly. 'I wrote several times. The
first letter was sent as soon as I reached shore. I
cannot conceive how my letters went astray. All the
time I was hoping desperately that you had received

them and would understand what had happened! I even suggested that you should seek Charlotte out so that you would not be alone—' He broke off, evidently not wishing to pursue that.

Eleanor shook her head. It was too late for recriminations now, too late to say that Charlotte had been away and instead she was forced to return to Trevithick House and the Dowager's vengeful accusations.

'Maybe your letters were lost, Kit,' she said. 'Where did you direct them?'

'To Trevithick House,' Kit said. 'I did not know where to find you, and I thought that at the least they would be waiting there for you, but...' He shrugged again. 'It is a mystery. But there is something more that I must tell you, Eleanor.'

Eleanor waited.

'My work itself took very little time. I was in a fever of impatience to return to you, but then something else occurred, something that kept me in Ireland far longer than I had intended. And that...' Kit paused '...is a matter that I fear I cannot disclose, Nell. It is not my secret to tell.' He took her hands in his, in a strong grasp. 'Please do not imagine that it is because I do not trust you. The reverse is true. But I gave my word of honour that I would not speak until the person concerned gave me their permission. I believe that the matter will be resolved soon, and when it is you will understand...' His gaze sought hers. 'Forgive me! It is a difficult matter...'

Eleanor wrinkled her brow. 'It is difficult for me too, Kit! If you do not tell me—'

'I know!' Kit's grip tightened on her hands. 'I have asked so much of you already and yet now I have to ask you to trust me further—for a little while longer. Can you do that, Nell?'

Eleanor did not look at him. She felt utterly bewildered. She had no doubt of the truth of what Kit had told her and she believed that whatever his secret, he must be keeping it for the most honourable of motives. Yet her heart cried out that it was not fair to ask more of her. The anger and bitterness his absence had created had not yet vanished and still she did not know the whole truth... The warm touch of his fingers in hers only served to confuse her further. She was not indifferent to him—she could not pretend that she was—and yet she did not want him to draw any closer to her. Any suggestion Kit might make for them to be married in more than name only had to be repudiated.

Eleanor shrank a little. 'Thank you for telling me this, Kit. I will think about what you have said—'

'Wait!' Kit held on to her when she would have pulled away. 'There is but one more thing, Eleanor!' He drew her resisting body closer until he had an arm about her. 'I should have said this long ago. I should have said it first! I am so very sorry for what happened. You must know now that it was never my intention to leave you, and I will never stop regretting it—'

'Oh, do not!' Eleanor could not bear any more.

'Say that at the least you believe that of me—'

'Of course! Of course I do!' Eleanor pulled away from him a little. 'But it is not so easy for me, Kit! I had a truly terrible time of it whilst you were away! Yes, I understand it was none of your intention and in time I am sure I can forgive—' Her voice broke. 'Pray do not ask any more of me for now!'

'Very well.' Kit loosened his grip and she stood up shakily. She could see the vivid disappointment in his face and the difficulty with which he mastered it. His tension was palpable.

'I must go and get ready,' she said uncertainly. 'We shall be late for the ball—'

'To hell with the ball and everything else!' Kit stood up. 'Eleanor…'

He swept her into his arms, holding her ruthlessly whilst his mouth plundered hers with merciless skill. Eleanor tried to free herself but he held her still. It was violent and frightening, yet beneath her fear, Eleanor felt the pull in her blood as her body answered his. When he finally let her go they were both breathing hard and she could not tear her gaze away from the compulsive heat of desire she saw in his eyes. He did not apologise for his actions.

'I must go,' she said again, shakily, and after a second Kit moved to hold the door for her with scrupulous courtesy.

Eleanor ran up the stairs, feeling the trembling in her legs at every step. Her thoughts were whirling and her senses scarcely less so, and uppermost in her mind was that she was going to have to be much more determined and strong-minded if she were to thwart Kit's intentions in the future. He was undermining her resolution at every step and what was worse was the fact that part of her did not care. Part of her wanted Kit's lovemaking very much, and it was only the memories and the fear that held her back.

Chapter Eight

'Marcus is in a very bad mood this evening,' Eleanor whispered to Beth, as they sat out a dance together at Lady Knighton's rout. 'Why, he snapped my head off when I asked how he was earlier, and when we danced the boulanger he spoke no more than half a dozen words! Whatever is the matter with him?'

Beth raised her eyebrows expressively and Eleanor smothered a laugh.

'Oh no! No wonder he is so cross-grained. He and Mama make a matched pair tonight.'

Beth shrugged lightly. 'I'll confess he was not best pleased when I refused him!'

'It has not made him relent yet,' Eleanor said. 'I saw Marcus turn his back very deliberately when Kit passed him in the card-room. You will just have to try harder!'

She looked across the room to where Kit was standing, deep in conversation with Henry Luttrell.

She had been introduced to the dashing Captain now
and had had two dances with him. Naturally they
had made no mention of Kit's recent sojourn in
Ireland, but it was uppermost in Eleanor's mind—
along with the discussion, and the kiss that had followed.

Beth nudged her.

'Nell, do you know the gentleman Kit is speaking
with? Is he an old friend?'

Eleanor laughed. 'I believe so,' she said, a twinkle
in her eye. 'That is Captain Luttrell. But what are
you planning, Beth?'

Beth got to her feet. 'I must go and speak to Kit—
and his friend. That will give Marcus something else
to think about!'

Eleanor shook her head, smiling slightly. 'I think
you have upset him enough for one evening!'

Beth smiled. 'I have a waltz with Marcus the
dance after next. It should provide the ideal opportunity to torment him a little further!'

She swept away, pausing to exchange a few ostentatious words with Kit as he came up with an iced
sherbet for Eleanor. Eleanor bit her lip. She could
see Marcus watching them with a face like a thun-
dercloud, and when Henry Luttrell bowed charmingly over Beth's hand Eleanor thought her brother
would explode. She devoutly hoped that Beth and
Charlotte knew what they were doing with their ul-
timatum.

Kit slid into the seat next to her and handed her
the glass. 'There you are, my love! I do not believe

it much melted, though it is very hot tonight. Are you enjoying the ball?'

Eleanor dipped her spoon into the ice. 'It is quite pleasant, my lord, although rather too hot for dancing. What do you think?'

Kit slid his arm along the back of her chair in a gesture that Eleanor found both proprietorial and rather pleasing. She was very conscious of his hand resting close to her shoulder. 'You know that I prefer the country to the town! I fear I find all these endless social events unconscionably boring!'

Eleanor giggled. 'Pray do not let the fashionable hostesses hear you, my lord! There are any number of people who make doing nothing a fine art form and would take offence at your words!'

Kit smiled at her. His gaze was warm as it rested on her face and Eleanor felt herself blushing a little.

'You should know that I would like nothing so much as to leave London for the country,' he said slowly. 'My aim is no grander than to live peaceably at Mostyn Hall with my family about me—children, perhaps... Maybe we could talk about it, Eleanor?'

Eleanor could feel his gaze intent on her, though she could not meet his eyes. She felt as though she was suffocating. Ever since Kit had kissed her earlier she had been pushing such thoughts away. She had wanted him then, wanted to feel his arms around her, wanted to forget all the bitterness between them. But there were some things that she simply could not give him... A stray breath of wind from the terrace made her shiver convulsively.

'I find that I rather enjoy the Season,' she said, in a brittle voice that did not sound her own. 'Surely there is no hurry to leave town!'

She saw Kit's gaze narrow too perceptive, too searching for comfort. She turned her face away, knowing with relief that Kit would not press her on this, at least not at the moment.

'I hear that Lady Knighton has engaged the services of a profile miniaturist tonight!' she said brightly. 'Shall we go and see his work?'

Kit got to his feet and offered her his arm politely. The easy intimacy that had been between them a moment before had vanished and Eleanor felt as though she was chatting to an acquaintance.

'They say he is very talented,' she rattled on, as they walked towards the room that had been set aside for the silhouettist. 'He cuts profiles from black card in a matter of minutes! They say he is a student of John Miers, who has his studios in the Strand—'

'I know the place,' Kit commented. 'Perhaps you should have your silhouette cut, Eleanor!'

Eleanor stole a glance at him. His face was closed and expressionless and her heart missed a beat from regret and pity rather than anything else. This was all so difficult! As soon as they had achieved their comfortable friendship it seemed that it had all been spoiled by the dangerous physical attraction that had flared between them. It was quite natural that Kit would assume they had reached a closer understanding and one that would lead in time to greater intimacy. Yet here was she, drawing back again, unwilling to take any further risk and quite incapable of explaining why…

The miniaturist had just finished a silhouette of Charlotte Trevithick when they arrived and there was an awkward moment as Eleanor and Charlotte stood admiring his work whilst Kit and Justin gazed studiously in opposite directions. The silhouettist was an earnest young man with intense dark eyes and flowing black hair, who clearly took pleasure in their praise of his work. Once the compliments had run out there was an awkward silence until Justin recollected that he and Charlotte were dancing the next waltz together, and Eleanor sat down. The silhouettist snipped away to produce a likeness and handed it to her in a matter of minutes. She smiled as she looked at it. He had made her appear very pretty, right down to the tender sweep of her eyelashes across her cheek, and the stray curl that caressed her neck.

Kit leant over the back of her chair to take a look and Eleanor, glancing at him over her shoulder, saw the genuine pleasure in his eyes at he looked on her likeness. Her heart gave another small lurch.

'Why, that has captured you precisely, my love,' Kit said, 'although…' He tilted his head a little, 'I do believe that your nose is a shade too long! Yes, decidedly a little too long for perfection—'

'That is because it is!' Eleanor said firmly. She smiled her thanks to the miniaturist and tucked her hand through Kit's arm. 'You are too partial, my lord.'

'There is nothing wrong in that!' Kit protested. He placed the silhouette in his pocket. 'I shall keep this—as a tribute to your beauty, my love, and to the fact that the miniaturist was evidently as much struck by it as I am!'

Eleanor blushed, disclaimed and felt even worse. She could not think of anything to say to lighten the situation and yet she felt a fraud responding to Kit's compliments. Some time soon she would have to make her feelings plain. It would be dishonest not to do so.

'Kit! Eleanor!' Charlotte Trevithick was hurrying towards them, her pale face flushed with distress. She put a hand on Eleanor's arm. 'I have lost my pearl bracelet! Have you seen it anywhere? I thought I must have dropped it whilst I was having my profile taken, yet it is not there! Justin will be so displeased, for it was a wedding present! I cannot believe I have been so careless!'

She looked as though she were about to cry. Eleanor put an arm about her.

'Oh, Charlotte, I am so sorry! Where have you looked?'

'Everywhere!' Charlotte was inconsolable. 'I should not have worn it, for the clasp was loose, but it was so pretty and now it has gone…'

Some curious impulse made Eleanor glance across the room to where her mother was sitting with Beth and Marcus. The Dowager's chin was sunk on her chest and she was not speaking, but was rocking backwards and forwards gently to the strains of the music. There was one empty rout chair by her side.

'Charlotte, were you sitting with Mama just now?' she asked casually. 'I see that there is a spare chair...'

Charlotte nodded miserably. 'We were all sitting together, for Lady Trevithick has softened towards Justin since his marriage, you know! But I fear she is not in good spirits tonight—she has scarce spoken a word and Marcus is also very morose tonight, so it has been a most subdued party!'

'You did not drop your bracelet over by the chairs, then?' Eleanor asked. She was beginning to feel rather cold at the direction her thoughts were tending. The last time she had seen a bracelet disappear had been at the Trevithick ball, and she knew exactly what had happened there.

Charlotte brightened. 'Well, I did not think so, but I had not checked. Perhaps I should take a look...'

Eleanor gave Kit an apologetic smile. 'I shall accompany Charlotte to look for her bracelet, my lord, but will be but a minute. Perhaps it would be better...' she paused delicately, '...were you to wait for me here?'

Kit bowed ironically. 'I will hunt up some company in the card-room!'

Eleanor linked her arm through that of her sister-in-law and they strolled over to the party from Trevithick House. At close quarters Eleanor could see the truth of Charlotte's words that the group was as sad as a wet Monday—Marcus and Justin were conversing together but there was a deep frown on Marcus's brow and at his side Beth was sitting flicking her fan with mock-innocence. The Dowager sat like a grounded ship, massive and a little apart from the others.

'Nell!' Beth said with a warm smile, 'how lovely for you to join us. Is Kit not with you?'

That gained her a glare from Marcus. Justin looked extremely uncomfortable. Beth smiled sunnily.

'No,' Eleanor said, trying not to laugh, 'he has gone for a hand of whist.' She turned to her brother and cousin. 'So perhaps the gentlemen should avoid the card-room.'

Both Marcus and Justin had the grace to look embarrassed and Eleanor felt a little spurt of pleasure. She might not be able to employ Beth and Charlotte's tactics but she could at least show them up for their bad behaviour. She turned to her mother.

'Mama, I believe that Charlotte has dropped her bracelet somewhere around here, and I wondered if you had seen it? She has searched everywhere else but it is not to be found.'

The Dowager had ignored the previous conversation but now she stopped rocking, opened her little dark eyes and surveyed her daughter calmly.

'I do not think I have seen it. That pretty pearl bracelet, was it? What a great shame! You should be more careful, Charlotte dear.'

'Yes, ma'am!' Charlotte shot a guilty look at Justin. 'I cannot see how I came to lose it!'

Eleanor looked her mother straight in the eye. 'For my part I believe that some unscrupulous person has taken it! What do you think, Mama?'

There was an odd silence whilst the Dowager's eyes narrowed on her daughter's flushed face. The others were looking puzzled but did not say anything.

'Perhaps if we were to search...' the Dowager Lady Trevithick murmured. She leant forwards on the chair and its spindly legs trembled. Eleanor could hear her stays creaking under the strain.

'You look, Eleanor,' the Dowager instructed. 'Down on your knees, girl, beneath my chair!'

Eleanor flushed. When she had started this she had had no intention of drawing the gaze of the whole room, and now she began to wonder if her suspicions of her mother could be in any way justified. Just because one bracelet had disappeared under mysterious circumstances it did not logically follow that her mother was a jewel thief, stealing to support her penchant for laudanum. Eleanor, who had shied away from this idea from the first, was now desperate not to pursue it. It felt wrong to impute such criminal behaviour to her own mother and she could scarcely ask Lady Trevithick to turn out her reticule or accuse her in front of the assembled throng.

But there was no need. Lady Trevithick twitched her skirts, there was a little thud, and the bracelet rolled out from under the chair to rest at Eleanor's feet. She bent to pick it up.

'It was there all the time!' the Dowager murmured. 'Beneath my skirts! I am sorry, Charlotte dear, I did not notice! Perhaps if you were to be more careful…'

'Yes, ma'am,' Charlotte murmured submissively. She gave Eleanor a grateful smile and clipped the bracelet about her wrist. 'I shall have the catch mended immediately!'

Eleanor smiled back. She deliberately did not look at her mother. She knew that it was only the combination of the Dowager's size and a lack of opportunity that meant that Charlotte's bracelet was not gracing Lord Kemble's pocket by now. No doubt her mother had been waiting for a chance to scoop the bracelet up when she was unobserved. Eleanor knew her mother had to be stopped—and that she had to stop covering up her behaviour…

She saw that Beth had picked up on her uneasiness, for her sister-in-law patted the seat beside her and deliberately broke the strained silence.

'Did I tell you that Lady Salome arrived this afternoon? She was too fatigued to join us this evening but asked me to tell you that she would call on you tomorrow…' The conversation eased into more comfortable channels and after a while Justin and Charlotte went off to dance, Lady Trevithick nodded off to sleep again and it was suddenly easy for Eleanor to imagine that nothing was wrong. Except, of course, that it was and she knew that she had to do something about it.

'Oh ma'am, was the ball so very glittering and romantic? Packed with handsome gentleman and beautiful ladies?' Lucy, her eyes sparkling, helped Eleanor out of the lilac dress and went to hang it in the wardrobe. 'Oh, how I wish I could have seen it!'

'No, it was not really,' Eleanor said on a yawn. She had been turning the problem of her mother's thefts over in her mind and come to no useful conclusions other than that she must speak to Marcus about it.

'To tell the truth, Lucy, it was a deadly dull affair and full of the same boring faces and tedious gossip! At this rate I shall be retiring to the country! I would rather stay at home and do my needlework.'

Lucy giggled. She gestured to the chair at the dressing-table. 'Oh, ma'am, I cannot believe that! If you would like to sit down, I shall brush your hair out. Do you wish to take your necklace off first?'

'No, please leave it for now.' Eleanor yawned again and sat down, her fingers touching the diamonds and emeralds at her throat. The Mostyn necklace glowed softly above the neckline of her chemise, shimmering against her creamy skin. Eleanor smiled. It was indeed a beautiful piece and the Dowager would never get her hands on it.

The maid started to unpin the flowers from Eleanor's hair and brush out the long, dark strands. 'Lord Mostyn looked so dotingly on you this evening, my lady.'

'Lucy, you may be in need of spectacles,' Eleanor said, a little wearily. The maid's romantic obsession was particularly hard to bear when her own feelings were in such turmoil. 'Pray do not imagine that my marriage is anything other than one of convenience! It is the way of the world to marry for money and position—'

'May I come in?'

Eleanor closed her eyes in mortification. She must remember to tell Lucy to shut the bedroom door properly, for here was Kit, standing in the doorway and eyeing her with an interrogatory look that suggested he had just heard her unflattering opinion of their match. This was disturbing, but more unsettling still was the fact that it was three in the morning and she was in her shift and Kit—Eleanor swallowed hard. Her husband was partially undressed, having removed his jacket, waistcoat and neck-cloth, and he looked so rakishly dishevelled that her heart started to beat a quick pit-a-pat. She did not believe that the current terms of their relationship quite allowed for this. Nor should it. This was where she had to call a halt.

Lucy bobbed a curtsey and laid the hairbrush down, and Eleanor caught her arm in an urgent grip.

'Lucy, wait! I need you to help me remove the necklace—'

'I can help with that,' Kit murmured. There was a wicked twinkle in his eye.

'And to brush my hair and to help me undress—' Eleanor rushed on.

'I can help with that too.' Kit sauntered into the room, holding the door open for the maid to depart.

Lucy, the romantic sparkle restored to her eye, sped out and the door closed behind her.

Eleanor stood up. 'My lord! Why are you wandering the corridors half-dressed and giving rise to servants' gossip…?'

'There is a bolt in place on the other door, my love,' Kit said, gesturing to the communicating door, 'so I was obliged to approach this way! As for being half-dressed, just be grateful that I am not in my dressing-gown!'

Eleanor was, but she did not wish to admit it. She sighed crossly.

'By what right are you in my bedroom in the first place, sir?'

'The right of a husband,' Kit said easily. He came towards her. 'You would not deny that, I think!'

Eleanor snatched up the hairbrush and held it to her breast.

Kit frowned. 'What do you intend to do with that, Eleanor? Brush me to death? You have no need to fear…' He took the brush from her clenched fingers and laid it down. 'I only wished to speak with you.'

'Can it not wait until the morning, my lord?' Eleanor said, a little faintly. Her defiance was weakening now that he was so close. 'It has been a difficult evening and I am tired and wish to retire…'

'In a moment. You need me to help with your necklace, remember? Turn around…'

Once again Eleanor closed her eyes as she felt him lift the heavy swatch of her hair over one shoulder so that he could reach the clasp. The air was cool on the nape of her neck. Kit's fingers were on the catch of the necklace; his touch grazed her skin, setting it alight. Oh, this was the most dreadful torture, but she had to withstand it. She did not want him to see that he could affect her so, for it would only encourage him to think he could ask for that little bit more.

She heard the clink as Kit laid the necklace down on the dressing-table, then his hands were on her shoulders again, warm and strong as they had been at the start of the evening when he helped her on with her cloak. Only then the action had been innocent. This time, her shoulders were bare. Eleanor shivered.

'There…' Kit's voice was a little husky. He was running strands of her hair through his fingers. 'Shall I brush your hair for you now?'

'No!' Eleanor snapped. She could feel the warmth spreading from his hands where they still rested on her shoulders, down her whole body, flushing her skin pink with desire, making her blood feel heavy in her veins.

'No,' she said again, trying to speak lightly. 'Boys always pull girls' hair. It is inbred from childhood.'

In the mirror she saw Kit smile slightly. He was rubbing his hands very gently up and down her upper arms, stroking, caressing. 'I could try to make amends for that,' he said softly.

His hands returned to her shoulders and the pressure increased slightly. Eleanor found herself sitting down again—she had to, for her knees would have crumpled otherwise. Kit picked up the brush. The long strokes were soothing and stimulating at the same time, from the crown of her head to the end of each thick brown curl. Eleanor's skin prickled with awareness. She closed her eyes briefly.

'I am sorry that you did not enjoy the ball,' Kit said gently. 'Perhaps in future matters will be easier. Now that we have reached an understanding...'

Eleanor bit her lip. Such a comfortable phrase hardly reflected her feelings at that moment.

'I am sure matters will improve,' she agreed, trying to strike the same bright note. 'I used to love the Season's balls and parties...'

'I remember...' Kit's voice was as soothing as the caress of the brush through her hair. 'And you dance so beautifully. It was always a pleasure to partner you...'

Eleanor looked at him in the mirror. His gaze was fixed on the reflection of her face and there was a turbulent heat in his eyes that made her feel quite light-headed. She had to put a stop to this.

'Enough, thank you...' She realised with horror that her voice had come out as a whisper and cleared her throat.

'Thank you,' she said again, not quite steadily. 'That will be quite sufficient.'

'That was nowhere near one hundred strokes...' She could hear the undertone of amusement in Kit's voice. 'I hope it is not because you are dissatisfied with my attentions...'

'No...' The word came out on a shaky sigh.

Eleanor took a deep breath to steady herself and stood up. 'You are a more than competent ladies' maid, my lord,' she said, as coolly as she was able. 'So much so that one wonders where you have learned your skill! I believe that is quite enough of your attentions for one night!'

'Ah,' Kit flashed her a grin. 'I am dismissed! But as to my skill, there is no mystery, my sweet. It is simply that I am prepared to be patient when there is something that I want so very much...'

Their eyes met again in the mirror. Eleanor watched their reflection as once again, Kit lifted the heavy curtain of her hair to expose one bare shoulder. She willed her feet to move, to carry her away from this insidious danger, but she found she could not take a single step. She did not want to. She shivered convulsively as Kit bent his head and she felt his lips touch the sensitive skin below her ear, then drift down the line of her neck to the hollow above her collarbone. She could feel his breath against her skin, the warmth of his hands holding her still. She leaned back against him. If he had let her go she was certain she would have fallen.

'I think that you had better leave...' Eleanor's words came out with about half the certainty that was required to make them sound even remotely convincing. She closed her eyes, wrapped up in the sensual spell that held her, and even as she did so she was aware that it could be her undoing. By now she did not care. Kit was kissing the smooth curve of her shoulder and instinct was prompting her to turn to face him so that he could kiss her properly. She remembered their embrace in the drawing-room and suddenly she wanted it very much. She tried to turn round but he held her still against him, her back against his chest, one arm about her waist.

'I remember that you mentioned you needed help to undress...'

Kit's hand had gone to the ties of her chemise, unfastening them so that her bodice was loosened. Eleanor felt it fall open and made a small sound of despair mixed with wanting. She opened her eyes and the reflections in the mirror stole the last of her breath—her hair was a tousled fall of dark, heavy silk tossed over one shoulder whilst the pale skin of the other was stung pink with Kit's kisses. Her head was thrown back, her eyes bright with a desire she could not hide. The open chemise showed the soft swell of her breasts and the hollow between them, whilst Kit's head was bent as he trailed a line of tiny kisses down the side of her neck, so frustratingly light and tender.

Eleanor wriggled, and succeeded in turning within the shelter of his arms. She felt Kit's mouth resume its agonisingly slow exploration, drifting from the line of her collarbone to the hollow at the base of her throat. When his tongue traced the curves there she could not prevent the small groan that escaped her—Kit's hands tightened momentarily on her arms, then slid round to the small of her back, holding her arched against him. Eleanor could feel the hardness of his arousal against her body and it was inexpressibly exciting. She tried to pull him closer.

Kit drew back, so suddenly that Eleanor felt dizzy. She looked at him uncertainly. His eyes were dark with a desire that was a mirror for hers and he was breathing hard. His gaze flickered over her, lingering on her parted lips, then dropping to the neck of her chemise.

'I must leave,' he said slowly. 'I do not wish to break my promise to you and in another moment that is precisely what I shall do.'

For a minute Eleanor could not even remember what that promise was, then a second later she realised that she was desperate for him to break it. She almost reached out to him, but he was already turning away from her, walking slowly towards the door.

Doubt crept into her heart, and confusion. The heat in her blood was cooling now and she folded her arms tightly across her chest, holding the chemise to her. At the door Kit turned, and his mouth twisted with wry amusement.

'Do not be afraid,' he said. 'I am gone.' He smiled at her. 'Good night, my love. Sleep well.'

The door closed softly behind him. Eleanor slid out of the chemise—an easy task now that it was so thoroughly undone—donned her nightdress and doused the candles but for the one beside her bed. She did not want to call Lucy back and she was certain that she would not sleep. She lay and stared up at the canopy above her head, listening to the sound of Kit moving about in the next bedroom, speaking to his valet in low tones. The sounds were oddly comforting but she wished that they were not.

She turned on to her side and hit her pillow with ineffectual anger. How close she had come to succumbing, and how soon it had happened! How easy Kit must have found it to seduce her! Eleanor rolled on to her back again. She was sure that Kit had set out to seduce her and she was only puzzled as to why he had stopped. Yes, they had had an agreement that he would not touch her against her will but he must have known from her response to him that she would not have objected...

Eleanor wriggled miserably, torn between confusion and unhappiness. Perhaps she knew the answer to that too, and at the thought, her body started to burn with humiliation rather than passion. Kit wanted her to want him. He wanted her to be frustrated with unconsummated desire, burning for his touch. As a strategy it had worked damnably well—it was still working, for beneath her mortification, Eleanor could feel a heat that was pure lust. She thumped her pillow with unrestrained force this time. Damn him! Damn him for his skill to arouse her and for his self-control in holding back! And damn her lack of self-control in still wanting him! The memory of their previous lovemaking still haunted her, overlaid with the excitement of the recent encounter. She was as likely to sleep now as she was to fly to the moon.

Eleanor clutched the pillow to her, putting both arms around it. It was only as she remembered the past, the natural outcome of making love, the desire Kit had for children, that the cold seeped into her bones, replacing the anger she felt with cold fear. She stared at the wavering candle flame. The house was quiet now; the sounds from Kit's room had gone. She felt lonely. To all intents and purposes she *was* alone, just as she had been in Devon when she had faced the appalling outcome of where her thoughtless passion with Kit had led her.

Eleanor turned her face into the pillow, breathing in its calming lavender scent and pressing its coolness to her hot cheeks. She could not bear such a thing to happen again. So she had to resist Kit's seductions. That was all there was to it. She would not let him so close again.

Chapter Nine

'Thank you so much for accompanying me, my dears!' Lady Salome Trevithick said, beaming at Kit and Eleanor as the town carriage conveyed them across London. 'I have so wanted to see the sights— why, it must be all of twenty years since I was last in town, and your mama, my dear Eleanor, was quite appalled at the thought of having to come with me to Westminster Abbey!'

Eleanor smiled. 'I believe that Mama's idea of sightseeing is to drive down Bond Street, ma'am! She does not have much energy for walking these days.'

'And I, alas, can only bear to go shopping twice a week at the outside!' Lady Salome said, sighing. 'We are most incompatible!'

Eleanor caught Kit's eye and could not help smiling. It was difficult to imagine finding someone who was compatible with the Dowager. Lady Salome, Eleanor's late father's sister, had arrived at the house in Montague Street just as they had been taking a late breakfast and Eleanor had been glad of the diversion. When she had arisen late that morning, she had vowed to treat Kit with a cool courtesy that would distance her from the events of the previous night. She had felt awkward and unsure how to go on. To her dismay, however, just the sight of him had been sufficient to make her feel all warm and disordered in the nicest possible way, reminding her as it did of exactly what had happened between them, and she had been hard put to it to reply to his conversation with any degree of sense. Kit had smiled at her, that slow smile that threw her into even greater confusion, then when the maid had gone out to fetch her breakfast, he had come across and kissed her with great deliberation. And all before Eleanor had had the chance to make it clear that any further intimacies between them were quite out of the question. Fortunately the maid had then returned with some warm rolls and honey, and before the meal had ended, Lady Salome had arrived.

Now, sitting across the carriage from her husband, Eleanor was aware that although Kit was discussing the tombs of Westminster Abbey very knowledgeably, his main interest was focused on her. His blue gaze moved over her thoughtfully, taking in the fashionable little hat perched on her dark curls, lingering on her face, moving down her throat to the modest neckline of her gown and on… It was enough to put Eleanor to the blush. She felt as though he was trying to learn her every feature.

Kit handed them both down from the carriage with a very proper attention, holding Eleanor's hand for longer than it was necessary. Lady Salome billowed ahead of them into the Abbey. Eleanor, who had not seen her aunt for several years, had forgotten the unusual dress sense that prompted Lady Salome to combine colours and styles with reckless abandon. Today she was wearing a scarlet evening gown with a royal blue spencer over the top and her head was crowned with some truly awesome ostrich feathers. The Abbey guide, coming to meet them at the door, recoiled slightly at the sight.

'I wish to see *everything*!' Lady Salome announced, surging up the nave. 'What a truly magnificent building! Tell me a little of the history, sir—' She turned to the guide, who seemed quite overwhelmed that for once there was a visitor who not only seemed fascinated but genuinely knowledgeable. They moved up the aisle towards the high altar and Kit offered his arm to Eleanor as they fell into step behind.

'I hope that you do not mind spending some time here,' he murmured in her ear. 'Lady Salome seems quite rapt and I have no heart to foreshorten her pleasure!'

'No indeed!' Eleanor was looking about her with undisguised interest. 'This may not be the sort of place one usually visits during the Season, but it is truly fascinating! Only look at those arches—and the ceiling! It is very beautiful, but a little cold...'

She shivered and Kit drew her closer to his side. Their footsteps echoed on the stone floor.

'And the shrine of Edward the Confessor!' Lady Salome's voice floated back to them. 'Only regard the stone carving! It represents scenes from the life of the Confessor himself, I believe.'

Eleanor stifled a little yawn. It was not that she was bored, but strangely the cold and the dark interior of the building were making her feel sleepy. They were the only visitors and it was very quiet. Then she had not slept very well last night, of course... She stole a glance up at Kit's face. He was looking straight ahead and his profile was as clear-cut as one of the tomb carvings. Only there was nothing particularly saintly about him. He turned his head and gave her a smile that both confirmed her opinion and made her heart skip a beat. If she had been confused the previous night, now she was even more at a loss. Cold resolution was no proof against Kit's determination, nor her own desires... Never had her body and mind been so thoroughly in opposition. She shivered again.

'Do you wish to go out into the sunshine?' Kit enquired. 'I believe that Lady Salome is intent on viewing the coronation chair, for she was horrified that the Westminster schoolboys had had the audacity to scratch their initials on it!'

Eleanor watched as Lady Salome, still talking volubly, disappeared from view behind a large pillar. Her voice, still talking nineteen to the dozen and quite drowning out the guide, echoed around the high ceiling and bounced back to them: 'Vandalism! Sheer wanton destruction! The youth of today…'

Eleanor laughed. 'Oh dear! It is fortunate those very youths are not now at Aunt Trevithick's mercy!' She turned back to Kit. 'Perhaps we could wait here, my lord? I would not wish my aunt to think we had forsaken her!'

Kit pulled her round and into his arms. 'Perhaps I may keep you warm then, Eleanor?' His breath feathered across her cheek in the lightest of caresses. 'I wanted to speak to you about last night and I can wait no longer.'

'Pray, my lord, you cannot behave like this here— in a consecrated building!' Panic rose in Eleanor and she struggled to free herself. She was not sure if she was more afraid of someone seeing them, or of Kit's actions, or of her own responses. Kit did not let her go.

'What better place? I am not ashamed of the feelings I have for my own wife—'

Eleanor made a slight, protesting noise that was smothered as his mouth came down on hers. She put her hands up to his chest, determined to push him away, and somehow found herself passing her arms around his neck to draw him nearer instead. For a long heart-stopping, breathless interval they were pressed close and oblivious to all else.

Kit loosened his arms a little and they stood looking at one another. There was the same dazed and wondering look in his eyes that Eleanor was sure must be reflected in hers, and at the same time there was a hopeless confusion raging through her body, for she knew that without a doubt she was falling in love with her husband all over again, and there seemed no way to prevent it.

'Eleanor…' Kit said huskily. He put out a hand to brush a stray curl back from her cheek.

'There you are!' Lady Salome's voice echoed down the aisle behind them. 'I am so sorry for keeping you waiting all this time. I hope that you have not been bored?'

'Not at all, ma'am!' Kit said, smiling at Eleanor.

Lady Salome's bright, observant gaze moved from Kit to Eleanor and lingered there.

'Goodness me, but you look very flushed, my dear!' she said. 'It is suddenly very hot in here—I have noticed it myself! Let us go out into the fresh air and pray that you will cool down!' She linked arms with both of them and shepherded them outside. Eleanor felt rather like a small boat carried along inexorably in the wake of a much larger ship.

'I was hoping to visit St Paul's Cathedral,' Lady Salome continued, 'but I see that it is time for nuncheon. Perhaps some other time, if you would care to accompany me?'

Eleanor had a sudden, heated vision of Kit kissing her in every church across London.

'That would be very pleasant, ma'am!' she said, and her hand trembled a little in Kit's as he handed her back up into the carriage. She resumed her seat in the corner and looked out blindly as the familiar landmarks passed by.

She was falling in love with Kit again and she could deny it no longer. Perhaps her heart had never entirely abandoned its feelings for him. She did not know. All she knew was that the thought elated and terrified her at one and the same time, but whilst she knew that a reconciliation with Kit was what she wanted now, it simply was not fair to him. Not when he might never achieve the family he so desired. She leant her head against the back of the seat and closed her eyes, feigning tiredness. She needed to think. But in her heart of hearts she knew the answer.

'So, my dear,' Lady Salome said, when she and her niece were back in the dining-room in Montague Street and were partaking of a luncheon of cold meats and fruit, 'it seems to me that there is an unconscionable amount of sorting out needed in this family! How fortunate that I have come up from Devon for that very purpose, but I scarce know where to start!'

Eleanor looked up in some surprise. Kit had gone to his club and she had been quite looking forward to a coze with Lady Salome, who had always been by far the most entertaining and least stuffy of her aunts. She poured them both another cup of tea. Now indoors, Lady Salome had discarded her royal blue spencer and the outrageous ostrich plumes, and the red ball-gown could be seen in all its glory, as could the diamond jewellery that adorned it. Eleanor thought about Lady Trevithick—and wondered.

'Whatever can you mean, Aunt? You have been here but one day to observe us!'

Lady Salome's eyes twinkled. 'I *hear* things, you know, my dear! And it takes but a few hours in your brother's house know that all is not well...'

Eleanor passed her a cup. She frowned. 'All is well with Marcus and Beth, surely? They are but new wed and very happy—'

Lady Salome raised an expressive eyebrow. 'Ah, marriage! Marriage! An honourable institution, as the Bible tells us! Yet how happy is a man when his wife refuses him entry to her bedroom no matter how he scratches at the door? And then there is your cousin Justin, who wears the expression of a man similarly afflicted. Both he and Marcus are decidedly cross and frustrated!' She saw Eleanor's scarlet face and patted her hand with her own, beringed one. 'I am sorry to put you to the blush, my dear, but I confess the matter intrigued me.'

'Oh dear!' Eleanor said faintly. She had quite forgotten her aunt's devastating combination of biblical quotations and outspoken sense.

'And then,' Lady Salome continued inexorably, 'there is the small matter of finding your mama in my room this morning about to relieve me of my favourite brooch...' She patted her ample bosom where the said piece of jewellery rested in all its splendour. 'A thief in the night! Or rather in the morning. She assured me that she had merely come to make sure that all my comforts had been se- cured...' Lady Salome crunched her fruit consider-ingly '…but I fear it was her own comfort she sought to achieve—by taking my diamonds. But then she is a slave to her laudanum, poor creature! We really must do something about that. And finally there is you, my dear…' Lady Salome tilted her head and looked thoughtfully at Eleanor.

Eleanor shifted uncomfortably, staring fixedly at the pattern on the carpet.

'I? I assure you, Aunt—'

'Oh, do not trouble to do that!' Lady Salome said blithely. 'It seems to me, Eleanor, my love, that you are mightily attracted to that husband of yours—and indeed, who would not be—but that you are not happy with your situation for some reason! Indeed, when I first met Christopher a few months ago and he was good enough to confide in me, I was struck by the difficult task he would have in regaining your love and trust—'

'Wait, wait!' Eleanor besought. Her head was spinning. 'You met Kit a few months ago, Aunt? He made no mention of it to me! I thought that you were meeting this morning for the first time!'

'Naturally, since I particularly asked him to let me speak to you before he explained,' Lady Salome said, smiling. 'A small deception, my dear, for which I apologise. Deceit is a bad thing, and I pray that I may redeem my soul from it, but in this case it was entirely necessary! Christopher had given me his word that he would tell no one of our previous meeting and I asked that he permit me to talk to you alone, so…' she made a slight gesture, 'here I am!'

Eleanor put her hands up to her cheeks. 'Aunt Trevithick, it seems that in a remarkably short time you know all our most closely guarded secrets!'

'I pride myself upon it, my love,' Lady Salome said complacently. 'One cannot spend as much time as I have upon Fairhaven Island without observing human life in all its glory!'

Eleanor was shaking her head in disbelief. 'So you know that Kit and I are not yet reconciled and that Mama is a thief and that Marcus and Justin are being stupid about reinstigating the family feud—'

'Ah, so that is what it is about!' Lady Salome said triumphantly. 'I could not imagine that Beth and Charlotte were…ah…withholding their favours for anything other than a good reason! But that is very piquant, as you will see when you hear my tale! Yes, decidedly we shall come back to that tale!'

'And as for Mama, she is under the influence of her laudanum and has taken to stealing jewellery to pay—'

Lady Salome shook her head sorrowfully. 'A nasty problem, that one! But we shall see!'

'And what do you have to tell me about Kit?' Eleanor eyed her keenly. 'He said that he was not at liberty to tell me the whole tale, but I thought, I assumed, it was a matter of business rather than a family affair…'

'Never assume, my love!' Lady Salome threw up her hands. 'Soon I shall give you a full assurance of understanding! Saint Paul's letter to the Corinthians, Chapter…well, well, never mind.' Lady Salome sat back. 'A delicious lunch, my dear. I find it helps the thought processes miraculously. So...' She exhaled her breath on a long and thoughtful sigh.

'As for this silly feud, I do believe that Beth and Charlotte will triumph in a very short time!' She twinkled at Eleanor. 'Neither Justin not Marcus have the temperament for a long abstinence, not when temptation is under their noses. Indeed, it is rather fun, like a morality play! As for your mama...' she sobered '...that is a more intractable problem, I fear.'

'Mama has been taking laudanum for years,' Eleanor said thoughtfully. 'Everyone does! Lady Pomfret, and Lady Spence and Mrs Hetherington... There is no harm in it.'

Lady Salome shook her head sharply. 'There I must beg to differ, my dear! Laudanum is the most pernicious dose and sadly undermining to one's moral fibre. Oh, I know that it eases the pain of the toothache or the bad head, but when one starts to take it simply for the beneficial feeling, when one becomes dependent upon it... Then it cannot be a good thing!'

'It is true that Mama doses herself up an unconscionable amount,' Eleanor admitted. 'And then her temper is uncertain and her health has been poor... But surely... I cannot believe that she is dependent...' She frowned, remembering the desperate look in Lady Trevithick's eye when she had realised that her bottle was empty at the musicale, her insistence that Kemble be asked to provide her with some more of the drug.

Yet everyone took laudanum for their ills... Why, Eleanor thought incredulously, if she complained to the doctor of feeling out of spirits, no doubt he would prescribe it for her himself! Yet if Lady Salome was correct there was a far more insidious effect and Lady Trevithick was in its grip. She would do anything to satisfy her need for the drug...

'Mama does not purchase her laudanum from the apothecary in the normal way,' she said slowly. 'I believe that one of her acquaintance supplies her with it and that she pays him for the privilege. Though why she would need to do so...'

'Quantity,' Lady Salome said succinctly. 'You may know, my dear, that the chemists will only supply a small amount at a time, for they fear that some sad wretches will use it to end their lives! But your mama requires more than the usual dose and so she obtains it elsewhere—and pays for it with other peoples' jewellery!' Lady Salome patted her diamonds protectively. She looked almost offended.

'It is not the first time,' Eleanor admitted. 'I fear that a piece of the Trevithick ruby set is gone, as was Charlotte's bracelet at the ball the other night...' And she related the tale of the lost bracelet and her insistence that her mother return it, and all the other occasions on which she had observed Lady Trevithick under the laudanum's influence. It was a relief to tell someone without feeling disloyal; Lady Salome listened, and tutted and Eleanor felt a little less alone.

'We shall have to see what can be done,' Lady Salome said, at the end. 'Certainly this man Kemble must be stopped and your mama rescued from her difficulties. It is not so simple... I must think!'

'Yes, Aunt. Another cup of tea?' Eleanor was suddenly aware that they had covered two of the three family problems and would be progressing inevitably to her own situation if she were not careful, and whilst she was curious to know how Lady Salome had met with Kit in the first instance, she did not wish to expose her own feelings to that lady's unerring scrutiny.

'Thank you, my love.' Lady Salome watched her thoughtfully as Eleanor rang the bell and sent for a fresh pot and some cake. 'You will be wishing to know, I am sure, how I met with your husband...'

'Yes...' Eleanor said warily. 'I confess it is uppermost in my mind!'

Lady Salome smiled. 'You are aware, of course, that Christopher has undertaken some small... commissions...for Lord Castlereagh in the past?'

'Yes,' Eleanor said. 'Kit told me so last night. Before that I had no notion.'

'Of course.' Lady Salome twinkled at her. 'For the safety of the nation one would hope we all go unaware of these things! As to my own involvement in this story, I confess that I had no notion why Christopher was in Ireland in the first instance, but it was fortuitous for me that he was! When we met,' she settled her bulk lower in the chair as she prepared to tell the tale, 'it was in early February and I know that he was anxious to return to you as soon as possible, my dear. He said that he had already been away too long and intimated that it was the most ill-timed and mismanaged business imaginable... But that is for him to explain. Perhaps he has already done so...'

'Yes,' Eleanor said, frowning a little. 'The only information he withheld from me was the nature of the delay, but I understand now, dear Aunt, that this was on your account?'

'Quite right, my dear!' Lady Salome nodded energetically. 'I confess that I was in the most parlous straits when I met Christopher. There is no concealing it.' She sighed. 'You may know that your Uncle St John Trevithick had been summoned from Fairhaven to Exeter last autumn by the bishop, who was not at all happy with St John's behaviour?'

Eleanor nodded. Marcus had mentioned months ago that their uncle, St John Trevithick, who was the vicar of Fairhaven, had been called to Exeter on unspecified church business. Now it seemed that the matter was more ominous than had first appeared.

Lady Salome resumed: 'Well, it was to be expected that the bishop would get wind of St John's problems, I suppose! The drinking and the sleeping in the church services and those long-winded sermons... The islanders of Fairhaven used to find St John amusing, but I knew he could not carry on, though we were at pains to conceal it from the bishop for pride's sake if nothing else—' She broke off.

'Forgive me, child, I am rambling. In short, the bishop sent St John on a visit to Ireland in January. It was made quite clear that this was my brother's last chance, but alas and alack, he made the most appalling mull of it! He was late for appointments and missed services and was drunk and querulous...' Lady Salome sighed heavily and Eleanor could tell how much the memory of it still appalled her.

'When Christopher happened upon us in our lodgings I was at my wit's end, for St John had spent all our money on drink and I did not even have the funds to pay our rent or the return trip. You can imagine that when I saw a kinsman I was utterly relieved and begged for his help.'

Eleanor frowned. 'Forgive me, Aunt, but how did you know that Kit was kin of yours? Why, until recent times the Mostyn and Trevithick families were the most staunch enemies imaginable!'

Lady Salome gestured widely. 'Indeed, and it was most fortunate they were, for it was that that made me recognise the Mostyn name. And of course I knew that Beth was to wed Marcus...'

'Oh, of course...' The pieces slid into place in Eleanor's mind. When Lady Salome had left Fairhaven to join her brother in Exeter, Marcus and Beth had already been betrothed. She would have known that the marriage had gone ahead and that there was now a tenuous but real link between the previously warring families. No wonder Lady Salome had applied to Kit for help in her difficulties—and he had responded as any true kinsman would… Eleanor felt a sudden, warm sense of appreciation for Kit's honourable conduct.

'It took several weeks for Christopher to untangle the mess that St John had made,' Lady Salome said sadly, 'and although I sensed that he was chafing to return home, he was the perfect gentleman and never sought to leave us to our own devices. Eventually one evening, when matters were at a very low ebb for both of us, he confided in me the story of your marriage, child…' Lady Salome's eyes were sad. 'I confess that I was shocked—oh, not that the wedding had come about as it had, but that Christopher had been obliged to leave you so untimely, and here was I, delaying him still further…' For a moment Eleanor thought her Aunt was about to cry, but Lady Salome was made of sterner stuff. 'I urged him to leave us but he would not. It was then that he told me of the letters he had sent you and how he hoped that matters would come right in the end…' She sat up straighter. 'And here I am, hoping against hope that that will be the case!'

Eleanor put both hands around her teacup, drawing comfort from the warmth. Now that she knew the truth, it was impossible to reproach Kit for his conduct in staying away so long, for he had put Lady Salome's problems first, no matter the personal cost.

Lady Salome was hunting in her reticule for her handkerchief, and gave her nose a hearty blow.

'I am so very sorry, my dear child,' she said gruffly. 'You will see now why I found it imperative to speak to you and to explain matters! Indeed, I should have done so before our trip this morning, but I confess I was a little nervous, and needed time to prepare…'

A sudden thought struck Eleanor. 'When was it that you returned to England, Aunt? Did Kit travel with you?'

Lady Salome nodded. 'Yes, my love. We all travelled back together at the end of last month and St John and I went straight to the bishop in Exeter. St John did the only thing he could, and retired from his living, so in the future we will both be settled in Devon.'

Eleanor let out her breath in a silent sigh. So Kit had been with Lady Salome until the end of April and then had returned to England, parting company with them and making his way up to London at last… She remembered the scrap of paper with 'St John at seven' written on it. An assignation indeed. She would never have guessed.

Lady Salome was looking much happier now, putting her handkerchief away with a briskly practical air, the tears now quite banished. She leaned forward and patted Eleanor's hand again.

'Pray do not hesitate to tell your husband that we have spoken, my love, for I know he cares for you deeply and I cannot but feel here…' Lady Salome pressed her hand to her breast in the general area of her heart '…that I am responsible for your estrangement! It was all so difficult! I swore Christopher to secrecy because I did not wish St John's disgrace to be known until he had resigned his living and I had the chance to tell your brother. As the head of the family Marcus had to be told first, but neither Christopher nor I really imagined the difficulties that would cause—'

'Marcus!' Eleanor cried. 'He cannot know that Kit helped you, Aunt, or he would never be pursuing this silly feud...'

Lady Salome's smile twinkled briefly. She got to her feet and embraced her niece fervently. 'No indeed! Your husband did not wish me to tell him, my dear! Some foolish matter to do with men and honour!'

Eleanor hugged her back. 'Oh, dear Aunt...' a thought had suddenly popped into her head '...I understand now what you meant when you mentioned that it was piquant that Marcus was pursuing the family feud! For if he were to know of Kit's involvement in your affairs—'

'He would feel obliged to repay him, never mind to thank him!' Lady Salome finished, her eyes gleaming. 'Indeed, it is very bad of me not to enlighten your brother, my dear, and I am tempted to do so, for all I gave Christopher my word! For now I feel that Beth's   solution   is   so   much   more... entertaining, so we shall see what happens! But be sure that the truth will out in the end! It always does, my love! It always does!'

Eleanor retired to bed that evening reflecting that it was typical that she had not been able to speak to Kit alone on the one occasion that she was desperate to do so. He had been tied up with his man of business that afternoon and had arrived home late, and as they were engaged to dine with a party at Lady Spence's there was no time to broach so serious a subject as Lady Salome's revelations before they left. At dinner she was seated as far away from Kit as possible and afterwards he had accepted Lord Spence's invitation to join him at Whites and Eleanor had returned home feeling tired and annoyed. It was not that she was expecting Kit to hang on her coat-tails, she told herself crossly, but it would have been pleasant for him to do so that particular evening when she had a special reason for needing him. She vowed to stay awake until he returned from Whites, then realised that to appear in his bedroom at that time of night would be somewhat equivocal, especially in view of the situation between them. Finally she retired to bed—Kit had still not returned—and fell into an uneasy sleep, only to awaken an unspecified amount of time later.

The house was quiet but for some reason she could not understand, Eleanor was wide awake. She slid out of bed and listened for sounds from Kit's room to see if she could ascertain whether he had returned, but there was no noise to guide her one way or the other. Eleanor reached for her dressing-robe. It was a plain no-nonsense affair, far removed from the light confections of silk and lace that Beth had purchased after her marriage to Marcus. Eleanor smiled to herself a little wryly; it seemed that she had moved from the innocent apparel of a débutante to the practical attire of a dowager with barely a pause in the middle. She tied the belt firmly. That was not precisely true, of course—there had been two nights of passion in between and even now the memory made her shiver, like a pleasurable spell that had not quite lost its power to charm. But that was the last thing that she should be thinking of at a time like this. Such pleasure must never be permitted to charm her again.

Eleanor slid back the bolt and turned the knob on the dressing-room door. The dressing-room itself was empty, as was the bedroom, although the candles were lit. Eleanor was about to turn around and go back to her own room, when the door opened and Kit came in, a candle in one hand and a glass of wine in the other.

Eleanor recoiled, clutching her dressing-gown under her chin. It was Kit who recovered himself first.

'Eleanor! Good evening! Could you not sleep?'

Eleanor came forward into the room slowly. 'No, I could not. That is, I wished to speak with you, Kit. It will not take long.' She drew herself up. 'Lady Salome has spoken to me and I now know the whole tale.'

'I see,' Kit said. 'Then there is no need to look as though you are about to run away again! Won't you sit down? Please?'

There had always been something about Kit's voice, Eleanor thought weakly, something persuasive, almost hypnotic, that made you agree to whatever he suggested before you had really thought about it. The timbre of his voice, low and mellow, was one of the first things that she had noticed about him. It had fascinated her, made her think all kinds of foolish things when he had spoken to her of love… And now it was set fair to undermine her defences before she had barely uttered a word. Yet it was too late to flee. Kit was placing a chair for her before the fire.

Eleanor sat down, curling up within the comforting bulk of the armchair, tucking her bare feet under her. Kit tossed another log on to the fire and made the flames hiss in the grate. Then he sat down. And looked at her. Eleanor's heart started to race. Here, in his bedroom, she felt so vulnerable that she could barely keep her mind on the matter in hand.

'Lady Salome has spoken to me.' She blurted out again. 'I know what happened in Ireland!'

Kit smiled a little rucfully. 'I knew she was determined to tell you! And indeed, Nell, when I realised what a coil my promise to keep silent had put me into, I was sorely tempted to break it and tell you myself.' He looked rueful. 'When I offered my services to your aunt and uncle in Ireland, I did not think the matter would take so long. More than once I cursed the delay, but I could not break my word. It was damnably difficult!'

'You acted most honourably, Kit,' Eleanor said, a little gruffly.

Kit smiled reluctantly in return. He got up and came across to her, taking her hands in his. 'So now it is all over. Do you forgive me, Eleanor?'

Eleanor's smile faded. She felt a little cold. She knew what Kit wanted and she could not give it to him. Forgiveness, yes. Reconciliation...

'Of course I forgive you, Kit.' She made her voice as steady as she could. 'I am glad that we have reached an understanding, for it makes it so much easier for me to say...what I have to say.'

She stopped. Kit was still holding her hands and the warmth of his touch was disarming. Eleanor struggled to blot it out. She would not be able to do this if she allowed herself to weaken even slightly. And she had to do it. She could not allow even the possibility of a reconciliation and she knew that they had been moving towards it gently, inexorably...

She saw the wariness in Kit's eyes as he realised that something was wrong. His grip on her hands tightened.

'Eleanor...'

Eleanor looked down at her lap. She could not meet his gaze.

'I think that our marriage should be annulled,' she said.

Chapter Ten

Kit relinquished her hands and stood up slowly. There was a strange, stunned look in his eyes, a mixture of disbelief and denial. He cleared his throat.

'Eleanor, I cannot believe that you really mean that!'

Eleanor clenched her fists. 'Oh but I do, Kit!' Her voice wavered slightly and did not have anywhere near the conviction it needed, but she ploughed on.

'I have been thinking on this for some time. It seems to me that our marriage was hasty in the extreme and that had we but exercised some sense in the first place, it would never have happened!' She took a quick glance at his face and looked away even more quickly. This was torture. Not only was she tearing herself apart but she was ripping Kit's feelings to pieces before her own eyes.

'No,' Kit said, and there was an angry edge to his voice now. 'At least do not pretend that we did not care for each other then, Eleanor!'

Eleanor tried to shrug. 'It was so, I suppose. At least, I thought that I cared for you—'

She saw Kit flinch and felt sick. For both their sakes she had to finish this quickly.

'And it is not that I do not care for you now...' Her voice wavered.

'Then what is it?' Kit's tone was harsh. 'For God's sake, Eleanor, tell me what has put this foolish notion into your head!' He took an angry turn about the room. 'Is it that you wish to punish me for leaving you? That even now, having heard my reasons and my apologies, you cannot forgive me? For if that is so—'

'No!' Eleanor cried. She just managed to resist the temptation to put her hands over her ears. 'I have no wish to punish you, Kit, but...' her voice sank to a whisper '...I cannot remain married to you. I am sorry.'

There was a silence.

'I, too, am sorry.' Kit spoke very formally now. 'I was under the impression that we wanted the same things. I thought that tonight we had achieved some kind of understanding and that in time, at least—' He broke off.

'It is for the best,' Eleanor said helplessly. 'You may be free to achieve the family that you wish and I shall also be free to go where I choose and do—' She stopped, unable to go on. She could feel his gaze on her, direct and angry, but also very perceptive. Too perceptive. Eleanor felt acutely vulnerable. She got to her feet.

'I must go…'

'Oh no,' Kit said smoothly. He caught her arm. 'Oh no, my dear. You cannot make so outrageous a demand as this without justifying your reasons! I want to understand you. I *need* to understand…'

Eleanor looked into his eyes and recoiled from the anger and pain she saw there. If she had ever doubted that Kit loved her she had her answer now— she had smashed all of his hopes and expectations with her words. The pain of it was tormenting her as well, yet she could not explain to him. Her fear was stronger than all else; fear that she could never give him what he wanted.

They gazed at each other for what seemed like forever, then the angry light faded from Kit's eyes.

'Nell…' His voice was impossibly gentle. 'What is this all about? I cannot believe that it is truly what you want—'

Eleanor evaded his eyes. 'It has to be—'

'It does not!' Kit's hands tightened fiercely and she winced. 'I do not understand! I could have sworn that you had feelings for me—that you were not indifferent! Yet now you suggest this…' His hands dropped away. 'Eleanor, look at me and tell me that this is what you want.'

Eleanor forced her eyes to meet his for the briefest of seconds. 'It is what I want, Kit,' she said tonelessly.

Kit stepped back meticulously, as though his presence too close to her was a contamination. Eleanor felt the cold seeping through her bones. She started to shiver convulsively.

'Very well.' Kit sounded almost calm, and looked it, but for the tight line of his lips and the hard expression in his eyes. 'I hear what you say, my lady. Now hear this. I do not believe your reasons and we will talk of them again. Further, I do not agree to the annulment of our marriage. Do you understand me? There shall be no annulment!'

With a sudden, violent movement he had sent his empty wineglass spinning from the mantelpiece to smash into fragments in the hearth. Eleanor flinched.

'You are right,' Kit said quietly. 'You had better go.'

Eleanor's legs managed to carry her as far as her own bedchamber, where she sank down on the bed and shook uncontrollably. Her mind was numb, dazed. She wondered why she had not considered that Kit would respond as he had. Had she expected him to agree to an annulment so easily when she would not even give him the honest reason why she wanted one?

Eleanor covered her face with her hands. She had been dishonest and cruel to both Kit and herself. She knew that he deserved the truth, deserved to know both about his lost child and her terror of losing another or of never being able to have more children... Yet she had locked that grief and fear so deep within herself that even now she could not tell him. He had gradually stripped away all of the barriers that remained between them until they were in a position where they could have started to rebuild their love. Instead she had told him that she wanted nothing of it...

With a sob, Eleanor curled up, wrapped her arms about herself and at last gave way to her tears.

When Eleanor woke up her head felt the size of a marrow and her eyes appeared to have been gummed together. At first she felt inclined to stay in bed, pull the covers over her head and pretend that nothing was wrong, but her feelings of misery could not be ignored. Although the bed curtains were drawn she could see that it was broad daylight and she decided instead to get up and do something—anything—to stave off her unhappiness rather than to lie there and wallow in it. A tear escaped unbidden from the corner of her eye and slid down on to the pillow, and that decided her. She jumped out of bed. She simply could not lie around feeling sorry for herself. It would give her too much time to think.

She rang the bell for Lucy, then saw her reflection in the mirror and regretted it. She looked dreadful and the maid would not scruple to tell her so. All Lucy's cunning ministrations would be wasted this morning, for Eleanor doubted if she would look anything other than wan and ugly.

Sure enough, Lucy almost dropped the can of hot water when she came into the bedroom.

'Oh! Oh, ma'am! Are you ill? You look quite dreadful!'

'Thank you, Lucy,' Eleanor said tiredly. 'I am not

ill, though my head aches a little. Pray make me as presentable as you can.'

A full hour later, washed, combed, curled and anointed with rose-petal cream, which Lucy swore would revive her complexion, Eleanor tiptoed downstairs. As soon as she set foot in the hall, the door to the drawing-room opened and Kit emerged. Eleanor felt her heart plunge as she saw him. He looked even worse than she did.

'Good morning, Eleanor.' He spoke distantly. 'I would appreciate it if you would spare a moment to speak with me.'

Eleanor shuddered. If Kit had reviewed his situation and was now prepared to agree to the annulment she did not really want to hear it and if he had not and wanted to discuss the matter further, she did not want that either. On the other hand, she could scarcely refuse his request. He held the door open and she went into the room with great reluctance, hearing the door click closed behind her.

After a moment, Kit said: 'I have been thinking all night about what you said, Nell. Is it still your wish that our marriage be annulled?'

Eleanor bit her lip hard. 'It is.'

She saw Kit's shoulders slump slightly, as though he had been hoping for a different reply. She could say nothing else.

'I see.' Kit's voice was steady. 'Your reasons?'

'I have told you—' Panic clutched at Eleanor's throat. She was not sure she could bear to rehearse all this again. 'I believe our marriage was too hasty! We should be given a second chance—'

'Is there then someone else you would prefer to marry?' Kit asked, almost as though she had not spoken. 'Is that what this is about, Eleanor?'

'No!' Eleanor burst out. 'How can you think such a thing, Kit? It was you I was thinking of—'

'How kind of you,' Kit said, with such cutting sarcasm that Eleanor had to swallow hard to quell more tears, 'but I cannot believe your altruistic motives, my love! There is something else here; something I am determined to discover. Yet you swear you do not intend it just to punish me—'

'No!'

'Though surely that is exactly what you are doing now.' Kit's quiet words silenced her. 'I am sorry, Eleanor, but I do not believe your reasons. I know there is something else—something I am determined you will tell me…'

Eleanor turned away so her face should not betray her. 'There is nothing else.' Her voice was muffled. 'This is for the best…'

Kit made a slight gesture. 'I will ask you again later. And again and again if I must.' He gave her a slight bow. 'I am going out now. Good day, Eleanor.'

When he had gone out Eleanor sank down on the sofa and wrung her hands. She was not sure how much of this she could bear. If Kit insisted on asking her, time after time, sooner or later she would give something away…

Eleanor jumped up. Waiting for the inevitable seemed intolerable. If she could just get away for a while…

She hurried back up the stairs, calling for Lucy as she went. The startled maidservant found her pulling the portmanteau out of a cupboard and hauling it up on to the bed.

'Lucy, we are going to Trevithick for a space,' Eleanor puffed. 'London bores me! I need to get away!'

'Yes, madam…' The maid caught the other end of the case. 'Is that a good idea, madam?'

Eleanor frowned at her. 'Certainly it is! Pray fetch all my dresses and fold them up…'

Lucy looked flustered. 'Will you need your evening gowns in the country, ma'am?'

'The day dresses!' Eleanor snapped. Suddenly she was possessed with a panicky urgency to be away. 'Walking dresses, promenade dress—'

'Your riding habit, my lady?'

'Oh, I will get all the clothes!' Eleanor said in exasperation. She felt strange—hot and fearful, yet cold at the same time. 'Fetch my underwear, Lucy! This need not take us long!'

As the maid sped away to open the drawers, the bedroom door swung open and Kit appeared in the aperture.

'What is all this feverish activity for?'

Kit walked straight into the bedroom and Eleanor realised that once again Lucy had forgotten to close the door. The maid was now standing, hands full of stockings and chemises, her mouth half-open.

'Lucy, please leave us!' Eleanor snapped. This was one occasion on which the maid could not possibly misinterpret the animosity between husband and wife. Kit was looking at Eleanor and at the portmanteau and his expression was cold enough to freeze water.

Eleanor bit her lip. She knew that she should have bided her time until she was certain that Kit was out of the house, but in her anxiety to be away she had overlooked his presence.

'Just what is going on here?'

Kit came up to her. His gaze swept over the portmanteau and the pile of clothes, and fastened on Eleanor's guilty face. She closed her eyes in anguish.

'I see.' Kit said politely, drawing his own conclusions. 'Did you have any particular destination in mind, my love?'

'I thought to visit Trevithick for a space,' Eleanor said, in a rush. 'It would be better to go away and we may put it about that it is for my health…'

'I see that you have it all worked out,' Kit remarked, in a tone that brought the colour into Eleanor's pale face. 'Have you already spoken to your brother about this?'

'No,' Eleanor flushed. 'I have spoken to no one…'

'So this is entirely your own idea.' Kit was watching her implacably. 'I am so very glad that I discovered it before it was too late! I should have been quite annoyed to be put to the trouble of searching various inns for you—again!' He paused. 'I take it that you were actually planning to travel alone?'

'I was intending to take Lucy with me!' Eleanor snapped, deliberately misunderstanding him. 'I thought that we had sorted out *that* particular disagreement, my lord—'

'I thought that we had sorted out many,' Kit returned, 'but it seems that I was wrong.'

Eleanor sat down heavily on the edge of the bed. 'Well, now that you are aware of my plans, do you not think that it is a good idea? I cannot stay here—'

'Why not?' Kit enquired, with a lift of an eyebrow.

'Well, because…' Eleanor floundered a little.

'Because we have disagreed over a point of principle?' Kit asked. 'I assure you, my dear, I *require* you to stay here and discuss the matter with me—again and again, until we have it clear! It is out of the question for you to leave London!'

Eleanor frowned slightly. 'You mean—you refuse to let me go?'

'Exactly. Indeed I would go further.' Kit smiled. 'I forbid you to go. In leaving this house you will be going against my express wishes.'

'In leaving the house!' Eleanor shot to her feet.

'Without my permission, yes. I cannot be sure that you will not run off, you see.' Kit smiled gently. 'Come come, my dear, it will not be so bad! I am happy to accompany you to balls and breakfasts, and once we have resolved our differences you may come and go as you please…'

'That is blackmail!' Eleanor said in a stifled voice. 'I have to agree with you or become a prisoner in my own home!'

Kit strolled over to the window and looked down into the street. 'You do not have to agree with me, you have to explain your own position.' He shot her a look. 'That is not unreasonable! I know that there is something you are keeping from me and I want to know what it is and how it pertains to our marriage! Is that so surprising?'

Eleanor did not reply. She clenched her fists, then forced herself to calm down and let her breath out on a long sigh.

'Oh! This is of all things intolerable. Am I then to be allowed visitors in my...prison?'

Kit laughed. 'There is no need to be so melodramatic! Life carries on much as it has done before, the only difference being that I am waiting for you to explain yourself. The remedy is in your own hands, my dear. Do you wish to talk about it now?'

They looked at each other. Eleanor was the first to drop her gaze.

'Very well then,' Kit said expressionlessly. 'Will you dine with me tonight or do you prefer to take a tray up here, my love?'

Eleanor was silent. She understood that for the rest of the morning and afternoon she would be confined to the house, or even to just her room. She would have no company, she would not be allowed out, she would have time to sit and think...and think. She raised her chin.

'Here, I thank you, my lord,' she said. 'I do not wish for your company.'

Eleanor ate her solitary dinner whilst trying not to think of Kit downstairs eating his alone at the huge polished dining-table. She did not think he had gone out, although she was not sure. Once the meal was taken she tried to read a book for a little but found her attention straying all the time. Eventually she realised that she would have to go down and play the piano. It was the only way to soothe her feelings—or try to soothe them.

This evening a fire was burning in the music-room and the candles stood ready to be lit, as though someone had anticipated that she would need to play. She took a stand of them over to the piano and sat down, her fingers straying over the keys, playing little melancholy tunes until the familiar melodies took her and she played the Bach cantatas one after another, losing herself in the precision and the feeling. This time Kit did not come in to see her and she remained undisturbed. But later, as she was preparing for bed, there was knock at the door and Kit came in. And this time he was in only his breeches and shirt.

'My lord—' Eleanor began.

Kit looked at her. There was a glitter in his eyes that made her nervous. She wondered suddenly if he were drunk.

'It occurs to me that I have been unconscionably patient with you, my love,' Kit said. He put the candlestick down on the dresser and came to sit on the edge of the bed. His gaze wandered over her thoughtfully, considering the tumbling dark hair, her pale face and the nervous pulse Eleanor could feel beating in the hollow of her throat. She drew the bedclothes up to her chin and clutched them there. Kit smiled.

'As I was saying…' there was a caressing tone in his voice now that made her shiver '…we are married, Eleanor, and the fact that we consummated that marriage before rather than after the wedding is…' he shrugged '…almost immaterial. You do know that an annulment is not easily granted? One of the grounds is impotence and that…' he smiled '…would be ridiculous and I cannot believe that you would expect me to agree to it. I have the rights of a husband and have shown considerable forbearance, not to say restraint, in not exercising them sooner—'

'We had an agreement!' Eleanor whispered. 'You swore you would not force yourself on me…'

Kit nodded. 'So I did. I did not promise not to seduce you, however. You know as well as I that I could have done so but two nights ago—or before that if I had not been so scrupulous!'

Eleanor closed her eyes briefly. She knew it was true and it was pointless to deny it.

'That being the case,' Kit continued, 'I find myself in something of a quandary. You see, Eleanor…' he plucked one of her hands from the coverlet and held it in his, stroking the back of it gently with his thumb '…I want you very much. I have done so since the moment I first saw you and certainly from the moment I came back. So…' he paused, looking at her '…I certainly do not feel able to agree to an annulment—under the circumstances.'

Eleanor screwed her face up. 'Kit, please…'

'No.' There was a note in Kit's voice that silenced her. 'I do not pretend to understand what is going on here, Eleanor, and you do not choose to tell me. Well, I cannot force you to do so, but I can put your resolve to the test. So I shall.' He leant forward and kissed her very softly. 'We shall soon see how set on an annulment you truly are…'

Eleanor made a small, piteous noise. 'Kit, that is not fair—'

'It is perfectly fair.' Kit sounded implacable. 'Since you refuse to speak to me this is the only approach I can take. You have only to have the courage of your convictions—whatever they may be…'

Eleanor knew that it was not that simple. In fact it was not simple at all. She knew it but she could not seem to focus on it, for Kit was kissing her again, ending both thinking and discussion. His mouth took hers in short, sharp little kisses that stole her breath. There was little of love in them and everything of desire and possession, but Eleanor still felt herself weakening. Her lips parted irresistibly beneath his and he kissed her again, with a deeper kiss that was slow and hungry this time. Eleanor let the coverlet fall from her fingers and caught hold of Kit's arms as much to steady herself as to draw him closer. The linen of his sleeve was rough beneath her fingers and she clutched it for dear life, but he sat back a little.

'You can stop me, you know, Eleanor. After all, I gave you my word. All it requires is for you to tell me to stop...'

'Yes...' Eleanor whispered. She was not at all sure what she was saying, but it certainly was not that he should stop. She could tell him that in a little while, perhaps. After he had kissed her some more...

There was a pause, then Kit pulled her to him again, teasing her lips apart with his tongue so that Eleanor caught her breath and he moved quickly to take her mouth completely. His hand tangled in her hair, tilting her head so that he could taste her to the full. She felt as though she was falling, tumbling down into a pool of the most desperate desire. This was so sweet and she had longed for it. Tell him to stop... Well, there was plenty of time.

Kit put his hand to the bow at the neckline of her nightgown and pulled the ribbon hard. It uncurled into his fingers. He eased the gown gently to her waist, dropping a kiss on the curve of Eleanor's bare shoulder. She shivered, a rose blush colouring her skin, then closed her eyes as she felt Kit cup one breast in the palm of his hand and bend to kiss its tight crest.

He sucked gently, first one breast then the other. Eleanor gave a small whimper of pleasure and almost fell backwards into the yielding softness of the mattress. Kit followed, leaning over to repeat his caresses with fingers and tongue, driving coherent thought even further from Eleanor's mind. It had been a long time and she had ached for him, and under the onslaught of her senses her conscious mind was quiescent, her fears stilled.

Kit drew the rest of the nightgown away from her so that she was lying on the coverlet, quite naked, her senses so dazed that she was utterly unselfconscious. Kit leant over her again, kissing her softly, tenderly. She was as innocent as when he had first taken her to his bed, her eyes slumberous with passion as she looked at him from beneath heavy lids.

'Kit...'

'Yes? Do you wish me to stop now?'

'No, but...' He saw her frown and bent his lips to touch the fullness of hers again, unable to resist. They were warm, damp and already swollen from his kisses. After a moment her eyelids flickered closed again.

Kit parted her lips with his own, touching his tongue to hers. She was not passive—she accepted his caresses with pleasure and responded with a shy hesitancy that excited him more than the calculated embraces of the courtesans had ever done. Nevertheless, Kit mastered his own desire. This was all about Eleanor. He would never discover the truth if he blundered on, intent only on satisfying his own needs. He had waited this long and he could wait longer if it meant that he could claim his wife at the end and solve this perplexing mystery of the annulment.

He pressed soft kisses gently against her neck and

the hollow of her shoulder, watching all the time for a sign that Eleanor was uncomfortable with his attentions, waiting for a clue to her fears. It seemed that the reverse was true. She moved beneath his caresses with evident pleasure; her skin was pink and flushed with desire. Kit trailed kisses down her throat to the upper swell of her breasts. She moaned softly. He took one nipple in his mouth again, flicking it teasingly with his tongue whilst he cupped and stroked her other breast with his fingers. The touch and taste of her satin skin and Eleanor's avid response were almost enough to drive him to the edge, but he concentrated hard on his predicament rather than his feelings. Unfortunately—or fortunately—he had not pushed her hard enough yet. There was more to learn...

He allowed his lips to drift lower, across the sensitive skin of her stomach. In the candlelight her skin was pale golden, soft but firm. Kit's fingers brushed across her thighs, softly parting her legs, subtly, so subtly stroking the soft, sensitive skin.

'Eleanor?'

An incoherent murmur was his only reply. Kit smiled and did not even bother to ask the question.

When he finally stole a caress at the burning centre of her, he was gentle and tender, watching her, revelling in her instinctive gasp of pleasure and the way she writhed on the coverlet beneath his hands. She made no move to pull away from him and after a moment Kit resumed the intimate caress. She was utterly lost in a realm of pleasurable sensation. With infinite care he parted her thighs still further and touched her again.

Eleanor shrieked, burying her face in the pillow. Her whole body went boneless, supine. Kit touched her again—and again, until she convulsed in sheer ecstasy. He no longer had any thought for anything other than the giving of pleasure—and the enjoyment it gave him to satisfy her so. At the end he rolled her into his arms and held her close, holding her sweet and softly scented body against his own aching one. Now... Surely now they could be reconciled...

'I love you,' he said, very softly.

Eleanor opened her eyes and looked at him. For what seemed like minutes her gaze was dazed and dark, then awareness crept back and with it horror. The colour came into her cheeks then fled as swiftly as it had come. She pressed her hands to her face, and burst into a storm of tears.

'No! Oh no!'

Kit was horrified. He pulled the coverlet close about her and cradled her to him as she cried.

'Eleanor? Sweetheart? Don't cry—everything will be all right...'

All he got in reply was a violent shake of the head and Eleanor cried all the harder. Kit gave up any attempt to speak and just held her closer, overriding her attempt to pull away. Eventually she started to speak. He had to bend his head closer still and strain to hear the words.

'This is just what I did not want to happen because

it is not fair…' Eleanor sniffed piteously. 'It is because of this that I have to go…'

Kit frowned as he tried to make sense of this. 'Why is it not fair, sweetheart? Fair to whom? You?'

'No!' Eleanor raised her head and looked at him angrily. 'It is not fair to you, Kit! Every man wishes to make love to his own wife—it is only natural…'

Whilst taking issue with the first part of this sentence, Kit knew that it was certainly true in his particular case. But it still did not make sense.

'True—which we have just done—'

'No!' Eleanor said again. She sat up and the coverlet slipped. Kit tried not to look at the nakedness it revealed, for she looked like a tumbled angel and it was doing terrible things to his concentration. He wanted her so much, but this was more important. He took her hands in his.

'Sweetheart, I am sorry but I still do not understand. Surely you are not telling me that you *still* wish for an annulment?'

'Yes, I do!' Eleanor cried wildly. 'To avoid precisely this happening again…' She started to cry again.

Kit stood up abruptly and thrust one hand through his hair. He could not believe it; could not believe that she was being so stubborn, could not believe that what had seemed so sweet to him—and in the end so simple—was not the same for her. He took her by the shoulders and shook her gently.

'Eleanor, look at me and tell me that you do not love me! Look at me!'

Her head came up slowly. Her eyes were wide, her expression bruised. 'I cannot tell you that, Kit. But it makes no difference!'

Kit let his hands fall away. He felt baffled and he felt furious. 'You love me yet you still want an annulment?'

Her answer was a whispered breath. 'Yes.'

Kit looked down at her bent head. 'Then you shall have what you want. I am too tired to fight this, Nell, when I do not understand what I am fighting.'

He went out of the room and closed the door quietly behind him. Through the bolted door to his dressing-room he could hear her crying and he almost went back to her, but in the end he did not and they both lay awake all night, on separate sides of the door, in silence.

Beth Trevithick was alone in her conservatory. It was very unusual to have time to herself, but this morning everyone had gone out and she, pleading tiredness, had snatched a few hours to herself potting cuttings for Lady Salome to take back to Devon with her. It was warm and airy in the conservatory and the scent of flowers was in the air. Beth was enjoying herself so much that she was quite annoyed to hear footsteps on the tiled floor—male footsteps, she thought, wondering if Marcus had returned early. She put down her gardening gloves and little spade in order to greet the newcomer.

It was not Marcus but Kit who came round the corner, and Beth smiled when she saw her cousin.

'Kit!' She greeted him with unalloyed pleasure. 'My dear, how delightful—and how brave of you to venture here! Is Eleanor with you?' She paused, looking at him more closely. 'Oh dear, you look quite dreadful! Whatever has happened?'

Kit did not reply. He took a seat on the cushioned bench beside the pond, and after a moment Beth came to sit beside him. She could tell something was terribly wrong—they were friends from childhood as well as cousins, and Beth knew Kit as well as she knew Charlotte. Kit was not normally profligate in his emotions, but now she knew he was building up to tell her something truly dreadful and her heart began to race with fear.

'I am only potting up some plants for Lady Salome,' she said conversationally, to give him time, 'for she wishes to have some cuttings for her own greenhouses. I do believe—'

'It is Eleanor,' Kit said abruptly, cutting across her as though she were not speaking. He swung round to look at her and Beth saw how haggard he looked in the bright morning light.

'She has asked for an annulment, Beth, and I have agreed.' Kit brought his clenched fist down on the arm of the chair with a force that made it shudder. 'I came here because I did not wish you and Charlotte to hear the news from Eleanor herself, or worse, from Trevithick. I wanted to tell you myself!'

'Kit…' Beth put a hand on his and after a moment he looked up at her, though she thought that he was not really seeing her.

'I cannot understand it.' Kit's lips set in a hard line. 'She will not tell me her true reasons yet I know that she loves me! She told me so herself! It makes no sense!' He shook his head. 'I even wondered last night if one of those so-called admirers of hers had hurt her in some manner...' he broke off, letting his breath out on an angry sigh '...yet I cannot think that true. I do not believe she has been with another man.'

He swung round, suddenly concentrating on her so fiercely that Beth almost flinched.

'Beth, you were with Eleanor during the time I was away. What happened to her?'

Beth closed her eyes briefly. From the very first she had dreaded this, knowing that one day Kit might ask her this very question, knowing that she loved her cousin and could not lie to him. Yet she knew that Eleanor loved him too and that it was Eleanor's place to tell him, not hers. But Kit had seen her hesitation now and his fingers bit into her wrist. His blue gaze narrowed on her.

'You know something, don't you! Tell me!'

'Kit, you are hurting me,' Beth said very steadily. 'Let go of me and pray keep calm, for I cannot help you if you terrify me!'

There was a moment of taut silence, and then Kit released her wrist and shook his head slowly, as though he were awaking from sleep.

'Beth, forgive me. I did not mean to hurt you, but I am half out of my mind—'

'I understand.' Beth said. She patted his hand

again. 'Listen to me, Kit, and do not interrupt, no matter how tempted you are. I cannot lie to you. Yes, I do know what happened to Eleanor when you were away and no, I cannot tell you what it was. No!' She held up an imperative hand as he was about to interrupt her. 'Eleanor *must* tell you herself! Now, I will speak to her and try to persuade her, but Kit, the matter is so personal to her—and to you—that it would not be right for me to intervene. But I swear,' she took his hand in a tight grip, 'that no one has hurt her. Not in the sense that you mean. This is a matter between the two of you only. And I dare swear also...' there were tears in Beth's eyes as she looked at him '...that Eleanor loves you most truly, but she is desperately afraid, Kit. That is all I can tell you.'

There was a silence, but for the splashing of the water into the ornamental pool.

'Marcus is hosting a dinner tonight in Lady Salome's honour,' Beth said, disentangling herself a little. She sat back and smiled at her cousin.

'I understand that it is the last thing that you would wish to do, Kit, but I beg you to come and bring Eleanor with you. It is very important. I believe that many things will be revealed.'

Chapter Eleven

The party that met at Trevithick House that night was hardly in celebratory mood and it was a tribute to Lady Salome that they were all there at all. The intention was for a family dinner followed by a ball for a small and select group of friends and acquaintances, and whilst the food was good the conversation was worse than stilted.

Eleanor, who had been placed next to Justin on one side and Kit on the other, was finding it impossible to make even the slightest attempt to talk to either of them. Justin's attention was focused on Charlotte with the single-minded avidity of a starving man who can see a meal just out of his reach. Kit was polite but so distant that he might as well have been an utter stranger. Eleanor nibbled her food and felt miserable.

Further down the table, Lady Salome was chatting blithely to Marcus, who was glaring at Beth. The Dowager Lady Trevithick was surprisingly animated and had two bright spots of colour showing on her cheeks. Every so often she would surreptitiously tip some laudanum from her vial into her wineglass. Even Beth and Charlotte looked vaguely strained and were avoiding looking at their respective husbands.

The dessert had just been removed and the ladies were preparing to retire, when Lady Salome stood up.

'I should like to say a few words to you all,' she said, twinkling at them roguishly. 'It has been a great pleasure for me to have my family about me this evening and I wish to thank you all, particularly as I know you would probably not have chosen to be at the same table could you avoid it!'

There was some movement around that very table as various members of the family shifted uncomfortably. Lady Salome had a talent for making them sound like difficult children.

'And it is for that very reason that I intend to right some wrongs this evening!' Lady Salome continued grandly. 'Vengeance is mine, I shall repay, saith the Lord! But tonight, my dears, I shall do the repaying!'

'Oh Lord,' Marcus said, under his breath.

Eleanor shot him a reproving look. She was glad that he was about to get his comeuppance. 'Marcus, hush! This is a serious matter!'

'At the beginning of the year I accompanied my brother St John to Ireland on a mission he was undertaking on behalf of the Bishop of Exeter.' Lady Salome said, casting her gaze down sorrowfully. 'I

think you all know now that the trip was a disaster
and that St John has subsequently retired. What you
do not know...' she paused for effect '...is that
whilst we were in Ireland we were beset by difficulties that I was unable and St John—sadly—incapable of rectifying. Personal and financial difficulties...' She let the sentence trail discreetly away.

There was a silence. Kit moved slightly in his seat.
Lady Salome turned to him.

'I know that you had no wish for this to be dis-
closed, my dear Christopher, but I can be silent no
longer! It pains me to see the unhappiness in this
family! Where there is discord, let me bring harmony! Where there is feuding, let me spread peace!'

Eleanor bit her lip, surprised by an unexpected
urge to laugh. There was no doubt that Lady Salome
was playing to the gallery. Everyone had turned to
look at Kit now, and he did not seem very pleased
about it. She made an instinctive move to place a
reassuring hand on his arm, and then drew back. No
doubt the last thing that he would wish was for re-
assurance from her.

Marcus raised his eyebrows. 'I infer that Mostyn
has rendered you some service that we are unaware
of, Aunt?' He sounded as displeased as Kit looked.
'You have us all on tenterhooks! Pray enlighten us,
if you please!'

'Certainly, dear boy!' Lady Salome said cheerfully. 'It was my good fortune to encounter
Christopher in Ireland. He was on the point of returning to this country and...' she smiled at Eleanor

'…a much desired reunion with his wife. I importuned him to help us—I do not believe we need the precise financial and personal details do we, Marcus?—and Christopher was honourable enough to put our needs before his own, most pressing, circumstances. I need hardly point out what a sacrifice this was for him, nor the troubles that ensued—'

Kit held a hand up. 'Dear Lady Salome, you have embarrassed me quite enough! I am sure your audience has all the information it needs!'

This time the silence around the table was explosive. Marcus's face was a picture. Beth caught Eleanor's eye and pulled an expressive face.

'You silence me, ma'am,' Marcus said, at length. 'Perhaps this would be an opportune moment for the ladies to retire? The gentlemen may then… ah…clarify a few matters…'

Eleanor sat irresolute. She did not like the thought of leaving Kit alone with both Marcus and Justin for it felt a little like throwing him to the lions. Her support was unlikely to be what he wanted, however. Beth was coming to take her arm with an encouraging word and a smile for Kit, whilst Charlotte had fixed Justin with such a speaking look that Eleanor almost felt sorry for her cousin. The ladies went out, Lady Salome lending the Dowager an arm to lean upon.

'Oh, I do hope everything will be well!' Eleanor fretted, as they took their places in the drawing-room and waited for the tea to be served. 'I could not bear it if they came to blows and made matters all the worse!'

Beth squeezed her arm. 'All will be well! I am confident that Marcus will behave as a gentleman ought and will apologise to Kit! And if he does not I shall never forgive him!'

'I confess I shall be glad that matters may revert to normal,' Charlotte said, casting a glance at the Dowager to make sure that she was out of earshot. 'These last few days have been very difficult! Not so much the...' she blushed, 'the *denial*, if you understand me, but the tensions it created! Why, I had to stab Justin quite hard with my embroidery needle yesterday to encourage him to desist in his attentions!'

Beth laughed. 'I understand you! I shall not be sorry either! But who would have thought that Lady Salome would spring such a surprise!' Her gaze fell on Eleanor.

'You are very quiet tonight, Nell, and you look very poorly. Very poorly indeed! Charlotte, does not poor Eleanor look positively sickly—'

'Yes, she does, Beth dear,' Charlotte said comfortably, 'but I do not think it will help Eleanor feel any better for you to keep repeating it! Come here, Nell, and sit by me.' Charlotte patted the sofa.

Eleanor sat, feeling rather uncomfortable. If Charlotte only knew what she had done to Kit she doubted she would be so friendly. Eleanor dreaded having to explain herself to Beth and Charlotte— both of them knew what had happened during Kit's absence and both of them had been the most stalwart of friends, but she suspected that she would be pushing their understanding by asking them to condone her demand for an annulment. Once or twice during the evening she had felt their gaze upon her and almost thought that they knew, but perhaps that was only her conscience making her feel guilty. Perhaps it was cowardly of her, but for now she was determined to keep quiet.

'As well as the comfort of reverting to normal in our behaviour to our husbands, it will be a relief to have the whole family united,' Beth said, making Eleanor feel much worse. 'I confess there were times when I thought it impossible to lay our quarrels to rest, but now I have real hope…'

Eleanor shifted and fidgeted on the sofa. The thought of ruining Beth's hopes of a united family made her feel quite ill. It seemed that as soon as they had achieved harmony she would spoil it all again. She had planned to approach Marcus for help tomorrow.

'Do you think Lady Salome has finished with us all yet?' she whispered, casting a glance across the room to where Lady Salome and the Dowager were chatting over the teacups. 'I have the most lowering notion that she has something else up her sleeve!'

Beth fixed her with a very direct look. 'You sound as though you are afraid of something, Nell!' she said acutely. 'And perhaps you should be, for I do not believe that Lady Salome has finished at all! Indeed I think that she has only just begun!'

By the time that the gentlemen rejoined them, the guests had started to arrive and Beth and Marcus went off to greet them whilst the others went through to the ballroom. Eleanor, who had expected to see at least a trace of constraint in Justin and Kit's behaviour, was a little taken aback to find them conversing with ease and a male camaraderie that left her feeling ever-so-slightly excluded. It was, as Beth would have said, quite typical.

Kit and Charlotte went off to dance, Justin stood up with Beth and Marcus led Lady Salome out, leaving Eleanor with a lingering sense of exclusion as she took a rout chair and sat the dance out at her mother's side. So now the entire family were on great good terms—except for herself and Kit, of course. He could have danced with her if he had wanted, but he had not chosen to do so. Eleanor concentrated fiercely on the detail of her fan and told herself that she should not be surprised. She was the one who had set a gulf between herself and Kit and could not now complain when he showed a coldness towards her. All the same, she felt lonely.

The dance seemed long and gave Eleanor ample chance to reflect on what would happen if she persisted in her demand for an annulment. The scandal would be huge, her family might well cast her off, and she would be alone... She was not sure that she had the strength to pursue such a course. Yet what was the alternative? Her eyes ached with unshed tears as she watched Kit dancing with his sister. They made a striking couple, so tall and fair, so at ease in each other's company, so *happy*… She could have been happy with Kit, if matters had fallen out differently.

'Would you like to dance, Nell?'

Marcus had returned Lady Salome to the chair at Lady Trevithick's side and was now standing before her, smiling slightly. Eleanor could see that a certain element of tension had already left him. He looked younger—and happier. Her heart felt like lead in comparison. Was she the only one left feeling miserable? But there was Kit, of course, whose misery was also entirely her fault.

She took Marcus's hand. 'Thank you, Marcus. I should like to dance.'

They joined a set that was forming.

'You are looking better, Marcus,' Eleanor said slyly. 'It must be a great relief to you that Beth will be…er…speaking to you again!'

Marcus's lips twitched. 'You knew about that, did you, Nell? I confess that that is one of the attractive aspects of the situation.' His smile faded. 'However, I believe I owe you an apology, before all else.'

Eleanor raised her eyebrows. 'Indeed, Marcus? Why is that?'

'Minx,' her brother said. 'You are well aware! I know that I have made matters very difficult for you and Mostyn these two weeks past, when they must have been difficult enough already, in all conscience! I am sorry.'

Eleanor's gaze flickered. 'It is Kit who is owed the real apology—'

'He has had one.' Marcus grimaced. 'I have seldom made a man so grovelling an apology in my life
and I hate to say that he was entirely gracious about
it! I think that I may appreciate him as a brother-in-
law after all!'

Eleanor looked away.

'What about you, Nell?' Marcus said suddenly.
His dark eyes were concerned. 'Are you happy?'

'I…Marcus…' Suddenly Eleanor's throat was dry.
This seemed like the perfect opportunity to ask
Marcus for an interview to discuss the annulment,
but she was not at all sure that he would be sympathetic. Probably he would not have been sympathetic before his *rapprochement* with Kit, and now
it was even more unlikely. She swallowed hard.
Marcus was looking at her quizzically.

'What is it, Nell?'

'Stop thief!'

Everyone froze and swung around as Lady
Salome's deep, throbbing accents rent the air. The
string quartet wavered on for a few bars then died
away and a hush fell over the ballroom. Marcus,
Eleanor and the rest of the family converged on Lady
Salome, who was standing like a vision of justice,
pointing the finger at Lord Kemble.

'That man,' she said grandly, 'has just stolen my
diamond brooch!'

'I have to admit that it was very clever of her,'
Marcus said later, 'for all that I wish she would not
do such things!'

The six of them were sitting in the drawing-room, taking a glass of wine to restore them after the trials of the evening. Both Lady Salome and the Dowager Viscountess had retired, leaving only the younger members of the party. Charlotte was sitting within the circle of Justin's arm and looking very happy, Beth looked relieved but tired. Only Eleanor and Kit were a scrupulous distance apart, in separate armchairs.

'I do not really understand why Lord Kemble did not simply blame Mama for giving him the brooch,' Eleanor said, a little hesitantly. 'Although I suppose it might have been something to do with the threatening manner in which you were standing over him, Marcus!'

'Can't stand the man!' Marcus said bluntly. 'If I had thought I could get away with calling him out—'

'And a very good thing you did not!' Beth said briskly. 'Matters have worked out quite for the best! Everyone is cold-shouldering Kemble, for all that he tried to pass it off as a mistake!'

There was a little silence. 'Do you think that Lady Salome deliberately left the brooch lying for Mama to find?' Eleanor asked.

It was Charlotte who answered. 'I am sure of it! I was sitting beside them but a moment before and Lady Salome was wearing it then! She must have slipped it on to the table, Lady Trevithick picked it up, and when Kemble came across to provide his usual supply of the laudanum...' She shrugged. 'There it was to hand as convenient payment!'

'Too convenient!' Justin said, with a grin. 'A neat strategy! Lady Salome is watching, realises that there are plenty of people who can testify to the fact that the brooch is in fact hers, and makes her accusation—'

'And Kemble cannot deny it is in his possession!' Marcus finished, a gleam in his eye. 'To pretend as he did that he picked it up off the floor in ignorance simply makes him look dishonest, if not an actual thief.' He sighed. 'I suppose it is better to let it go at that...'

'Of course it is!' Beth said sharply. 'We do not wish to draw any further attention to your mother's part in this, Marcus!'

Eleanor fidgeted. 'I do feel responsible for not telling anyone of Mama's thefts before now! I am so sorry, Beth...' she turned to her sister-in-law '...the Trevithick ruby bracelet is gone and it is my fault! It is simply that I could not believe it at first...'

Beth shook her head. 'I think that we all misjudged Lady Trevithick's desperation, Nell! Oh, we all laughed at her with her little bottle of laudanum and the way she was forever taking a draught, but we had no notion of how harmful it was becoming! It was only when Lady Salome explained to me just how damaging are the effects that I realised...'. She stopped. 'It is all most distressing. What can we do now, Marcus?'

'I think that Mama will have to go away for a space,' Marcus said, grim-faced. 'Perhaps when we return to Trevithick and she has a new grandchild to occupy her and is away from town...'

There was another silence. No one seemed very hopeful. Thinking back, Eleanor realised that she could not remember a time when her mother had not been dependent on her little bottle of laudanum. To deprive her of it now might cause untold harm.

She got to her feet, yawning. 'I am sorry, but I must go home! It is late and I am monstrous tired!'

It was the signal for the group to break up. They went out into the hall, Marcus and Justin discussing with Kit the possibility of meeting up the following day for a visit to Tatersalls. Beth raised her eyes to heaven.

'You would think that they had never been at odds!' she whispered to Eleanor. 'But it is fortuitous, for I *must* speak to you, Nell! It is most urgent! May I call tomorrow— Oh!'

Eleanor made a grab for her arm as Beth slipped, but it was too late. Her sister-in-law lost her footing and tumbled down on to the marble floor, letting out a little shriek as she fell. Eleanor, ashen-faced, fell to her knees beside her. The floor was slippery with candle grease and Beth was lying awkwardly, twisted on one side.

'Beth!' Eleanor grabbed her hand. 'Beth, are you hurt?'

There was a dreadful moment of quiet, and then Beth moved a little gingerly and started to sit up. She gave a groan. The others, who had frozen with shock for a brief moment, now hurried up. Marcus cradled his wife to him with such tenderness that Eleanor caught her breath.

'Beth—'

'I am all right, Marcus!' Beth spoke shakily. 'There is no harm done!'

Marcus tightened his grip. 'Are you sure you are not injured?'

'I feel perfectly well,' Beth said more firmly. 'Or at least I will do when you stop squashing me! I have not twisted my ankle nor do I feel remotely unwell. It was only a spot of grease and a minor tumble.'

'But the baby—' Marcus began.

'She will be quite all right.' Beth tried to get to her feet. 'Oof! I feel a little short of breath, that is all!'

Charlotte bustled up. She had nursed her first husband and his comrades on campaign in the Peninsula and was a staunch support in any emergency.

'Beth, keep still and do not try to rise. Marcus, can you carry her upstairs? I am sure she will be quite well, but it might be safer to send for the doctor. Justin, if you would send one of the servants...'

Within ten minutes, all was organised. A footman had run for the doctor, who appeared with great promptitude. Beth was carried up to her chamber, protesting volubly, and Kit and Eleanor were left to kick their heels in front of the fire in the drawing-room and wait for news.

Eleanor sank down on the sofa and knitted her fingers together to stop them shaking. She felt cold and vaguely sick. If Beth lost her child... But of course she would not, she *could* not... Beth was strong and the fall had only been a little one...

'I could not bear for it to happen to someone else!' she said. She missed the searching look that Kit directed at her down-bent head, the sudden stillness that held him for a moment before he went over and threw another log on the fire. He came to sit by her.

'Why do you suppose she thinks it will be a daughter?' he asked.

Eleanor blinked at him. 'I beg your pardon?'

'A daughter.' Kit smiled. 'Beth referred to the baby as ''she'' just now!'

'Oh!' Eleanor smiled. Suddenly she felt a little warmer. 'I think it is because she is determined to have a daughter first, and then a son! She said that she wanted her daughter to be first in order to give her a natural superiority when the son inherits the title—and of course, because girls are better behaved than boys!'

They smiled at each other. 'I am sure it will be a girl then,' Kit said. 'It would not dare be otherwise!'

'I am sure they will love it, whatever sex it may be!' Eleanor said. Her voice wavered a little. Kit took her hands. 'Nell. It will be all right.'

Kit's grasp was infinitely gentle and comforting. He slid an arm around her and drew her close to him, stroking her until her shivering stopped. Eleanor leaned her head against his shoulder and closed her eyes. She had not thought but to accept the comfort that he offered. Kit's arms were a haven against the world and her own fears, and she felt her body relax a little.

The door opened. They both jumped to their feet as Charlotte came in.

'Well?' Eleanor demanded.

Charlotte smiled. She looked relieved. 'Beth is very well. The doctor has said that there is no cause for alarm but that she should be careful for a few days. Naturally she is already making the greatest fuss about being confined to her bed! I hope that you will both call tomorrow to try to distract her! She will be the most tiresome patient otherwise!'

The journey back to Montague Street was a short one and was accomplished mainly in silence, but when they reached the house and Eleanor wished Kit a good night and made for the stairs, he put a hand out and touched her arm lightly.

'Eleanor, a moment.'

Eleanor looked at him, surprised. 'Kit?'

'May we speak?' There was something closed and watchful in Kit's face and Eleanor hesitated. Her emotions were still close to the surface, dangerously so.

'I am very tired, Kit,' she said, knowing she sounded reluctant. 'In fact, I feel exhausted! It has been such a difficult evening—'

'A glass of wine would restore you and help you to sleep,' Kit suggested. 'Take one with me.'

He held the door of the drawing-room open and after a moment Eleanor joined him. The thought of a drink was pleasant and she told herself that she need not stay long, nor be drawn into a difficult conversation. This was no time to pursue the subject of an annulment, for she was sure that she would simply burst into tears and flee at the first mention of the word. She hoped that Kit would not take advantage of her evident distress to push his case.

Kit took her cloak from her, installed her in an armchair and lit some of the candles from the one branch that was already burning in the room. The light was soft and pleasing, as was the warmth of the fire. Eleanor felt herself start to relax. It was only now that she realised how tense she had been during that dreadful episode after Beth's fall. She watched Kit covertly as he moved to pour them two glasses of wine. He did not call the servants and somehow this added to the sense of warm familiarity in the room.

Eleanor took her glass of wine from him, her fingers brushing his. She turned her thoughts aside from the intimacy of that touch, trying to keep at bay the loneliness that always dogged her now.

'Eleanor,' Kit had taken the chair across from her and was leaning forward, watching her intently. The ruby wine swirled in his glass, rich red in the firelight. 'There was something that I wished to ask you…'

Eleanor opened her eyes wide. 'Oh? Then ask it, my lord.'

Surprisingly, Kit still hesitated. He looked away, then directly at her. Eleanor felt the power of his glance and felt also the first pang of apprehension as his tension communicated itself to her. She narrowed her eyes, puzzled.

'When we were in the drawing-room after Beth had had her fall,' Kit said slowly, 'you said that you could not bear for it to happen to someone else.' He shifted slightly. 'What did you mean by that, Eleanor?'

Eleanor sat stock still. She felt nothing—no shock, no despair, no surprise. She wondered vaguely how she could have given herself away so easily when she had tried so hard and for so long not to do so. And she heard herself say lightly:

'Did I say that, my lord? I do not recall.'

'You did say that.' Kit was remorseless and she knew he would not let it go now. Fear nibbled at her stomach. He was watching her still. She shifted uncomfortably.

'I am not entirely sure what I meant...'

'I do not believe you.' Kit put his glass down. 'You meant that you could not bear for someone else to lose their baby, did you not, Eleanor?'

Eleanor closed her eyes for a moment. The firelight danced behind her closed lids.

'Eleanor, please answer me.' Kit's face was in shadow, his voice steady, and she sensed his resolve. 'Please.'

Eleanor opened her eyes, momentarily dazzled by the light. Once again, she found herself responding to that hypnotic tone. This would be easy if she kept it light and did not give too much away. Well, perhaps not easy, but it need not be too bad. And it need make no difference to the annulment...

'Eleanor?' There was an edge to Kit's voice now, ruthless, inescapable. She looked him straight in the eye.

'I was thinking about myself. I was thinking about me and about our child. Our child, Kit! The one I lost while you were away! I—' At the last moment, she was able to pull back from the brink before the whole terrible tale came tumbling out. She took a steadying breath.

Kit's mouth was set in a hard line, his face pale. 'How did it happen?'

Eleanor shrugged. 'It just...happened. No reason, not a fall, like Beth's. I hear it is not uncommon in the first few weeks. The doctor told me...'

Kit got up, thrusting his hands into his pockets, pacing across the room with all the restlessness of a caged animal.

'Were you ever going to tell me about this, Eleanor?'

Eleanor watched him with dull eyes. 'I thought not, no.'

'I see.' She could read nothing from his tone. He came across to her chair and stood close to her. Eleanor shuddered. The words broke from her and try as she would, she could not prevent them:

'I am sorry, Kit... I am sorry I lost the child...'

'Nell...' Now she could read his tone and the gentleness in it made her shake all the more. He went down on one knee beside her chair, his arms going about her softly, rocking her.

'No, it is I who am so very sorry that I was not with you when you needed me, Nell—'

Eleanor rushed on, heedless, the tears spilling down her face now.

'I told myself that I did not care, but I did! Oh, it hurt so much I could not bear it! For a while I thought I would run quite mad, and you were not there…I did all those other imprudent things and got myself into such foolish situations and it was all horrible—'

Kit held her closer still, stroking her hair. 'You did nothing that was foolish, sweetheart…'

'I was confused—'

'I understand. You have nothing with which to reproach yourself.'

'And then you came back and I was so very angry with you!' Eleanor shuddered, gasping on a sob. 'I hated you for leaving me, Kit, and then I hated you for coming back! But it was not easy…' She gave a little hiccup. 'You made it very difficult for me to dislike you, Kit!'

Kit did not answer. Her face was in the curve of his shoulder, so close that her lips could touch his skin. He smelled distractingly good. Eleanor snuggled closer.

It was several minutes later that Kit said, muffled: 'Eleanor, much as I would love to stay here all night, I am losing the sensation in my arms! If you will allow me—'

He scooped her up and transferred them both to the armchair by the fire. Eleanor rested her head against his shoulder.

'Kit, you do understand—'

'Yes.' Kit was stroking her hair. 'I am sure I would be the last person in whom you would wish to confide, mistrusting me as you did! Oh Nell—' There was a bitter edge to his voice, 'I will never forgive myself for leaving you so carelessly like that to face such things alone—'

'I had Beth and Marcus.' Eleanor said. She smiled a little. 'They were so good to me, but I made them promise never to tell…'

Kit's jaw set in a hard line. 'I understand your brother's attitude much better now, I confess. Had our situations been reversed I fear I would have put a bullet through him!'

Eleanor smiled again. She rubbed her fingers tentatively along the stubble of his cheek, revelling in the rough touch.

'Mmm. Well, this is a matter between you and me, not Marcus,' she murmured. 'Though I am glad that you have settled your differences now…'

Kit turned his head and kissed her palm, but his eyes were still serious.

'Eleanor, about the annulment…' He felt her stiffen and held her still. 'Please, my love… I *must* know. Why do you wish us to part?'

Eleanor fiddled with one of the buttons on his coat. In the exquisite relief of letting go of her secrets she had forgotten this one last matter. She was silent.

'If you are afraid,' Kit said huskily, 'then I swear I will not push you to do anything you do not wish. But Eleanor, I have been thinking that I cannot let you go! I will fight it with every breath in my body—'

Eleanor could not bear the anguish in his voice. She shook her head abruptly. 'No Kit, it was not that, though I confess I was a little frightened... When you made love to me the other night I wanted so much more, but yes, I was afraid...'

She saw him smile then. 'Nell, I promise I would never rush matters—'

Eleanor shook her head again. 'It was not that,' she said again. She sat away from him a little so that she could look at him properly. 'Sometimes I think that it is that I am afraid of everything,' she said candidly. 'I am afraid in case I conceive a child and lose it again, but I am more afraid that I may never have children.' Her eyes, dark and sad, sought his. 'The doctor tells me that it is by no means certain that I may have a family,' she said slowly. 'And you were so anxious to set up your nursery, Kit.'

There was a silence. Kit pulled her back close to him, his arms tightening about her. He did not speak.

'Kit—' Eleanor struggled upright. 'I am right, am I not? And with an annulment—'

'There will be no annulment.' She had never heard so much determination in his tone. 'It is out of the question.'

'But—'

'Eleanor.' Kit's voice was low and firm. 'There is no way of determining whether or not any man and woman will have children before they try, and you have not been told that it is impossible! And even if you had…' he held her so close that she could barely breathe '…there would be no annulment.'

Eleanor's throat felt thick with tears. She thought her heart would burst. 'But Kit, you need an heir—'

'Pray do not argue with me. If you are not to be the mother of my children then I want none.'

'That is not in the natural order of things,' Eleanor said uncertainly. 'A man needs an heir—'

'And I need a wife. This wife.' Kit held her away from him. 'Eleanor, I love you! Surely you cannot think that I would let you go and marry someone else just for the sake of begetting an heir! The thought is monstrous!'

'I do not know.' Eleanor's voice was small. 'I have struggled with this for so long that I am not sure what I feel any more! And Kit, I am so unhappy and afraid! If we…if I…were to conceive another child only to lose it again…' Her voice broke. 'You must see that I thought it simpler for us to part!'

'I understand why you believed it might be so,' Kit said, 'but I fear that I cannot agree, Nell. Whatever happens, we shall deal with it together. Which means that there shall be no separation and no annulment. Are you in agreement?'

A little smile curved Eleanor's lips. She was almost persuaded. 'Well…'

Kit shook her gently. 'Nell, I will lock you up if it is the only way to keep you!'

Eleanor looked at him. Her body, softening against his, gave him the answer. 'I do not believe that there is any need to be so medieval, my lord!'

Kit drew her close into an embrace that precluded any further discussion. After a moment, Eleanor was obliged to object.

'Kit, you are crushing me half to death!'

Kit loosened his grip and they looked at each other. 'I suppose I should let you go now,' he said reluctantly. 'It has, as you said, been a very long evening!'

Eleanor slid to her feet and Kit stood up too. She knew that he would let her go alone, if that was her wish. Despite his determination that there should be no annulment, he would not hurry her into a physical intimacy that she did not want and she loved him for it. She walked slowly over to the door and turned back to look at him. He was watching her, his expression unreadable.

'Kit,' she said slowly, 'I find I do not wish to be alone tonight. Please stay with me.'

Chapter Twelve

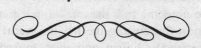

'I suppose I shall just have to seduce him!' Eleanor said glumly. 'I have tried everything else! Why, when we went to the masquerade last night I chose to wear my lowest cut dress and all Kit could say was would I like a scarf as the nights were still a little cold!'

'You could just tell him how you feel,' Beth said. She was sitting up in bed and eating a plate of toast and honey. 'It is easier in the long run than all this worrying. A simple statement of intent—that you would like Kit to make love to you—should do the trick!'

Eleanor stared, the colour slowly mounting to her cheeks. 'Oh Beth, I know that I have made great strides in overcoming my natural modesty, but that is surely a step too far. Of all the brazen things… Why I would have to be drunk! Or taken with the laudanum, perhaps!'

Beth grimaced. 'Well, there is plenty to spare. We

found an entire bottle hidden at the back of one of your mama's drawers. She had evidently forgotten it was there!'

'I hope that she will be happy in the dower house at Trevithick,' Eleanor said slowly. The Dowager was even now packing her belongings for the remove. 'I realise that it is wise for her to leave town for a little until the talk dies down, but I cannot see that being in the country will help improve her situation! Unless the laudanum travels with her...'

Beth finished the toast and licked her fingers. 'Perhaps that is the kindest action. To forbid her it now would be cruel and probably dangerous.' She sighed. 'It is like an illness, is it not, and a problem not easily solved. Lady Salome is hopeful that Dr Wentworth in Exeter may be able to help her... But do not turn the subject, dearest Eleanor! We were speaking of you—and my cousin...'

Eleanor sighed. On the night that she and Kit had had their final confrontation, they had retired to their separate rooms and had prepared for bed with an odd sort of decorum. Eleanor had pulled the bolt back on the dressing-room door and opened the door shyly to allow Kit to come through. Then they had sat in her bed and had talked and talked. All the anger, all the frustrations, all the fears, had come out in the intimate dark, until she had fallen asleep in Kit's arms from total exhaustion. It had been an extraordinarily profound experience, far deeper than making love. And in the morning Kit had said gravely that he was happy that all was now resolved but that he felt they now needed a little time before anything else happened between them. Eleanor had been bitterly disappointed and a tiny bit relieved, but she had agreed to what he had suggested. Perhaps Kit himself needed time before they resumed a deeper relationship or perhaps he thought that she did. Worse, she might have made him so afraid of hurting her again that he would not approach her. Whatever the case, they had spent a week in the pleasantest of pastimes, driving together, walking, talking, attending the Season's balls, and it had been delightful but somehow…unfinished.

'You have no qualms, then, Nell?' Beth asked now. 'When the time comes, I mean…'

Eleanor shook her head. 'No. I trust Kit to stay with me and I love him with all my heart. If we have children I shall feel truly blessed, but if not… I shall still have Kit.' She shrugged lightly, 'To tell the truth I am a little nervous of how we get to that point…if you understand me…'

Beth laughed. 'I do! Which is why this delay is unsettling you, Nell. The anticipation—'

Eleanor laughed too. 'Well, it is pleasant, in a rather disturbing way! I shall think about your advice, Beth!' She stood up. 'Who knows, I may be able to summon up the will to tell Kit how I feel. Now, you will be wanting your maid sent up if you are to be ready for dinner. Though how you may eat it after that plate of toast—'

'Oh, I am forever hungry!' Beth said cheerfully, 'and most excited at being allowed to get out of bed!

Of all the torments—to be confined here whilst everyone else is out enjoying themselves!'

'We are just happy that you are quite well,' Eleanor said feelingly, kissing her sister-in-law before she left the bedroom. 'I shall see you at dinner.'

Eleanor went slowly downstairs, turning over in her mind what Beth had said. She did not consider herself shy, precisely, but to state her wishes to Kit in so blunt a manner did seem somewhat bold. On the other hand if she did not take the initiative she might be fretting herself to flinders for days whilst she waited for Kit to take the hint. It was difficult.

They were taking dinner that evening at Trevithick House and following that with a visit to the theatre. The whole family, with the exception of the Dowager, were to make up the party and it promised to be a better-tempered experience than the previous dinner at Trevithick House. Eleanor had just reached the hall when the outer door opened and Kit came in, talking to Marcus. Eleanor thought that Kit, in buff pantaloons and a cinnamon-coloured coat, looked quite devastatingly handsome that afternoon. She watched him openly as he crossed the hall. After all, no doubt Beth would tell her that if one could not stare in open admiration at one's husband, one might as well be dead.

Kit saw her, exchanged a quick word with Marcus, and his brother-in-law clapped him on the shoulder before hurrying off upstairs, no doubt to visit Beth. Eleanor tried not to laugh. Such harmony between the Mostyn and Trevithick families was still something of a novelty.

'Eleanor, how are you?' Kit had taken her hand now and was pressing a kiss on it like the most ardent of suitors. Eleanor shivered pleasurably, her thoughts returning to their earlier topic.

'I am well, thank you, my lord.' She gave him a look from under her lashes. Once upon a time she had been able to flirt rather well and perhaps she had not lost the skill…

'I have a small present for you,' Kit continued. 'To wear to the theatre tonight, perhaps?'

He produced a small posy of violets, velvet soft and sweet-scented, and handed them to Eleanor. She buried her nose in them.

'Oh, how lovely! Thank you, my lord.' Eleanor stroked the petals with a gentle finger. They were soft and smooth, and the faint perfume filled her senses, making her feel curiously aware… It was like the sun on your skin, or Kit's touch… She blinked.

Kit was speaking. Eleanor raised her gaze to his. 'I beg your pardon, Kit, I was not attending. What did you say?'

'I was asking whether you would care to travel to Mostyn with me in a few weeks,' Kit repeated, brows raised. 'The Season is almost at an end and your brother and Beth are removing to Trevithick… Are you quite well, Eleanor? You seem a little distracted today.'

'Oh!' Eleanor blushed a little. His eyes were such

a deep blue, warm with laughter... 'Yes, well, Beth and I have been talking too...about returning to Devon, I mean, and I am sure it would be very pleasant...'

'Good.' Kit frowned slightly. 'You look a little flushed, my love. Are you sure you feel well enough to go out tonight?'

'Oh yes!' Eleanor gave him a melting smile. 'I am quite well, Kit!' She took a deep breath. 'I am very sorry if I appear a little *distrait*—it is simply that I was thinking of seducing you!'

Kit had half-turned away, for the front door had just opened to admit Justin and Charlotte. Eleanor saw the precise moment that her words impinged on him. He turned his head sharply and looked at her, his eyes narrowed in puzzlement as though he thought he had misheard. She gave him another, brilliant smile. There was a flash of heat in Kit's gaze as it rested on her, he looked as though he were about to speak, then bit off what he was going to say as Charlotte and Justin came up to greet them. Eleanor, reaching up to kiss Justin, saw out of the corner of her eye that Kit was still watching her. She took Charlotte's arm and moved away to the drawing-room, well satisfied.

There was no chance of private conversation after that. They were joined by Marcus and Beth and finally by Lady Salome, and went into dinner informally, chattering amongst themselves.

Eleanor was delighted to see that Kit was quite preoccupied during dinner. Twice he stopped eating altogether and a third time he almost knocked over his wine. Lady Salome, who was sitting on his left, had the greatest trouble in sustaining a conversation with him. Every so often his gaze would rest on Eleanor and she would give him the demurest of smiles before applying herself to her food once again. She knew what was distracting him; he knew that she knew. It was definitely working... Eleanor gave a little shiver of nervous anticipation.

When they were all in the hall gathering their cloaks prior to going to the theatre, Kit caught her arm in an urgent grip and drew her to one side.

'Eleanor, did you have to initiate that topic of conversation at the precise moment when you knew we would not be able to discuss it?'

'Which topic was that, my lord?' Eleanor queried, her tone light. She could not quite meet his eyes.

Kit gave her arm a little shake. 'You know full well! Devil take it, I have thought of little else since we last spoke!'

'Oh,' Eleanor gave him a little smile, 'I do believe that is the problem, Kit! Sometimes you think far too much when you should simply...act!'

She whisked her arm out of his grip, smilingly accepted her cloak from the footman's hands and hurried out to the carriage, wondering how she had the audacity to tease her husband like this. But she had started and so she was determined to finish.

The play was *She Stoops to Conquer* by Goldsmith and had always been one of Eleanor's favourites, but tonight it seemed to drag. She was very aware of Kit sitting behind her in the box and although she could not turn around to look at him, she was sure that his attention was on her and not the play. When they reached the interval, Kit offered her his arm.

'Would you care for a stroll, my love?'

The press of people was great, for plenty were taking the opportunity to stretch their legs. Neither Kit nor Eleanor spoke at first, but she was very aware of him beside her and of the brush of his body against hers. After they had walked the length of the corridor, Kit said:

'When you said earlier that I thought too much, what did you mean?'

Eleanor gave a little sigh. This was proving more difficult that she had imagined. It seemed ironic that Kit, who had not troubled to conceal his desire for her in the past, should now prove so difficult to persuade. Without pausing for thought, Eleanor tugged his arm and pulled him behind the shelter of a huge pillar. It was hardly private but it afforded more seclusion that the theatre entrance hall.

'It is simply that if we wait until we both think that it is an...appropriate time...' Eleanor took a deep breath and pressed on, 'well, the time may never come!' She put both hands against Kit's chest. She could feel the beat of his heart beneath her palm. 'Stand closer!' she said urgently.

Kit obligingly bent closer to her. His breath stirred her hair. Eleanor resisted the urge to run her fingers along the line of his jaw.

'If you are taking care because you have no wish to frighten me…' the colour came up into her face and she stood on tiptoe so that she could whisper in his ear '…then I pray you, do not! I want you to make love to me! And please do not ask me to make it any more plain to you because I cannot!'

And before he could say another word, she had whisked out from behind the pillar and was making her way back to the box with determined step, not looking behind her.

Kit followed slowly. It was going to prove impossible to concentrate on the play now—not that he had been giving it his full attention before. From the moment that Eleanor had made her outrageous statement about seducing him, back in the hall at Trevithick House, he had been utterly incapable of focusing on anything other than that thought. He could not remember a single thing about dinner, for his entire attention had been rapt in his wife. She had looked so demure, so innocent and so wholly seductive. Deliciously so, outrageously so. And every so often, she had cast Kit a look that had said that she knew exactly what he was thinking and she wanted him to want her. She wanted him to make love to her… Kit reached the box and almost cannoned into Lady Salome in the doorway, so intent was he in his own thoughts. After making his apologies he resumed his seat, and looked at Eleanor. She had cast him one swift glance as he had come in and was now making conversation with Beth, but there was a colour in her cheeks and a sparkle in her eye that he could not miss. She was wearing a pink dress with a modest décolletage and one dark ringlet was resting in the hollow of her shoulder. Kit's fingers itched to touch it.

In fact he had been aching to touch her for what seemed like weeks now. This latest abstinence he had laid upon himself, sternly abjuring himself to do the gentlemanly thing and not to hurry Eleanor, not to press his attentions on his wife when they were so recently reconciled. But now... Kit shook his head a little to try to displace the images that seemed to be running riot in his brain. It was no good. The figures on the stage were pale and unreal in comparison to the vision of Eleanor as he had seen her stretched out on her bed. He had to take her home and they had to go now. Except that there were still two acts of the play to go... Kit almost groaned aloud.

By the time the play ended he felt as though several days had passed. Then there were the farewells to the rest of the family, the arrangements to meet the following day, the business of sending for the carriages... It seemed that every delay was designed to add to his torment. He could smell Eleanor's faint perfume as she stood beside him; he could feel the brush of her hair against his shoulder. He wanted to kiss her senseless and instead he was obliged make polite conversation whilst Eleanor and Beth and Charlotte discussed at endless length the plan to go shopping the following day. By the time it finished he would have happily traded half his fortune to see his sister and his cousin in Hades.

Eleanor was well aware of Kit's impatience as she discussed arrangements with Beth and Charlotte. He positively vibrated with irritation and she suspected that she knew the cause—her plan to engage his interest was working exceptionally well. And now she had to deliver what she had promised. It felt quite curious, as though she had deliberately let a predatory animal out of its cage and now could not restrain it. Not that she wanted to, of course, but she knew that eventually there would be a price to pay. What she could not decide was whether eventually would arrive too soon—or not soon enough.

She did not look at Kit and an edge of nervousness made her spin out the farewells as long as she could. Soon it was impossible to delay any longer, however. Kit's hand was imperative on her arm as he helped her up into the carriage. He installed her in the corner then sat next to her rather than opposite, as was customary. Eleanor tried to appear casual and yawned delicately. Kit raised an eyebrow.

'Did you enjoy the play, my love?' he asked politely. 'I seem to remember it as one of your favourites.'

'Oh it is.' Eleanor cast him a sideways look. Her heart was beating rather fast. Surely he did not intend to commence his seduction in a carriage? Or did he?

'I fear I found myself oddly distracted tonight, my

lord!' she said slowly. 'I was not as drawn in as usual.'

She could not see Kit's face in the darkness but she heard him laugh. 'Is there anything that I might do to help your powers of concentration, sweetheart? You need only say the word!'

Eleanor's heart not only speeded up, it skipped a beat. 'Well, I do not know… Yes, perhaps you might…'

In reply, Kit caught her up in his arms and pulled her to him. He stopped with his mouth an inch away from hers.

'You have been teasing me all evening, my love—'

Eleanor wriggled. 'That is true, but—'

'No buts. Now you have to make good your words.'

Kit bent closer until his lips touched hers lightly. Eleanor leaned into him, grasping the lapels of his coat to hold him to her when the movement of the carriage threatened to pull them apart. After a moment she felt him slide a hand round behind the curls at her neck, holding her to him as his mouth explored hers, slowly and deeply. Eleanor felt the world start to spin around her; her senses reeled. She had spent the whole day imagining what it would be like and now the reality transcended both her memories and her dreams. Now there were no barriers between them, no misunderstanding and no bitterness. Now there was only sweetness—and longing.

The carriage jolted over a rut and broke them

apart. Eleanor fell back against the cushions, and Kit followed, trapping her body beneath his, claiming her mouth again in a fiercely demanding kiss.

'Kit…' When she could speak at last, Eleanor was moved to protest. 'We are in the carriage!'

'And?' Kit sounded amused.

'And…' Eleanor struggled to sit upright and after a moment he shifted sufficiently to allow it, 'and I do not wish to be seduced in a carriage—at least not on this occasion!'

'You have considered it for a future occasion then?' Kit questioned.

'Well,' Eleanor smiled to herself, 'I confess I had thought about the possibility!' She smoothed her gloves down demurely. 'Along with the drawing-room and the conservatory—'

In reply, Kit tumbled her back into his arms and kissed her with a thorough slowness and a heat that threatened to melt on the spot. When the coach drew up in Montague Street she allowed Kit to help her down and did not demur when he put an arm about her, for her legs were still trembling a little. In the entrance hall, Carrick came forward to take their coats, then hesitated, clearly embarrassed.

'Excuse me, my lord, but there is a small matter of business which I must draw to your attention—'

Kit's face was a picture. Eleanor very nearly laughed.

'Good God, Carrick, can it not wait? It is near midnight and I am anxious to retire—'

Eleanor could tell that Kit was trying to erase the

impatience from his voice but he was not quite succeeding. The butler hovered.

'I am sorry, my lord. It will not take long.'

Kit cast Eleanor a speaking look. 'My apologies, my dear. If you wish to retire—'

'I think I shall go to the music-room and play for a little,' Eleanor said, suddenly reckless. 'I am in the mood for a passionate piece—'

She saw the flash of desire in Kit's eyes before he turned away and gestured to Carrick to follow him to the study. Eleanor hurried across the hall and into the music-room. The piano was waiting and nothing but Beethoven would do. She closed her eyes and plunged into the music.

She did not even hear Kit come in, nor the click of the door closing. The first intimation she had that she was not alone came when she felt Kit brush aside the curls at the base of her neck and plant a kiss against the sensitive skin uncovered there. Eleanor shivered abruptly, opened her eyes and broke off in the middle of the music.

'Enchanting,' Kit murmured. He drew her to her feet. 'And very, very passionate, my love.'

'What did Carrick want?'

'Oh…' Kit did not sound remotely interested. 'He had a urgent letter for me from St John Trevithick, settling his debts. Which will please your brother, my love, since I refused to take payment from him no matter how he urged it upon me. But I do not really wish to speak of that. Tell me…' He was touching her hair again, entwining a curl about his finger before he released it again, 'did the music-room feature on your list of places suitable for seduction?'

Eleanor's throat dried. 'No...' She whispered.

'Hmm, a pity.' Kit sounded thoughtful. 'Would you like to reconsider?'

Before Eleanor could reply, Kit had bent his head to kiss her, the touch of his lips once again driving out any other thought from her mind. This kiss was tender but no less disturbing for that. The slow, sure passion of it made Eleanor quiver with anticipation, the hardness of Kit's body against her own yielding softness was desperately distracting. She was shaking; she leaned back for support, feeling the edge of the piano hard against the small of her back. A second later Kit had caught her about the waist and placed her so that she was sitting on the piano top. She could feel the smoothness of the polished wood beneath her skirts and caught the edge to steady herself.

'Kit, what on earth—'

'I'll show you...'

'Oh!' The word was driven from Eleanor with a mixture of shock and wicked pleasure, as Kit, suiting actions to words, slid the gown and chemise from her shoulders. The height of the piano had changed their relative positions and he did not even need to bend down to disrobe her. Eleanor felt his hands on her bare waist, above the material of her bodice, and then his lips traced a leisurely path across the bare skin that he had exposed, to brush the upper slope of her breast with the lightest of touches. He moved in closer and Eleanor felt the weight of his body force her thighs apart under her silken skirts. Then his mouth was at her breast.

Eleanor trembled, closing her eyes. This was exquisite torture, and pinned here on the piano's smooth surface, she felt strangely vulnerable and at his mercy. Kit's hand traced the curve of her breast before his lips followed the path of his fingers, teasing, tormenting, making her skin shiver. The searing touch reduced her to desperation and she caught him to her, running her fingers into his hair.

'Kit, please—'

In answer he slipped one hand beneath her skirt to stroke the soft skin of her inner thigh. Eleanor wriggled desperately and slithered straight off the piano top into Kit's arms.

'So now you may add the music-room to your list for the future.' Kit's voice was husky. His hands closed about her waist again and slid her down the whole, hard length of him. 'I just wanted to demonstrate the potential. But now—' He swiftly rearranged her bodice, 'Now, I fear, my dearest Eleanor, that I can wait no longer. I want to take you to bed, for neither the carriage nor any other location can do justice to what I have in mind tonight.'

He swept her up in his arms, and threw the music-room door open. The entire servants' hall appeared to be lined up outside, making no pretext whatsoever of doing any sort of work. Kit merely grinned.

'We do not wish to be disturbed,' he said, and took the stairs two at a time.

'You might as well have made a public announcement,' Eleanor said drowsily, much later, as she lay naked in her husband's arms. 'Indeed, you did make a public declaration—'

Her words were cut off as Kit kissed her triumphantly, his hands sliding to cup her breasts in a gesture of possession that set her trembling again with an echo of the passion that had so recently subsumed them. Kit propped himself up on one elbow and looked down at her, brushing the hair tenderly away from her face.

'There is no shame in that. I want everyone to know how much I love you, Nell…'

Another blissful interlude followed this affirmation. Eleanor twisted beneath him, running her hands over his chest, fascinated by the feeling of hard muscle beneath her fingers, revelling in his warmth and the scent of his skin. She turned her lips against his shoulder, bit him gently and heard him groan.

'Nell… No, don't distract me! Keep still, you minx!'

Kit caught both her hands in one of his, restraining her innocently erotic caresses, and rolled her into his arms.

'Listen to me, Nell. I want to be quite sure that this is the right thing—'

Finding her hands captured, Eleanor pressed tiny

butterfly kisses against his chest. 'Sure? Can you be more sure than this, Kit?'

Kit moved to trap her beneath him. 'Then if you are still happy—'

'Oh yes…' Eleanor freed her hands and slipped her arms about him, stroking the smooth skin of his back. 'I do not believe I could be happier…'

She tilted her head to kiss him, parting her lips beneath his, touching her tongue tentatively to his. She could feel the coiled tension of desire in his body again, see the concentrated, passionate heat in his eyes. It thrilled her that he wanted her so much. She wriggled down, her hair spilling over the pillow to entwine them both in its silken bonds. Kit drew her hard against him, her breasts pressed against his chest, his mouth plundering hers ruthlessly as his hands moved over her. Each movement was intense, gentle and demanding by turn as he set out to learn her body all over again. Again and again. Eleanor felt weak at the thought.

'Nell, look at me…'

Eleanor opened her eyes and looked at him, half-fearful of drowning in the intense light in Kit's blue eyes. The blissful sweetness was building inside her now, demanding release. She arched against him.

'Kit…'

He took her then, with a mixture of exultant demand and exquisite tenderness that made her ache with pleasure. And when it was over she slept in his arms, utterly confident that he would always be there when she awoke. No fear of the future could ever touch her now.

Epilogue

I͟t was a week later and Eleanor was sitting in the garden when Carrick announced that Lady Salome Trevithick had called to see her. That redoubtable lady swirled across the lawn in a dress of green taffeta adorned with diamonds, and came to rest under the canopy where Eleanor was reading *Guy Mannering*. She had paid another visit to the circulating library the day before and was forced to admit that reading was a far more enjoyable pastime than she had previously imagined. Really, it was very absorbing indeed.

'My dear Eleanor!' Lady Salome bent to kiss her. 'Here I am come like a *deus ex machina* to put everything right for you and I find you have no need of my help! You look radiant, my love! Am I to infer that All Is Well?'

Eleanor blushed. 'Yes, I thank you, ma'am! Kit and I are reconciled, and in no small part due to your plotting!'

Lady Salome dismissed this with a wave of her hand. 'I do my poor best! But I am glad to see that no more of my interference is needed here!'

She sat back. 'Now that your mama is to retire to the country and this foolish family feud is finished, I find there is little for me here. I shall be returning to Fairhaven Island in a couple of days. My work is done!'

Eleanor sighed. 'We shall miss you, Aunt, although I do not believe that we shall be far behind you! Kit and I plan to retire to Mostyn Hall at the end of the Season, but up until then we shall scandalise the *Ton* by being quite hopelessly in love!'

There was a hint of a tear in Lady Salome's eye. 'Bless you, my dear,' she said gruffly. 'Well, I have kept you from your husband quite long enough! And as I see he is coming to join you now, I will take my leave. But first, I had something for you. I was helping your mama to pack this morning and I found these at the back of one of her drawers...'

She was groping around in her reticule and emerged, brandishing a handful of paper triumphantly.

'Here you are! Letters for you, my love! Well, I must be away.'

She dropped the letters into Eleanor's lap, bent to kiss her again, and swept away across the lawn, meeting with Kit on the edge of the terrace and stopping to engage him in conversation.

Eleanor picked up the letters in some confusion. She could see that they were addressed to her, and at Trevithick House, and that they had been opened. She unfolded the first one.

My dear love
Forgive me for leaving you so suddenly and without a word. I had no intention of this... Pray seek my sister's help until I may return and I swear it will not be for long... Forgive me, my love...

Eleanor let the letter sink slowly back into her lap. Lady Salome and Kit were still talking on the terrace, although Kit was looking across the garden towards her. Eleanor picked up a second letter.

My dearest Eleanor
I can scarce bear to imagine what you are thinking of me by now, alone and friendless as I have left you. I think of you every day, no, every moment of every day, and long for that time when we will be together. I imagine you reading my letter and hope from the bottom of my heart that you will forgive me... I love you...

Eleanor remembered the Dowager railing against her marriage, intent on an annulment, desperate for her to marry Kemble. She thought of her mother reading Kit's letters secretly and hiding them away from the one person for whom they had been intended. She thought of Kit, honour bound not to tell her why he had to delay, and of the Dowager telling her that her husband had abandoned her and had never loved her and that he was a rogue and a scoundrel. She picked up the last letter.

My dearest love
I know of nothing to say other than that I love you so dearly and count the days until I may be back with you. I love you... I love you...

The letter blurred a little and a fat tear dropped onto the paper. Eleanor wiped her eyes. She was smiling and crying at the same time. She saw Kit take his leave of Lady Salome and start down the steps towards her. She got to her feet. The letters fell to the ground. Eleanor could not tear her gaze away from Kit. As he drew closer she saw that the urgency in her own stance had somehow communicated itself to him. He started to hurry towards her just as Eleanor started to run—positively run—across the grass to him. They met in the middle and Kit swept her up in his arms and spun her round, before setting her back on her feet and looking into her face.

'Eleanor?' He touched a gentle finger to her tear-stained cheek. 'What has happened? What is the matter?'

'Nothing!' Eleanor said. She smiled radiantly at him and flung her arms around his neck so that she could reach up to kiss him. 'I love you, Kit! There is nothing the matter at all!'

*   *   *   *   *

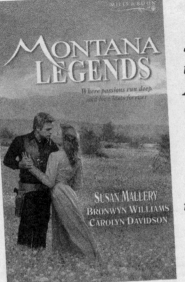

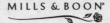

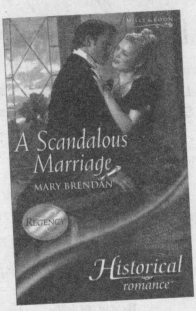